I pounded on my chest and clawed my neck trying to force oxygen into my windpipe, but nothing worked.

"That's it." Tally's voice sounded tinny and far away. "Take control of it. Mold it how you want it so you can force it back out."

It was clear she'd never been on the receiving end of her wicked staff from Hell.

I managed to draw in a single breath through a very closed airway, right as a soft tremor rippled through the dirt beneath me.

The movement was just enough to catch my attention.

Did you feel that? My wolf ignored me in favor of snapping and ripping at the magic consuming us. The hybrid demon magic had manifested as a thick, dark mass in my mind, and as it cascaded over my eyes I was launched into total darkness.

I'd indeed captured the magic, but I couldn't mold it. I couldn't do anything with it. And it was taking over as fast as it could.

My wolf managed to tear a small patch of clarity open in my mind and I sucked in another gulp of air as quickly as I could. I was still on my knees, but surprisingly, my body had started to shake in rhythm with the ground tremors.

The vibration running through my body hummed like a musical note.

I wrenched my head up, but I still couldn't see anything through the dark magic covering my eyes. *Do you hear that?* My wolf stopped what she was doing, her ears up and alert.

Someone was yelling and the only thing I could make out was my name.

Then two more words.

"Don't go!"

By Amanda Carlson

Full Blooded

Hot Blooded

Cold Blooded

Red Blooded

RED BLOODED

Jessica McClain:
Book Four

AMANDA CARLSON

orbit

www.orbitbooks.net

Copyright © 2014 by Amanda Carlson
Excerpt from *House of the Rising Sun*
copyright © 2014 by Kristen Painter
Excerpt from *The Shambling Guide to New York City*
copyright © 2013 by Mary Lafferty

Orbit
Hachette Book Group
237 Park Avenue, New York, NY 10017
HachetteBookGroup.com

Printed in the United States of America

RRD-C

First Edition: September 2014

10 9 8 7 6 5 4 3 2 1

Orbit is an imprint of Hachette Book Group, Inc. The Orbit name
and logo are trademarks of Little, Brown Book Group Limited.

The Hachette Speakers Bureau provides a wide range
of authors for speaking events. To find out more, go to
www.hachettespeakersbureau.com or call (866) 376-6591.

The publisher is not responsible for websites (or their content) that
are not owned by the publisher.

Library of Congress Cataloging-in-Publication Data

Carlson, Amanda, 1969-
  Red blooded / Amanda Carlson.
    pages cm — (Jessica McClain ; book 4)
  ISBN 978-0-316-40433-4 (paperback) — ISBN 978-0-316-40434-1 (ebook)
1. Werewolves—Fiction. 2. Vampires—Fiction. I. Title.
PS3603.A75274R44 2014
813'.6—dc23
                                                    2014008025

For Paige.
You amaze me every day.

1

The force of the blow shot me out of the circle. My body crashed into the concrete wall, three ribs broken this time. Blood trickled down the back of my neck, tickling my skin, my head wound closing quickly. Instead of standing, I leaned back and rested my shoulders against the cool wall. My patience had evaporated a long time ago.

It had been five days and I'd had enough.

"Get up and do it again," a commanding voice ordered me for the tenth time that morning.

I spread my arms wide. "What's the point? I already told you I don't care if the circle holds me. All I need to do is get down there and back. I don't see why this is still an issue."

"And I've already told *you* that the circle is the only protection you're going to have in the Underworld." Tally's neatly clipped nails drummed along her hips. Her long frosty-blonde hair was tied back in a low ponytail, a military fatigue cap pulled tightly down around her eyes. She was clad in black, right down to her

Nike cross-trainers. How could someone so small still look tough in yoga pants and tennis shoes? "When you get yourself into trouble—which by the way is a for sure rather than a maybe—the circle will be the only safe place you'll have in Hell. And in case you've already forgotten, we're going to be working our asses off up here to keep the magic running while you're down there. So the very least you can do is act like you care. Now get up and do it again."

I stood immediately. "Of course I care," I retorted, barely resisting the urge to stamp my foot in frustration. "But this is taking too long and you know it." I paced toward her. "The Underworld operates on its own timetable, which you've already mentioned more than a dozen times. A week here could mean a year there and vice versa." Anger welled in my throat and I swallowed hard, trying to get past the knot that formed every time I thought about my brother being held prisoner there. "Waiting around is killing me, and it's literally killing Tyler. I don't want to waste another moment. I'm willing to go now and I'm prepared to take my chances once I get there."

My twin brother had been kidnapped and taken to the Underworld by none other than the Prince of Hell himself. No one needed to tell me Tyler was in serious danger. The demons would torture him for any information he had and toss him away like garbage. And they would be merciless about it.

My brother was in agony and I was trying to stay inside a witch circle.

Tally strode over with purpose, stopping directly inside my personal space. She had to tilt her head up to address me, which gave me some brief personal satisfaction. My wolf growled at the intrusion, but I stilled her. I wanted to hear what Tally had to say.

"You're not going to be worth anything to him dead," she declared. "Which I know you're smart enough to figure out on your own. It's very simple. If you can't hold the circle, you die. It's the only lifeline you'll have in a very dark, very dangerous place. If the demons knock you out of the perimeter, you lose, which means you don't come back. And neither does your brother." Her irises sparked deeply, her emotions right at the forefront. Seeing her feelings so close to the surface surprised me, since originally she had refused to help us.

Once we had all returned from New Orleans, banged and bruised from a fight on multiple fronts, she'd informed us the witches were out. She wasn't willing to risk putting her Coven in jeopardy by helping me go up against the demons, who were the witches' natural enemies. But a few days later something had changed her mind.

I glanced to my right at the rosy-cheeked child playing in the corner with her dolls. Maggie immediately glanced up at me and smiled. My best guess was that Maggie had told her mother something important, and that information had ultimately changed Tally's mind. When I'd prodded Tally about it later, she'd refused to divulge the reason she'd had a change of heart, but whatever it was, Tally had agreed to help my team get to the Underworld, and I was trying hard to be patient.

It wasn't exactly working.

I sighed as I ran a hand through my hair, turning in a full circle, frustrated. "Listen, I understand what you're telling me, but since the day we arrived on your doorstep none of this has gone according to plan." I faced her again, hands braced on my hips. "I can't stay in the circle, none of your spells have changed my signature, I can't bring any real weapons with me, and your organic ones disintegrate before I have a chance to use them. Your witches haven't been able to create anything strong enough to stun the Prince of Hell anyway—so what are we really doing here? We're wasting precious time that could be better spent saving my brother."

"This is hardly a waste of time." Without taking her eyes off mine she yelled, "Reaper, get in the circle!"

"Fine," Ray grumbled from the sidelines. "But I'm leaning toward Hannon on this one. We've been at this for days and none of us can hold the circle, including the Vamp Queen. We aren't witches, and the power you're hitting us with feels strange. It's slippery and it comes on too fast." Eudoxia, the Vampire Queen, had taken the morning off. Being in a house full of cranky witches who had balked at the vampire intrusion was beginning to take a toll on everyone.

The Vamp Queen had actually arrived a few days ago. The promise of my blood and a step toward godhood had finally been enough to sway her, but she wasn't happy about it. She'd brought several of her minions, and keeping the witches and the vamps from killing each other was proving to be a full-time job for everyone. The house was so tense you couldn't sneeze without someone cocking their weapon or snapping down their fangs.

"All you have to do is pay attention and do what I tell you," Tally said to Ray, who now stood at attention in the middle of the circle.

We were situated in a room deep under the Coven. The circle to the Underworld was a permanent fixture here. Nothing like having a gateway to Hell in your basement. But I didn't have to live here so I couldn't really complain. It was just a ten on the creep-o-meter, if anyone had bothered to ask me. A thick line about six inches wide and a foot deep was etched into the raw earth. The circle was about ten feet in diameter and it'd been filled with a white powdery substance that I assumed was chalk from the smell. One of the witches had told me it made the connection to the Underworld super strong. I hadn't doubted it for a moment. Heavy magic swirled around the room and made my chest thump like I was too close to an amp at a rock concert. Whatever was meant to happen in this room was intense. I'd also been told the walls were over five feet thick and the door was made of several inches of steel with a silver core.

"The only thing I've been doing this entire time is paying attention," Ray complained, his arms up. "Do you honestly think I enjoy having my ass thrown against a wall over and over again?"

"When I hit you with the demon magic, you have to absorb it," Tally ordered, ignoring his snark like a pro. "Don't try and shield it away from you. Take it fully into your body. Reaper, you eat souls for a living, eat this, and when you're done, eject it." Without any more instruction she aimed an ugly, gnarled wooden staff at Ray. It was covered with gruesome, howling faces, all of them with reptilian eyes. Tally incanted something under her breath, and a current of energy manifested in the air and rushed forward like a lightning bolt.

It hit Ray squarely in the chest.

But instead of flying backward as he had in the past, he flung his arms wide and started to shake like he was possessed. After a few seconds he doubled over, straining, the magic clearly taking hold. His new fangs snapped down and his face began to shift downward in that awful vamp slide—his facial bones elongating, making his skin appear to be made of hot wax.

Something I wasn't fond of witnessing, but it couldn't be helped.

Ray had recently become a potent mix of vampire and reaper. The reaper piece had been a total surprise and the best theory any of us had was that my blood had brought his latent reaper genes to the forefront. I'd also inadvertently become his vamp Master after feeding him my blood to complete his transition—much to the chagrin of both of us. But because Ray was pigheaded and ridiculously ornery, the relationship hadn't solidified fully yet. Something new had been forged between us, however—something I was certain was going to be a work in progress until the very end of time.

I observed him now with morbid curiosity.

He was a strong, stubborn son of a bitch, and right now he was going to show me up or die trying. That kind of pure tenacity had earned him a grudging respect from everyone, including me. He was a brand-new supernatural, but there was no denying he was powerful.

"You will get it in no time, *Ma Reine.*" Naomi came to stand beside me. "I have no doubt you will learn to harness the magic as you have done before."

"That's the problem." I turned toward her, tearing my eyes off the spectacle of Ray. "I don't feel like there's anything to harness. Whatever Tally is throwing at us isn't full demon magic. I've felt the dark, smoky demon essence before, and I've shaken it off. But this is a hybrid of some kind and it shocks my system. It comes too fast and before I can think about mounting a defense, I'm out of the circle."

"It's concentrated on purpose," Tally said, overhearing our conversation perfectly. "If the Prince of Hell wanted you dead, it would hit you with the equivalent of a loaded handgun. This is cannon fire." She shook her staff. "When ten demons hit you at once, it will feel like a wrecking ball smashing into your body. This is me getting you used to it the hard way." She gestured at Ray, who was still doubled over in the middle of the circle. "Demons can't physically pass through the circle boundaries, but their magic can. They will do everything to try and knock you out of your only protection, and once you're out, you're free for the taking."

Only organic matter could pass through a witch circle.

I'd been told that if demons tried to cross the boundary their blood boiled in their veins, killing them instantly. I glanced down at my hemp fatigues. I wore the witches' standard combat uniform. It was dark green and formfitting, and it held a little stretch, courtesy of some natural rubber plant woven between the fibers for ease of motion. The outfit was also spelled to act like a shield against some of the lesser demon magic, but it didn't seem to be repelling much of whatever Tally had tossed at me.

Ray made a low strangled noise and began to stagger back and forth, bobbing and weaving like a drunk, his arms cartwheeling in front of him. He came close to the edge of the circle a few times but never crossed the line. Then, without warning, his chest bowed toward the ceiling and he bellowed, and a second later he doubled over and vomited all over the ground.

Thick, black sludge hit the dirt floor in a rush.

"Ew, Ray," I coughed, covering my face with the inside of my elbow as bile rose in my throat. When I'd taken in the magic Tally had thrown at me, it had never manifested physically like that. *We're not ejecting anything, so where does our magic go?* I asked my wolf. She gave a sharp bark and shook her head. I took that to mean she had no idea either. *Maybe it passes through us and that's why it's not working?*

Seeing it come out of Ray was sobering.

Before Tally could congratulate Ray on finally gaining control of the magic, a sweet child's voice piped up from my right. "It's okay to have a tummy ache. Demons don't like you." She pronounced the word "demon" like *denims* in her two-year-old cadence. "You are very strong."

"Maggie," Tally cautioned, the tenderness in her voice reserved only for her daughter, "you need to stay back. Mommy told you this was a very dangerous place. I agreed to let you come here at your insistence, but you have to follow the rules or go back upstairs."

The child had indeed wandered to the edge of the circle. She pointed to Ray as she took a step backward, listening to her mom like a champ. "Reaper." She smiled and clapped her hands together. "He did it."

He had indeed done it.

Ray stood there with a big grin on his face, a smear of black sludge across his chin. "Take that, huh, kid? The demons won't get me now."

Maggie giggled before she abruptly sobered. "Demons are bad."

"You got that right." Ray strode out of the circle. As he crossed the line a crackle of power ran through the room, making my ears pop.

"Maggie, take another step back," Tally ordered. The toddler hadn't gone back to play with her less interesting toys. "This circle is too dangerous for little girls. You can't stand so close. Go and play with your dollies while Mommy finishes her work. I'm almost done. There's only one more person to try." She arched a pointed look in my direction.

The child took a few more reluctant steps backward but was not interested one bit in playing with her dolls. Once she was situated a little farther away, she raised her chubby little finger at me. "Time for you to go."

I chuckled. "Oracles don't do time, remember, Maggie?" I edged toward the circle, resigned to yet another try. "But just for you, I'll let your mom blast me one more time. How does that sound?" As I walked by her, I patted her on the head.

"Kitty be mad."

She'd been calling Rourke "Kitty" ever since we arrived and it made me smile every single time she uttered that word. We had no idea how she knew what he was, other than she was an oracle and probably knew everything. But he'd indulged her the entire time, never correcting her. She'd even spent a few meals perched on his lap. The size difference between them was comical; he was the giant to her Tinker Bell. Witnessing him being so careful and patient with her was nothing short of heart-melting. He'd admitted to me later that he'd never held a child before. But it didn't matter. He was clearly cut out for parent duty. My wolf made a sound that sent chills racing up my spine and I had to shake it off quickly or I'd leave right now and go search for him.

Instead of having fun with Rourke, I sighed as I entered the circle for what felt like the hundredth time. I turned around and faced the bystanders, Tally, Naomi, Ray, and Maggie, who all stood on the outside, certainly hoping I would finally succeed and we could move on with business. "Kitty's not very happy with me today, is he?" I asked Maggie as I readied myself for the assault.

The child shook her head solemnly.

After he had witnessed me repeatedly ejected from the circle, receiving constant contusions and broken bones, and engaging in intense hand-to-hand combat training, it was decided Rourke was no longer allowed in the Circle of Fun room. His snarls and threats were making it hard for everyone to concentrate, including me.

Incapacitating a demon had been much tougher than I'd ever expected, because their true nature was serpentine and they had extremely hard skeletons. The demon dummies the witches had built were made of some sort of spelled metal and they were a bitch to destroy. I was always left bleeding and exhausted at the end of the day.

It didn't help that Rourke was still grappling with the fact that he couldn't accompany me to the Underworld.

It consumed our daily conversation, and truth be told, he had begun to wear me down. I was on the verge of allowing him to accompany me, even though the demons would know his signature the moment he crossed over. I couldn't deny that he was my strongest ally and undoubtedly the best man for the job. And, ultimately, I wanted my brother back, and having Rourke with me in the Underworld would give us the greatest odds of achieving that goal.

The door to the circle room opened with a loud groan and I glanced over, half expecting to see Rourke barging in. I knew he was close because my blood rang with his tension. Once the door was open I could scent him, but it wasn't him.

"Hiya," Marcy called as she shut the door behind her, using her backside. "How goes the training?"

"It sucks, as usual," I replied wryly, readying my stance to take the magic Tally was about to launch at me. "Your aunt is a wicked taskmaster and she thinks I can channel hybrid demon magic, but it turns out I can't. It's too strong and it keeps blowing me out of the circle."

"That's where you're wrong. It's not too strong." Marcy's tone was decisive as she strode forward. "You're just a wimp." She smiled as she bent over and swept Maggie into her arms. "Hi, Cherub. Fancy meeting you here." She planted a kiss on the child's cheek.

One of Maggie's arms snaked behind Marcy's neck. "Kitty be mad," she told Marcy in an earnest voice. "He be mad at me." She placed a chubby finger on her own chest.

Marcy raised an eyebrow at me.

I shrugged.

"No way, Big Kitty loves you. He'd never be mad at you," Marcy crooned. "Besides, cats don't get mad at people, they just get annoyed, and then all you have to do to fix it is feed them and they're totally over it. We'll get Big Kitty a nice sucker and he'll be good as new. How's that?"

Maggie didn't look convinced, but nodded anyway.

"Are you ready this time?" Tally asked me pointedly, bringing us all back to task. "It's my daughter's naptime and I'd like to wrap this up, if you don't mind."

"Oh, she's ready." Marcy smirked. "Look at her face. That's her determined look. See the way her lip is quirking up at that odd angle and her head is tilted slightly to the right? That's her game face, and it's *on*."

"You pain me. Right here." I pointed to my backside, keeping it clean for Maggie. I knew Marcy would appreciate the gesture. "And it makes me want to use this." I pointed to the bent knuckle on my middle finger. "And if I'm so wimpy, why don't you come in here and give this a try, huh? We'll see how long you can stay in the circle with demon magic up in your grill."

"I can't do that. You see, it's a sliding wimp scale." She re-adjusted Maggie on her hip while trying not to laugh too hard. "And my wimp runs strong. One blast of that demon juice and I'd be a goner. And once I was dead, you'd have one angry were-wolf up in your *grill* and you'd wish you were already in the Underworld." She chortled. "The demons would be delightful compared to the wrath of my guy. He'd rip this place apart trying to avenge my dead, broken body."

James and Marcy were mated in every sense.

And she was right. If something were to happen to her it would shatter him. "Angry" would not be an apt term. "Ballistic" would be closer to the truth. The two of them had come back unified from their ordeal with the sorcerers, but the only information I'd managed to pull out of her so far was hazy, involving "near death" and "best sex ever." It was typical of Marcy to keep it light and not delve too deeply into the trauma, and because she hadn't ventured into the nitty-gritty on her own, I hadn't pressed her. More than likely, being kidnapped had shaken her to the core and she wasn't ready to discuss the details yet.

On the flip side, along with terrifying her, it had also brought out a magic streak I'd known she had inside her all along.

No more tentative Marcy. This was kick-ass Marcy with new, twitchy fingers. The Coven was already in discussions to finally vote her in after she'd schooled a few of her old nemeses once she'd arrived—including Awful Angie, whom Rourke and I had the misfortune of encountering the last time we'd been here. Rourke was determined to strap Angie onto the ancient Vespa she'd forced us to use when we were running for our lives and send her into the lake as payback. But so far our paths hadn't crossed. It was likely Tally had sent her away on purpose, which had been a smart move.

"I don't have to worry about a pissed-off werewolf," I countered. "I wouldn't let you in this circle anyway—"

The blast from Tally's staff struck me so hard, my breath lodged in my chest and I collapsed to my knees. I grabbed on to my neck and gasped like a fish out of water, but I'd managed to capture the magic this time, so that was a win.

Tally's element of surprise might've been the ticket, but the only problem was I couldn't breathe. I pounded on my chest and clawed my neck trying to force oxygen into my windpipe, but nothing worked.

"That's it." Tally's voice sounded tinny and far away. "Take control of it. Mold it how you want it so you can force it back out."

It was clear she'd never been on the receiving end of her wicked staff from Hell.

I managed to draw in a single breath through a very closed airway, right as a soft tremor rippled through the dirt beneath me.

The movement was just enough to catch my attention.

Did you feel that? My wolf ignored me in favor of snapping and ripping at the magic consuming us. The hybrid demon magic had manifested as a thick, dark mass in my mind, and as it cascaded over my eyes I was launched into total darkness.

I'd indeed captured the magic, but I couldn't mold it. I couldn't do anything with it. And it was taking over as fast as it could.

My wolf managed to tear a small patch of clarity open in my mind and I sucked in another gulp of air as quickly as I could. I was still on my knees, but surprisingly, my body had started to shake in rhythm with the ground tremors.

The vibration running through my body hummed like a musical note.

I wrenched my head up, but I still couldn't see anything through the dark magic covering my eyes. *Do you hear that?* My wolf stopped what she was doing, her ears up and alert.

Someone was yelling and the only thing I could make out was my name.

Then two more words.

"Don't go!"

2

Don't go where? Where do they think we're going? My wolf didn't respond. Instead she cocked her head to the side, listening. The ground beneath us began to quake faster. Words were trying to force their way into my mind, but I couldn't make them out.

Someone screamed.

I shook my head, trying to clear the cloud of demon essence, but it was useless. It was too thick and concentrated. *Focus on the sound*, I told my wolf. I pushed outward, trying to break through whatever had encapsulated me.

With a resounding *pop* he came through in a rush.

Jessica, JESSICA! Listen to me. Don't go yet, you're not ready. Please. Throw the magic back out. Tally said you have to eject it. Dammit, listen to me! You have to get rid of it and get the hell out of that circle!

Rourke? How did you get in here? I must've been out of it longer than I'd thought. *What's going on?*

I felt your power shift so I kicked the door in, but it doesn't matter!

The circle is activating and taking you on its own. Tally thinks your magic, combined with the demon essence she threw at you, has triggered something. You have to rid yourself of the demon magic. Eject it before it's too late!

I'm trying, believe me. I staggered to my feet, my arms flung wide to the sides for balance. Ray had just been doing this very same thing, and now I knew exactly how he'd felt. This stuff was vicious.

With a start, I realized I was breathing again and the magic wasn't trying to choke the life out of me anymore. It was there, swirling around inside me, but it had settled like a thick fog around my senses, almost like it was waiting for something. *Rourke, I don't understand what's happening. Can't I just walk out of the circle? Once I'm out, Tally can suck this stuff out of me with her staff.* I took a few steps forward and abruptly smacked into something solid. It buzzed with the same magic that was now in my head. *Rourke, can you hear me? What's going on?*

Jessica, you closed the circle. There was anguish in his voice and he sounded very far away. *The magic you're emitting is mimicking demon magic. You fully absorbed whatever Tally threw at you and the circle now thinks you're some kind of powerful demon. It's about to give you a one-way ticket to the Underworld. You have to try to eject it.*

I stopped moving.

I had no idea how to get rid of it. *We have to harness it like Tally told us before,* I said to my wolf. She growled at me, giving me a look.

She was right. There was nothing to harness. The demon essence had begun to sink into me, mingling with my own magic.

Jessica, can you hear me? Rourke's voice shook as he pounded on the edge of the circle.

I can, but I can't see anything. The magic has completely settled over me. It feels strange. And there's a weird buzzing in my head. I can't find anything to grab on to. It's not threatening me—just the opposite. It's beginning to feel like my own.

I could hear him explaining it out loud to others, but his voice was muffled. Then he shouted, "I don't care! You have to help her. You have the fucking staff. Break the circle open and yank her *out of there.*"

The Kitty was indeed mad.

Tally's voice was calm. She was nearer or her voice projected better, either way I could hear her. "I can't do that. She's more powerful than this staff right now. She just has no idea how to wield the magic inside her."

No shit. *Okay, we have to figure this out on our own,* I told my wolf. *We have to dump this magic.* I raised my arms and pressed my palms against the inside of the circle, the same circle I had inadvertently activated. It felt hot and sticky, but totally solid. It curved slightly upward. I cleared my voice and yelled, "Can you hear me?"

"Yes!" Marcy answered first. "Jess, you have to get out of there. I don't care how you do it, but you need to get it done." Her voice was just short of frantic, which was a lot of emotion for her. "You can't go to the Underworld without any protection. Come on! There's no need to show any of us up and be all powerful and scary. Just dump the magic into the ground and the barrier will drop. Easy as pie."

My body began to shake like a tuning fork in tandem with the ground. The magic inside me grew stronger by the second. There was no pie here. It swirled through me in a massive current, a big haze of golden darkness, leaving nothing for me to hold on to.

I think we're feeding the circle, I told my wolf. *It's coming up from the ground and through us and back like a transformer. We're going to have to break the circuit the same way we did with Vlad's sword.*

"Focus on the ground," Tally ordered. "The earth will take the magic and disperse it for you. That's why we set the circle here. The reaper ejected it one way, yours will be another. You don't have to manipulate the magic, or try to change it, just take it as it is and dump it into the ground."

"Yeah," I muttered as I dropped to my knees, "because it's easy like that, but unfortunately there's no magic to hold on to." I plunged my hands into the dirt anyway. My claws were sharp and I realized I was in my Lycan form.

"Jessica, please." Rourke's voice was low. "I can't let you go to the Underworld by yourself." There was enough bitterness in that statement to last a lifetime.

"Harness the mass, Hannon," Ray yelled. "It was a big cloud of dark shit in my mind. Get your magic around it, and once you have it, squeeze it."

There was no cloud. Mine was a hazy brackish swirl that was now thoroughly mixed with my own magic. "There's nothing to grab on to, Ray." I panicked as the ground beneath me started to feel like a washing machine in its final cycle. "It's all one big… mass."

"That's impossible." Tally's voice held a hint of desperation. "The magic is its own being. It can overcome you, smother you, but it can't become a part of you."

"Tell that to the damn magic." I coughed as I plowed my hands deeper into the ground, hoping it would help me.

"*Ma Reine*," Naomi said in a worried tone. "You are starting to glow."

"Jessica!" Rourke yelled. "Hold on." His fists continued to pound against the barrier. The reverberations rang through me as I felt his sorrow beat against my chest.

There was more commotion as another voice entered the room. Danny's worry jumped in my blood. We were bound together. I was still his Alpha and his need to help me was strong. "This is a bloody travesty!" Danny shouted, joining Rourke on the outside of the circle, their combined blows resonating like thunder claps in my eardrums. "You can't go to the Underworld without anyone to aid you. How are you going to defeat the Prince of Hell, then? With your fists?"

"I'm…doing my best to stay here," I panted. *Did the color of the magic just change again?* I asked my wolf. The hazy darkness of the combined magic had turned a shade lighter. The ground below my knees kept up its frantic tremors and I knew instinctively that once the vibrations reached a crescendo it would be too late and I'd be on my way to the Underworld. I flexed outward, trying to send all the magic in my body into the ground.

"That's it," Tally urged. "Keep doing that. When you do that I can feel the barrier weaken."

I took a big gulp of air. "I'm tossing everything out but it keeps coming back too quickly. My body has done something to the demon magic. There's no separation anywhere I can see."

"You have a special ability to morph magic," Tally said. "It helps you fight off an attack, and it's truly remarkable, but I don't want you to do it right now. If the demon magic becomes a part of you, I have no idea what will happen."

"What did you *think* would happen when you pumped me full of this stuff?" I continued to push outward. But it was dawning on me that I wasn't breaking the circle, I was still feeding it.

"Clearly not this," she retorted. I was certain she had her hands on her hips and a wary look on her face. "The magnitude of power I shot into you was supposed to teach your body how to defend against such a force. You take the power in, harness it, and eradicate it. It's magic defense 101."

"Well," I said, "I guess I missed that class."

"There has to be some way to get the magic out of her system," Rourke snarled at Tally. "Do something to help her, witch."

"Cat," she replied, "I would if I could. But if what she says is correct, her body has completely absorbed the demon essence, and now it's changed into something unknown. There's no precedent for such a thing. Her own magic is fueling this circle. It thinks she's a demon."

"*Jesus Christ!*" he shouted. "I don't care about any of that or who's fueling what. I refuse to believe there are no other options." I felt his tension and his love. This was killing him. "What was your backup plan, witch? There has to be a way to break this circle open if something goes wrong."

"There is no *backup plan*," Tally huffed. "No witch can do what she's doing. Even if they were somehow chock-full of demon magic they couldn't activate the circle on their own. And if this were a real demon, they would know how to drop their magic to stop fueling the circle."

"Tally," I said, "I'm not a demon and I don't know how to stop it."

"I'm picking up on that," she answered. "It weakened when you first threw your power into the ground, but now the energy is circulating again. As much as I presume to know about demons, I've never spent any time with one. Witches eject power, but maybe demons do not. Instead of grounding it back into the earth, try to suck it back into yourself and see what happens."

"Isn't that what got me here in the first place?" I growled, my body still quaking in time with the ground. Suddenly I wondered if anyone else felt the earth shaking.

It pissed me off that I still couldn't see.

"Try to channel it where you keep your own magic," Tally ordered. "It's possible you can store it somehow. But you have to hurry."

I had no idea where I kept my magic. It had always just been there. I usually left the power grabbing to my wolf, who did it instinctively, because that was her role in this partnership. *Do you know how to do what she's talking about?* My wolf yipped. *Where do we put it?* I asked. My wolf started pulling back the magic we'd been channeling into the ground and began to funnel it into us, but I couldn't detect any secret spot she was stashing it. It just felt normal. I began to help—by doing what felt right, like stretching my muscles after a long run.

The force of cycling it back into us launched me forward onto my face. *"Oof."* I spit out a mouthful of dirt and braced myself back up on my arms. *Holy crap*, I said to my wolf. *There's no way we can harness all this. Plus it feels like it's growing.* The magic kept piling up on me, continuing to build. I was too new and unskilled to stop it, and my wolf was completely overwhelmed by how much was in our system. She abruptly stopped and sat down with her ears pinned back. And I knew once the magic reached a pinnacle, the circle would activate completely and we would be sent to the Underworld and there was nothing we could do to stop it.

The demon essence Tally had hit us with had inadvertently started something I had no idea how to control.

"Jessica." Rourke's voice was urgent. "Listen to me. If you go, I'll be right behind you. I swear. The witches will get me there right on your heels. Just hang tight until I get there. Find a place to hide."

"Rourke," I gasped, trying to push myself completely upright. I managed to stand and stagger a few feet. "You can't come after me. Give me your word you won't go to the Underworld. Once I get there, I'll have some reasonable cover, but you won't. They'll probably think I'm a demon with all this demon essence inside me. But they'll know your signature once you land. Please, you need to stay here."

A vicious sound erupted out of his throat. "Nothing is going to keep me from going after you. Nothing. I don't care if they send a thousand demons to hunt me down, I promise I will find you." His fists continued to pound against the edge of the circle. I knew they were battered and bloody by now. "If the demons find me, I will wreak havoc on the Underworld and give you the best distraction you'll ever get down there. I will gladly let those bastards catch me if it gives you a chance to escape."

"No," I argued, pain in my voice. "Please, Rourke. Let me go alone." Images of him being torn apart by demons raced through my mind. "We need to stick with the original plan. It's the best chance we have to get Tyler out. You need to promise me you'll stay here."

"She may be right," Tally stated quietly. "If her signature has changed now that she's taken in the demon magic, she may indeed be undetectable once she arrives. She will be able to navigate undercover for a time. It might be enough to find her brother."

"Arrives where?" Rourke bellowed. "Where exactly is this circle sending her, anyway?"

"There isn't one place it lands," Tally answered. "When the witches fuel it, we can pick from a number of designated places that are known to be low traffic. But we aren't doing this, she is. It's going to be keyed to wherever she directs it."

"Then you need to give her directions," Rourke said, his voice low and menacing. "And do it now. I want her in a 'low-traffic' area. She's going to need all the help we can give her."

The ringing reached a fever pitch in my mind.

It blocked out everything else around me. I could barely hear the conversation. I cupped my hands behind my ears and strained to hear Tally and Rourke, but almost nothing came through. "You're going to have to tell me now!" I yelled. "We only have a few more minutes at most. I can barely hear you!"

"Giving you directions is not going to be that easy," Tally shouted, her voice projecting. "In my lifetime, I've only sent two witches to the Underworld, and both of them were seasoned spell casters. And they were only there for moments at most, just to do recon. We have very few concrete details about the Underworld. The demons keep it secretive for a reason. We're only grasping at straws here."

"All that doesn't matter now," Rourke urged. "There has to be someplace that will guarantee her the best chance of survival. Where were you going to send her in the first place?"

"The trash heap."

"The what?" Rourke said.

I strained to hear Tally's answer. "Demons are fastidious about their persons, as you saw with the Prince of Hell. No hair is out of place, no button undone. They go to great lengths to keep their home life as sterile as possible. But they generate a fair amount of trash. We've figured out, over time, that they bring it to one single area. It's approximately ten miles wide and twenty miles long from what we can gather. It's also well away from their normal habitats. It's the best chance she has."

"Fine," Rourke answered. "If that will keep her off their radar, it works for me. She can hide in the garbage until we get there."

"It's not exactly like that." Tally hesitated. "We were going to arm her with spells. The area is still watched. I'm not sure if it's the best—"

"Hello!" I called. "It's not like I have a better option, and I hate to tell you this, but we're out of time." The circle quaked so hard, it rattled my bones. "Tell me what to do and you're going to have to yell it because my head is filled with a shrieking noise."

I heard her shout to others in the room and I could sense movement. "We're going to try and direct you to the garbage dump," she called, "but be on the lookout because there are demon beasts that eat the trash. I've never seen one, but I've heard they are formidable."

"What kind of . . . beasts are you talking about?" I asked.

Small ones, I hoped.

"The common term on our plane is chupacabra, a mix between a reptile and a dog, but in the Underworld they are simply referred to as hell beasts."

Lovely. My teeth had been clenched so long my jaw ached. The waves of sound and motion began to overwhelm me completely. My body was now shaking with enough force it felt like I was going to break apart, and the noise in my head sounded like a high-pitched siren. "How do I get to the dump?" I shouted, unsure my voice was being heard.

Outside the circle there were frantic calls and more footsteps. Tally's voice rang out. "Join hands," she ordered to someone, likely her witches.

The ground undulated beneath my knees like a roiling ocean. Tally's voice came in and out as she yelled, ". . . try to . . . deserted lands . . . farthest from She'ol . . . demons' prized city." Then Tally's voice addressed me directly, shouting, "Jessica, we will act as a beacon! When you fall, push your magic back up through the circle and search for us. We will try our best to show you the way!"

Time was up.

The crashing vibrations consumed me in one huge powerful wash of energy. My body shook and my teeth rattled. I plunged my hands deep into the earth one last time, hoping it would keep me rooted in this world.

But nothing I could do would stop the tide now.

I was going whether I liked it or not. A tornado of power

swirled around me, lifting me up before it sucked me into a vortex, sending me spinning end over end. I was on my way to the Underworld.

"Jessica!" Rourke roared. "We will be right behind you!"

The last thing I heard before I popped out of existence completely was a small voice that cried, "Bye-bye, wolf."

3

The pressure inside the vortex was so intense it felt like a vise was clamped around my entire body. While the crushing force came from outside, my insides felt like they were going to bust out of my skin.

As I fell, I tumbled in circles, my wolf emitting a low, continuous keening howl.

I tried to calm her. *We have to focus on sending the magic back up to Tally. I'm sure the travel time will be short and I really need you to focus. This is not a great time to lose your mind.* Her ears were still pinned back, her eyes unfocused, and she didn't respond at all.

Shitsocks. Landing us in the right place was going to be up to me. The air was weighty and it gave the strangest feeling—like experiencing g-force in a cloud. I pulled on my power and immediately realized my wolf had pushed it all outward instinctively like a shield. I had to give her credit. She'd obviously prepared us the best she could before she checked out. I couldn't bring my arms down, but her focusing our magic outward might have been the only thing keeping our vital parts inside my body. Tally had told us a supe had to be strong enough to make the trip; maybe this was what she'd been talking about. Without enough power, this vortex would rip you apart.

The problem was I had no idea how to send magic up when we were using it to protect us. I grabbed a single strand of muddy gold in my mind and unraveled it from the outside as quickly as I could. A small portion was going to have to be enough. *Can you get it together and help me? We need the witches' help and this is all we can spare. I'm going to shove it outward and hope we reach them. Without it, we risk landing in the middle of the demon city hall.* My wolf blinked and shook her head. *Snap out of it!* I yelled. *If we arrive in their most populated place, we lose our only chance to find cover.* She clicked her jaws at me and growled. *Good, glad you're back, now help me with this.*

Together we shoved power into the strand and sent it out into the vortex. We were still spinning, so it was almost impossible to know which way was up.

After a moment, a small tug pulled along our senses. *Did you feel that?* In the next instant a grid spread out in my mind with a yellow blinking dot in one spot. The witches were scary good. *We're going to have to home in on that one spot. Any idea how to do that?* My wolf rose and took a step forward, her nose lifted, scenting.

The air current began to change.

Strange smells and sounds started to creep into my consciousness. *We're getting close. We need to pinpoint a landing place quickly.* The pressure pushing on my head made it hard to stay focused. My wolf's ears perked up and she growled. We needed to send more magic into the vortex to get a better read on the grid. *The only choice we have is to weaken the magic shield protecting us.* My wolf had shaken off her fear of falling and was now on high alert as we both gathered magic by reeling it back into us, and as we did it, the shield diminished and the crush of the vortex pressed down like an anvil on our chest. My wolf took over as I struggled to breathe. *Don't take too much more*, I gasped, *or we won't be able to take in any more air.*

Passing out now was not an option.

In one heave, she shot all the magic we could spare forward in a rush.

It plunged into the vortex, seeking a clue to our destination. *Concentrate on the dot in our mind. We need to link the two together.* The witches' directions were still clear, glowing like a three-dimensional hologram in my mind. I had no idea if we were linked to them through magic or if they'd burned the map into my mind with a spell. It didn't matter. We had what we needed.

It's working. The dot in my mind turned blue once my magic connected with it on the plane below us. *Can you see that? We found it. It's to the left. We have to force ourselves to fall that way.* I willed us to move that way with everything I had and the beacon miraculously came closer.

With a snap of power, our magic fully engaged with our destination and a tether formed in the air between us, the magic connection guiding us. The witches were brilliant and I owed Tally my life for this.

We were closing in on the destination fast.

Smells, sounds, and lights started to whip by us as we flew at high speed into the demon atmosphere. *The demons must know how to slow down*, I told my wolf. *We don't. We're going to crash hard. Try to brace—*

We hit a pile of something with the force of a cannonball.

Large chunks of what appeared to be some kind of plastic flew in an arc around us as we plunged all the way to the bottom of the stack, hitting the ground so hard starbursts of light erupted in my vision and my brain felt like it had been scrambled. If the trash hadn't slowed us down, we would've splattered all over the ground.

I was just happy we hadn't lost consciousness.

I took in a few breaths and tried to steady myself. *What is this stuff?* We were covered from head to toe. It was impossible to know how much was on top of us, but the stuff surrounding us was oddly shaped and smelled strange. I moved my hand to grasp an edge of the plastic and a chain reaction of movement followed, causing a tinkling like dominoes. *Are these TV trays?*

Luckily for us, the trash was lightweight and angular. It resembled a kind of cafeteria tray, which made pockets of space around me. There was an odd light filtering in from above. Judging by the awful, pungent stench radiating from around us, there used to be something alive on these trays. On closer inspection, some of the trays also had bite marks out of the ends and residue that was bloodlike.

We had indeed landed in a trash heap. It also appeared that every demon here ate the same thing. And it didn't smell at all appealing. I gave an inward shudder. Time to move.

A sharp growl erupted from somewhere outside the pile.

Another joined it.

Those must be the chupacabras, I told my wolf. But she was way ahead of me. She'd already contained the magic that had been outside us during the vortex ride, and had begun to fortify a shield. *They must eat the leftover crap on the trays.* I wasn't looking forward to my first introduction to a chupacabra. *Let's sit tight for a minute and see if they leave on their own.* Fighting a hell beast when my body was healing from the landing was not on my top ten list of things I wanted to do at the moment.

But of course that was wishful thinking. In less than a minute, there must've been twenty of them growling and pacing out there.

Okay, we need to rethink. I believe the best thing we can do is try and outrun them. Judging by the light, we're in some kind of building. The demons must keep them locked up in here, but if we can get out of the building we may have a chance to lose them.

My wolf was not convinced.

Do you have a better idea? The trays started to shift around us as the beasts started to paw at the pile. *We're out of time. We run for whatever door we can find. Go!* We dove out of the mess, aiming for the least smelly area we could find. Less putrid hopefully meant fewer beasts. The trays scattered around us like dried leaves as we leaped. I hoped it was enough of a distraction to give us a head start.

We emerged and quickly rolled. I tried to find my footing but hit a few trays and inadvertently slid over the slick floor, using them like skateboards. I jumped off and spun in the air, landing in my fighting stance.

Right in front of thirty snarling chupacabras.

Jesus, they look like something straight out of a horror flick. Meaning they were some of the ugliest things I'd ever seen. But I shouldn't have been surprised. We were in Hell, after all. The only positive thing was that they weren't much bigger than a full grown pit bull. *Look at their creepy eyes. They're tiny and matte black.* But the most freakish part wasn't their beady eyes. It was that their front legs ended in hands. Hands! Little creepy black monkey paws with opposable thumbs.

I had to quiet my inner shriek quickly, but it wasn't easy. Their delightful appearance didn't end there. Bony spires stuck out of their heads and ran all the way down their backs. As they moved toward me, hissing and growling, I saw that only a portion of their skin was covered in spotty fur the color of death. The rest was translucent. Their organs beat right under their hide. One of them opened its maw wide and flashed a few rows of mismatched teeth—some long, some short—all sharp.

I growled back, flashing my own teeth, and edged slowly to my right.

They don't seem to have any urgency to attack us. A few of them were openly scenting me, their horrid snouts in the air. *Maybe I smell too much like a demon? Or at least enough like one to fool them?* I flexed my inner magic, pushing the muted gold, my signature mixed with the demon essence, outward.

If the chupacabras thought I was a demon, it was my lucky day. But before I had time to decide what to do, a roaring noise erupted overhead and the ceiling began to move. Slowly, a portion slid open to reveal some kind of weird-looking chute.

As one, all the beasts glanced up.

We have to move. We can't be spotted if this is some kind of surveillance apparatus.

I stumbled backward as plastic trays and food began to rain down from the chute above. Hearing the noise, the chupacabras took off after their next meal, slobbering as they went. They attacked the new pile of garbage, twenty feet from where I stood, like the rabid beasts they were, clawing and snarling their way to the top to get the choice pieces. A few of them began to fight one another for what looked like hunks of decayed meat.

Whatever it was, it was limp and gray and highly disgusting.

No wonder it smells like death in here. They're consuming rancid meat and they all smell like it. Good gods. This place wasn't going to get any easier, either. The Underworld was already proving to be tons o' fun. *Once they're done with that, they'll be back on us. We need to move now.*

I started to race in the opposite direction of the feeding frenzy. There had to be a door somewhere. The hazy blue light above made it hard to see. There were piles and piles of trays in every direction, some reaching the ceiling, which was made up of a shiny material that didn't look like anything I'd ever seen before. Not metal, not wood, something completely artificial.

Honestly, as long as we weren't in some kind of alien embryo, I could deal with it.

My wolf barked and I darted to the left, following a thin pathway between a few heaps. We had run no farther than fifty yards when I heard shuffling and angry growls behind me. The beasts had finished their meal and were coming after us. I picked up the pace, dodging the errant trays as best I could. *It's like a slippery hamster Habitrail in here*, I groused as I darted around another pile. *Is that a door up ahead?*

As we gained on it, I saw it was indeed a door. It was located in what seemed to be some kind of an elevator shaft, or something like it, because it was right in the middle of the room. I raced toward it with preternatural speed. The chupacabras were quite a few yards behind me. They were slower than I was, which was a benefit. Their long, creepy hand-paws must get in the way of securing a good grip on the slippery floor. Ick.

I slid to a stop in front of the door. It was like something out of an old army barracks. It was iron—or seemed like iron—and covered in rusted bolts. I placed a tentative finger on the handle to see if it was spelled. Nothing tingled back at me, so I grasped ahold and yanked the door open. It swung toward me freely with no resistance.

To expose a gaping void.

It was total darkness inside. No walls, no floor. Nothing.

Where are the walls? We clearly weren't in our world any longer. This was the best wake-up call I could possibly have had so early in the journey. Thinking the Underworld was like our plane was going to get me into trouble. I had to get my head in the game and take it as the warning it was.

Something nipped at my leg.

I'd taken too long and inadvertently let a chupacabra get too close. I kicked it away, and without thinking jumped onto the back of the open door and swung it closed with my body, my sharp claws digging in to keep us attached. *I hope the door doesn't disappear once it's closed.* Falling into another vortex to gods knew where wasn't on the list.

Nothing happened. I clung to the inside wondering what to do next as the beasts growled and scratched on the other side of the door. They knew I hadn't gone anywhere. *If we can get the beasts to jump in here they would disappear into the vortex. How do we do that?* We needed bait. *Too bad we don't have any rancid meat handy. The chupacabras aren't very tall. Maybe we can climb up to the top of the door and swing it open, and then jump over them and look for some meat? Once we find it we can run back here and throw it in and hope they go in after it?* Before I could implement my master plan to rid ourselves of the chupacabras, a human-ish voice shouted on the other side of the door, surprising me.

"What are you doing, you filthy beasts?" it shouted. "Move away from that portal door at once." The voice was guttural and unrefined. The only demons who would choose to speak English in the Underworld, as far as I knew, were imps. Imps were born on our plane, usually the offspring of human mothers, but many of them came here once they were old enough.

I could take an imp if I had to. I'd done it twice before. My wolf snapped her jaws in agreement. But showing ourselves would put us at a disadvantage. *Did that imp just say "portal door"?* I asked my wolf. I glanced behind me at the gaping void. "Portal" usually meant an easy way to get from one place to another, likely still on this plane, and from what I understood, was different from a vortex.

It would be risky to jump in and see where we landed. It might send us to a populated area, but it might not. My wolf cocked her head at me. *Don't give me that look. Just because I don't want to plunge through a portal if we don't have to doesn't mean I'm a wimp. For the moment I think it's wiser to wait and see what's going to happen here. This building is probably out of town and we can use that to our advantage. We need secrecy, not public portals that could potentially spit us out in someone's living room. The imp may leave on its own, let's give it a second.*

She snapped her muzzle at me, impatient with my humanness.

On the other side of the door there was a crack of what sounded like a whip and a whine from one of the beasts. "I said get back, you filthy mutts"—snap—"away from that door," the voice ordered. "We won't have a repeat of last time. I was flayed for that little stunt. Portals are not for you mongrels."

The imp had stationed itself right on the other side of the door.

My wolf stood at attention. Not a muscle on our body moved.

"What is that horrid smell?" The imp sniffed at the door like a dog. "Have you been naughty again?" Another crack sounded, followed by a wounded snarl-hiss. It was hard to feel sorry for chups, but they hadn't seemed overly ferocious. They were just trying to survive in this wretched place, and weren't we all? "Did one of you get in here and take something with you? It's the middle of the day out there," the imp muttered. "If you rouse the conclave by baying in the streets, it will be my head this time, not just my back."

Middle of the day was good. Was there a sun here? Demons hated sun. "Baying in the streets" also meant outside, not inside. Outside was good. Outside was not another enclosed space.

The door handle moved.

I slid one hand to the lever and tightened my grip to keep it in place.

"What's going on? Why won't this open?" The imp rattled the

lever. "Portal doors are never restricted!" More barks and growls erupted.

Time to make a decision. *I think we have to take our chances in the portal. You win*, I told my wolf. *Even if we fight this imp successfully, once we're done we have to fight that entire pack of chupacabras to find another way out.*

My wolf snarled in agreement and adrenaline shot through our system, fortifying us for what was going to come next. Reluctantly, I let go.

I heard the imp yell, "You little bastards will pay for whatever you did to this door" as we tumbled backward into the void.

4

Falling through the portal felt nothing like spinning through the vortex. It was empty space. Nothing touched me. There was no wind and no pressure—until I hit the ground.

Flat on my ass.

"*Ooof*," I gasped, my teeth snapping together. *Good grief, I thought it would be a longer ride than that. We were in there for less than thirty seconds.* My wolf ignored me in favor of scenting for danger.

I glanced around. We were sprawled in the middle of a doorway, half inside and half outside what appeared to be a low concrete building. The portal exit led into some kind of alleyway. Another building, which looked the same as the one I was currently hanging out of, sat directly across from me.

I gazed upward. The sky was a strange, muted purple.

I didn't want to admit it, but the color was sort of amazing and beautiful, even though it felt threatening and ominous at the same time. Oppressive energy pushed down on me as I studied my surroundings, trying to gauge what to do next. *There's enough light out here for it to be daylight, but I'm not sure if "sun" is the correct term on this plane. Let's move slowly.*

I stood, glancing around me like the fugitive I was, and tugged the portal door shut behind me. I made a mental note of where I was and knew I could find it by scent if I needed to. I couldn't detect any movement anywhere. Daytime hopefully meant downtime for demons, but I didn't want to get overly excited until I was sure. It was a lucky break I'd landed now and not in the middle of the night. I had a feeling night would be worse.

I crept forward, heading toward the edge of the building closest to me. There wasn't a street at the mouth of the alley, instead a field of lemon-yellow grass spread out as far as I could see with a lone tree positioned squarely in the middle.

Is the grass moving? I bent my head and narrowed my gaze.

It was in fact wiggling.

The tree was also strange. It was gnarled with no leaves. Instead it had bloodred flowers dotted all over its massive branches. And it was huge. Bigger than the largest redwood tree in our plane.

I slid to the very end of the building. Directly in front of me was the field of wiggling weirdness, and behind me and on both sides sat more buildings. All the same, row after row, for what seemed like miles.

I'd landed at the edge of the city.

The ground under me was paved with the same flooring as the dump, slick and perfectly flawless. It wasn't concrete, it was something demon-made and totally foreign to me.

Tally had been right. This environment was extremely sterile. There was no dust, no dirt, nothing out of place—exactly how demons kept themselves.

Scenting the air, I couldn't detect anything particularly strange, because it all smelled strange. The air held a lot of sulfur, but there were also many complicated layers on top. One of which was plum. *Why would the Underworld smell like plums?* Not normal plums, of course, but acidic, rotten ones. But my wolf wasn't interested in debating the smelliness of Hell with me. She barked, urging us on. *I know you hate it here. I do too, but we can't leave until we find Tyler. Let's try and scent him through all the rotten egg plum sauce. If he's here, his signature should stick out like a wolfy sore thumb. Raw animal smell in the midst of demons should be easy to track.*

With supreme caution, I peered around the corner of the building nearest the field. No one was around. Oddly, the sprawl of buildings reminded me of rows at the supermarket. Each building was the same size and the same distance apart as far as I could see in any direction.

Tally had referred to the main demon city as She'ol. *And something tells me we shouldn't walk on the grass.* Yellow was never a good color. That grass was basically waving a danger flag in front of us that said: "Step Here If You Want to Die."

We had no choice but to turn around and head through the buildings and into the city of She'ol. There wasn't a better alternative. We just had to make sure we did it carefully.

I stepped out of the shade of the building and into a sliver of sunlight, and sharp tingles raced along my skin. The light was intensely hot. I glanced down at my hands and watched as blisters began to form.

I ducked back flat against the building and brought my hands up. They were beginning to regenerate slowly, but they weren't clearing up nearly as fast as they should. *This is why no demon is outside right now. We'll have to use the daylight hours while we still can. I don't think the sun is going to do us any long-term damage, because our skin is already healing, even if it's doing it slowly. There's enough shade to weave our way through the buildings. I'm assuming eventually we'll hit some kind of town center or hopefully a building marked* Hostages, *but regardless, we have no choice but to move forward.*

I hadn't felt my connection with Tyler at all since I'd landed. He had to be here, but I wasn't picking up on anything from him specifically.

Tyler? I called in my mind, just to be sure.

Nothing.

Who knew how our mind powers worked on this plane? I wasn't expecting anything to work right.

It was time to move. I ducked along the building, hugging the walls to stay in the shade. Once I reached the end of the first building, there was another one about ten feet away. I raced toward it, the sun barely singeing me because I moved so rapidly.

Once I was clear, I started to jog. I darted through the sun when I needed to, but it was easy to keep to the shade in between. None of the buildings I passed had any windows. That made it easier not to worry about being spotted. As I ran, I held my nose in the air.

Do you see that break up ahead? Looks like the buildings are coming to an end. There was a definite change of scenery. *Once we make it to the last building, we need to gauge the sun and see how much more time we have left. We'll need to find good cover by the time it goes down. That's when Demonville must get active.*

A shudder ran through me. I was not looking forward to seeing a bustling Underworld.

Once we reached the end, I placed my back up against the side of the building and stuck my head out. The alleys I'd been running through had apparently dead-ended into a town square of some kind.

No yellow grass in sight, instead the entire square was covered in neatly clipped green turf, which I knew wasn't real grass, but the demons were obviously trying hard to mimic what we had at home. Surprisingly, the open expanse in front of me looked remarkably quaint, but incredibly off at the same time. The town center, from what I could gauge, was roughly the size of two foot-ball fields. The far side was flanked by a much bigger building, which looked fairly official. It was about as long as five of the regular buildings, and twice as high, and held a clock tower. I was happy to see it. "Official" meant I was closer to finding Tyler. To the left and right of the square were more regular buildings, evenly spaced apart.

But the most interesting aspect of the square, by far, was the number of white gazebos it held.

There were hundreds of them dotted all over the place.

The small structures appeared polished and shiny and seemed to have been lifted right out of some small town in Maine. The entire area looked like a decent place to take a Sunday stroll—if you were on the East Coast of the United States and not in Hell.

Look, all the gazebos have low railings. We can duck into one of those. I say we make a run for it and once we get out there, we can see the layout of the square better. They're also shaded. My wolf was hesitant and a low growl issued from her muzzle. *What, do you have a better idea?*

She flashed me a picture of us scaling the side of the build-ing and landing on the roof. I turned and craned my neck up. The walls of the building were smooth, but if I launched myself between the two with enough momentum, I could literally bounce between them and propel myself to the top fairly easily.

The building was no more than twenty feet high at most.

You're always thinking, I praised my wolf as I backed up. *Let's give it a try.* The top of the building would keep us concealed if we could duck below a lip, and it would give us a great vantage point to scout the area. I just hoped there was some kind of shade or we were going to burn up. *If there's no cover, we'll have to make it quick.*

I took a running leap and pounded off one side of the building and jumped to the other, and back again until I was within reach of the top. On the last leap, I stretched my hands up, grabbing the edge. I hauled myself onto the roof and readied myself to spring onto the flat surface, but stopped myself just in time.

Holy crap, what are those? My wolf howled in distress. The roof was covered in dark cone-shaped structures. They were roughly the size of mailboxes. The sun burned my skin and it started to blister as I stood gaping at the display, riveted in place.

I turned, shielding my eyes from the sun, and scanned the horizon.

Every rooftop as far as I could see held the same structures. And the buildings never seemed to stop.

Then the smell hit me.

Oh, good gods. *These are devil bat houses. They must come out after the sun sets. We have to get out of here right now.* I'd come in contact with the dreaded *Camazotz* already and I'd managed to purge their wicked poison from my veins, but this many would surely kill me. *Back to the original plan. We go scout out the gazebos, but it was worth the trip up, because now we know we can't stay out here. We'll have to search for a way inside the big building. Come nightfall this place is going to suck boatloads of ass.*

If the distance was right, the sun was going to set in ten to fifteen minutes at most. We barely had any time left to find cover.

My exposed skin was bubbling in earnest now.

I turned and jumped, landing cleanly in a crouch between the buildings.

With a sigh, I leaned back against the building closest to me and gave myself a few precious moments to heal. *If we can't find an easy way in somewhere, we're screwed. Once the sun goes down this place will be crawling with demons and devil bats and who knows what else. We go out there*—I gestured to the gazebos—*and try to find a way in or a good place to take cover until nightfall. We have no other choice.*

I took off before my wolf could argue and sprinted across the short expanse, hoping that if a demon spotted me they would only see a blur. I barreled into one of the small structures, hopping the rails in one jump. I immediately lost my footing, slipping in something on the floor and crash-landed under a bench, my body sprawled beneath me. *What just happened?*

The smell was putrid.

I gagged, rolling over, banging my head on a bench seat that ran all the way around the small space. I was covered in gunk. I brought my hands up and grimaced. *Good gods, what is this crap? It's all over.* My wolf snarled, her lips curled back to expose her canines.

We were lying in leftovers of a kill of some kind.

There were bits of rancid meat and blood all over me and the floor. I sucked in a shallow breath and prayed my breakfast stayed down. *This is where the demons must eat. That's why there are so many structures. These are outdoor cafeterias.* I lifted myself up, staying low, slapping the big, sticky parts off my body.

Something chirped above me.

I didn't want to look.

I looked.

Mesh netting of some kind separated me from what looked to be hundreds of small piglike creatures. They were roughly the size of large rats and they all began to squeal in earnest, crawling all over one another in fear as they spied me peering at them.

This place keeps getting worse, I complained to my wolf. *We have to find Tyler soon and get out of here.* I'd only seen a small portion of this world, but I never wanted to set eyes on it again. *Why would anyone* ever *choose to come here willingly?* We'd only been in the Underworld an hour and I was totally disgusted.

The little piglets were covered in scales and a coating of short, coarse hair. As these ones stirred up a racket, more gazebos started erupting in similar sounds. *They think it's feeding time, and we're here to eat them, which it will be soon if I'm not mistaken. Once the sun goes down, it must be a dinner free-for-all.*

There was no way to quiet them down.

I poked my head over the rail, scanning the fronts of the buildings, searching for a way out, or at the very least a hiding place that wasn't covered in bloody bits and squealing piglets.

Each building facing the square had a row of ten doors. *Once darkness falls they must open those doors.* I knew without a doubt that was how the demons were released. *And we're standing right in the middle of their dinner party. We'll have to go back to the chupacabras. I can't believe I'm saying it, but that's a safer bet. We can wait there until—*

I spun around to exit the gazebo and crashed to one knee.

We're caught in something. I bent over to check, and even though I hadn't felt it, it seemed my foot had slid into a manacle of some kind. Before I could do anything about it, the floor shook and a small compartment in the middle of the gazebo slid open to expose two rows of stacked TV trays. The same kind I'd seen at the dump. *Okay, I'm not liking this.*

The cuff that held my ankle had obviously risen up from the floor prior to the trays, but I'd missed it because of the piglets' shrieking. I counted ten sets of manacles total and they'd all been engaged. My ankle had just been in an unlucky spot. *We must have triggered something to start the dinner process. The demons must get wild when they eat.*

If not, I didn't really want to know why they had restraints under all the seats.

I wrapped my hands around the strange material gripping my ankle and tried to pry it open. It was smooth and slick just like everything around here and I couldn't get a good grip on it. The metal, or whatever, was unforgiving. It made sense it had to be super strong if it was meant to hold a struggling demon, but that wasn't helpful to me.

Fur sprouted along my forearms as I increased my effort. The squealing above me didn't make it any easier to concentrate. *Send us more adrenaline.* My wolf obliged and my muscles tightened like granite beneath my skin. *I think it's coming loose.* With a pop, the thing cracked, but it wasn't enough to open it completely. The piglet squeals reached a fever pitch above me. Something was happening.

I glanced upward just in time to see the netting give way.

Ducking quickly, I covered my head with my arms as roughly two hundred scaly rat-piglets were dumped onto my head. *Crap!* They bounced all over me, squealing and oinking—if you could call it oinking. It sounded more like hissing. *Swat them back, we don't know if they're venomous.* As they fell, the railings along the outside of the gazebo morphed together like something out of a sci-fi flick, solidifying the enclosure so the tasty demon treats didn't escape.

I slapped the piggies off me as fast as I could. My ankle was still stuck, so I couldn't do much more. But the luckiest part of being covered in scaly demon piglets was that they didn't seem interested in me. After their initial fall, most of them had scurried under the benches as fast as they could. They wanted to escape their fate as much as I did.

Join the club, little piglets from Hell.

They aren't biting us, but don't look into their beady little eyes. Let's just focus on freeing this thing from my ankle. I went to work on it again. *Once we get this off, we're going to set these demon pigs free. They can serve as a distraction while we find our way back to the portal door we came through from the trash heap.*

I glanced up at the sky. The sun was setting too quickly for my liking. As the sky eased into darkness, the purple hue turned into a magenta twilight and misty clouds began to fill in above me. There were no stars that I could detect, which made it seem like we were in a huge horror-filled gymnasium and not actually outside.

The shackle wouldn't budge any farther no matter how much strength I used. I leaned over to examine it. It was completely melded together with no discernable seam. It looked like it was one housing, and it probably contained some magical demon essence I knew nothing about.

I stopped working and searched for something that might be able to help me, like a release button of some kind. After the demons had eaten their fill, they had to be able to get free of the manacles. *Look for a lever. When the demons are done feasting they should be able to turn the horror show off so they can go back to doing their regular business.* Whatever that was. Where did one go after group ravaging?

I didn't want to know.

I really didn't.

Everything in the gazebo was whistle-clean, except for the floor. There wasn't a crack in sight and I didn't see any buttons or levers. My wolf barked. Her muzzle nodded upward. I followed her direction. On one of the pillars, toward the ceiling, I spotted a small button built into the structure. Unfortunately, it was attached to what appeared to be a speaker box.

We can't risk hailing anyone. I instantly pictured a demon receptionist with a beehive hairdo and pointy glasses trying to understand our issue on the other end. *We can't use that. Look again. There has to be some kind of unlock button. I bet there's something that will get rid of the piglets too, in case they don't eat all of them or have an emergency during dinner.* Who knew, maybe the demons went into a rage as they ate? I glanced up and studied the mesh that had held the creatures. There had to be a trigger for that.

Then I saw it.

Two grooves, barely identifiable, right by the connection point of the roof and the mesh. *That looks like something. They have to get these piglets in here somehow. I bet there's an elevator or another door in the floor, and I bet that switch opens it up.*

Finding the piglet button was helpful, but that still left the problem of the shackle attached to my ankle.

If I couldn't get it off, I couldn't engage the switch to see what happened, because I couldn't reach it. The piglets scurried back and forth, giving me a wide berth, squeaking like mad. I'm sure they were confused as to why I wasn't tearing them to shreds with thirsty abandon.

I refocused my energy on my ankle. "Get out of my way," I muttered as I swatted one of them. A few of them were becoming a bit too curious. As I worked, my hand accidentally struck the underside of the bench. *Did you feel that?* I quickly rolled onto my back and stretched myself under the bench across from me. Sure enough, each seat had its own release button. It was seamlessly made and almost undetectable, integrated into the material, just like everything else around here.

I slid out, trying not to cringe too much about my choice to roll around in the muck again, and ran my hand under the bench closest to my ankle. I felt the shallow depression and jabbed my finger in it.

Nothing happened.

I pressed it over and over like an irritated salesman ringing a doorbell. *Dammit, why isn't this working?* I finally stopped and all at once the shackle popped off.

Victory at last. I whipped my leg out and stood as quickly as I could. The rails had stayed closed and the piglets continued to alternately cower and zip around the small space. The first order of business was to set them free.

I punted one away from my foot and strode to the entrance, which was now solid from the waist down like the rest of the gazebo, and brought one foot up and rammed it into the material. Hard. It splintered, but in a funny way, like a crack in a block of ice.

One more kick and a big chunk flew out. It was a hole big enough for the little beasts, so I was satisfied. I turned, thinking they'd all be lined up behind me waiting to scurry to freedom.

Not one of them moved.

"Shoo!" I yelled. "Get out of here." I backed out of the way so they could run. When they didn't react, I bent over and waved my arms, trying to spark them into action. "Go free and be my diversion! While the demons worry about you, I'm going to make myself scarce."

A few of them waddled up to the opening and sniffed, but none of them ventured out.

It appeared they were smarter than they looked.

I had to give them some credit. I didn't want to go out there either. But before I could toss them out one by one, a tremor shook the ground, followed by a loud hum. It sounded like a hundred elevators had engaged at once. I glanced around me, somewhat surprised. The sun had set and I hadn't noticed. I'd been too busy trying to free myself from the manacle.

The humming sound whirled for about ten seconds. The piglets began to squeal like never before. Their cries held an anguish I was beginning to feel myself as I watched all the doors across the all the buildings slide open at once.

5

I was frozen into place as I watched hundreds of demons emerge from the newly opened doors. They filed out into the square in orderly rows. They were all dressed alike in the same outfit, a dark-colored jumpsuit with what appeared to be zippers up the sides. They could've been strips of metal, but I couldn't see the small details because the twilight made it too hard.

Every demon exiting the buildings had very precise features. Human, but too sculpted. No flaws, hair perfectly slicked back, skin shiny. They clearly mimicked their leader in their appearance. It was surprising they weren't in their more reptilian forms. The Prince of Hell had been glamoured on my plane, so here, on their home turf, I'd expected to see the demons in their truest forms. It seemed like a lot of work to be glamoured all the time. But there was no mistaking it, they'd all been ordered to look the same—exactly like the Prince himself.

It was super strange and more than a little unsettling.

My wolf snarled, snapping me out of my stupor. I dropped to the floor of the gazebo. We were out of time. None of them had spotted me, as far as I knew, which was a miracle. But then, they hadn't been expecting an intruder. Having a fugitive in their midst had likely never happened before. But they would scent me soon enough. I was covered in rancid piglet juice, so that helped. It was weird to be thankful for putrid blood and guts, but at this moment I was. I also smelled, at least partially, like a demon. I hadn't triggered any of their alarms yet, so it was safe to assume whatever magic had mixed with mine was keeping me cloaked for the time being.

Before I could decide if I should flip the lever in the ceiling, clear liquid started pouring over me from small sprinklers that had just emerged from strategic points around the gazebo. A beat later small drain valves slid open in the floor. As the strange wetness coated me, a voice came over a loudspeaker in a language that was clearly Demonish, followed by English, likely for the imps: "Cleaning commencing. Please wait in an orderly line."

The liquid flowing over me, however, wasn't water.

It was thicker and slimier—like water mixed with gelatin. The bits and blood attached to my body coagulated and slid right down the drains, cleanly and efficiently. *We have to escape before the cleaning is over. This has given us a few minutes grace period, but we have to move.* The piglets scurried around squealing and slipping in the liquid gel as they struggled to find some traction.

I shimmied on my belly, batting them away from me, and made my way over to the TV trays. The hatch was just big enough for my body to squeeze through. It would've been nice to know what was down there ahead of time, but it had to be better than what was up here. I didn't have to worry about convincing myself for long, because there was no way I could take on a legion of demons myself. It was exactly like what I'd told Tyler and Danny when we'd scaled the mountain to Selene's lair. An army of *anything* could defeat even the strongest supernatural.

The plastic trays had to have been stacked by something, so that meant a workroom or assembly line below. That equaled places to hide until daylight. The demons had come up in elevators, so their habitat had to be underground. Going below was my only option now that the horde was here for their evening meal.

I grabbed a handful of trays and lifted them out, trying to slide them as quietly as I could under the benches. Instead they shot like Frisbees around the slippery mess and the piglets hissed at the intrusion. I ignored them. Luckily the clatter was covered up by the still-running sprinklers in all the gazebos. The cleaning process was loud, and all the other piglets had started shrieking like never before, knowing dinnertime was upon them.

The trays were piled shoulder-deep in the hole. Once I reached the end of the line, I could see they'd been stacked on a hydraulic lift of some kind. I grabbed the last few off and tossed them to the side right as a red light on the bottom started to blink and a low noise issued from the lift. *This thing is going down to refill. Let's go.*

The trapdoor started to close on its own. I dropped my knees in, ducking low, barely making it before the hole sealed up from the top. As the lift started moving downward, I realized a good portion of my hair had caught in the seam. "*Ow!*" I cried, as I reached up to rip the ends away before it was torn completely out of my head. There was no time to lament the loss. I was away from the legion of hungry jumpsuited demons, so that was well worth the cost of some hair—hair that would regenerate within moments.

I crouched on the lift, making myself as small as I could. But I wasn't achieving inconspicuousness, because I was dripping wet. Thick, pudgy water droplets lazily rolled off me and plunked somewhere below. If anyone was down there, they would be alerted to something strange by the unexpected shower from above. But I had to admit, it was a relief to be wet and not bloody.

Not only had the liquid bathed me, it had also somehow eaten away any blood and guts that had been left behind.

I was squeaky clean.

The lift began to slow. The ride hadn't been a long one. *We take the element of surprise.* Before it came to a full stop, I dropped into a small dimly lit room filled with equipment and cages and cages of squealing piglets. I did a full scan, staying low in my fighting stance.

There were no demons in sight.

At my arrival the chatter of the little beasties increased. The lift came to a complete stop, engaging with a long, motionless conveyor belt that went between the walls, likely linking the gazebos together. I crouched next to it and ran through a row of supplies parallel to the conveyor. The room was stacked full of trays and strange-looking implements. The cages lined the back wall. I stopped, peeking my head above a low shelving unit. This room was about the size of a modest living room. The conveyor belt ran the entire length and disappeared through a cutout in the wall.

All at once the thing whirled to life.

I stood slowly, examining it as it started to move. It was more streamlined than anything I'd seen, sleek with lots of shiny metal. Most of the noise it made was drowned out by the continued squealing of the piglets.

Time to make my exit.

There was only one door. As I rushed over to it, I realized it had no handle. Voices echoed from out in the hallway and I ducked behind it three seconds before it opened. From the gap, I could see two demons enter the room, both of them in jumpsuits. They were speaking Demonish and didn't glance behind them.

They both stopped in front of the lift I'd come down on and started chattering in earnest. The door they'd just entered was closing and I wrapped a single finger around it to keep it in place.

I needed a distraction. The beasties were still making a racket, but I needed more than that if I was going to make a clean getaway. I didn't have any spells on me and I couldn't shoot any magic. I could try to throw power into a verbal command, but that would defeat the purpose of being stealthy.

Instead, I plucked a can of something off the shelving unit next to me. It was heavy and that made me happy. *We have to make this count.* I didn't have a lot of space to prime my arm, but I was a supernatural, after all. My wolf flooded me with adrenaline as I hurled the can straight at the biggest cage I could see across the room, aiming for the locking mechanism.

The can exploded on impact, sending the contents, which were pea green, splattering everywhere, and popping the door to the cage neatly open.

A beat later everything in the room erupted into total chaos.

I blew out a relieved breath as the beasties began to flood out of their trashed cage as quickly as possible, crawling over one another in an effort to get free. And to turn things even more in my favor, several piglets dropped from the ceiling above onto the lift. It seemed the ones from the gazebo had found a way out, or the floor had opened up—either way, they were raining down from above.

Each of the demons sprang into action. One went for the cage and one jumped onto the lift to try to contain the masses as they started bouncing like plump treats onto the conveyor belt.

I used my advantage and ducked around the door and zipped out of the room.

There were no demons lingering in the hallway. *These lucky breaks are going to stop very soon*, I told my wolf. *We need to find a place to lie low until we can figure out where we are.* The hallway ran both ways. I chose left. *We need to make our way to the big building. I'm fairly sure we take a left, and then another left, but I'm not sure. Do you have a better sense of where we are right now?* My wolf barked and flashed a perfect picture in my mind of the view from the roof, marking our current location on the map. *You are so very handy. I love that about you.*

Once we were out of the this particular hallway, we would need to keep left in order to arrive at what I hoped was the main building in She'ol. I raced by a bunch of closed doors. I could hear piglets chirping and hissing behind every one of them. The assembly line was in full swing; I could hear the conveyor belts going. *There's a door at the end that looks promising. It's bigger than the other ones.*

This one thankfully had a handle.

It was a detailed knob with what looked like a devil head carved into it. I put a single finger on the handle, testing for power or spells. It was clear. I palmed it and turned. It opened with no resistance, and to be as cautious as I could be, I put an ear to the space and scented the air. I heard nothing. I was certain I would run into something eventually, but my hope was that most of the demons who didn't run the food service shift were up top for suppertime. It seemed like everything was regimented here, so it was a good bet they had all gone to dinner.

I snuck around the corner, and into a very strange land.

Well, this is…unexpected. Or maybe the neat gazebos and innocuous buildings were unexpected and this is what we should've expected all along? My wolf growled, her ears twitching. The sulfur smell was so strong I had to cover my nose and mouth with my hand. On closer inspection, I could see sulfur water seeping out of the walls. No wonder.

We had just entered the true bowels of Hell.

No more buildings and seemingly normal structures. This was what the real Underworld looked like.

This tunnel was much larger. I was guessing it had to be one of their main arteries. It was wider, likely to accommodate more traffic, but I also knew it was a primary thoroughfare because it seemed almost *alive*. Dark red porous rock jutted out all around me. It was hot and humid and the walls were bumpy and coarse, with tons of wide holes resembling coral. Fluid leaked everywhere. There were smells I've never scented before—all of them ghastly. I moved forward cautiously, stepping over a huge channel that ran down the middle of the tunnel to catch all the runoff, and once on the other side, I started to jog.

I had no idea where my final destination was, but the image in my mind, courtesy of my wolf, kept me focused. I passed door after door as I ran. All of them plain and unassuming. They looked completely out of character nestled into the red, bleeding rock.

Look for another big door with an ornate knob. Can you scent anything? If this was a major passageway, like I guessed, Tyler's scent should be lingering here somewhere. When the Prince had arrived back in Hell with my brother as his prize, he would've had to walk somewhere down here.

As I ran, the tunnel meandered right, and then left. After a long curve, it straightened out for a short distance before it abruptly ended in a T. I slid to a stop and listened. I heard voices down both corridors. Once the tunnel had straightened out there had been a smattering of a few more doors. *Let's duck behind one of these doors until it's clear. We can't risk sounding the alarms yet. Cross your fingers we find something nice inside instead of another set of beasties.*

I backtracked to the last door I'd passed. It looked the same as all the others. I didn't have time to test the handle, because the voices were getting louder. I grabbed the knob and it swung open cleanly. I stepped in cautiously, clicking it closed softly behind me.

The room was pitch black.

I placed my back against the door and slid down into a crouch. My nose rose in the air and I scented the space. My skin prickled.

We weren't alone in here.

Something moved directly in front of me. *Do we stay and fight or should we flee before it figures out who we are?* The decision was made for us when multiple voices erupted right outside the door. A moment later alarms sounded. Whooping sirens echoed all around us.

They knew I was here.

Before I could decide if I should fight the unknown in front of me, or race back into the tunnel and take my chances, a low red light started to blink next to the door and a voice came over a loudspeaker, speaking Demonish and then English: "Alert, alert. There is an intruder in our realm. We must stop it at all costs. All demons to your armament stations."

Armament? That didn't sound good.

"They're talking about you," a voice in the darkness purred. "But you knew that already, didn't you?"

I sprang to my feet, trying to make out the details in the room via the blinking red light, but there only appeared to be solid rock in front of me.

That couldn't be right.

"I am here, but you must part the curtain of darkness to see me."

The voice was decidedly female.

Demonesses were rare. From what little I knew about demons, there were only a handful. But honestly, what did I really know? Everything I knew about the Underworld had been gathered from tidbits from other supes, myths, and old books I'd read as a child. The entire Underworld could be run by demonesses and none of us would've been any wiser. No supernatural I'd ever known of had ventured here before.

"And how do I 'part the curtain of darkness' and why would I want to?" Establishing a motive was the first step.

She chuckled. It was a strange sound, tinkling coupled with a coarse undertone. "And where will you go now? They have filled the tunnels. Can you not hear them? Soon they will have the hell beasts scent your precise location and you will be found. Without my help you are completely lost."

"The chupacabras aren't that fierce," I muttered. "I could handle them if I had to."

"Then you have not met their mothers."

Mothers? The garbage dump was filled with baby chupacabras? Well, that explained why they hadn't torn me to shreds. *Dammit.* "Why are you in here?" I asked. "And why are you hiding behind the mysterious 'curtain of darkness'?"

"I am a prisoner. As you will be very soon."

A prisoner meant dangerous. I immediately wondered what you had to do to be arrested in Hell. It had to be something big. When I didn't respond she continued, "You are the girl they are so worried about, am I correct? The she-wolf who is fated to rule our lands?"

"Hmm, the ruling part is totally wrong. I want nothing to do with this place. If the demons could finally get that through their thick, reptilian exoskeletons, my life would be a whole lot easier."

"That's where you are wrong," the voice said. "Our Scriptures are never written in error. They were composed in the Time of Lucifer. If it says you are Fated, that means you are strong enough to rule Hell. Whether you do so or not"—she paused—"may ultimately be up to you, but that doesn't make you less of a threat in our eyes."

"It seems counterproductive for the Demon Lord to want me here in the first place, then, don't you think? Why lure me to the Underworld if I'm the biggest threat to the Prince's rule?"

"He is very shrewd but compelled by his quest for supreme power. You stand solely in the way of that. As every demon child knows, what is written in the Scriptures must come true. The Prince must dispatch you or his rule will remain in question for the rest of eternity."

Snarling and barking erupted right outside the door.

"Hurry," she urged. "You are almost out of time. You must come to me or you will be captured and contained. I am your only hope of escape."

My wolf growled and snapped her jaws, shaking her head. *I agree, it doesn't feel like exactly the right choice to move forward*, I reasoned with my wolf, *but what other options do we have?* My wolf flashed me a picture of us running back to the trash heap. *We can't get there now, the sun has set. If we leave, we have to deal with the demons outside our door first, and even if we don't get caught out there, we won't last outside with all the demons and the devil bats. And if we get caught we're no use to Tyler.*

"If you do not come to me, all will be lost," the voice said.

"We have to make some sort of a deal or I'll have to take my chances elsewhere. My priority is to find my brother and get back to my plane, and if you don't make a pact with me now, I can't trust you'll help us without betraying us."

"In your world you may swear oaths; we do not do such things here," she answered.

"Well, what do demons do, then? And why would you want to help me, anyway?" I asked curiously. "Why not let me get eaten by the beasts? You should have no stake in what happens to me."

More barking and snarling filtered in through the door. *There must be forty of them out there.* My wolf howled and gnashed her teeth.

"I do have a stake. I will help you, because you are my only ticket out of this place. Fine, we will make a formal agreement, then," she said. "I will lead you to your brother, and to freedom, and you will agree to take me along to your human realm when you return."

"Wait...what...*what*?" I sputtered. "I can't agree to bring you home when I have no idea who or what you are. That's insane."

"Your brother is slated for execution this eve." Her voice was stone-cold. "He has been...less than agreeable." I could hear movement, but it was strange I couldn't see her. "If you do not free me, all is lost for you *and* your kin."

The beasts were right outside the door. Vicious snarls erupted as they began to claw at the material. Multiple demon voices rang out and footsteps were running from all directions.

I couldn't let Tyler die, and there was no way to know if the demoness—if that's what she was—was telling the truth or not. "I'm not going to agree to bring you back to my plane right now, but I *will* agree to consider it. And you have to swear to"—what could I say to bind her to me?—"follow my rules with no exceptions as we move forward, and after that we decide from there."

"I agree to this," she answered. "But you must swear to give me fair appraisal, as I risk my life to help you. My deeds must not be done in vain. As is custom in your realm, it is the same here, all favors in the Underworld are paid in return of equal value. If I save your life, and your brother's, you will owe me at least one favor of my choosing."

"I swear," I agreed. Technically she was right. If she saved my life, I would owe her a life debt. But I could argue the payment, and I could choose to grant it later.

It gave me a small out.

"Now you must hurry, they are almost upon us," she urged. "Step forward and wave your hand in front of you. The curtain will part to allow you through, and once you are on my side, you will be concealed."

I took a bold step forward, the snarling and scratching intensifying on the other side of the door. My wolf howled her displeasure at my choice to trust in the unknown, but I ignored her. What other options did we have? My main objective was to find my brother. And getting captured by these demons was not going to achieve that.

I stretched my hand out in front of me as the door crashed open behind me.

6

The texture of the air was strange, like invisible feathers brushing along my fingertips. As the door behind me exploded open, the demoness seized me by the wrist and hurled me behind her in one clean toss.

I crash-landed behind a dresser. At least I think it was a dresser.

Demons stormed into the room I'd just been in, barking orders in a frenzy of guttural voices. I peeked out from behind a shiny metal structure. It was light enough to see in here, not total darkness like out there. The demoness faced the invisible curtain, watching the demons swarm. It was like looking through a smoky screen.

"They cannot see in here until they part the curtain," she said, not bothering to turn and face me.

I poked my body up farther. There had to be twenty of them out there. From behind, I could see that the demoness had long blonde hair tinged with metallic green strands. It shimmered slightly as she moved, the green combined with the blonde like flowing liquid. I hadn't thought she'd have blonde hair, or of any demon having blonde hair for that matter, so that was a surprise. I was going to have to refer to her as a *her*, not an it, because she was so clearly female. I was going to assume she was a demoness until she told me otherwise. She had a curvy figure and delicate hands. I quickly overlooked the fact that she was dressed in a bizarre gray jumpsuit that, at least from the back, appeared to be made of a latex-type material. It wasn't exactly like what I'd seen the other demons wearing, but similar enough. The shiny material gave her a definite ninja look. Again, I hadn't been expecting anything like this. The demons were totally surprising me. I'd pictured reptilian horrors, sort of like you'd conjure from all the B movies, half man, half reptile. Instead they were glamoured humans who wore strange jumpsuits. Hardly terrifying at all. My wolf barked, ending on a growl. Well, sort of terrifying in an odd creepy way.

Alarms began to ring as steam shot up through the floor. The invisible curtain must be dropping. I ducked back down behind my small cover.

Immediately the demoness engaged in a violent argument with whoever had broken in to find me. They were all speaking Demonish, so I had no idea what they were saying. I couldn't see anything from my vantage point, cowering behind the furniture.

All of a sudden there was a huge explosion and the demoness flew back in a shower of sparks. She crashed against the far wall of the cell and fell limply to the ground. There was more yelling, but then, surprisingly, the footsteps retreated.

The demoness lay there, in my sight line, breathing heavily, head down at a strange angle. I had no idea what had happened and I had no idea if I should try to help her. I made a move and my wolf snarled, snapping at the air in front of her decisively.

Okay. Fine. Have it your way. We'll wait. Instead of helping the demoness, I readjusted myself against the cool wall and slid from my crouching position into a sitting position, eyeing her as I made myself more comfortable.

Everything around this place was cold and slippery in the strangest way.

I moved my back in a circle and it slid against the wall like the surface was made of butter. I turned and placed my fingertips against it. *What do you think it's made of?* My wolf ignored me in favor of keeping her eye on the demoness. *Well, it's not made from any material we have at home, that's for sure. There's no residue, but it feels organic, not artificial.*

The demoness made a noise and I turned quickly, watching as she brought her head up. Her features from the front were pristine, very sculpted and angular. She had a long, slim neck and her skin was shiny like the Prince of Hell's, but there was a marked difference.

She appeared to be more human somehow.

Moaning and in obvious pain, she turned toward me and met my gaze straight on. *Good grief, she's beautiful.* My wolf snarled. She was gorgeous in a foreign way—as in, I knew she was beautiful, but I couldn't explain why.

I extended my power outward, trying to get a better read on her signature.

"Your power feels demonic," she said, her eyes pinned on mine. "That is very peculiar."

Her power was heady and strong, but again, different from the Prince's. "I'm assuming you're a demoness. Are you glamoured?" I asked, ignoring her comment about my signature. I had to figure out a way to make this work between us—demoness and wolf—if that was even possible.

She chuckled. Her eyes were arresting. They slanted upward at the outer corners and her pupils weren't full serpentine slits like I'd glimpsed when the Prince of Hell's glamour failed. They were more like cat eyes, with a wide oval pupil surrounded by a sea of brilliant sapphire. "I am a demoness and I am not glamoured."

I raised my eyebrows, not sure whether to believe her. "I saw the demons above. They were all glamoured. And I know a demon's true nature is not human. Why would the demons here choose to look human in their own world?"

"All demons are required to be glamoured at all times and have been for nearly three hundred years."

"Why?"

She shrugged as she braced herself to stand, using the wall to aid her. Once she was up, she began to rearrange herself as best she could. Her latex jumpsuit had been severely damaged from whatever blow she'd been dealt. She came forward, stopping at the dresser to open a drawer. "They are glamoured because the Prince deemed it so. A demon's natural appearance is unrefined by nature and with glamour we can become anything we want. The Prince has chosen to have our race represent itself in a pleasing manner, and what you glimpsed above is what he's chosen."

"But you said you weren't glamoured," I pointed out as I stood, eyeing her from head to toe as she grabbed a new outfit and paced to a small utilitarian bed covered in a single gray blanket—which appeared, unsurprisingly, to be made of a strange shimmery material. "You're not a full demoness, are you?"

She glanced at me over her shoulder, her eyes narrowing, her oval pupils thinning, making the entire eye appear blue. "You are an extremely curious creature, aren't you?"

"It's not hard to deduce. You speak perfect English," I said, turning away to give her privacy as she disrobed. Out of the corner of my eye, however, I noted her spine looked sharper than any human's, signifying she was at least half demon. My guess was that the other half was something supernatural, not human.

I strode out from behind the dresser, still keeping my head

bowed, running my hands along the top as I passed. I absent-mindedly brought my fingertips together to see if they were sticky. They weren't. "You can't be an imp, though, because your power signature is too strong. So I'm guessing the other half is supe, something from my world, judging by your accent. And because of your striking beauty, my next guess would be nymph or pixie. That's why glamour is unnecessary for you." Not that I'd ever seen a real live nymph or pixie, but that sounded like a good theory based on pictures I'd seen. Nymphs were usually drop-dead gorgeous and had strong abilities in the seduction area.

She turned to face me, zipping up her new, exactly-the-same-as-before latex jumpsuit. "I'm no nymph. But what I am is not important. Escaping this place is."

By her dismissive tone, she wasn't ready to give me any more than that right now. I glanced around the room. We were in a fifteen-foot-square space. Other than a dresser and the bed, there was no furniture. The floor was tiled in large squares. "How did I pass through the curtain so easily? I didn't feel a ward."

"It is coded to me alone. All others can pass through."

"Why?"

Her pupils pulsed. Like a small heartbeat in the middle of her eyes. I'd have to watch for that. "Because I am dangerous."

She said it so matter-of-factly, it sounded like she was telling me she enjoyed afternoon tea. "You don't say." I walked toward the curtain and she followed behind. "So you're telling me I can just walk back out the way I came and you can't follow me?"

"That is correct." She stopped shoulder to shoulder with me as I peered out at possible freedom that didn't include promising any-thing to this creature. "But I wouldn't advise it. As I said before, I am your only hope of escape. I was not telling an untruth."

I glanced at her. "What did they do to you when they blasted you into the wall?"

"They hit me squarely in the chest with the equivalent of a bazooka in your world."

My eyebrows lifted. "And why did they do that?"

She turned her body, addressing me directly. "Because I told them to fuck off."

"How come they left so quickly? All they had to do was search the room. I was crouched behind the only cover in the entire cube." I nodded behind me at the dresser. "It wouldn't exactly be hard to sleuth me out."

She shrugged. "Because I would have killed them if they had tried."

This time I openly gaped. "So what you're telling me is, I stumbled into the *only* cell in all the Underworld that holds the *only* prisoner who will be able to keep me safe? Or maybe I'm wrong and every prisoner is just like you?"

Her arm swept out in front of her as she gestured to the curtain. "You are welcome to go find out. I'll wait for you over here." She turned and strode to the bed. Once there, she lay down, clasping her hands under her head like she didn't have a care in the Underworld. "Of course, it'll be a long wait if the chupacabras find you first. But if you happen to get past the beasts, and the guards, and get to the next prisoner, they may toy with you for a while, depending on whom you stumble upon, but likely not before they rat you out. It's very easy for us to summon the guards. They have buttons all over the—"

I held up my palm, effectively cutting her off.

I went to the dresser and leaned against it and crossed my arms. "I've had enough of your games. I'm not really in the mood, in fact I'm in a hurry. We need to get down to business..." I didn't know how to address her. "What do I call you?"

"Lily."

"*What?*" I shouted, then tried to rein in some of my incredulity. "Your name is *Lily*?" It was so human. How could there be a demon named Lily?

She smirked as her blonde hair, dappled with its green highlights, spread over the pillow, seeming to dance against the shimmery material. "Demons never give their true birth names to anyone. If you had my real name, you could summon me against my will. Names are sacred in the Underworld." She didn't need to end with "duh," because it was implied. "So you'll have to settle for Lily, whether or not you deem it demonic enough."

"Um." I coughed. "Yes, that does make some sense now that you mention it. You'll have to forgive my total naïveté about the Underworld. I'm pretty much befuddled that I'm actually here in the first place."

"While you're gone investigating the other prisoners, trying to find someone more reputable and trustworthy to help you, I'm going to take a nap and finish regenerating from a nasty bazooka blast to the chest."

She was shrewd, I'd give her that.

My wolf snarled, still unimpressed. She wanted us to leave the way we'd come. *We can't do that. I can still hear the guards out there. She's intelligent, but she wants something from us. I'm going to use it to our advantage.*

"I'm not leaving," I said after a moment. Her nonchalant attitude didn't fool me. She needed my help as much as I needed hers. "Although it sounds very tempting, I'm not going to investigate the other prisoners." Lily gave off a strange vibe that made my wolf hyper-aware. "I realize you're playing this all very cool, but you need me more than I need you." She gave me a bored expression, which I ignored. "As I see it, I'm your only ticket out of Hell. And if the demons are willing to blow a hole in your chest, which didn't even seem to harm you, *and* you can tell them to fuck off and they scurry away, it means you're über-dangerous. I may find another way out of here if I go searching, but you clearly don't have that option." I folded my arms across my chest, satisfied.

"I already told you I am dangerous. I'm not trying to hide it."

"If you want my help, you're going to have to tell me why you're in here." I glanced around the tiny room to remind her where she was stuck. "And I want the truth this time."

"I'm residing in this cube because I've tried to kill the Prince of Hell"—she paused for effect—"often."

"Why are you still alive? I would think the Prince would obliterate you as quickly as possible."

Her eyes flicked to the wall and back. "Because he...secretly enjoys the challenge of holding me prisoner. When he can."

"But this time you went too far? Is that why you can't escape?" I was grasping at straws, but it made sense. She'd surprised me with her admission, and she held a quiet desperation about herself that told me something had gone very wrong with her last attempt. "You did something so bad the Prince decided to give you no more chances, and you're biding your time until you're to be executed?"

"Yes."

That was all she was going to give me.

"I know I agreed to give you a fair appraisal, and possibly take you back to my plane in exchange for your help, but I have to set up some ground rules before we move forward," I said. "If I didn't, I'd be a fool. You're too dangerous and I don't know you."

She sat up. "If you want my cooperation, you must agree to take me back to your plane if I prove worthy. There is no other way I will aid you. If you agree to consider this request, I will guide you to your brother, and once we have him, I will lead us to a portal."

"I have a way back with the witches." I couldn't be that dependent on her or this wouldn't continue to work in my favor.

She shook her head. "A circle will not work. If they haven't found the way you entered the Underworld already, it means we are the only two left in Hell. They will have masked all communication by now and cut the witches off. But there are three portals on this plane. A regular demon cannot pass through any of them. They are for imps and...others..." Admitting that she was, in fact, other. "We will have to use one of these."

There was no way to know if what she was telling me was the truth or not, but with nothing else to go on, I said, "If I end up agreeing to bring you back, you would have to swear an oath to me at that time. You would be my responsibility once we arrived in my world, and mine alone. You would stay voluntarily under my control and follow my rules, no questions asked. If you broke that oath, I'd have the right to have the witches send you back here, and you'd suffer your fate at the hands of the Prince."

Her eyes flickered, the pupils pulsing almost too quickly for me to see. "If that's what it takes, I will agree to bind myself to you. For a time."

"Wrong answer. You will bind yourself to me until *I* decide to change the rules."

"What exactly would you have me do? Give you my blood? I will follow your rules. I will behave. I am willing to do this because I need to be free of this land or I die. I have no other choice, it's that simple."

There was more movement in the hallway. The demons hadn't stopped the hunt. If anything, they'd ramped it up. And if they were smart, they'd charge right back in here with heavier artillery, like rocket launchers.

"If you end up saving my life, or my brother's, you will agree to swear an oath to me, whatever my terms, in the end, or there is no deal."

The demoness knew she was running out of time. "Fine. I will swear an oath, like you do in your world. Will that satisfy you?"

"Yes, for now." My wolf growled. *We don't owe her anything yet and she's agreed to help us. It's the best I could do.*

There were noises coming from outside. Lily's head turned toward the curtain. "They have come back with reinforcements. They did not believe I wasn't harboring you."

A strange roaring, keening noise erupted right outside the door. "What's making that awful sound?" I asked.

"That is the hellhound; it is part of the beast horde. It will devour us whole once it enters. Its piercing teeth skin you alive, and then it laps your blood until you take your last breath. It is the worst beast we have and it is rarely used because it's so hard to control."

"So how do we get out of here?" I asked.

"Through the floor," she answered.

I immediately glanced down. The floor tiles fit together like a big puzzle. Each of them notched to fit exactly with the pieces they lay next to. I squatted down. *Do you smell that?* I asked my wolf. Air was flowing up from between the two tiles beneath me and it smelled peculiar. I shot my power into them and picked up on something, not attached to this room, but down below.

"There's a catch, right?" I asked, nodding my head at the floor. "It's like the veil. This room is completely spelled against you, including the floor." I brought my nose close and sniffed, smiling. "But I can get through it no problem."

Her face changed from shrewd to impassive. "Yes, that's correct. But before you get any ideas about going without me, they house our beasts below. You would not survive on your own. The reason my cell is located in this region is because, on occasion, they must keep me in line. To do so, they bring the beasts up from there." She pointed to the piece of flooring I hovered over. "And I can promise you, it is less than pleasant in the bowels of Hell."

I didn't need convincing. I knew it would suck down there. I'd seen my fair share of tunnels today and I was already sick of them. I could only imagine what lurked beneath. The thought of climbing down to another one made my head pound.

I had to remember that there was a big difference between being weary and being dead. I had to survive.

Not only did I have to survive, I had to get my brother back. Even if that meant crawling around in every tunnel in this godforsaken world. "If this is where they bring the beasts up, why didn't they just send the hellhound up through here?"

There were more noises and shouting from outside. We had only moments left.

"Because the hellhound is too big, The hole beneath you is meant for creatures to torment me, not devour me whole." Several thumps sounded against the door, followed by some demonic howls. "They are having trouble controlling the hound as we speak or they would be in here already. It is a wicked thing with long claws and hideous teeth. They are taking no chances with you."

I curled my claws around the seam in the floor. The separation was barely there. I had to dig my nails in hard to get between the tiles. Once I got a grip, I tore the piece of flooring up in one pull and tossed it to the side.

I'd exposed a smooth, open cylinder under the floor that appeared to be made of something like PVC. It was white and just big enough for a human to slide through.

The roaring outside became louder. We were out of time. The demoness rushed forward and pushed me toward the chute. "Go, go! You must take a lock of my hair." She ripped a chunk off the end. "Once you reach the bottom, put the hair in the mouth of the chute and say these words in Demonish: *Dys swez kytaf hozz.* Do you understand? It's the only way to break the spell keeping me here."

"Okay," I said, taking the hair in my fist.

The door burst open behind us and a vicious howl rent the air. The demons rushed the curtain, their faces furious. Their loathing of Lily was clear.

"Why are they so angry?" I asked right before I slid down.

Her face was grim, but resigned. "Because I am the devil's concubine."

7

The ride was short and fast. The chute plunged downward at an extremely steep angle. I landed with a gigantic thud into something soft and squishy. It took me a moment to gather myself, and then the smell hit me.

It was atrocious.

I brought my hands up in horror, shaking the gunk off. "Are we sitting in *feces*?" I yelled out loud. I couldn't help it. It was the worst smell I'd ever encountered and it was indeed from excrement of some kind. I glanced around, taking a quick inventory of the place. From what I could gather, before the beasties were shot up this pipe, they must have lost whatever was in their bowels.

There was no other explanation.

I scampered out of the pile as fast as I could, which meant I slopped my way out of thigh-high muck slowly, scraping the putrescence off me as I went. "This is completely disgusting," I muttered. "And did I just agree to consider a deal with the Prince of Hell's mistress?"

A horrid scream echoed from above through the tube.

"*Dammit*, I forgot to throw the hair in!" I frantically sloshed back through the pile of crap. I'd inadvertently let go of the hair while I was trying to get the feces off me. I pawed at the pile, searching, and then I spotted the long locks half covered in a nearby clump. I snatched them up, hoping it didn't matter if they were covered in goo, and tossed them into the pipe and spoke the words.

Almost instantly Lily came shooting down the tunnel.

She was covered in blood.

"Oh, good gods, are your fingers missing?" I gasped as I took in her appearance. Reddish-purple liquid flowed freely down her arms and onto the heap.

"Yes." She took a deep breath and arched her head back, closing her eyes for a brief moment. "It was better to lose them than my neck. They will regenerate. Come, we must go. They must harness the hellhound first, but they will follow soon." She stood, wobbling slightly. She seemed unfazed by the large pile of feces we were standing in, and waded out without comment.

She'd done this before.

I followed, still swatting the crap off me, trying not to take in too many breaths. Lily walked purposefully to a door I hadn't noticed before, as it was artfully concealed in the rocky wall.

This level of Hell was covered in charcoal-colored rock with specks of something dotting throughout that looked like flint. Whatever it was made the walls glitter in the low light. Lily placed her broken and bloodied hand onto a flat surface next to the door and muttered something under her breath. After a moment she tried again. Nothing happened. She swore. "They've locked me out." She stepped back. "You must break this ward or we can go no farther."

"Me?" I said. "How do I break the ward?"

"Your magic signature contains demon essence, as I noted before. It should be enough to break this ward. We are on a lower level of Hell and the security here is less than above, because none willingly venture here. The beasts provide their own security."

"It's that easy to break?" I didn't believe it was. "How can I possibly get through something you can't?"

"I have done it too many times already." She shrugged. "They have found a way to keep my magic signature out. But I know you can do this, and you must. They will be arriving shortly, which means we have a limited time to get to the Sholls. If we do not, we die. It's that simple."

I switched places with her reluctantly. "So many ways to die, so little time," I grumbled as I placed my palm on the flat surface as she had done. A strange pulse immediately needled at my skin, pulling and scraping across it like sharp fingernails. "What is it *doing*?" My wolf snarled, wanting us to pull back, but a powerful suction had glued my hand to the wall. If I yanked it back, I would tear it open.

"It's trying to figure out what you are," Lily said patiently.

"Then what?" I asked as I envisioned a demon face with very large teeth coming out of the wall and gobbling me whole.

"You must force it to acquiesce."

"How do I—" A gurgling sound shot out of my throat as I morphed into my full Lycan form. The plate had tugged raw power out of my body so fast it had plastered my palm to it with the force of a cyclone.

"You must push your power against it. It thinks you are a demon, so use it to your advantage. Throw your magic into it," she ordered. "Hurry."

I gritted my teeth. It felt like my hand was being skewered open. My wolf barked, angry at me for doing something so stupid. *Instead of griping, help me get our hand back*, I told her. *Throw*

our magic at it. Together we shoved magic into the wall. It immediately bounced back and we had to force it outward again. Very
slowly magic began to seep into the wall. "I think . . . it's working."

"You must override it now. You will not get another chance."

My wolf howled and we shot a big burst of power into the wall.
The energy exploded into the wall, knocking me back, finally
freeing me. The force of it sent me reeling into Lily.

The wall panel was smoking.

Before I could regain my footing, the door slid open like something out of a sci-fi movie, exposing what appeared to be another
dark, dank tunnel. I righted myself and glanced down at my
hand. It was totally healed. No damage whatsoever. It still tingled
a little, but that was minor, especially since I'd thought it would
resemble raw hamburger. "What do we do now?" I asked.

"Now we go. And it's a good thing, because we have no more
time to lose." She exited through the doorway and I followed.

I immediately noticed the new tunnel walls were veined
with something other than flint. Instead of being glittery, these
walls had long, tubular vessels spreading out in every direction.
I squinted. It almost appeared as though *blood* were pumping
through them. "Why does it look like this rock has blood-filled
veins?"

Lily grabbed my shirtsleeve and tugged me into an alcove. She
punched a button and the same watery gel as in the gazebo coated
us, cleaning us instantly.

Lily pressed another button and a fan dried us in moments.
"To answer your question, the cave walls are alive and those *are*
veins. They bring nutrients to the rock."

"What do you mean, *alive*? As in living, breathing, with a soul?"
I asked, trotting behind her as she took off down the tunnel.

"No." She tossed her head back at me in exasperation. "Alive, as
in like a tree or a flower."

"Flowers and trees don't have blood running through them," I helpfully pointed out as we turned and ran down another passageway, the creepy veins intertwining all around us. "If the cave is alive and grows, it must constantly shift." I had to admit it was a little hard to wrap my mind around living rock.

"Yes, the cells here shift," she said absentmindedly as we ran faster. "They must be maintained, but the benefit outweighs the effort. The beasts housed here can feed directly from the wall themselves, so they require very little upkeep. It is a harmonious pairing."

Harmonious? How about...strange and...weirdly primal? We started to pass row after row of short, solid doors. Various noises and snorts were issuing out of all of them. I did not want to find out what was inside.

"What's the plan?" I called. "You said something about going to the Sholls?"

"Yes, we are heading to the Sholls. It's located in the in between and is the only place that will provide us cover."

"I'm sorry, what?" I almost tripped. Heading into an "in between" sounded tricky, but going in between the Underworld and gods knew where sounded bad.

"It is the only way," she urged. "Come, we must hurry."

"This 'in between' doesn't sound like a great idea to me," I said. "Isn't there a place here we can go? I came in through the garbage dump and there wasn't much action there."

"In order to lose the guards, we must become undetectable, and to do that we have to leave this tangible plane. Once we are there, we will cross to the courthouse where your brother is being held and go back through a portal. Not only is it necessary to lose our tail, but it's efficient as well." There were shouts in the distance. "Very few demons know the way to the Sholls, and once they enter they cannot navigate it. But I am not one of them, so this is your lucky day."

"It's not feeling lucky," I muttered. "This trip has not gone according to any plan we'd formulated."

"Really? And what exactly was your master plan? Arrive in the Underworld and defeat five hundred thousand demons by yourself?" She turned a corner quickly and the topography changed instantly. This tunnel had a blue hue and no veins. It resembled water. I wondered if the beasts drank from this rock.

Tally had never mentioned how many demons lived on this plane, but five hundred thousand seemed like a lot. Most Sects were lucky if they had numbers in the hundreds. "No, that wasn't the plan," I answered as I jogged behind her. "But I was supposed to have some of my team with me and, at the very least, spells if I ran into trouble."

"Witches' spells are useless here. They are only effective on us when we are on your plane, because our own magic is lessened there. There are a few demon varieties who will fall victim to a witch spell for a short time here in the Underworld, but overall, they do not affect us much."

That wasn't great news. "How many demon species are there, anyway? It's tough to see any differences when you're all glamoured to look the same."

"We are in She'ol," she answered as she turned down yet another tunnel. This one was still blue, but a lighter hue. As I inspected it more closely, it appeared to have small sapphires dotting the walls. "All the demons here are what we refer to as true demons. We have many kinds of demons in the Underworld: fire demons, water demons, horned demons, incubi, and succubi, to name a few, but they all live on different levels of Hell."

"What's the difference between a true demon and the rest?"

"True demons contain pure blood magic. They can glamour themselves, and their blood is potent. Other demons have different abilities. A fire demon can produce fire, but cannot spell. An incubus can seduce, but cannot glamour. We have arrived." The demoness stopped in front of a bland-looking wall. This particular chunk of rock was brown and dead-looking, unlike all the vibrant blue we'd just passed.

Multiple shouts in Demonish and fierce growls erupted behind us. "They're coming."

Lily turned toward me. "Hold on to me, whatever happens. If you let go, you will be lost to the in between."

My wolf snarled, clearly uneasy.

Lily aimed her already regenerated fingers at the wall and shouted something I didn't understand. Immediately following there was a pulse of energy that almost sent me flying. The demoness reached out and grabbed my wrist, yanking me into the vortex right as a full-grown chupacabra turned the corner.

Holy crap! It was five times the size of the ones in the trash heap, eyes glowing, saliva dripping, teeth as long as swords.

The vortex sucked us in like a vacuum an instant before the beast took a swipe at me with its horrendous claws, howling its outrage.

The last thing I saw as my head disappeared was a dozen demons rounding the corner, a look of shared horror on all their glamoured faces. I didn't have time to figure out if they were horrified by seeing me or by seeing that we were entering the Sholls.

But it was too late to back out now.

Oh…my gods…I'm not sure we're going to survive this. My wolf roared her displeasure right back at me, sending huge currents of adrenaline washing through our system to fortify us. I was in my full Lycan form, hands clutching Lily's waist for life, but it felt like pieces of my body were being ripped apart.

Then, just as suddenly, it was over and I was on my back, panting.

The ride had been short, but extremely painful.

My eyes were firmly shut. I could already tell my mind and body were not on board for the Sholls. The air was thick and musty, and strange vibrations ran through me like physical sound waves, making my insides quiver and jump.

I knew I wasn't going to like what I saw when I opened my eyes.

Beside me, Lily stood. Her breathing was labored. "Come, we must go. There are creatures that lurk here in the shadows. They are not demons. They are other and we cannot linger."

I reluctantly opened my eyes.

I *so* wasn't prepared.

My wolf howled, gnashing her teeth and snarling, urging us to go back the way we'd come—so much so that I fell backward as I tried to rise. The air wavered around us. The sky was a muted gray streaked with burnt orange. Things were off-kilter and at haphazard angles.

We sat in the field behind the buildings.

I leaped up, expecting the yellow grass to be wiggling beneath me. Instead here the ground was cracked and broken, emitting what smelled like toxic gas through the millions of holes the wormlike grass had occupied on the other plane.

Everything around me looked awful and menacing. "What is this place?" I whispered as I loped after Lily, who had already started to run. My body wobbled with every step as I tried to find my balance on this strange plane. My insides felt heavy and each time my legs hit the ground it felt like my organs were going to plummet to my feet.

"I told you, we are in the in between," she answered.

"That doesn't mean anything to me. How is an in between even possible?"

"There are vacant spaces on every plane—" Something large dropped from the top of one of the buildings. I couldn't see what it was, because it was gone in the next instant.

But it hadn't been a winged devil. *That was way too big to be a devil bat,* I told my wolf, as I crouched low, hands out in front of me.

Lily had stopped and braced herself against the wall, hands splayed, eyes alert.

That wasn't a good sign.

"What was it?" I asked, panting in the thick air. The beast had evaporated into thin air. I glanced all around me, heightening my senses as much as I could. My body was still undulating on the inside. I put a tentative hand out in front of me and brushed the air back and forth. It moved like invisible smoke. It was barely detectable, but I could see it. It was freaky. "The air is actually moving. I think that's what's making my insides feel like—"

"*Shh,*" the demoness hissed.

"I'm pretty sure the smoke monster knows we're here—" Something had me by the throat. It threw me up against the wall and I gasped, my head hitting the building behind me hard enough to draw blood. My hands scrabbled at my neck, but there was nothing there to hold on to. I tried to take in a breath, but I couldn't get any air into my windpipe. Lily was suddenly in front of me, a look mixed with horror and irritation flowing across her striking features. Then her pupils elongated as she uttered some words in Demonish, her palms open and facing me. Something like static electricity shot out of her fingers and the creature I couldn't see roared and let go.

I fell to my knees, gasping in the putrid wet air. I was so sick of having my airflow cut off. "What...was...*that*?"

"There is no time to explain. We must get to the other side of the square. Now." She yanked me up by the arm and we began to run.

Up ahead I spotted the gazebos. On this plane they were bent and withered, appearing grotesque in the gray landscape. "Tell me what attacked me." I panted as I ran, the thick air sticking in my throat. "And if you're not around next time, how do I defend against it? It had no magic signature that I could sense. In fact, it felt like dead air was strangling me." I couldn't die if I passed out from lack of air, but I'd be vulnerable to an easy death once I was unconscious.

"We call them wyverns and you are correct when you say dead air. They are truly dead beings and they only exist on this plane."

"You're not talking about demon ghosts, are you? Please tell me that's not what you're saying." If the demons had an equivalent of a vampire Screamer, this entire foray into the Sholls was hopeless. There was no way we could defeat a dozen demon Screamers.

"Not exactly," she answered as we neared the main square and slowed to a jog. "When a demon dies a true death it enters into what we call the Unknown. The Sholls is known. If a demon comes here instead, they have become other after their death… changed. Many believe it's not a true death, but a half death. Their serpentine side takes over, much as if you became a rabid wolf for all eternity."

"No." I shook my head emphatically. "That wouldn't be the right equivalent. An equal comparison to what I just saw would be if I died and became Bigfoot and could turn invisible whenever I wanted. That thing was as big as a dragon. Ten times the size of a regular demon. How can something that big become invisible and have no substance or magic signature?" Whatever had latched on to me was like a ghost.

"That's the way it hunts. It has to become corporeal to spot its prey," Lily answered. "When it is solid for those few moments, it is vulnerable to attack. Then as a ghost it can kill you without worry or harm."

"But you took care of it when it was invisible." We'd stopped by the corner of the last building before the square with all the weathered gazebos. The slabs on the buildings were jagged and decidedly unsmooth. The polar opposite of what it looked like on the demon side. The sky was still dark and nasty and everything was hazy and hard to focus on. The air made everything distorted.

"That's because I knew where it was." She eyed me intently. "It was choking the life out of you. That"—she paused—"and I have a special gift." She shook her head to steel herself in order to divulge information she didn't want to, which I knew demons were loath to do. They liked to keep their secrets close.

I took in a shallow, labored breath, waiting for her to answer.

"I alone can banish the wyverns."

8

I glanced at the demoness, my eyebrows arched. She was no normal demon. That wasn't even up for debate. She clearly had vast abilities. Whatever supernatural she was mixed with made her extremely potent. And by her own admission, she'd managed to charm the Prince of Hell into submission and become his lover.

"So that's why the demons looked horrified when they saw us heading here?" I asked. "They can follow us if they wanted to, but no demon wants to die a horrible death being ripped apart by the ghost wyverns?"

"That is one of the reasons," she answered, appearing nonchalant. "The other is that if they die here, they stay here in a half death, and none are willing to risk it. But it makes it a perfect place to escape, because other than the wyverns, we can walk here unmolested."

I chortled. "I don't think 'unmolested' is the word you're looking for. Nor would I deem this a 'perfect place' for anything." I rubbed my aching neck. That thing had a powerful grip.

"Duck!" Lily shouted.

I hit the ground with preternatural speed.

A spell shot through the air. "We must go now before more descend." I stood slowly. Lily kept her hands up, aimed right above me. "The openness of the feeding grounds will make us more vulnerable, but we have to cross them. There's a portal on the roof of the courthouse that will take us inside to where your brother is being held."

"Won't the demons know where we're headed and be ready and waiting?" It seemed logical.

"No," the demoness answered stonily. "There are several safer routes to traverse. They will be guarding those, assuming we would choose the easiest path. This one is...treacherous, and because of that, few know of its existence."

"And why wouldn't they know about it?"

"Because anyone who has tried to pass through here has perished." Before I could respond to that she took off. "Follow or die," she called over her shoulder.

My wolf snarled as I ran after her, pumping my legs and arms as fast as I could. *You heard her, Tyler is just across these...feeding grounds.* I shivered as we dodged our way among the gazebos. *We can't forget why we came here.*

We were halfway through the square when I felt movement all around us.

The air shifted quickly, back and forth, creating a strong breeze. Running in a straight line was very difficult to manage, even with super strength. I felt inebriated, lunging one way and then another.

"Stay low and start changing your position constantly," Lily called.

"Changing my position is not a problem," I yelled back. "The air is already doing that for me."

In front of me, Lily dodged gazebos, changing her posture from low to high. I followed, making sure I did the same, varying my pace as much as I could. A few times I felt a huge burst of movement beside me and I wondered how many of these guys we had evaded. I hadn't seen any of them flash solid again, so they were only guessing where we were.

"They are coming!" the demoness shouted.

"What do you mean coming? Aren't they already here?"

The air suddenly blinked with more wyverns than I could count. They dotted in and out of existence like bursts of lightning and they were closing in like sharks circling a school of exactly two sardines.

They were about to pick us off easily.

Lily skidded to a stop and leaped into one of the gazebos. "Hurry," she called, beckoning to me. "Get inside."

One jump and I cleared the railing, but before I could get fully inside, something sharp raked my back. I landed, evading it, and slid into what looked to be the remains of something too big to be a piglet. The wyverns ate in these gazebos too. Old habits must die hard.

Jesus, this place sucked *so* bad.

"Get behind me," the demoness shouted.

"There is no behind," I snarled. "We're in a goddamn circle."

"Just stay down. We're going to have to wait until they've all gathered. Once they do, I'll unleash a big blast. We'll only have moments to get to the rooftop of that building." She gestured to the side. "Wait for my lead."

I crouched low, glancing out into the square. The building she gestured to sat about fifty yards away. It seemed to be faintly glowing, but it was hard to tell in all the moving air. But I wouldn't put it past this place to have a glowing building.

Lily threw her head back and stretched out her arms. She was gathering power to herself as she uttered something under her breath. Heady breezes were whipping around us, so I knew the beasts were flying and swooping around. They'd stopped popping into existence for now, but they knew they had us trapped, so why bother?

I searched around me, trying to find something to help, but only found old bones littering the floor. I picked up what looked to be a giant femur and tried not to gag. It would probably break on impact if I used it against the wyverns, but it might give me a few seconds—and every second counted.

The demoness began to move in a slow circle and I inched out of her way. Something shifted to my left, much too close. I sprang to get out of the way, but it was too late.

It had me in its grasp before I could blink.

Its claws raked down my arm as it began to drag me out of the structure. I reached out at the last possible moment and hooked my elbow on a pillar as I gave out a strangled howl.

Before Lily could blast it, it ripped into my arm and blood began to spurt freely out of a gash that ran from my shoulder to my elbow.

The wound was jagged and hurt like a mother. "Get it... *OFF*," I roared, clinging to the side of the gazebo with everything I had as it tried to yank me out.

A moment later a sonic boom exploded all around us.

The power of it almost lobbed me out into the open. My grip failed at the last minute, but the beast had fled and I managed to turn myself inward, falling to the ground inside the structure. I collapsed to the floor and rolled, holding on to my arm. It was regenerating slowly, but it still hurt insanely bad. "What the... *hell*," I panted, glancing up at the demoness, who had her hands on her hips in front of me like we hadn't just been surrounded by a bevy of wyverns waiting to tear us to shreds. "There must be hundreds of those things out there. How can you be so blasé? And how can we possibly make it to the roof from here? You said we only had moments to get there, but there's no way we can traverse that much ground before they attack again."

"I have blasted them soundly back. Some will be injured. When one is injured others will prey upon it. But they will pick each other off quickly, so we have to leave now. Get up."

"There's something you're not telling me about this," I said as I stood, the pain in my arm subsiding. I shook it out, ignoring the throb, trying to ready myself to run. "And I'm not going out there until I know the whole story." Which was sort of a bluff, because where else was I going to go?

"The portal here is unused because it's in a very bad location."

"How bad?"

"It sits in the middle of their nest."

The demoness was out of the gazebo before I could form a rebuttal, and I had no choice but to follow. Damn her. As I ran, I glanced behind me and saw the beasts intermittently blinking into existence in a huge circle. They were indeed gorging on one of their own and I was happy it wasn't me.

The demoness moved quickly. She was a blur, and I increased my speed to catch up. Once she reached the building she began to scale the wall. I was more apt in that department, my animal instincts aiding me, but with my arm still regenerating I was forced to move more slowly. The structure was broken and warped, which made it easier to find the footing we needed. It just would've been nice if my insides weren't quivering like I was in a tiny boat at sea on top of everything else. It made it more difficult than it should've been.

I followed her to the top, rounding over the lip easily. By the time I hit the roof, my arm healed.

What lay before us was total chaos.

Bones and nest material were littered all over; scarcely one foot of roof was showing, the rest was debris. There was one particular heap of matted bones stacked twenty feet high. It had to be the queen's nest or the king's or however the hierarchy worked for wyverns. It was massive and sat right in front of the clock tower.

Lily stilled beside me. I could tell she was formulating a plan in her mind. "Don't tell me the portal is the clock tower." I pointed toward the huge nest. "That's not why we're standing here waiting, is it?"

"The clock tower is the portal," she replied. "Just let me think. That nest was not here the last time."

"How long has it been since you ventured here?"

"Two hundred years."

"What!" I would've clapped my forehead at that news, but I didn't want to waste my energy. "And you didn't stop to think that maybe things might've changed a bit since then? I'm pretty sure the momma wyvern or whoever lives here isn't going to just let us waltz up to her nest and dig through it on our way to the portal."

"There are no wyverns up here at the moment." The demoness swept her long blonde hair off her shoulder as she turned to peer at me. "We can get through if we move now."

"How do you know for sure it's clear? One could be taking a nap."

"Because I don't sense any."

"Hmm," I muttered. "And we're trusting your inkling to be correct because...why?"

"Because there is no reason to doubt my sensing abilities now." She started for the nest without looking back.

I trailed behind her, trying not to complain about our awful situation, but not quite achieving it. "When they come back, we will literally be standing in the belly of the beast."

"I'll have my power at the ready." She flexed her fists as she walked purposefully toward the base of the nest. "Stop worrying."

Most of the bones I glimpsed here were bigger than those of the largest human or demon I'd seen. I gave a futile glance around me, wondering what else lived in the Sholls. Whatever these wyverns fed on was huge.

Lily started yanking apart the nest, tossing pieces of it behind her, uncaring of where they landed or how loud a racket she made.

"Why don't you just zap the nest out of the way with your power? This is going to take all day," I said.

"If I use my magic, they will come. Stop grumbling and help me." She grunted as she tossed a large mass of what looked to be cartilage connected to half a skeleton away from her.

I started prying bigger parts away. "You said before that other than the wyverns, we were safe in the Sholls. But they feed on something huge. This bone came from a bruiser of a beast." I yanked a large bone out and examined it.

"They consume something that resembles a rhinoceros in your world, but is too slow to be of harm to us, and they don't live in this area. They are called *xer tottod* and they gather in small groups far from here. The wyverns only venture out when they have to. Mostly they just scavenge on the small beasts, ones that cannot harm us."

Once we cleared away more of the nest, I spotted what looked to be an outline of a door in the surface of the clock. The hole we'd made was now big enough to enter, so I ducked my head and went in. The only light from outside was putrid gray and very little of it filtered in here. It was like picking my way through a thicket when I was a kid. Only back then I was actually having fun; now I was in Hell trying not to get eaten by a dragon.

The demoness gave a shrill scream behind me, knocking into my back, sending me sailing forward into more bones and twigs. "They have come back. Hurry—"

There was a terrifying screech as the thing landed and the nest above us quaked. I risked a glance behind me and saw more than one gigantic talon blink into existence.

"Go, go!" Lily pushed me again.

I raced forward as fast as I could, yanking things out of my way and crawling over bones that lay across my path like downed trees. "Am I going for the door?"

"Yes," she said. "Put the palm of your hand in the middle of six."

"Six what?" I shouted, confused.

"The number six! On the clock!"

"Will that activate the portal?"

"It will open the first door, and then I'll do the rest."

Above us the wyvern started to dismantle its nest by ripping it apart. Pieces flew everywhere, raining down around us between the gaps. It kept shrieking its anger and two beats later the roof bounced again as several more landed.

"There's no more time left, Lily!" I yelled. "They will be on us in a minute."

She shouted something in Demonish and a pulse of energy shook our small tunnel, collapsing it around us. She gave a frustrated howl of anger and grabbed my back, swinging me aside in one motion.

She was a lot stronger than she looked.

She took the lead, diving for the number six, and I was right behind her. She slammed both her hands into the bottom loop of the six right as the top of the nest sheared off.

My wolf was in overdrive, howling and barking. I had my magic at the ready, but if the wyverns became incorporeal it wasn't going to help me. "That's it!" I yelled, encouraging her. "Give it more power."

"I don't have any more to give. It's stuck!" she cried.

I reached around her and jammed my palm into the same circle and blasted my magic along with hers, trying to focus on the dark demon essence I had incorporated into my own signature and pull it forward.

The wyverns gave a mighty howl. I glanced up. We were completely exposed. This was it, we had to open it or die. *The portal wants the demon magic*, I told my wolf. *Pull only the black signature*. Frantically my wolf siphoned off the darkest part of our magic and blasted it into the clock.

The portal shook.

One more time, I shouted. More magic came forward in a rush, and with a loud groan, the portal began to open. Lily went first, grabbing on to my arm as she tumbled through. As my body fell, I turned to see the roof one last time.

Right as a wyvern blinked into being, a millimeter from my face.

9

"If I never see another wyvern again, I'll be a happy girl," I declared once we'd landed. "I think the portal closed on that thing's head."

Lily lay next to me, looking spent. It was actually nice to see she wasn't as invincible as she portrayed herself. "They are fearsome beings. With my luck, I'll probably come back as one."

"That wouldn't be something to look forward to." I stood up, clapping off the debris that had followed us in. "Just so you know, I'm not entering the Sholls again, so if we get cornered, you'll have to come up with another plan."

The demoness rose slowly next to me. We appeared to be in a large closet of some kind. I leaned over and fingered what looked to be a bottle of cleaning solution on a shelf next to me. "Did we land in a storage room?"

"No. We are in what we call a mending cell, or a *tyfkefr laat* in Demonish."

"A mending cell?"

"This is where we take a demon that has broken the law and try to 'mend' it—meaning we try to force it to think like the horde once again, and if that doesn't work, we use that"—she pointed to the bottles I'd just been grasping—"to kill it."

I snatched my hand back. "Do they make the demons drink this stuff?" For the first time I examined the space. We were standing behind a partition. I took a step and peeked around it, spotting an evil-looking cross between a bathtub and a bed sitting in the middle of the room. There were restraints all over the place, including ones for the head, arms, legs, and what looked to be . . . the groin.

Well, now I knew demons had all the working parts.

"No, they don't drink it." The demoness sighed. "We pour it over them and they disintegrate into a bubbling mass as it eats away at their hide."

My eyebrows furrowed as I glanced back at her. "This is not what they're planning to do to Tyler, right? If they decide to kill him, it won't be in a torture chamber like this? Please tell me they are not going to tie him down and pour acid over him."

"Likely not," she answered. "But it's hard to know. This room is only one of many and they all have particular ways to eradicate errant demons. These rooms are attached to our courthouse and are made especially for the demons who stand trial and are found guilty. But we have mending rooms all over She'ol, some of them very crude. One would be lucky to go this way." She gestured to the bottle of solution. "It is painful, but it is over quickly. I've heard of some demons being 'mended' for years."

I shuddered. "You know, this entire world is the worst. Is there any beauty or happiness here? Or is it just all horror and sadness?" There was a definite pall over the Underworld, like an ongoing depression nagging at me.

She bowed her head. "There is beauty, but it is hard to see. I have been happy here until recently."

"You mean before you turned on the Prince of Hell."

"No," she said quietly. "Before he turned on me."

I didn't really want to know, but curiosity got the best of me. "Why did you choose to sleep with him in the first place?"

She shrugged. "I have been here for many years and he is very powerful, as am I. It was a coupling of strength at first, but it turned into something much deeper later. He has feelings. Demons are not devoid of emotion. In fact, they have a fair amount of feelings. They just choose to keep their true wants and needs concealed."

Thinking about the Prince being intimate was more than a little disconcerting. But knowing he had real emotions made him seem a little more . . . normal. "It's hard to believe what you're telling me since he has the outward appearance of a robot."

"I assure you, he is no robot. He can be very sensual."

I held my hand up. "Okay. It's time to move on." I walked toward what I thought was the door, but in this place it was hard to know. It didn't look like a door, but more like a cutout in the wall. It wouldn't have surprised me if we had to slide through another tube to get free of this torture chamber. "Are all demonesses mixed race like you?" I asked. Maybe demons had to breed with other Sects to have females? It wouldn't be unheard of. "Or are there full demon females?"

Lily followed me, so I kept moving toward the cutout. "There are indeed pure-blooded demonesses, but only a few are born every century. They are treated like queens here." Did I detect a little cynicism? "But mixed-race demonesses, as you referred to them, are much rarer. One is only born once every thousand years or so."

I stopped in my tracks, turning with my mouth open a little. "Are you telling me you're the only female of your kind?"

"Yes, I am the only one," she answered. "Imps are always born male, and from human mothers. Most other supernatural Sects are not compatible genetically with demons and cannot produce children, but my mother's race is strong and fierce."

I closed my mouth, thinking. "You're part witch, aren't you." I said it more as a statement and less as a question. "Magic of the earth and magic of the blood together in one body." I made an involuntary shushing noise in the back of my throat, before continuing. "That makes you one very powerful supernatural. That's why you can't or won't take a witch's circle out of here with me. If the witches know about you, it would be war the moment you stepped foot on my plane."

There was no way I could bring that kind of danger home with me.

She shooed my words away dismissively with her hand. "I don't have a beef with anyone, and they have none with me. I was not lying before. The demons will have disarmed the circle already. It has nothing to do with if I can use it or not."

"Bull," I retorted. "You have vendetta written all over you." I made a sweeping gesture up and down her body with an open palm. "I bet you were cast out of your Coven when you were young—why else would you be here? Your English is flawless, so you must have spent your formative years on the human plane—before what? They found out what you were? Or you rebelled? Maybe your demon side took over? You must have been quite a menace—"

She held me by the throat before I could move to defend myself.

A second later she tossed me across the room. I hadn't expected her to attack, so it was my bad. My wolf howled at my foolishness. *I hear you*, I muttered. I flew twenty feet and smashed into a rack of something that broke apart instantly. Bottles and cans bounced all over, rolling around on the floor. Luckily none of them burst. I stood immediately, wiping blood off my lip with the back of my hand. "So I uncover your true self and you choose to fight me?" I asked. "Fine. We can fight. But it ends here. No more deal-making or aiding one another. The winner walks though that door alone."

She sauntered over to me, loathing etched across her features. "You think you're extremely smart, don't you? That you have me all figured out? The reincarnate wolf enters our realm to save her poor brother...but what's this?" She arched a hand behind the back of her ear and stuck her neck out. "She has demonic magic running through her veins? Sound the alarms and call the guards!" She faked a gasp and thumped a hand over her heart. "It seems this wolf has turned out to be a much greater threat than any of us had originally thought. And when they finally catch you, they will bring you into a room just like this one." She spread her arms wide. "And if he's not dead yet from his own stupidity, they'll drag your brother in to watch. And once the deed is done, and they've killed you in the most horrendous way imaginable, they will send him home with his tail between his legs—but, of course, not before they inflict as much *damage* on him as they possibly can. Your brother will be sent back as a warning to all others, broken and out of his mind. Anyone who comes to Hell to avenge your death will pay the same price. They will *all* die and the demons will win. They always win."

I didn't think. I launched myself at her, my wolf snarling and snapping her jaws as images of Lily being torn apart flooded my psyche. I was in my Lycan form when we collided, my fist swinging at her face. It connected hard and her neck whipped back, followed by a satisfying crunching noise. Her body connected hard with the wall behind us, denting it. But before she could recover or throw me off, I yanked her down to the ground, snarling right in her face, flashing my teeth. "No one is torturing anyone, do you hear me? I'm freeing my brother and getting us both out of

Hell. In one piece. And if I have to kill you, I will, with no hesitation." Before she could respond, my fist flashed down, connecting with her throat.

She gurgled as her windpipe imploded.

Without pause, she brought an arm up and backhanded me. I knocked into a rack next to us from the force of her blow. This time a single bottle fell to the ground and cracked. Liquid seeped onto the floor around us and started to smoke. I glanced down at Lily, whose neck was regenerating quickly—quicker than mine had—and whose blood was all over.

It was red, a witch's blood color, not the oily stuff that came out of the Prince.

I wondered in that moment whether she was more witch than demon.

"You can try to kill me all day." She gnashed her teeth, bringing a hand up along her cheek, smearing scarlet. "But I won't die, no matter how many times you try. My magic is something you've never encountered before. It makes me stronger than any witch or demon, and something you can't best no matter how strong you are."

"We'll see about—"

Before I could retaliate there was a loud crackling noise coming from the PA system, followed by a voice that filled the room around us. "Attention, attention. We know you are in the building. We will find you. Turn yourself over, female wolf, or we will dispatch your kin. You have three minutes to respond. Thank you."

It clicked off.

Lily pushed herself up and I let her go, a grim smile playing on her lips. "Still willing to risk your brother's life by fighting me? I've never lied to you. I'm still the only chance you've got, no matter what I am, or how strong. And the sooner you realize that, the sooner we can move on." She gestured toward the door as she stood. There was movement in the hallway beyond it. "I am the only thing that can defeat what lies out there. And because of what I am—a witch *and* a demon—they all fear me. And because they fear me, they will hesitate to react. I alone can get you and your precious brother out alive. Me." She placed a single finger on her chest. "And you have one minute and forty-seven seconds to make up your mind."

My mind raced. "There's no way I can trust you, and the only way you're going to keep helping me is if I agree to take you back to my plane. That's not happening, Lily. You've proven over and over again how dangerous you are. Your powers are unique and strong, I get it, but that makes you a serious threat. Too serious to risk bringing you back."

She took a step toward me, her pupils expanded to form a perfect sapphire oval. "I've repeatedly told you I'm dangerous. I've never kept it a secret. I also told you I would swear an oath to you that I will not harm anyone on your plane. I am purely looking for asylum and nothing more. I will still swear that vow to you now, if only to prove to you my intentions are innocent."

I peered at her hard. "If you really want to prove to me you're *innocent*—then prove it by freeing me and my brother. Earn my trust and my favor and stop asking for it."

She opened her mouth and for the first time I saw that some of her back teeth were pointed. "Fine. I will continue to earn your trust, as I have already done, but when this is over, and I have led you both safely to the portal, you will owe me. But your brother's life is in jeopardy. There is no more time to argue—"

A horrid scream rent the air.

It was Tyler's.

I didn't hesitate. I spun, kicking the door in, and bounded through. I knocked several demons out of my way as I blindly followed his voice down one corridor and through another.

The demons would come after me, but I didn't care. If Lily was true to her word, she'd take up the rear. The demons had already sounded the alarms. There was no way around it. By acting now, I had the element of surprise. It would take the demons time to organize, and if anything, I might be able to exchange myself for Tyler. I just knew I had to stop anything more from happening to him. His cries of anguish were real.

The tunnels I raced through appeared deceptively normal. They mimicked hallways in buildings where humans conducted business. I flew past several demon underlings, each one looking more surprised than the last. I plowed right by them in a blur, moving fast, a haze of red covering my eyes. The new speed I traveled at surprised even me. But I knew it was fueled by terror, thinking I might be too late to save my brother.

My wolf worked overtime as we ran, feeding me power and urging me on.

I made one last turn, following his continued screams, and found several demons standing in front of what appeared to be a door to another "mending room." These demons didn't have any beasts with them, but I was too preoccupied with saving my brother to be relieved.

One of them stepped forward and tried to block my path, bringing its hand up. "Halt. You...come with...us," it said in broken English. "You are...our prisoner...now."

"I don't think so," I growled as I charged forward, spinning at the last moment and catching this particular demon in the chest with my foot. I wished I had my throwing knives for one brief, sorrowful moment.

The demon I'd kicked collided with several others and they sprang apart, crashing around the hallway. They were clearly taken off guard by my hand-to-hand combat. Judging by their surprised expressions they had not expected me to fight. And, luckily for me, these demons were not skilled at all. They must settle everything by trial or magic down here, but it was clear demons were not used to engaging physically.

I used it to my advantage. "Get out of my way!" I yelled, hauling another demon away from the doorway by the scruff of its neck, its jumpsuit tearing as I tossed it behind me with little effort.

Once the door was clear, I brought my leg up, but before I smashed it open, it swung from the inside and a startled demon met my furious gaze. I reached in and grabbed it, throwing it behind me as I made my way in.

"Tyler, oh my gods. No!" I shouted as I raced forward. My brother was strapped to an ugly-looking chair with several demons surrounding him, one of which was in the process of administering something that resembled a giant leech to his neck via some sort of nasty pliers. The black bug whipped back and forth as it headed closer to my brother.

With horror, as I moved farther into the room, I saw there were already several of those things secured to his face.

Tyler was straining, but awake. He was covered in his own blood.

I sprinted forward, swatting demons out of the way with my fists, taking the one with the nasty slug by the shoulders, my claws sinking in. I whipped it around, seething, "What are those?" I shook the demon. "Tell me what you're doing to him!"

The demon was too stunned to answer so I raised my hand in front of its face, my claws sharp and pointy. "If you don't spit it out in the next second, I will sever your jugular. And if you don't have a jugular, I will rip your head off. Now tell me!" I shook it harder.

It stammered, "We…we are applying these to drain his strength." This one's English was better.

"What are those leeches doing to him? *Specifically?*"

"They—" it sputtered.

"Their damage is not lasting," Lily finished as she grabbed my slug-toting pal and knocked it out in one punch.

She hit it below the belly button. I had to remember that.

The demon went down hard. She picked it up by the neck and tossed it out, slamming the door behind it. She turned back to address me. "The leeches dampen your brother's strength or he would be fighting. They have had to keep him very well contained because he is so strong. He will recover as soon as they are all removed." She stopped and punched something into a code box on the wall. "They will be here with reinforcements very soon. These demons here are like doctors in your world. But the guards will have been alerted now to your location. This was not the best plan, you realize. Now we have no choice but to fight our way out."

I ignored her and bent down in front of my bleeding brother. I grabbed one of the slugs stuck to his neck and pulled. "Tyler, can you hear me? I'm getting these off of you." It finally came off, but I had to yank hard.

There was a loud sucking noise, followed by a current of blood. These things had either thinned his blood or inhibited his healing, or both. He should've been able to regenerate from the bite instantly, but it wasn't closing yet.

Tyler grunted and smiled. "Jess, it's so good to see you." He reached out and touched my hand, which was positioned right next to his shackled wrist. He was weak, but once he brushed me, our connection sprang to life. Almost like someone had flipped an on switch. It was such a relief to feel him again. "You finally got here. I was beginning to think you weren't gonna make it." He closed his eyes.

"What do you mean *finally*?" I asked him after I'd removed a few more of the disgusting leeches. "It's only been a few days."

He shook his head as I reached for another one that was stuck under his shirt collar, and for the first time I noticed he was dressed in a jumpsuit like all the demons.

"No." His breath hitched as I tugged it off. "It's been over two months."

"*What?*" I leaned back so I could meet his gaze. "You've got to be kidding me." I knew time worked differently here, but that was unsettling. If I'd waited another week would he have been gone almost a year? It was unthinkable.

"I'm not. It's been a long-ass time," he replied, trying to smile. "There's a few more of those goddamn things under my shirt. They make me feel weird and they hurt like—*ow*."

I took the wiggling thing in my fingers and dropped it into a jar Lily had just produced. The jar held the ones I'd gathered up and discarded on the cart next to my brother as well. As soon as I'd dropped it in, she screwed the lid on. "What?" My gaze was questioning. "Is it going to jump back out at us?"

"Yes." She nodded. "In fact it will."

My eyes widened. They were so sluglike, slow and lethargic in their movements. They didn't look like they could morph into attack bugs.

"They're drunk on his supernatural blood." She nodded toward my brother. "But when it wears off, they will want more. These things"—she rattled the jar and they flopped around—"can jump ten feet, and they have fangs, which is mostly what caused your brother's discomfort. They suck power from a supernatural like a vampire bat feeds on blood."

"Christ," I muttered as I reached down the front of Tyler's jumpsuit to get the last embedded bloodsucker.

"Who's the blonde, mildly scary female?" my brother asked,

nodding in Lily's direction. "I haven't seen any women so far. I was beginning to think they didn't exist down here."

Before I could answer him, the ground shook and there were several screams of terror on the other side of the door. Then a familiar voice echoed in my ears like a slimy oil slick.

"What is the matter with all of you fools?" it boomed. "You let them escape... *twice*. I will see your deaths for this. Now get them out of that room!"

The Prince of Hell had arrived.

And he was pissed.

"Tyler, meet Lily," I said. "She's the Prince of Hell's concubine... and possibly our only ticket out of this crappy inferno."

10

"How do we get my brother out of these cuffs?" I asked Lily. "And how are we going to get by the Prince of Hell when he's right outside the door?"

Lily hit a button on the wall and Tyler's restraints popped open. "It will be difficult to get by him, but not impossible."

Once Tyler was loose, he staggered to stand. He was a big wolf, blond and brawny, with broad shoulders and sky-blue eyes—the only trait we shared. I was happy to see his were clearing and his strength was returning.

I placed my hands around his waist to steady him. "Give it a minute," I urged. "The demoness said those vampire slugs sucked your power dry. It's going to take a second to regenerate. How long were they on you?"

He ran a hand over his face.

I let him go and tossed him a rag off a nearby cart so he could mop the blood off his face. "They put the ones on my chest a while ago, but they added more today," he answered. "I honestly didn't think you were going to show. It was hard not to lose hope. Every single day here is like a day void of any joy. This place is fucking miserable."

"Me showing up was never in question. I'd been training for about five days, trying to get ready for what to expect down here, but I ended up triggering the circle too soon. But there really isn't a way to prepare for this and it's lucky I came when I did," I said. "Did they do anything else to you?"

"No, not much," he answered, "which surprised me. But these guys are total pussies. They can't fight worth a damn and every time I growled or flashed my teeth, they scurried out of the room. But they did take blood, hair, and tissue samples ad nauseam. I've been picked over like a lab rat."

"The reason they feared you is because those who were tending you were only one step away from imp," Lily said, somewhat impatiently. "True demons do not work, nor do they do menial labor. Powerful demons live on a different level of this city and rarely venture here. This place is like...what do you call it?" She snapped her fingers. "Ah, yes...a labor camp of sorts."

"Well, that certainly explains why it's been easier to evade them," I said. "And why everyone is wearing a similar jumpsuit?"

"The suits are coded per demon rank and have tracking and stunning abilities." She indicated the sides of Tyler's suit. "Those metal strips can fell a demon in its tracks."

"Great." My brother whistled. "So they can zap me if I try to run?"

She looked at him appraisingly. "Yes, they can, and they will."

"We'll have to get it off you pronto," I told my brother, scouting around for something else in the room for him to wear, but finding nothing.

There was more commotion on the other side of the door and I didn't really want to think about the Prince of Hell being out there. "Why hasn't the Prince blown the door off its hinges and come in after us?" I asked.

"Because I am here," Lily said smugly. "He must wait until his guards arrive. He won't risk me harming him while he is hunting you."

I assessed her. "What choices do we have now?" I asked, starting to pace as I ran a hand through my hair. "We have Tyler, so now all we have to do is get to a portal. That can't be too hard, right?"

For a second I even contemplated taking him back through the Sholls.

It was an ugly second.

"Wrong," Lily said. "Not with the Prince standing outside waiting for you. He came for you himself." She gestured at me. "He's never in this area, except for a high trial. He didn't even bother to oversee any of my torture." Her voice held bitterness, but I wasn't so sure having the Prince of Hell missing your torture was a bad thing. "It's too late to squeeze by him. The only chance you have is if I can distract him long enough to give you an edge, but he will be expecting it, so whatever I do must be big."

"If you fall to the Prince, you forfeit your chance to leave with us," I pointed out, appraising her. "I thought escaping this place was your only motivation to help us?"

She shrugged. "It's a risk I'm willing to take, mostly because I believe there is almost no chance you will succeed and you will need my assistance later. By my estimations you will be captured and taken to trial. If not, and you manage to escape, I've missed my chance." She raised her palms upward. "But by doing this, I've proven to you I am dedicated to your survival, and you will owe me for that. Once you are caught, I will aid you again if I am able and after that we will discuss compensation."

She was right. If she sacrificed herself for our cause I would be indebted to her. "Are you positive there's no other way out?" I glanced around the room again. "It seems there's always a hidey-hole in this godforsaken place."

She shook her head. "Other than that specific mending room we entered, all are sealed in this place. If there were another portal in this building I—of all demons—would know it."

Tyler interjected, "We don't need a portal. We can break out of here. These guys are pushovers. If you show us the way out"—he nodded at Lily—"we can fight. It shouldn't be too hard to overwhelm them. Use your magic against the Prince, and let us do the rest."

Tyler, can you hear me? I reached out to him via our internal connection. *Watch out for Lily, she's dangerous. My wolf is very leery of her, and no matter how much she tries to convince us she's on our side, she still hasn't proven enough to me yet.*

Tyler smiled, showing off one of his killer dimples. *I can hear you, Sis. But it's all wavy, like we're underwater.*

His voice sounded strange to me too, coming in and out of pitch. *Yes, like radio interference. This place is nuts. But, but we tread lightly with Lily. Agreed?*

He nodded once and turned to Lily, sizing her up, glancing back at me. *She doesn't look too dangerous. Her signature is not over the top, but she has a weird look to her.*

She's either cloaking her power or it's muted, because she's extremely strong. She's half witch, half demon, and that may contribute to her "weird" vibe. But whatever she is, she's fierce and crafty.

His expression turned to one of wonder. *I've never heard of a half witch, half demon before, but man, that's a killer magic combination.*

It is killer, I said. *That's what she specializes in—killing. Stay clear of her.*

Got it. Now let's get the fuck out of here.

We both turned toward Lily, and found she was studying us. By her expression she knew something was up, not quite what. Her voice held an edge when she said, "We can't fight our way out. So far, you've been dealing with the equivalent of *janitors* in your world, but the alarms have been sounded and everyone knows you're here in this very room. There's no way to sneak out. And once you're captured"—she nodded to me—"the entire city will tune in to watch. Everyone has been waiting for this day. There is no leaving undetected any longer."

A rap of knuckles sounded on the door. "Come out, come out, wherever you are." The Prince's voice held menace. "There is no escape for you. *Any* of you. My minions have been lacking, but my full guard has amassed. We have surrounded the building and there is no other hope." He paused in a gleeful way. "If I have to blow the door in, I risk killing you all and that wouldn't be any fun, now, would it?"

Lily went to the door, the back of her hand gliding along the smooth surface in a swirling motion that could only be defined as a caress. "But, darling, that *would* be fun—if only you could achieve it. But alas, you cannot. Be truthful now, or it's not a fair game," she teased. "And it's such a shame, because the Prince of Hell should be much stronger than that. Being bested by me always makes you look foolish."

There was a snarl from behind the door, followed by a rush of orders in Demonish.

"What's going on?" I asked, moving toward her. "Why can't the Prince blow in the door? Wouldn't he just want to be done with this?"

Lily gestured at us with a flick of her wrist. "He can't blow us up, because I've warded the door. Now move behind the partition. It won't be safe in about ten seconds. He's ordered his ward breaker in—a half demon, half dwarf. That little shit has a gift for decoding magic. Once he breaks the ward, the Prince will indeed blow the door in. Then I will attack. Once I do, race to the right down the hallway and keep going." She arched a pointed glare at us. "There is a front door if you can find it, but there will be guards everywhere. The only thing that may give you an advantage is if it's daylight. But according to my internal clock there is still over an hour of darkness left." She glanced at me pointedly. "If you had waited just one hour, we might have succeeded."

"I wasn't going to let my brother die," I answered her stonily. "You heard what they said."

"They wouldn't have killed him."

"He was screaming."

"Torture is different from death." She dismissed me, turning toward Tyler, giving him a sweeping glance. "And he looks to me like he could've withstood a hell of a lot more than they gave him."

"They told me I was going to die," he growled, backing me up. "They said those bugs would suck me dry, and then they would 'disassemble' me. My sister did the right thing. Pack protects each other. That's what we do. When one is in trouble, the other comes to their aid. We risk our lives for each other daily. It's called honor." He crossed his arms, his biceps straining through his ridiculous jumpsuit.

"Well, your little *Pack* better get ready to spend some quality time in Hell," she responded in a bored tone, "because the real deal is here. You've been in limbo waiting for your sister to come free you, and it's clear it's dulled you to the peril you're actually facing. Once the demon guards bring you to the detaining rooms, the Underworld will be a much different experience, I guarantee it. Now get back behind the minimal protection we have or you may be harmed in the blast. You won't die, but while you're regenerating from the nasty damage, you'll be caught with no chance of escape."

There was tapping along the outside of the door, along with quiet murmuring, which sounded like a chant. I kind of wanted to see what a half demon, half dwarf looked like.

But then again, I could live without it.

I grabbed Tyler's sleeve and tugged him back behind a partition, where all the supplies were kept. In the other mending room there had been a bathtub crossed with a bed. This one held the chair Tyler had been in, which resembled an evil-looking dentist's chair, and contained nothing else, except a strange metal cabinet.

"Let's shove the cabinet in front of us," I said, grasping one side as I moved past it. It was solid, but not crazy heavy. "I have no idea what the blast will be like, but she's right, I don't want to spend any time regenerating."

Tyler took the other side and we slid it forward together, placing it right in front of the partition. Coming around the side, he whispered low, "Listen, Jess, the demoness may be right. If I was just in a holding cell, we may be in for much more. I can't help but feel like this is all some kind of weird game." He glanced around, eyeing everything with distaste. "Like we're standing in the middle of a chessboard and someone is about to say checkmate."

He was right. It did feel like that. Wolves are up-front in everything they do. Conniving and trickery are not in our nature. There is no reason to beat around the bush when simply crushing your nemesis with your fists is enough. "I totally agree," I said. "Something's off. I had to go through some craziness to find you, but come to think of it, the entire city should've been on lockdown once you arrived. They knew I was coming. And once the demons saw me escape to the Sholls, there should've been a red alert issued then. We had to come back here eventually. And why are the janitors running the courthouse? You should've been under heavy guard. My first thought is they knew I would come to you, so this is not a surprise, but why wouldn't the guards and beasts have been waiting for me in front of your cell? It's all strange. Demons do their own thing, but this feels too orchestrated. But we're not going to find the answers until it's all over."

"I hear you." He turned. "Now help me get out of this monkey suit." He had the front zipper clasped between his finger and thumb. "It won't give."

I reached up to grasp it and it gave me a little shock. "It's spelled." I pushed some of my magic into it until there was an audible pop. Then I yanked the zipper down and Tyler peeled it off. "After seeing you on a street corner not too long ago in your Calvins." I chuckled. "I hadn't thought I'd see you in them again so soon."

"Very funny," he grumbled. "At least they left me my underwear. They're very cleanly around here. They made sure I was washed daily with this weird gel. It cleaned whatever it touched. I didn't even have to get undressed."

"I know," I said. "It's cleaned me off twice so far. It eats everything. We could certainly use some of that at home. It would make life a lot simpler. I'm deeming it the only good thing about Hell."

"Yeah, it works great at home, until it accidentally disintegrates my pet cat." Tyler wadded up the jumpsuit and tossed it in a corner. His boxer briefs were black and luckily covered him well.

I laughed. "You don't have a cat," I said pointedly. "So it won't be an issue."

"Well." He shrugged. "You have one, so I thought maybe I

might get one too. You don't own the market on cats, you know. Maybe the rest of us are searching for our own furry cuddle pal."

I thumped him in the chest. "That's not funny. My cat is going to be cranky I'm not back yet." I missed Rourke like crazy, and for my wolf it had been almost intolerable. I had to block out her constant yearning or it would have been overwhelming. Being apart was hard for both of us, but I knew it was harder on him at the moment. Being separated from a mate felt like an open, aching wound. I just prayed that if he was coming after me, he would show up soon. I didn't want him here alone.

There was a loud thud against the door, but not a blast.

"Is that all you have, sweetheart?" Lily called. "That wasn't very—"

The explosion burst my eardrums and sent both Tyler and me flying backward. We smashed into the wall, the metal cabinet bursting through the partition to land on top of us. It had indeed taken the brunt of the blast. Tyler kicked it off and we both sprang up and ran. "Lily!" I called, squinting through the dust the blast had caused as I sprinted toward the door. "Where are you? Are you okay?"

She was nowhere to be found.

She'd been right in front of the door, so it was possible she'd been vaporized. There was commotion out in the hallway. I poked my head out. It was hard to see anything through the dust, but her voice carried: "Well, what are you waiting for, idiots? Run!"

I cursed myself and my internal human mothering.

Tyler grabbed my sleeve and propelled us forward. "Let's go!" He shoved me in front of him and we raced down the hallway.

We ran hard. After maneuvering through two hallways I called, "There's no one here. This can't be right!"

"We have to keep moving no matter what. This place is a maze, but I bet there's only one front door. Here, let me go first." He came up beside me, but I grabbed his arm.

"Wait," I said, slowing. "This doesn't feel right. Maybe we should duck into one of these rooms. Something's definitely off, just like we stated before. I bet Lily lied and there's another portal somewhere and she directed us to right into a trap." Once again I contemplated the Sholls. The mending room we'd come out of was close by. I could smell my scent trail, but surviving the wyverns would be next to impossible without Lily.

"Jess, we need to keep moving. You're right, this is too easy, but what else are we going to do? Come on," he said, dragging me along behind him at a quick clip. He brought his nose up to scent the area. "I'm getting a read on something different up ahead."

I followed him cautiously, trotting along. "Different is not good in this place."

"You're telling me. I want out of here so bad it hurts, and I also want a bacon cheeseburger, a regular shower, and—" He held his hand up and switched to internal. *There's movement around that corner.*

We both stopped, but I couldn't hear anything substantial. Tyler began to inch forward again. *Tyler, wait. My gut is telling me not to go.* Not to mention my wolf, who had begun to howl.

He stopped, turning to me. *Fine, but what do we do? Are there any windows in this place? They haven't exactly given me a tour.*

No windows. In fact, the sun here burns the skin. We're going to have to duck into one of these rooms and think of something else. I moved toward a door. This one had a knob.

It turned slowly. No movement. I braced my shoulder against the door.

Nothing.

Try the next one, I told him, gesturing down the hallway.

"That one won't work either," an arch voice said from behind us.

My head whipped around.

The Prince of Hell stood very regally at the end of the long hallway. He was dressed in a three-piece suit, hair shellacked, precise in all ways.

Except for one thing.

A line of fingernail tracks running from his cheek to his chin.

11

The Prince's wounds were closing fast, but that didn't bode well for Lily. Drawing blood, or in this case motor oil, from the Prince of Hell was no small feat. As my brother had learned the hard way. Though the demoness was already in hot water, so maybe it didn't matter.

"You will not escape through any of those doors." The Prince took a step forward. "They are impassable. I had not thought you would encounter"—he flourished one of his hands—"the *demoness*, and that meeting has thrown everything off. But make no mistake, we have been awaiting your imminent arrival. We've made plans, but in your...eagerness...to make another defiant alliance you have managed to throw a wrench in them. So, I am once again forced to come here and take care of things."

"My eagerness?" I scoffed. "Of course I was eager to save my brother. And I'd pair up again with anyone who would help me. And I'm sorry, but *I've* ruined everything?" I sputtered. "In this situation"—I waved an arm between us—"you definitely win the spoilsport award. If you hadn't kidnapped my brother, I'd be home right now curled up with my mate under the covers watching reality TV. Instead I'm here fighting my way through the horrors of your world. And, by the way, this place *sucks*. You need to redecorate and possibly import some sunshine that doesn't blister off the skin."

"The Underworld is an extremely pleasant plane to exist." The Demon Lord continued down the hallway at a slow gait. "I took your kin, because you must face your crimes. There was no other way."

"I beg to differ. I haven't committed any crimes that will hold up in any real court, and you know it." I took a bold step forward, Tyler behind me, a continuous low growl emitting from his throat. "I defended myself, which is acceptable in any supernatural realm. But when you kidnapped my brother, you forced me here—and if it weren't for you, I wouldn't be involved in any demon business at all. The Underworld wouldn't even be on my radar."

"It was fated you would come," the Prince responded calmly, though I could tell I was affecting him. "It was only a matter of time. I simply sped things up."

"I think not," I contended. "If it weren't for your stubborn visits to our plane and your constant aggression, I never would've come here."

His eyes did the reptilian flash where the pupils elongated, making me curious once again as to why the demons were glamoured in their own realm. It would take much less energy to just be a regular demon, whatever that looked like.

"It was written. Everything that is written comes to pass. Do not question our Scriptures, you lowly mutt." The Prince took another few steps forward. "It is offensive."

I was tired of being called a mutt or a mongrel. If you wanted to get technical, I wasn't a mutt, I was a reincarnated *purebred*. My wolf howled her agreement. "If me coming here was documented in your Scriptures, then your interference should be noted in there as well," I countered. "Does it say, 'The female wolf will descend to the bowels of Hell to wreak havoc, but only if she is provoked by the idiotic Prince of Hell'? Because that's how it should read."

"How dare you mock me?" His eyes narrowed as he continued to stroll nonchalantly toward me. The Prince's face had already healed. Only faint lines of dried residue marred it now. "I did nothing but seek to make you pay for your atrocities. Killing our beasts and our imps is a direct crime against us. You are dangerous and will pay dearly for your actions."

Jess, there's something coming from behind and I'm beginning to hear movement behind all these doors. We are totally surrounded.

I was laser-focused on the Prince, who was taking his time reaching us. Twenty more yards.

Tyler continued, *The bad news is I don't know what's coming at us from behind. They don't smell like the regular demons I've been dealing with, but whatever they are, they are nasty as hell.*

My wolf inhaled while I kept my eyes on the threat. *Those are the chupacabras,* I told my brother, *but these smell different from the babies and there's an undertone of something else. There may be other beasts with them.*

Babies?

Long story, but the chupacabra adults are vicious. I don't know how we're going to get away from Mr. Nasty here, so I'm just going to keep talking to buy us some time.

Yeah, he chuckled, *because that's working really well for you. Why don't you tell him his pants are on fire from being such a liar, liar?*

I bristled. *And what exactly would you have me say?*

I don't know, maybe tossing some honey on this mess would work better for us.

It was all I could do not to turn around and gape at my brother. *You want me to sweet-talk* the Prince of Hell? Wolves did *not* sweet-talk. *I can't believe you just said that!*

Well, he said defensively, *whatever works, right? How else are we going to get out of here? There's a threat in every direction and we're on a Hell plane with no backup. I'm up for doing whatever it takes to get out f here.*

I swallowed a softball-sized gulp. Sweet-talk the Demon Lord? Right. My wolf snapped her jaws. *I know, but Tyler makes a fair point. Even if I used my combined magic to get by the Prince, I don't think we can get Tyler out too, or defeat all the beasts coming at us from every direction. We need more time and some... sweet talk might get us... something.* The question was, what? Less torture? A kinder trial?

But it would buy me more time.

"I sense your defeat." The Prince took a long breath in. "And it smells divine. You are finally realizing that there is no hope for you any longer." The Prince thought I was worried. He had no idea I was incensed with my brother's suggestion to be nice.

I played it up. "That's not exactly it," I hedged. "But maybe I am having a teensy change of... heart?" I swallowed. "This has all been incredibly... overwhelming, you know? The Underworld has been almost too much to handle in such a short amount of time." Like turning into the only female wolf on the planet and proceeding to fight off every supernatural Sect in the world had been tons easier for me than being here.

Way to lay it on nice and thick, Tyler chuckled. *The Prince is going to be putty in your hands after that heartfelt admission.*

Shut up. Don't forget, this was your idea. The least you could do is back me up.

The Prince of Hell stopped walking.

He stood only ten yards from us. My wolf wove our magic around us like a shield, readying us for a fight we knew would happen. I loathed being nice to the Prince of Hell, even if it bought me a few more moments, but I knew this wasn't going to end without a fight.

"A change of heart?" he said, cocking his head at a weird angle, in only the way a supernatural could, mimicking a bird listening for worms. "Do my ears deceive me? The great female wolf warrior is giving herself up? Without a fight?" The Prince spread his well-manicured hands wide. "This day must be recorded in our history."

I gritted my teeth. "I didn't say that…exactly. But perhaps we've both been a bit"—I managed—"overzealous in our attempts to"—I took in a big breath—"win this battle between us. Maybe if we both come at this from a different angle it could be"—I exhaled—"beneficial to us both."

"Oh, and what *angle* would that be, pray tell?" he snickered, obviously not buying anything I was selling. "The angle where you come willingly and I don't kill you or your kin? Or the angle where I bring you down no matter what?"

This is a shitty-ass plan, I said to Tyler. *We're going to have to fight our way out. There's no other way.*

Just tell the Prince something he wants to hear, Tyler urged. *Something that will get us an escort out of this fucking hallway and hopefully toward better odds.*

Like what?

Like you don't want any trouble and you're just here to clear your name.

I'm here to free you, remember? I said. *I'm not here to clear anything.*

That's good, add that too.

That's really helpful.

The Prince had his gaze locked on me. He wasn't smiling. He knew something was up. I would have given anything to have my ghost pal Ben here to help me right now. There was nothing better than being inside the head of your enemy to win the advantage. But I hadn't seen or heard from Ben since we'd left New Orleans.

"No," I said, clearing my throat. "The angle where I admit to your head council that I did…some wrong, but that I ultimately want nothing to do with your kind and pose no further threat. I will then…pay restitution to the demons…and promise never to visit this plane again."

"You *will* pay restitution." The Prince grinned. "In whatever form the court deems appropriate, and if I hazarded a guess, it would involve something where you are…laboring"—he eyed me up and down—"…quite hard…for a very long time."

Ew. I wasn't sure if that was a double entendre or not, but it was still awful.

My jaw clenched and my wolf howled, gnashing her teeth. "Listen," I told him, shaking my finger in a scolding way as I took a step forward. "You're not going to get any more from me than I just offered. I will come with you…willingly. But it's not possible for me to be held here indefinitely and you know it. My team will come, or I will break free—but whatever happens it won't bode well for you or your kind. There will be damage once this is over. Lots and lots of collateral damage. So I would advise you to listen to what I'm telling you and come up with a new plan, one that takes me as a cooperating *visitor*, instead of a prisoner. I know we can work this out so everyone will be happy. If not"—I grinned, because I couldn't help it—"you're not going to like the repercussions."

You were doing pretty well there until that last part, Tyler piped in as I felt his power jump. He was readying for the fight we both knew was fast approaching. *I think it's safe to say that wolves weren't meant for sweet talk. You were terrible at it.*

Whatever. I'd like to see you give it a try. It burns like sandpaper being scraped against my tongue, and with that last compromise, the honeypot is officially dry. The only one who was ever going to get sweet-talked was my man, and when I did it for him, I would mean it.

The Prince's pupils elongated and stayed that way.

Power pinged between us up and down the hallway.

Get ready, I told my brother.

Already there.

"You are outnumbered in force and power," the Prince raged. "You cannot possibly escape. You will come with me, as you stated, *willingly*, or you will come harmed. But you will be leaving on my terms one way or another. I am the master here, you will do everything I decree."

I made a split decision and pivoted in a blur, swinging my leg around and plowing it, along with my demon power, into the door nearest to me. If there were things behind these doors, then they were about to become my newest diversion.

Tyler, hit the doors, I yelled.

He didn't pause to ask if it was a solid plan; he was already in motion while I arced my foot into the next one. I'd knocked down two, exploding them open with enough force to shatter them completely, before the Prince reacted, physically shaking himself.

"What are you doing?" he boomed. "You cannot win! Leave those doors alone."

"Whatever you're keeping locked up behind these doors is about to come out and join us," I yelled as I moved forward toward another one. "I hope they're not your pets, because I want things to get nice and ugly for all of us."

Jess, Tyler whispered in my head, *these aren't his pets.*

"You are an absolute menace," the Prince snarled, moving forward. I had backed away from him as I kicked in the doors, and he was almost to me when something big stepped out of the door I'd just obliterated, coming between us.

I stumbled back to get out of the way. This thing had to duck to get through the doorway. It was gigantic.

The Prince of Hell was forced to come to a standstill in front of it.

This creature wasn't happy, either. It gave a long groan, which sounded like a roar mixed with a battle cry.

It seemed we'd just freed some of the Prince's prisoners and they were pissed.

Is that a . . . troll? I asked Tyler, still backing out of the way, putting more separation between us and them. *Why would a troll be in the Underworld?* I'd never seen one before.

Beats the hell out of me, but if it stays focused on the Prince I'm all for it. Let's keep moving backward.

The troll's skin was sallow and sagging and its pace was sluggish. This was clearly not its normal habitat and it looked like it had been down here for a very long time.

It was also seven feet tall and as wide as the doorway itself.

"Get back." The Prince shooed it with his hand. "Go back into your cell, you dirty beast. This fight is not yours."

The troll didn't move.

Instead it started to keen and rock, the high-pitched sound coming from its throat surprising me. But before the Prince could use any magic on it, a shadow fell on the open doorway a few paces to my right.

I moved away quickly, not knowing what it was, and collided with Tyler's chest, his hands steadying my shoulders as he walked us both backward.

"What is it?" I whispered, trying not to call attention to us in any way.

He leaned over and murmured, "I think it might be...a *ghoul*."

"A ghoul?" I gasped. "Are you sure? I didn't think they really existed."

"Me neither, but look at it. What else would it be?"

He was right.

As the thing eased out of the doorway, it appeared to be haunted—as in just-from-the-grave ghostly. Its skin was gray and peeling. It resembled a human, but a very dead one who had come back to life as something else. Ghouls, from myth, were dead bodies reanimated by powerful necromancers. And once a ghoul came back to life, only its necromancer could control it.

"I thought ghouls were like puppets," I whispered, both of us continuing to take hefty steps away from the brewing melee. "Only controlled by a master, like a zombie on a leash?"

"Who knows," Tyler said. "I've certainly never seen one before and I don't know much about them."

The Prince of Hell roared, "Get back, necromancer! You are not needed here. Go back to your cell if you do not want one final death."

The troll took a giant step toward the Prince, who was now openly clenching and unclenching his fists, just short of losing it completely.

"Well," I said to my brother. "I guess now we know what a dead necromancer looks like. They must come back as a ghoul themselves once they die."

Tyler elbowed me. "When the troll takes a swing, we start running."

"Sounds like a plan," I said.

The troll took a swing at the Prince and we both turned.

Straight into a bevy of snarls and howls.

"Freeze!" The demon guard aimed an ugly-looking weapon at our heads. He yelled in heavily accented English, "Put your hands up." The gun resembled some kind of mini rocket launcher, and to make matters worse, the demons behind this one were juggling two grown chupacabras on straining leashes, snapping their pointy teeth at us.

They were incredibly massive with huge incisors and spiny backs with lethal-looking points.

My brother and I lifted our arms.

The Prince of Hell shouted once more, and then a shock of power hit the hallway, reverberating around like a seismic tremor.

We turned around to see the poor troll give a strangled yell as it crashed to its knees, making the floor jump. It fell prone on the ground and lay there unmoving. The ghoul went next in another rush of power, its body smashing against the wall as it crumpled to the floor like a bag of rotted bones.

With the troll down I could see the Prince's face clearly. If the Demon Lord could've willed us dead, we would've been toast. "These creatures didn't need to die!" he boomed. "They were of use to me! Now you will pay dearly for their deaths along with all the others."

"I would happily free your prisoners again," I called. "They didn't look like they were enjoying their extended stay in Hotel Hell anyway. I wonder if keeping supernaturals prisoner for this long is against High Law? I hardly believe that troll came to the Underworld on its own looking for trouble."

I noticed now that three of the other occupants had wisely chosen to stay inside their rooms rather than face the angry Prince, even though their doors had been destroyed.

The Prince of Hell stepped over the troll and came straight at us.

Before I could get another word out, he raised his hands and power shot into the air with lightning speed. I heard Tyler yell in terror as the Prince's dark essence hit me squarely in the chest, tossing me backward.

Blackness pulled me under, filling me up immediately, until there was nothing else.

12

I awoke with a gasp, my body jolting upward like I'd been shocked. My hand went straight to my chest, where the Prince had blasted me, as blood pounded in my ears, sounding like a rushing ocean with a heartbeat. My wolf paced back and forth in my mind. It was obvious she had been waiting for me to wake up for some time.

What happened? I asked her as I blinked and glanced around, trying to get my bearings.

She flashed me a picture of us being consumed by darkness.

I saw that part, but how did it happen? I had defeated the Prince of Hell's magic before, and now that I had demon essence inside me, I'd been certain I could defeat him again—or at the very least hold my own in a fight. *Where did the blackness go?*

I glanced down at my hands like they would somehow give me answers to my burning questions, but of course they appeared perfectly normal. My fingernails had seen better days, but they weren't falling off or streaked black with demon juice.

I rested one hand on the cool, slippery white floor beside me while I rubbed my other absentmindedly over my chest. *Where are we?*

After a moment, I stood slowly, turning in a full circle. The room was all white, and unlike in Lily's cell, there wasn't a scrap of furniture to be found. No bed, no dresser, which to me indicated no long-term stay.

I was taking that as a win.

There weren't any doors either, and this time there wasn't even a cutout where a door should've been. The room seemed to be hermetically sealed. I knew this wasn't true, but it was still unsettling. I had to find a way out.

I paced forward, searching.

That wasn't an ordinary shock of magic the Prince hit us with, I told my wolf. She didn't answer. She was too focused on sending our power out now that I was finally awake. *Either the Prince has always held out on us, or something else happened back there. I should not have fallen so easily to his magic.*

It bothered me. I'd bested the Demon Lord before, so why was this time any different?

In my short experience as a wolf, I'd learned that magic had to go somewhere. When a supe was blasted with foreign magic, as the Prince and Tally had done to me, it either had to flow out, which is what Tally had hoped I'd do with it—or it had to be forced out like Ray had done when he vomited.

In my case alone, it stayed inside.

Most supes could transfer power easily, as my brother had to me when I'd needed it, but power wasn't raw magic—it was energy, like giving a car a jump so it could grab its own juice. A supe needed power to make magic.

Magic was alive.

It was your signature, something that manifested from deep

within you, and it made you unique. The stronger the supernatural, the more power they could generate. Thus their ability to control their magic was more potent.

This was what Rourke had been telling me all along.

The stronger the supe, the higher they were on the supernatural food chain. A supe with less power did not engage those with more power very often. But, on the other hand, if a pixie had been born with my kind of power she would have been fierce, able to wield her own magic to a much higher degree.

That's what the sorcerers had wanted—to siphon off my power to enhance their own magic. But that wasn't possible. A power transfer only worked in the short term, but it wasn't something they could harness and keep.

My wolf barked, interrupting my thoughts. She motioned to the wall and I ran my hands along it as she pushed our senses out to find a weakness or some escape pod. The walls were sterile and smooth, kind of like marble, but more porous. The texture was warm and sticky, but once again, there was no residue.

Not finding anything in the walls, I stepped back and glanced up at the ceiling, but only found more of the same.

Tyler, can you hear me? I called out in my mind. *Are you out there?*

Nothing.

Our connection was still blessedly there, however. I could feel he was alive, but I wasn't picking up on anything else from him. The demons had a way to stanch communication or they had put him to sleep somehow. They had no real reason to hurt him, since I was here, but that wasn't saying much. I had no idea how he reacted once I went down.

The Underworld was nothing like I'd imagined. Fire and brimstone would've been too clichéd, but office buildings, courtyards with gazebos, and demons wearing jumpsuits hadn't been anywhere near my radar. It would've been nice if this place had been a little more predictable, because as I thought about escaping, I realized I had no idea how to do it or what I would encounter. It made it hard to prepare.

I sat down in the middle of the room and wrapped my arms around my knees. *We have to be thoughtful about this*, I told my wolf. *We're probably being monitored right now.* I peered into all the corners, trying to locate anyplace they could've mounted a camera, as one hand wandered to my chest to rub the small ache that still lingered. *We should've been able to take on the Prince's magic.* I was having trouble letting it go. My wolf growled in agreement. *We went down too quickly. And I wonder if Tyler tried to defend us? I'm sure he did and they better not have hurt him.*

I hated not knowing.

There was no doubt in my mind Tyler had tried to protect me, but how much had they punished him for it? Before I could formulate a new plan, a *ding* sounding like a doorbell sounded and a voice rang out in passable English: "Prisoner, you will stand trial in three hours. You must prepare yourself."

Prepare myself? "And how am I supposed to do that?" I called. "Shouldn't I be meeting with a lawyer?" Did they have demon lawyers in Hell? "Or see someone who is going to try my case?"

No response.

Instead a drawer slid open on the far wall.

I jumped up and went over to investigate. Inside lay a single jumpsuit, neatly folded. I glanced around me, hands on my hips. "I'm not wearing that, so you can forget it," I called. There was no way I was putting on something they could control me in. I still wore the witches' hemp fatigues and they'd proven to be very durable and flexible—even after all the blood and guts, and subsequent water dump baths I'd taken.

"You must wear the appropriate garments," the voice stated in an even tone.

"I'm not putting them on," I insisted. "You can tell whoever's in charge they can go to Hell." Then I laughed a tiny bit maniacally because we *were* in Hell. How many times in your life can you say that while you're actually standing in Hell? Never.

Or almost never, in my case.

Instead of my donning the required garments, my leg shot out and connected with the drawer, slamming it back in the wall so hard it cracked the facing. I bent over to investigate the damage when a blast of something shot straight into my chest. It was so strong it tossed me back against the far wall, knocking me silly and pinning me there.

But what had hit me wasn't magic.

It was air.

The fire hose of wind held me for a few moments, and then abruptly shut off. I dropped to my knees. *Do you see where the air jets are coming from?* I asked my wolf. She growled, but shook her head. "You're going to try to take me down with air?" I shouted into the room. "I don't think so!"

I stepped forward and another blast shot into my abdomen. Before I knew what had happened I was plastered up against the wall once again.

The pressure was intense.

At this rate it would bore a hole through me. *We need to stop it.* I gritted my teeth. My wolf shot power through us and I managed to angle my hand in front of the brunt of the jet. I was in my Lycan form as I cupped the air into my hands. Fighting it with all my strength, I managed to direct it away from my body. It took both my hands and all my strength.

Using the power of straight-line winds, clocking in at easily a hundred miles per hour, was actually brilliant on the demons' part. Air wasn't magic. I couldn't combat it with anything except pure force. I took a step forward, gnashing my teeth, my hands still shielding the blast away from me.

This might be able to stop a lesser demon in its tracks, but not a pissed-off werewolf.

Power tingled in my hand as my strength beat back the airflow. I continued to push forward, searching for where it was coming from. *Let's make it look like we're struggling more,* I told my wolf as I took another small step forward and staggered a bit. *We need to find the source so we can destroy it, but we can't move too quickly or they'll amp up the flow.* The room was obviously rigged with things like drawers and air jets, so it wasn't completely sealed, which was great news.

I continued forward, making each step appear like a feat of mankind. My magic helped ward off the impact and damage to my body. The stream suddenly jumped a few more miles per hour and I was forced to take a step backward.

They were testing me.

Okay, new plan. We rush the jet and crack through the wall. Everything in here is seamless, so we need to act fast while the air is still flowing. My wolf agreed by sending a huge jolt of adrenaline washing through us. It jumped in my veins as I dashed forward, one hand and my chest pushing the air back with all my might, the other fisted above me, ready to pound the wall.

I reached the source in a few seconds, ramming my fist into a place that appeared completely unmarred. The white wall exploded around me, revealing a rocky surface where three small air jets were embedded. How the air came through the wall was a complete mystery, but demon technology was crazy like that. The air jets immediately turned off and a bell pinged in the air.

"Cease and desist, prisoner. You will don the proper attire and await your trial."

"Or what?" I shouted, moving quickly toward the drawer. It had to be set in the same rocky wall, and they had to be able to fill it from the other side. If I destroyed it completely, I might be able to crawl through. I smashed my foot into the broken face and the rest of the components flew apart, scattering through the small space like Tinkertoys across an icy expanse. I ripped the remaining pieces out and tossed them behind me as I squatted in front of it. The jumpsuit lay at the bottom and I bunched it up and threw it to the side. I crouched low, peering into the darkness of the small hole. I couldn't tell where it led, but it was out of here and that was all that mattered. It wasn't quite big enough for me to get through, but I could kick more of the stone out of the away to make it bigger.

"Stop!" The intercom crackled.

"Sorry, too late," I called as I positioned myself on the floor in front of it to do some serious damage. "I'm not staying in here any longer than necessary, and I don't see anyone here to stop me." I brought my knees up and kicked one side of the hole. My feet encountered rock, but it broke easily, crumbling around me.

A few more kicks and I would be free.

I knew the demons would be on me as soon as they could, but I was prepared to keep fighting my way out. There weren't any other options at this point.

"If you do not stop, we will *kill* him." This voice was harsh, not like the last one.

I froze mid-kick.

The ambient lights in the room flickered once. The space was backlit. I turned slowly as all the walls around me blinked twice and seamlessly morphed into screens.

"Tyler," I yelled. "No!" I jumped up and raced to the nearest one and slapped the edges of my fists onto the picture in front of me, frustration that I couldn't reach him raging within me.

No leeches this time. They were preparing to cut him up or do something equally appalling. He was out cold and strapped on a harsh-looking bed. There were huge implements lined up on a counter next to him.

One of them looked like a sickle.

"Fine!" I screamed, backing away from the wall. "I'll do whatever you want. But you have to promise not to hurt him."

Another drawer opened up near the one I'd demolished, containing a new jumpsuit. I walked over and snatched it out. "I'll put this on," I seethed, turning in a full circle. "But you have to keep the live feed going so I know you're not hurting him."

The screens flickered off.

I raced up to the nearest panel and pounded my hands against it. The walls were hard, but they cracked in the places my fists landed. "I'm not going to cooperate unless you show me my brother is alive! I will tear these walls down, so help me." My wolf howled along with me, both of us maddened by what we had seen.

"The next time we show you your brother, you won't like what you see." The voice was low and menacing. This demon spoke perfect English. They weren't messing around. "If you want to save his precious soul, don the garment and sit down." It was a command.

Goddamnit! For the first time, I wished Lily was here. At least she would know if they would follow through or not. She'd already told me they would torture him but not kill him. I needed to know if that had changed.

But in my heart, I knew they had no reason to keep him alive. They would probably enjoy killing him and reaping his soul.

I put the jumpsuit on.

A few hours later a portion of the wall slid back and I jumped to my feet. I'd managed to don the damn jumpsuit against a myriad of loud, ugly protests from my wolf. It'd been more than three hours since they'd shown me Tyler, and it had all gone by fairly uneventfully. During that time my wolf and I had come up with several plans, all of them flawed.

But the time hadn't been totally wasted.

Being forced to focus inward for more than five minutes had aided me dearly. I smiled thinking about it. The Prince was going to be in for a little surprise.

Five demons dressed in jumpsuits, these ones silver with black stripes, strode in. They appeared like carbon copies, hair slicked back, all the same dark color, all the same height, their features eerily similar. They looked like quintuplets. The only thing that gave them away was their eyes. *A few of them are scared*, I told my wolf. *I can smell their fear.* A ripple of excitement ran through me and my magic jumped.

Both sets of magic.

In my alone time, I'd managed to separate the demon magic completely from my own. It had been a tedious endeavor, like picking individual thistles out of nest of thick fur. The effort it had taken me had made me sweat, but once I'd figured out how to pull the black flecks out, I'd parceled them away in a different place from my own magic—and they had stayed separate. So far, so good.

If I wanted to survive this ordeal, accessing the darkness on its own would be essential. The realization had come an hour after I'd started worrying about Tyler, achieving nothing. I couldn't stop thinking about why I'd succumbed to the Prince's magic in the hallway.

It had literally come down to the magic running through my veins.

The Prince of Hell had absolute control of his minions, which made sense. If he couldn't control his demons, what kind of leader would he be? I'd had that same demon magic in my blood, given to me by Tally. It had mixed with my own, and when the Prince blasted me, the demon magic inside me had instantly succumbed, like I'd been one of the Prince's own demons. Had it been separated, and I could've fought with my own magic alone, I think the outcome would've been different.

But I wasn't going to take any chances. I wasn't going to let it happen twice.

I clenched my fists as I walked toward the demon guards. I had wound my golden signature around me tightly, fortifying me, and the demon magic moved like an oil slick in my system, powerful, waiting for an opportunity to strike.

A demon grabbed my arm, an ugly-looking needle clutched in one hand. "What's that for?" I asked, tugging my arm back roughly.

"It is called *deviek bely*," he said. "Liquid fire. If you move the wrong way, we will put this in you, and you will not like the consequences. If you survive, you will be forever damaged." Its English was good.

"I'm not going to make any trouble," I said, stepping back as far as I could. "As long as you tell me my brother is fine."

"He lives."

They shuffled me through a ten-foot stone tunnel. It would've been mighty hard to break out of this fortress, and ultimately I was glad I hadn't wasted my time. My new plan was much better.

Kill the Prince of Hell, and free my brother.

13

The demons maneuvered me through a few more tunnels, each one different from the last. "You know, you could really use some continuity around here. Maybe hire a few decorators? One hallway looks like an office building, and the next looks like lava flows freely down the corridors. It's a little unsettling." I sidestepped a huge granite-colored rock with red veins, doing a double take. "Was that one just pulsing?"

"Quiet, human," a demon snapped, pulling me forward.

"I thought we were already in the courthouse," I said. "Where are we going?"

One of the demons chuckled and it was a strange sound, like a squeaky helium balloon barking. "Once our Prince brought you down"—there was pride in the demon's voice—"you were transferred. Your trial is out of the ordinary."

"So where are you taking me?"

"The High Court of Mephistopheles."

"And where's that?" I pressed, wanting as many details as possible.

"You will remain quiet, prisoner." They jostled me forward, the needle still visible.

I shut my mouth.

The Prince had already told me I had a date with the High Court of Mephistopheles when he visited Selene's lair. It must be the equivalent of the demon Supreme Court. That didn't put the odds in my favor.

We have to believe that if we take out the Prince, the demon population will fall into chaos. They're so regimented, and they look to the Prince for absolute assurance. This entire place reminded me of an anthill. One huge, well-placed interruption would send the ants scurrying everywhere. *But if this court is made up of powerful Demon Lords, it may be trickier than we anticipate.* My wolf barked her agreement, her ears perked, eyes on the tunnel in front of us. *We should've asked Lily what specifically was in the Scriptures. It would've been nice to know exactly why they fear me.*

We came upon a massive door, taller than any other I'd seen. It was carved in ornate detail and had circular handles that were set too high to reach.

There was murmuring behind it. Lots and lots of murmuring.

This place is full of demons. My wolf snarled, her ears low. *Everyone has turned out to see the female wolf stand trial. That's why they took so long to come and get me. They were waiting for the masses to arrive.*

The demon guards stopped in front of the door and made three lines, with me in the middle. I was flanked by a guard on either side, one in front and two behind. We stood quietly for a few minutes. "Why aren't we going in?" I asked.

"Quiet!" a demon barked.

"*Ah*," I said. "You guys want pomp and circumstance. I'm

supposed to make a grand entrance, is that it? The big baddie up for trial needs to be paraded through the crowd in shame. All the better for your master's case against me."

Before another demon could reprimand me, a huge gong sounded. It was so loud, my chest vibrated with the echoes. Once the reverberations died down, all the sounds on the other side of the door stilled.

I swore under my breath. *I don't want to sound hopeless, but it feels like we're never going to escape this place. We can't take every demon from Demonville out on our own. Even if we kill the Prince, this is too public. Just the way he wanted it.* It made me furious thinking the Prince could outsmart us. I made a silent wish for backup for the first time since I'd arrived. If Rourke was coming, he had to be on his way by now. But time was so screwed up here, there was a chance he wouldn't arrive for months. My chest tightened. *If he waited too long we're in trouble, and he's in trouble.* My wolf flashed me a picture of us using the newly concentrated demon magic. *I know, but what if it's not enough? It sounds like there are thousands of spectators in there. The only option is to defend our case the best way we can. If I can talk my way out, or demand a retrial, I may be able to hold off at least until our backup arrives. If they arrive.*

No more time to strategize. The huge doors slowly creaked open on their own to expose row after row of seated demons. We stood at the top of what looked to be a massive coliseum. That was the only word for it. The room before us was gigantic, with a large domed ceiling and huge gilded pillars running around the far walls.

The demon guards dragged me to the head of a steep row of stairs. The steps led down through levels of gathered demons to the bottom of the amphitheater, where seven lofty chairs were positioned behind a long, continuous bench of what appeared to be polished wood of some kind.

The Prince of Hell sat in the middle, his chair elevated the highest. Six other Demon Lords fanned to the left and right, three on each side.

"Are you telling me the Prince of Hell is the judge?" I gasped. "This isn't a trial, it's a hanging! I thought you guys were all about rules and fairness. What happened to a well-worded defense giving me a chance to go free?" Anger raced through me, threatening to overpower me. "As it stands now, I could form the best defense the supernatural world has ever heard and the Prince of Hell would still find me guilty. It's a mistrial already."

"The Prince is Master of Court, of course," the demon beside me growled. "His decisions are law."

"Master of Court, my ass," I muttered. "Then why all this formality for nothing?" I glanced around at row after row of assembled guests. "The Prince will sentence me to something horrid in five minutes and everyone will go home. This won't be a fair trial, no matter what happens." I struggled against the guards for a moment as I contemplated making a break for it. Then one of the demons raised the needle and I stopped moving. "Where is my brother?" I sighed. "I want to know that he's safe."

"He is not in attendance."

"How do I know he hasn't been harmed?" I asked. "Am I supposed to take your word for it?"

Instead of giving an answer they prodded me down the steps.

We began to descend the massive stairway. As I placed a foot on the first step, a low hum began and every demon in the place turned to stare at me in unison.

As I continued down, I noticed the demons were split into hierarchies.

The black jumpsuited janitors sat in the back. They must be the working-class demons. In the middle were demons clad in black and silver. They looked a bit more professional. Maybe white-collar demons? They wore the same outfit as the guards, but I didn't think they were all guards. It was a long way down, but once I was closer, I spotted what must be the upper-class demons. They all wore three-piece suits, hair slicked back, hands clasped in front, just like their big bossman.

The only surprise sat in the very front row. I landed at the bottom to find six demonesses in formal, high-backed chairs facing the court.

And they appeared nothing like Lily.

They were all clearly glamoured, each of them with identical long raven hair and hawkishly precise features, much like the Prince of Hell's. They were dressed in black dresses with high collars and their eyes tracked me as I was escorted to a standstill in front of the high seats.

Other than the Prince himself, these demonesses were clearly the six biggest threats in the room. Incredible power zinged off each one of them. True demonesses were few and far between, as Lily had said, but I hadn't realized how powerful they'd feel.

Fuckerdoodles. We can't kill all these demonesses with the power we have. It's no match for all these threats. We need to—

The Prince of Hell cleared his throat for a long moment before he spoke. "You will address the court's questions in a clear, concise manner. Once we finish our questions, we shall decide your fate and you will accept our rulings. The High Court's decisions are always final."

I glanced around, making sure everyone took note of me before I spoke, which wasn't a problem since every eye in the place was on me. "So where is my defense lawyer?" I mocked, searching the room. "Or someone who is assigned to plead my case? If this is a fair trial, by supernatural High Law, I want representation."

"There are no lawyers in Hell," the Prince answered, a toothy grin spreading across his pointy features. "Demons know if you tell the truth. You will answer our questions and your guilt will be determined as such."

"As such—you mean by you? Let me guess. You're going to ask me if I killed an imp, and I'm going to say yes. But you're not going to ask me why." I made eye contact with each of the Demon Lords as the crowd behind me began to murmur. "You're not going to ask me if the imp committed a crime, or if my killing it was in defense against bodily injury or not. This is not set up to be a fair trial—if it were, you'd know that an unbiased supernatural High Law judge should be in attendance, not you, and I should not be tried by my extremely biased accuser." I had no idea if that was true or not, but I guessed that none of the demons here knew either.

The Prince of Hell half rose from his chair, scowling, and placed his palms on the wooden platform in front of him, his skinny fingers splaying and curling out in front of him. Not a single piece of his hair moved. "We are in the *Underworld*. Your crimes are against us, and us alone. You will answer on our terms." His pupils jumped. I was pissing him off and getting under his reptilian skin, as usual. I smiled. "There is no more debate."

"Yes, I'm currently in the Underworld"—I took a step forward—"but I'm not a demon, correct?"

"No, indeed you are not."

"Then why should demon law apply to me?" I turned to gauge the crowd. "No one would ask a demon to answer to shifter laws." I raised my eyebrows, glancing directly into the rows behind me. "Or witch laws." There was an increase in the whispering. "If I did break a *supernatural* law, I should be judged by those laws, not demon laws—because, as you just told the court, I'm no demon. As a supernatural, I am allowed to defend myself against bodily harm, as well as protect humans if we fear our secret will be exposed. Your imps were out of line. One attacked a human child in view of other humans, the other attacked me unprovoked—"

"Silence!" The Prince's voice carried to every corner of the huge auditorium. "The imps matter not! They are but a small piece of your infractions against us. You killed our cherished pets and you took the life of a goddess who was under our protection. You will answer for those wrongs here and now!"

"I did you a *favor*," I countered. "Admit it. You wanted Selene's soul and her servitude and you didn't want to wait an eternity to get it. And she's the one who traded her soul for your beasts. If anyone should pay, it should be her. She allowed those beasts to roam alone in the human realm." Audible gasps came from the crowd. "They attacked us on her command far from her home. I challenge *any* supernatural not to defend itself against a deadly threat. Nothing you're accusing me of would hold up in any supernatural court except this one."

The Prince balled his fist as he gathered his power. With supreme effort he pulled himself together. His hand wandered to his tie to readjust the perfect knot at his throat.

Behind me the demonesses grew agitated. They rocked in their chairs as their combined power whipped along my body, pricking me with its pressure. I hazarded a glance in their direction, and one of them made eye contact with me.

Did that demoness just wink at us? I asked my wolf. *That can't be right.* But before I could either confirm or deny any wink, the demoness peered forward, hands clasped demurely in her lap.

The Prince's voice was just short of a bellow. "Bring her out!"

My head snapped to the right as a struggle broke out in the corner, but I couldn't see anything yet because the giant wood panels were in the way.

"Get your filthy hands *off of me!*" a voice shrieked.

Oh, good gods, I cried to my wolf. I had hoped Selene was dead due to her own stupidity. I'd imagined her contesting and fighting every order the demons gave her until they finally gave up. *Maybe this is not such a bad thing. Let's use it to our advantage. I don't think these demons understand the saying "Hell hath no fury like a woman scorned," but they're about to find out.* Once Selene saw me there were going to be dramatics of the highest degree. She was going to tear this place apart with her fury alone.

They yanked her out from behind the wall of seats. Her face was covered with some kind of cloth. Once she rounded the end of the gallery she stilled. Her head went up. "You!" she screamed. "You will die for what you did to me!"

The Prince put his hands together. "Goddess, you will remain quiet and answer the questions directed at you. Nod if you understand my directions."

I noticed for the first time that her hands were bound with some kind of black string. It almost looked like dried tar. I'd been right, she must be a hard-to-handle prisoner. The thought made me smile. I hoped she was getting her ass handed to her at regular intervals.

Selene remained still, unmoving.

"Goddess, you must answer the question or you will be punished. Severely. Do you understand my orders?"

One slow nod came down.

"Good," the Prince continued. "Then we shall proceed."

"Wait just a minute," I sputtered. "If Selene is going to testify against me, I want my brother to testify in my favor. He was a witness to this altercation. You can't bring in one without the other."

"We will do no such—"

"We will allow it." The voice behind me was clear and certain. All the Demon Lords' faces took on strained looks and they shifted in their seats. The voice had come from one of the chairs behind me. I turned my head, trying not to show my surprise.

"But, Your Highness, this is unprecedented," the Prince reasoned. "We cannot allow our laws to be manipulated by this being. If we do so, we are setting a precedent we cannot support."

Your Highness? Was that his *wife*?

I gaped because I couldn't help it. Things had just turned in our favor in about seventeen different ways. Relief flooded through me. If the Prince had a Princess, and Lily on the side, this soap opera had just gotten incredibly interesting.

Now I understood the wink.

This demoness was going to use me to her advantage and I was going to let her. *She can use us like an old wet rag for all I care*, I told my wolf. *All we need to do is pay careful attention.* My wolf yipped her agreement, her eyes pinned on the demoness in question.

"You will not argue my ruling," the demoness stated confidently. She sat in the middle of all the others and definitely held a queenly air. Her English was better than most of demons I'd heard. The demons I'd encountered had understood me, which meant they must have been forced to learn English at some point. "What this wolf has stated is all correct according to High Law as we know it. She is no demon. And you have brought in"— she gestured toward Selene—"an unusual guest to this trial. Our court has never received a guest, so it is you who has made this unprecedented." The demoness inclined her head at the Prince in a very small challenge. "We all understand the intent, but I am curious to hear from…another who was witness to the events if we are indeed to decide this wolf's fate today."

The Prince ground his sharp teeth together, his glamour flickering.

I was utterly astonished. If the Princess could overrule the

Prince, the demonesses must be cherished in a way I didn't understand. The Prince was clearly the ruler in Hell. His signature was more powerful than that of any of the demonesses, including his Princess, yet she held sway over him.

My eyes ran over all the other demonesses. None of them had moved or spoken. But they would stand by their Princess, I had no doubt. Maybe the Underworld was preparing itself for a little women's lib? And maybe the Prince didn't want to agree to try me in front of such a huge demon audience, but had no choice?

"Bring out the male wolf," the Prince bellowed. "But keep him in his chains."

In the time it took to retrieve Tyler, I studied Selene. She hadn't rebelled, but her power was so low it almost didn't register. That was surprising. They must be muting it somehow. *We can't ignore Selene, even though the Prince seems to be*, I told my wolf. *She's been here for at least a year, maybe two, and there's no way she hasn't been plotting her revenge. Me being here is too delicious for her to pass up, and she'll strike as soon as she gets a chance.*

There was a loud commotion and Tyler was hustled around the side. "What is he tied in?" I demanded. Tyler appeared to be wrapped in a horde of rail-thin snakes. They were moving and hissing.

"Those are our *chains*," the Prince said, his distaste over my ignorance very clear. "They are spelled to keep any supe's powers at bay, and if he rebels, they will bite him. And it will hurt."

"I'm not in chains." I held my arms up. "And clearly I'm the biggest threat in the room. So why don't you be a sport and take them off of my brother."

"We will not. This wolf has caused too damage already. He will remain in chains for the duration of this court session. Consider yourself lucky he is in here at all." The Prince ended on a hard edge. He wasn't going to discuss this further.

I turned toward my brother. *Are you okay?* I asked Tyler. *What happened?*

Nothing.

The chains must keep all his abilities constrained. He nodded at me, inclining his head slightly, letting me know he sensed me but couldn't respond. He was fine, but looked tired.

"I trust you are satisfied." The Prince nodded toward the demoness. "The wolf is here and we will continue as planned—"

A shrill scream hit my ears as Selene broke free of her captors, and then the best three words I'd ever heard rang loud and clear through the auditorium.

"Jessica!" Rourke yelled. "We're here!"

14

The entire proceedings were thrown into immediate chaos. Selene launched herself at me right as Rourke's bellow filled the arena. As Selene raced forward, the cloth covering her tore free, revealing her face.

I was too stunned to react for a split second.

She was completely bald. But that wasn't the worst of it. An ugly network of scars lined her face. Some were deep, others were fresh. Supernaturals did not scar. "See what they've done to me! I'm going to make you suffer for this." She was almost to me when my brother turned and rammed his foot into her side, sending her flying into the bench, causing the Demon Lords to jump up in unison.

She crumpled to the ground and stayed there.

The Prince of Hell was furious at the double intrusion, but his shouts went unheeded as panicked demons started to race every-where. They flooded down from the seats in a distressed mess, shouting in both Demonish and English.

"Save the demonesses!" they cried.

"Run for cover!"

"The animals are loose!"

"The Scriptures are true."

I slammed into the two demon guards who stood beside me and sent them flying, pivoting toward my brother at the same time. I grabbed the snake chains and shot pure demon essence into them. The things were blessedly not real, and they withered from the force of my magic and slipped off him in an instant. *That worked well*, I congratulated my wolf. It was the first time we'd used only the pure demon magic. *I guess our work paid off. Yay, us.*

"Damn, Jessica," Tyler said, shaking the remnants. "Why couldn't you have done something like that back in the hallway?"

"Because I didn't know how to wield this crap until about an hour ago." The dark mass inside me remained slippery and hard to hold on to; it was going to take me some time to learn how to master it.

I turned, glancing up the long stairway. Rourke and Ray were fighting demons at the top. They were battling the guards who had come in the doors behind them. Tyler and I turned to aid them.

"Not so fast." The Prince's voice was hard as stone. "You are not leaving this hall until your guilt is proven."

I turned back around very slowly. The Prince stood alone behind the wooden bench, towering over the proceedings in disgust, his Demon Lords long gone. Watching his minions flee must have been maddening.

I calculated the odds of racing up the steps to Rourke before the Prince could blast me with his magic. He'd likely zap me halfway up and that wasn't going to help matters. I knew I could fight him off this time, and likely not succumb, but it was still an unknown. If I did fall to his magic, Rourke would be in danger if he came after me, which of course he would.

"I shouldn't need to remind you," the Prince intoned, "that you are being tried for your crimes, and you will be sentenced *today*. I have waited too long for this." He stood tall over his fleeing domain, his hands clasped in front of him like he didn't have a care in the world. Power whipped between us. The Prince was ready for a fight, and suddenly I realized this was it. If I fled despite his direct order, he would have a solid excuse to kill me. He might have been waiting for this the entire time.

I glanced around me. The demonesses had left sometime during the melee, which was mildly surprising.

When I didn't answer him, the Prince stepped down from behind the bench to face me on the floor. Instead of running, I watched with interest as Selene rose from her position, stumbling to her feet. I met my brother's gaze and nodded once. He understood my meaning and I felt him ready himself.

Selene's face contorted in rage as she stood to face us. She had clearly lost some of her faculties, if not all of them. The Underworld had not treated her kindly. The Prince sauntered toward me, coming from around the corner, either not noticing Selene or ignoring her altogether.

The Prince of Hell stopped in front of us and Selene lunged.

She took hold of him from behind, her hands going to his neck, screaming, "I will kill you once and for all! You can't hold me against my will any longer!"

Oily blood gushed from the wounds, but the Prince didn't flinch.

I wasn't going to stick around and watch, because this diversion was exactly what we'd needed. I had no idea what Selene was going to do, attack me or the Prince, but either worked. Tyler and I turned at the same moment and raced up the steps toward the boys, who were still fighting in the back.

There was a loud noise behind us as the Prince shouted, "You have been a thorn in my side since the day you arrived. I will tolerate it no longer. I will happily rid the Underworld of you once and for all!"

Power swirled around the room and the few remaining demons fled, shouting their fear in Demonish. Their Prince had clearly lost it and everyone had received the memo.

"You can't get rid of me that easily," Selene raged. "I am a goddess!"

"Not any longer."

There was a boom, followed by a thunderous amount of power that rippled through the arena. Tyler and I reached the top, ignoring what was happening below, focusing on the destruction in front of us instead.

Ray smiled at me from across the landing, his fingers forming a small salute off his forehead. It was so good to see him. And now that he was here, I felt my connection with him jump in my veins for the first time. "These guys can't fight worth a shit," he shouted, gesturing to the demons lying on the ground in a pile around him. "They were a piece of cake to take down, but I have no idea if they're actually dead or not." He touched one with the tip of his boot. It didn't move. "I'm guessing they're not dead. That would be too easy."

"Jessica," Rourke yelled, leaping over several downed demons and moving toward me. He scooped me up in a tight embrace, his hands covering my back and neck, his lips falling by my ear. "I'm so glad you're in one piece."

He smelled so good. My wolf howled in pleasure. It was hard not to attack him, but that had to wait. We were still very much in danger. "I'm fine," I said, running my hands along his chest like they'd suddenly been magnetized to his skin. I hadn't let myself realize how much I missed his touch, missed him. "You got here quickly—more quickly than I thought possible."

Before he could answer, Ray's voice piped up: "He dove into the circle the moment your energy zipped out. I had to fight to get in there with him. He threatened the witches within an inch of their lives." Ray chuckled. "They had no choice but to send us or risk his wrath."

Rourke growled, his lips still lingering near my ear. "He held on to my leg like a child and wouldn't let go." His grudging respect for Ray was apparent. "So he came by default."

"What about Eudoxia?" I asked. The Vamp Queen was supposed to have joined our little party.

"I have no idea." Rourke shrugged, letting me go reluctantly. "If she wants your blood, she'll get here." He glanced down at me, his irises radiating a delicious soft green. "Now we have to get out of here. This place reeks of nastiness." He grabbed my hand, leading me toward the big double doors I'd first come through.

I turned before we exited, glancing down in to the arena. The Prince was grinning over Selene's broken body. As I looked on, his gaze slowly landed on mine. It was piercing even from this distance.

"There is no place you can hide from me here," the Prince roared. "You will not get away." His magic grew as he spoke. He might be able to hit me with his blast, but he couldn't hit all of us at the same time. The Prince was going to have to regroup and get his guards together and come after us.

I tore my eyes off the angry Prince, ignoring his wrath for now, to discover my brother was nowhere in sight. I broke from Rourke's grasp. "Where's Tyler?"

"I'm here," Tyler answered, striding back into the auditorium from the hallway. "And look who I found milling around outside."

He had Lily by the arm. She looked disheveled but alive. Once she saw us, she jumped into action. "We must hurry, you only have moments to leave here. The army is on its way," she told us.

"You were given a very small window to escape. No one will be coming for us, but we must move quickly."

"What are you talking about?" I asked, grabbing ahold of her jumpsuit in my fists. I shook her a bit, wanting her to answer me. "Where did you come from? And who granted us a window and why?"

Her face was grim. "The Princess of Hell freed me moments ago with the order to get you out." Lily met my gaze straight on. "All of us. Take it or leave it. The hag wants me out, and this will be the only gift you will ever receive in Hell, so I suggest you take it."

"I thought the Prince killed you," I accused.

"He can't kill me."

"Because you're too powerful?"

"No," she answered, turning toward the doorway. "Because he's still in love with me. Now come on, we have to go."

We all crowded into the hallway after her because we didn't have a better plan. She was right, there were no demon guards in sight. It seemed we might indeed have a real chance to get out of here.

Lily turned, her hands guiding the massive doors easily. When they were almost completely closed, the Prince yelled in a strangled howl. His voice was as maddened as I had ever heard it.

He only spoke two words.

"Ardat Lili!"

15

I slowly turned to face her.

Ardat Lili. *Handmaiden of Lilith.*

Everything came crashing down around me as my brain spun, my wolf snarling and gnashing her teeth. The boys stilled beside me.

She met my angry gaze proudly with her chin up.

"Please tell me you're not a child of Lilith?" I demanded, already knowing full well the answer was yes. When she didn't respond, I added bitterly, "I guess I can take full blame for not figuring this out sooner." I'd been so very, very stupid.

Tales of Lilith were some of the most ancient in supernatural lore. Lilith was the first femme fatale, a seducer of demons, a killer of children, and rumored to be the first wife of Adam. According to legend, she was thrown into the Underworld for all her sins. She lived out her days in Hell constantly seeking ways to procreate and build a sacred race. Over the years she'd been rumored to have birthed many powerful children, all of them part demon of some kind, but she hadn't been seen or heard from in a thousand years.

How incredibly dumb could I be? We were in the Underworld! And the demoness had told me her name was Lily, and stupidly, I hadn't connected her to Lilith.

"The myths are highly exaggerated," Lili answered, dismissing my concerns as the doors slammed behind her, drowning out the Prince's irate ranting. "Do not believe all you've heard or read, as the legends are highly inaccurate. Now, if we don't get moving, we will miss our golden opportunity, so I suggest we move." She brushed past me.

"Um, we're not going anywhere with you and that's not an answer," I countered, grabbing her arm to stall her. "And I'm not taking you back to our plane. So if you're expecting a ride home in exchange for helping us, we need to separate right now. I'm not making any deals with a daughter of Lilith, no matter how wrong or inaccurate the myths are."

She knocked away my hand. "Then you're a bigger fool than I'd thought possible. The only reason the Prince of Hell is not bashing down those doors right now is that the Underworld mandates he go to his *Qeby* and make sure she is okay. And just to make sure he does so, his wife has summoned him. He cannot resist her. They are bound by a firm supernatural link. The Princess alone has given us an out. The only real out I've had in centuries, and you are mistaken if you think I'm not leaving this plane—with or without your help." She leaned into my personal space, my wolf snapping her jaws. "And for your information, I can leave here on my own. But if we go together, you will have some control once we arrive on your plane. Which will it be?"

My wolf urged me to fight her, to eliminate her altogether. She shoved adrenaline through me like a hypodermic full of juice. It raced through my body and my fingernails ached, my claws an inch away from springing. It was everything I could do to rein my wolf in. *I know this is bad, but let me handle it. If the Prince couldn't kill her, we may not be able to either. And I'm not killing anyone in cold blood until we know the full story.*

I cleared my voice, trying to stay calm. "We've already covered this, *Lili*—if you could've left, you would've already. You're stuck here, and according to the myth I'm familiar with, it's for a damn good reason. I'm not going to be the one to unleash you in our world, so if you can manage to get to our plane on your own, and cause trouble, I'll figure out a way to deal with you then. But I'm not willfully bringing you with us. So you need to stop asking."

She shook her head. "That's where you're wrong. I've stayed here by choice, because I didn't want to leave. I had a good life up until—"

"The Princess of Hell found out you were banging her husband?" I finished as Rourke growled behind me, moving in closer. He sensed my distress, but had no idea what had happened between me and Lili thus far. I appreciated his patience, especially when I knew all he wanted to do was get rid of the threat and hurry us home.

"I've been 'banging' her husband for eons. That's not the issue." She shooed my comment away. "We're not attached to our... *mates*...here"—she glanced behind me at my imposing significant other—"like you seem to be. The demoness seeks power, and she feels it is her time to rule. But she cannot do it if you or I stay behind. We are a distraction to the demons and our power is greater than hers. In order for her to ascend to power and take the Throne of Astaroth from the Prince, we must leave this plane."

That was new, game-changing information. "If the demoness is truly seeking power," I countered, "then we should all stay here and help her win the throne. Even though I want nothing more than to escape this plane, leaving before it's all finished will guarantee the Prince will go on another manhunt to find me if the Princess doesn't win. And if you think I'm going through another mock trial, you're wrong. When I leave here, it will be for good. The Underworld is never going to interfere with my life again. The demoness either takes the crown and sets us free, or we kill the Prince ourselves. If we achieve either, she will be in our debt and set us free. But whatever the outcome, I'm still not taking you with us. She's going to have to find another place for you to go."

Lili crossed her arms. "You have no choice in the matter."

"Excuse me?" My wolf snapped her jaws.

"The reason I was jailed wasn't that I was an insufficient lover. It was that I discovered something just before you arrived. Something that has shaken the internal fabric of the Underworld to its very core. Because of this, things are moving on their own and we are just along for the ride. It was no mistake you found me when you did and it's no mistake we're standing together right now. The sooner you accept that, the sooner we can all leave this place forever."

I glanced around the group to see how everyone else was taking this information. Ray appeared stoic, Tyler concerned, and Rourke's mouth was set in a determined line. "And what exactly was the big news you uncovered?" I asked, turning back to Lili. "If I truly have no choice, you're going to have to do some heavy convincing. And I'd suggest you start with the truth."

Lili was speaking of Fate, there was no question. And we all knew that if we were in the middle of Fate's true choice—for me to bring Lili home—it would be very hard to veer from that path.

"There was more to the Scriptures than any demon originally thought," she started. "When I happened to uncover more of the Old Writings in their entirety, I was as shocked as anyone. Once I gathered the impact, I took them to . . ." She paused as she glanced down at her hands.

It wasn't hard to guess she had broken her allegiance to her lover, so I took the most logical path. "You took them to the Princess, instead of the Prince," I finished. "And when the Prince of Hell discovered your betrayal, you fell from his grace. He unceremoniously kicked you out of his bed and had you put into prison. I see where this went wrong, but that still doesn't explain the facts to me. What did the sacred Scriptures say exactly?"

She smirked at me. "Are you always this disagreeable?"

"I'm disagreeable to those who try and continually manipulate me, which you've done from the very start. You could've told me the truth—if this even is the truth—when we first met, but you chose not to. You have done very little to gain my trust, why should I believe anything you tell me now?"

"There was no time to explain the entirety of it," she huffed. "We've been on the run since you first walked into my cell. Not only that, the demoness had forbidden me to say anything up until twenty minutes ago, when she freed me from the horrors of a mending room."

"And why did the demoness have such a sudden change of heart?" I asked, remembering our little wink session a few short minutes ago. "And if you're so much more powerful than she is, why didn't you just escape on your own?"

"Because in order for this all to move forward in the direction Fate has determined, and for the Princess to ascend to power, you needed to be paraded in front of the entire city. Your presence here had a purpose. It was meant to launch the demons into a civil war—to separate those who believe in the old Scriptures from those who will embrace the new. Your birth has been marked in our books for centuries. And every demon in that audience knew this day would come. Now that it has, and your presence is known, you have triggered a huge, unstoppable change. One that was meant to happen. But now it means you must leave the Underworld quickly, or run the risk of dying. There will be upheaval and turmoil for years to come. This is just the beginning."

I was livid. My eyes flashed as I demanded, "Do you mean to tell me that it was your goal all along to 'parade me' in front of the demons to launch a civil war? If that was your ultimate plan, you weren't ever leading me to my brother or any real escape. Why bring me through the Sholls if I had to end up in there"—I gestured angrily to the coliseum doors—"and why not let me in on what was going on from the very beginning? I would've agreed to aid you in a plan to defeat the Prince and put the Princess on the throne. I despise the Prince!"

She stared at me like I had lost my mind, which I was beginning to think was quite possible. "Fate is at work here," she cried. "And in case you haven't guessed, it's not as easy as you think to defeat the Prince of Hell. But if you must know, I only uncovered the Scripture a few days ago when I was in the Great Library searching for something else. There was no time to formulate any solid plans, and as I told you when we parted, I guessed you would be caught. Again, I never lied. How you were going to get to this place"—she pointed toward the doors—"was just as much a mystery to me as it was to you. But you're here. The die has been cast, you've done your part, and now it's time to leave."

Tyler stepped in, placing a hand on my arm. He rang with tension. "Jess, I know all this is important and we need to solve it, but I hear movement and smell something rancid in the air. Let's move out of this area. We can figure this out as we go." He eyed Lili up and down. "And, honestly, one wrong move from you, demoness, and we take you out, understood? I don't comprehend everything that's going on here, but if my sister doesn't want you on our plane, you're not invited. Got it?"

I began to hear shouts and movement too. I sighed, addressing Lili. "Take us somewhere safe, if such a place actually exists here. I'm going to process everything you've told me, but I'm not going to make any decisions until I have all the information. And I mean *all*."

"I will lead you to safety, which was granted by the Princess," Lili agreed. "And, once there, we can settle this. But lingering in the Underworld is not advisable. As I've told you, we only have a short time to escape."

Rourke tugged me to the back of our procession by the hand as we followed Lili down a tunnel carved out of rock that had been polished with care. "I understand what's going on up to a point," he murmured. "But if the demon Scriptures say Lili goes with us, it might be unavoidable."

I smiled at him, braiding my hand through his tightly. Gods, I'd missed him. "I agree, but I'm sure you noticed that she hasn't divulged any particulars of what the writings actually say, only the doomsday disclaimer that I will start a civil war." While we walked, I gripped Rourke's forearm with my other hand, leaning in to him and drinking up his scent. "When I first met her, she assured me she could free me and Tyler and get us out quickly." I filled him in on what had happened and shook my head. "We are definitely missing pieces to this puzzle. She and the Princess must've had a prior agreement. What's worse is my wolf is rabid whenever she's around. That's a very bad sign."

Up ahead Ray asked Lili, "So what gives with these demons? They can't fight worth a damn. I thought once we got here we'd be ducking and running, trying not to get ourselves killed. But it's like a comedy skit out there. They have no idea what they're doing and have no business being on the front lines."

Lili inclined her head toward him. She was likely trying to figure out what kind of supe he was, but a vampire reaper wouldn't be on her radar. Ray was one of a kind. "Only the demon army is taught defense. Much like everyday humans, we have no need to learn to fight. We are well protected here and are insulated from outside threats. Not many supernaturals, besides witches or sorcerers, ever come here. Most wouldn't know how. You were fighting the equivalent of the home guard. Not our army. The troops who fight for the Underworld lie outside of She'ol."

"But demons have raw power, I can feel it," Ray continued. "They should naturally pack a better punch than that. Back there was like taking down women and children. It was just sad."

Lili chuckled. "Well, we also depend on our beasts for our protection. The demon army will bring them out shortly if we don't hurry, and then you will be able to see how demons really defend themselves."

Tyler turned. He was dressed in the same sort of jumpsuit as I was. "We should take these things off," he said, fingering the zipper. "They can track us, right?" He'd directed his question to Lili.

The demoness stopped and motioned to my brother to come forward. "Here, turn around," she ordered. Tyler obeyed with a skeptical look. He didn't trust her. Instead of grasping the zipper, she placed her hand along the metal strip running up his side and said a few words under her breath. The thing literally melted off into her hand and she tossed it away. It made a pinging noise as it bounced off the rock wall. She beckoned to me. "Let me free you too."

I walked over and she did the same thing. This time I heard her words. They were in Demonish. "You can spell in both languages." It was a statement, not a question. Crafting spells was technical. Just how technical, I had no idea. But words, names, and pronunciation mattered. Spells were attached to the very sound of the words uttered. The language used needed to be precise.

Her pupils pulsed, elongating, reminding me she was very much a demon no matter how human or half witch she appeared. "Yes. I've been here for too many years to count. More than enough time to master demon spells."

"Can regular demons cast spells?" I asked as we all started walking again.

"Only some," she replied. "As I said before, there are many different kinds of demons in the Underworld. Demons we call *zhydd pozsylz*, their specialty is to cast spells, as well as the Prince, and all the demonesses."

"Why don't the spell casters act as the demon guards? That seems more logical," I said. "They would have a greater advantage in situations like this."

"They do not live in this city. She'ol is considered an urban center. They are what humans would refer to as living 'out in the country' by choice. They are very powerful and can be very dangerous. I wouldn't say they are shunned, but other demons don't like to encounter them. They also refuse to use glamour, so they are not allowed into the city limits very often."

I shook my head. This place was incredibly strange. "What about Selene?" I asked. "She didn't look very good. Did the Prince kill her back there?"

Lili slowed by a curve in the tunnel, listening before she beckoned us forward. My wolf was on alert, but I didn't detect anything crazy around the corner, though that wasn't saying much. Anything could pop out of this place.

"How do we ultimately leave here?" Tyler asked me. "I never asked how you arrived. Is there a circle nearby?"

"I landed in the dump," I said. "I literally plunked down where the demons throw their trash." I turned to my mate. "How did you get here?"

"We landed out in a field somewhere," Rourke answered. "It was covered in weird moving grass. We ran until we picked up your scent."

"Was it daylight out there?" I asked.

"It was just breaking. Strange colors here," he mused. "Everything was purple and yellow."

"It was lucky you landed when you did," I commented. "The sun burns the skin and the bats were probably already back in their nests. If you had come at night, it might've been a different story."

Lili glanced back, tilting her head, appraising me once again. "The sun here will not affect them. And it should not have affected you, because you are not a true demon." Her eyes narrowed. "I've been trying to puzzle this out for a while—why you smell like a demon and why the sensors categorize you as such. You must have demon blood running through you somewhere. Maybe a long-lost ancestor?"

I wasn't going to divulge my abilities to Lili, who was obviously in the dark, so I settled on, "It has to do with my magic abilities."

"I don't understand," she said. "You cannot absorb our magic."

Rourke stepped in. "Our business is not yours, demoness. What we need from you is a relatively safe place to regroup until we can figure out what do to next." He glanced at me. "I'm not opposed to heading back to our plane and dealing with the fallout later, but I know that's not what you want. It could be centuries before anything happens with the Prince, and it may be the safer alternative. But once the demoness leads us to a safer destination, we can throw around our options."

"It could be centuries or it could be a matter of days," I said. "I seem to unhinge the Prince whenever I'm around. Now that we know what the Princess is after, making sure she takes over, especially since she has already granted us some favors, seems like the best way to rid ourselves of the Underworld indefinitely. When we get back to our plane we'll have enough to worry about. The sorcerers and the fracture pack aren't going to give up." I turned to the group. "Now that we're together, we can solve this once and for all—"

A shrill screech erupted and half a beat later something darted around the corner of the tunnel.

Selene had me by the throat before any of us knew what had happened.

16

Yelling and commotion surrounded us instantly. I wasn't frightened that Selene could do any harm, since she barely had any power. But I had to admit I was a little shaken she'd managed to take us all by surprise.

She had literally come out of nowhere.

"Now you die, bitch," she snarled in my ear.

"What...are you...*doing*?" I sputtered, batting her hands away from my face. We rolled on the ground. "You can't take me on and win, Selene. You don't have any power or magic."

Before she could answer, she was plucked off me by a very angry Rourke. He tossed her against the other side of the tunnel, snarling, "Enough! We've already gone through this with you, Lunar Goddess. If we kill you here, you die for real, and I'm more than ready to do the deed for the final time." He cracked his knuckles, positioning himself between her and me.

She rose to her feet in seconds, her features rabid. She seemed even more unhinged than she'd been a few moments ago.

"You can't kill me," she spit. "I've already tried it a dozen times myself and I keep coming back to life in this wretched place." She turned her furious gaze on me. "Do you see what they've done to me?" She pointed at her face and hair. "I can't die, but I won't heal either! They've taken my magic and my power and this is all your fault." She pounded forward, swinging her arms, only to be scooped up by Rourke again and tossed back. "You horrid mongrel, you made sure I'd rot in this place for an eternity. This was your plan all along."

I brushed off my jumpsuit. "This had nothing to do with me, Selene. You kidnapped my mate, almost killed my friend, and then tried to kill me. You deserved everything you received and then some." I clapped my hands together. "And don't forget, I wasn't the one who suggested you sell your soul to the demons. You did that all on your own. What did you think was going to happen? That Hell would be all unicorns and rainbows? The penance you're serving is what you justly deserve, brought on by no one but yourself."

She deserved more, since she was still breathing. Rourke hadn't relayed to me the horrors of what had happened when she'd captured him, but I knew it had been bad. When I'd found him, he'd been eviscerated. It pained me to even call up the memory.

"The Prince sounded like he finished you back there," Ray helpfully added. "How'd you manage to slip away and recover?"

Selene shot him a malicious gaze. "He did kill me. But I told you, I always come back."

Lili stepped forward. "That is not typical," she said. "If the Prince of Hell kills you in the Underworld it is a true death... most of the time. It's completely unusual for anyone to survive, especially after so many attempts."

"Most of the time?" Tyler commented. "If you don't die a true death, then what can possibly happen to you?"

Before the demoness could answer, I replied, "It seems some demons have a half death. Instead of going to the unknown, they go to the Sholls." I eyed Selene. "When a demon dies a half death, they come back as their serpent selves. They call them wyverns."

"I'm clearly no demon, and I'm not an undercover serpent," Selene sniffed in her haughty tone. "But they can't kill me and I know the real reason: it's because I'm a goddess." She looked accusingly at me. "You couldn't take that away from me when you sent me here. A goddess doesn't just simply lose her godhood, she *survives*."

I took a step toward her. "But you're completely changed. Your power is vastly diminished to the point of almost nothing and you're not healing. You've become something else. Maybe you belong in the Sholls. At least there you'd be safe from further demon abuse, and the wyverns are nasty, but they can't kill you." She appeared aghast at the suggestion, but I ignored her and turned to Lili. "If we took her to the Sholls can she get back out herself?"

Lili studied the former goddess for a moment. "Perhaps, through a portal, but why would she want to? Her life right now in the Underworld is far worse than it would be in the Sholls."

"Is there more to the plane than what we saw?" I asked. "Is the Sholls big?"

"Of course," the demoness replied. "It's as big as the Underworld. The wyverns occupy the city, but there are likely...other areas which can be utilized. To tell you the truth, no one knows. A demon doesn't go willingly to the Sholls. I have ventured there, but have never taken the time to scout anything out."

"Then that's the perfect place for her," I concluded. "As long as there are no portals to other planes there."

"There are not," Lili said. "The Sholls is tucked inside the Underworld, like the middle floor of a house. Any way you go, the exit is through Hell first."

"Wait a minute," Tyler said, shaking his head. "If we let Selene off the hook and send her to this place, won't she just be plotting her revenge from a safer place? That doesn't sound right after what she put us through."

"Tyler," I said. "Did you hear what Selene just told us? We can't kill her. The Prince of Hell can't kill her. I'd much rather put her someplace where she can't do any real damage and can't escape, rather than risk the possibility of her getting back to our plane from here." I turned to peer closer at Selene. "But she's not going to retaliate once she gets there, she's going to settle in and make a life for herself." I wasn't going to describe the Sholls in detail.

It wouldn't be a pretty life, it would just be one with less torture.

"And why wouldn't I plot my revenge?" Selene asked, hands going to her hips. "It will be my life's quest to get off this wretched plane and have my retribution. Nothing will change that."

I took a step closer. "No you won't."

"Like hell I won't," she insisted, snarling at me.

"Nope," I said. "Because you're going to swear an oath to us you won't. And for helping you escape this ongoing torture, you will forswear your revenge on us. Plus"—I rolled my eyes—"it's not exactly revenge when you're the one who started it. This is all on you. Keeping that in your mind would be incredibly helpful."

"I will swear no such oath," she snapped. "I refuse to stay in this hellhole and you can't force me to say the words."

"Selene," I explained as patiently as I could, "we're talking about giving you a *gift*, and in return you will help us defeat anything we encounter on the way. The Sholls is actually the perfect place for you." I waved a hand in front of her unhealed face and shaved hair. "You should be able to start a new life...in a cave somewhere...we know how you love them. But if you stay here you will be killed again and again and subsequently come back." Exasperation leaked around my voice. "And it wouldn't hurt you to take some time out to figure out why you're such a stone-cold witch." Before she could interject, I raised my hand. "And, really, it's the only option, so you've got so stop arguing."

"Jessica is right," Lili offered. "You infuriate the Prince and your very nature makes you highly uncooperative. No one can discipline you adequately, and since you cannot die, you will get no relief in Hell. It will continue to be...hell. It's my guess that you haven't seen the worst of our tortures yet or you would not be opposed to leaving. I would choose the Sholls over the Underworld if I were not welcome here. It's a gift to get such an opportunity."

Rourke crossed his ample arms over his chest, matching my stance. "Why are we standing here making deals with her? She needs to suffer for what she did to us. Daily. I say we give her back to the guards. Or tie her up here and let her be found." His eyes yielded a kaleidoscope of emotion. He was remembering what he'd gone through under her ministrations.

The man had a point.

"If we could kill her, I would agree with you," I answered. "But if the Prince can't, I don't think we'll be successful. The Sholls is no picnic, believe me. She will have a hard time carving out a place for herself, but she will be out of our hair with no chance of escape."

Ray stepped in. "What if I took her soul? She might die then."

Selene stamped her foot, reiterating how childish she'd always been. She was the quintessential supernatural who'd never grown up. "You can't make decisions for me when I'm standing right here." Her fists were balled. She was infuriated she had no power, and she knew that if she struck against us, it would be futile.

But if she could've, she would've blasted us all without a second thought. "I will not let any of you manipulate me like this."

I gave her my full attention. "Would you like to continue your happy fun time in Hell? Or would you like another option? I think we all deserve medals for even discussing this." No supernatural I was aware of knew anything about the afterlife. There were ghosts, but no one knew what really happened when a supe died a true death. "My mate wants to leave you for dead, but if we could give you true death would you take it? Or do you prefer the option of fending for yourself in the Sholls?"

"I prefer neither," she cried as she launched herself at me.

Old habits die hard.

I swatted her away like a mild irritant. It was hard to remember her in her former glory. She hardly resembled the porcelain doll full of vigor who had just, a short time ago, made my life a living nightmare. My wolf snarled at my humanness, which she considered my weakness, wanting me to end Selene once and for all. In the realm of the supernatural, having mercy was atypical behavior.

Before she could come at me again, Ray scooped her up, keeping his arms firmly locked around her waist. She struggled for a moment and then gave up.

I met Ray's gaze. "Do you think you can take her soul?" I turned to address Lili. "Her soul is promised to the Underworld, correct? Do we rob the Prince by having Ray reap her soul right here?" That plan didn't sound half bad.

Lili shook her head. "Something has gone wrong with her capture, anyway. I think no one here one understands why. But whatever you do, you must do it soon. We have to leave this area. It's a miracle no demon has found us. The Princess must be keeping them occupied, but it won't last for long."

"Ray," I asked. "What happens when you take a living soul?" Ray had just figured out he was a reaper and had taken down a Strigoi, the equivalent of a vampire ghost. But he had never sucked a living soul out of a body before that I knew about.

"I have no earthly idea," he answered as Selene started to squirm. "But my body is telling me I can do it, and her soul is screaming for a release."

I walked forward, placing a hand on Selene's arm. She tried to shake me off. "Don't touch me," she snapped.

I ignored her and nodded to my brother. He moved forward and grabbed Selene's other arm. Rourke stepped in behind me. He'd been silent but I knew this was his vote. I placed a hand on Selene's carotid artery. She tried to move her neck away, but Ray held her still.

I sucked in a sharp breath.

"What is it?" Rourke asked.

"I know why they can't kill her. You're not going to believe this—but I think she's already dead." As I spoke I sent my magic into Selene and found darkness, with only traces of her vibrant red magic signature scattered here and there.

"What are you talking about?" Selene barked. "I'm clearly not dead, you beast! I'm alive and breathing."

"It seems your godhood is holding on to a shell, Selene." I shook my head. "I think the only thing left in there is your soul. You must have an incredibly strong one."

I dropped my hand and turned to Rourke. "I can't let Ray harvest her soul. None of us understands what's going on here, but she's clearly already dead. I can't help feeling like finding her like this was supposed to happen." I glanced at Selene. "How did you know where to find us? None of us sensed you were near. We're some of the most powerful supes on the planet and we detected nothing from you." I angled my head back and took in a deep breath, along with my brother, just to be sure.

We both snapped our heads up at the same time.

She carried no scent.

For the first time, Selene appeared a little flustered. "I...I..." she stuttered. "I don't remember. The Prince killed me again... and when I woke up, I heard your voice, so I followed it." She brought a hand to her forehead for a second. Ray dropped his hold on her waist and stepped back, surprise lining his features, which certainly mimicked our own expressions. "But I can't be dead. I'm not supposed to...die. Dying is for humans and... weak supernaturals. I'm above that. I am *immortal*."

There was a shout in the distance.

"We can't linger here any longer," Lili said. "It's only a matter of time now."

Rourke prodded the small of my back. "Come on," he said. "We need to move." He ushered me forward, glancing at Selene as we passed. "If you know what's good for you, you will follow us. Of your own accord. We can decide what to do with you when we have more than a minute to spare."

Lili started down a new tunnel and we all followed. Including Selene.

I had no idea what we had just uncovered, but I was certain it was a one-of-a-kind situation. And to be very honest, I was damn tired of one-of-a-kind situations. They were sticky and hard to deal with. But the good thing was that nothing surprised me any longer. Unique experiences seemed to follow me by the truckload and I had to make my peace with it or go crazy. *Do you know why this happens to us?* I asked my wolf. *Why do we attract all these unexplainable things? My mate is one of a kind, now so is Ray. Lili and Selene. Naomi is the only vamp I know without a bond to another vampire, and Danny is the only wolf on the planet whose Alpha is female. Things in my life are always complicated.* I had to believe this was all working toward a purpose. I just had no idea what it was. My wolf shook her head, flashing a picture of us surrounded by our family. *I know, I feel the bonds too. I guess we're just going to have to wait and see.*

"Where are you leading us?" Rourke interrupted my thoughts as he asked Lili. We had gone down several tunnels and a few stairways, each one seeming smaller and more remote than the last. "We need to move faster."

"We are heading to the Prince's private quarters," she declared airily, not entirely pulling off unaffectedness.

"What? Are you kidding?" I exclaimed. "How could you possibly take us into his home? How will we not be detected? That doesn't sound like safe haven, that sounds like a hijack."

"It's not a hijack," she assured me. "You're talking to someone who is intimately acquainted with Hell and its ruler. Going to his personal rooms will take us far under their radar. Once there, I will be able to get a message to the Princess. It's literally the only place that will give us cover where no one will look."

"If we're in his quarters, and the Prince comes back, how do we flee?" Tyler asked. "I'm not letting my sister in there if there's no way out."

"There's a secret passageway, known only to me and very few others. It will keep us concealed if need be," the demoness assured us. She stopped. "You're going to have to trust me or this is never going to work."

"Lili," I said patiently. "Trust is earned." Everyone's face was set. "But we don't have another choice at the moment, so we will follow you. But be warned, if you're leading us into danger we will retaliate."

"I have no doubt you will." She eyed Ray specifically. "But the warning is unnecessary. I'm not about to screw this up." She started to move again; this time she began to jog.

We followed. The tunnels kept meandering. How did the demons ever remember how to get from one place to the next?

The last tunnel we turned down abruptly changed scenery about halfway through. Ray was ahead of me, his head swiveling. "What is this? Some kind of funhouse? One minute you have rock and the next it looks like we're walking through a tree?" It did look like we were in a tree, if bark grew on the inside.

"We are passing through the living parts of Hell," Lili said as she ran. "They are scattered within the demon-made parts. There are a number of levels and areas that grow organically and this is one of them." She made a quick turn at the end. "We just need to go about five hundred yards more—"

The demoness stopped in her tracks so abruptly, we all had to pull up so we didn't crash into her. Once I saw the reason we'd stopped, I gaped.

There, standing at attention at the end of the hallway, was the biggest dog I'd ever seen.

It had two heads and a tail that hissed.

17

"What in the good goddamn is that?" Ray bellowed as we all peered at it. "And whatever it is, it's blocking our path."

"That is an orthrus," Lili answered calmly. "And it was left to guard the Prince's chambers."

The thing growled at us, swishing its snaky tail around in circles. The tail actually flicked its tongue, arching over the dog's back to stare at us.

"So," I said. "This plan is turning out to be awesome. You guys have a run on scary beasts here, but this takes the cake as far as I've seen. That thing is huge."

"I can take care of an orthrus," Lili said firmly. "I just need a few things first."

"Like what?" Tyler asked. "A one-way ticket out of here? Or a rocket launcher? That beast looks like it can tear us apart by breathing on us. It's as tall as the damn hallway and just as wide."

"It won't attack unless we move forward and try to gain entrance," she assured us.

Which was exactly what we were trying to do. "Well, that's comforting," Ray retorted. "I'm sure we can just stay here for a while and nobody will notice. And why wouldn't that thing charge us? We're an obvious threat. This place is backwards."

"It's trained to guard the entrance to the Prince's private rooms and nothing more. It actually can't see very well," the demoness replied. "Which is why I need something like a blanket to cover its eyes."

"A what?" I cackled. "You're going to bring the scariest beast I've ever seen to its knees by covering its eyes with a *blanket*? It looks like Cujo there could eat us all for a bedtime snack."

The thing paced back and forth and huffed out of its double snouts. My wolf had her muzzle open and a snarl on her lips. My fingertips tingled. I was close to changing.

Lili glanced at me like I was clueless. "A blanket and this." She pulled a tiny vial out of her pocket. Her latex jumpsuit apparently had pockets.

"Is that a spell?" Ray asked.

"It is indeed a spell," she answered. "It's a special concoction I made long ago for some of the beasts here, including the orthrus. It will put it to sleep, but it needs to be ingested."

"And how exactly are you going to get that thing down its gullet?" Ray asked.

"It's a curious beast," she answered. "If I can get close enough I can toss it, and then follow with the blanket to subdue it before the dose takes effect."

"I don't like the sound of that. Why does it need to be subdued?" Rourke asked. "Shouldn't the spell take effect immediately?"

"They are very large creatures," Lili said. "It must absorb the entire spell... and before the potion takes effect there may be a few... complications."

"Just spit it out already," Tyler insisted. "What complications? What happens to it when it ingests the spell?"

"It will go a little crazy for a while," Lili admitted with a sigh. "Which is also why we need something to shield both sets of its eyes. It can become quite...rambunctious."

"Rambunctious in a small hallway isn't going to work. Is it venomous?" I asked.

"Only the tail," she warned. "Stay clear of it."

"That sounds easy enough," Ray snorted. "You've got to be kidding us, lady. There has to be someplace else to go."

"There is no other place in all of Hell to go," Lili countered. "This is it. We are in a secluded hallway that most don't know exists. This orthrus has been stationed here likely since my first arrest. The Prince thinks even I cannot best it. But he is wrong, as usual." Her voice was bitter. "He underestimates me at every turn and it will cost him dearly."

The orthrus stamped its huge clawed feet and let out a dangerous howl. Its tail was as thick as my thigh and slashed back and forth over its shoulder. It truly was an awful monster.

"I shouldn't have to mention this, but we don't have a blanket," I said. "I mean, who really carries a blanket around, anyway? Unless you have some demon ultra throw in your jumpsuit, Lili, you're out of luck."

Rourke moved between us, tugging off his shirt in one motion. "We're getting this over with now," he declared. "Not only are you going to get that vial in its mouth"—motioning to Lili and the potion—"but we're going to hold that thing down until it goes to sleep. I'm not going to risk it damaging us. None of us have time to heal." He glanced at Ray and Tyler. "Are you with me?"

"We're with you, brother," Ray said. "Whatever it takes."

"I'll take the tail." Rourke motioned to Ray. "You take the

heads." He nodded at Tyler. "You take the flank. Get it to the ground as quick as you can."

It wasn't the best plan ever, but it might work. I nodded my head grudgingly in agreement. Tyler turned to me, squaring his shoulders. "Once we get it down," he added, "you three move down the hallway and open the door. This thing is going to make noise. We need to be out of here quickly if any demons come running."

"Got it," I said, glancing at Selene. Her expression was still only one step away from shell-shocked. I guess finding out you're already dead is a lot to take in, even for a queen bitch. A teensy bit of sympathy welled up in my mind and my wolf snarled, snapping her jaws at me. *I know, but she's pitiful. Why do we have to bear witness to her unraveling? That doesn't seem fair.* My wolf flashed me a picture of us with power, taking down evil. *I know it's our job. I also know that if Selene were at full strength she'd be trying to kill us and exact her revenge. I'm sorry, but that doesn't make this any easier to tolerate. Did you get a good look at her face?* My wolf gnashed her teeth. *It doesn't make me weak, it just makes me human. And guess what? I like being human.* My wolf glanced away, nosing her muzzle at me. For a supernatural diva, that was a hard compromise. I understood why, but forgiveness and empathy were the only two things keeping me rooted in reality. And once I lost those, I didn't want to think about what the world would look like.

Lili took Rourke's proffered T-shirt. "I guess this will have to do. It's bigger than anything else we have." She shook it out.

Yes, yes it was.

"There's no time to debate this," Rourke said. "Let's move. I want Jessica safe." He eyed the orthrus. "If we make this a concentrated effort and act at the same time, we can best it, at least for a few moments. If that spell doesn't work, it will be a different story."

"It will work," Lili said. "I swear to it."

"I can help," I added. "If I morph to Lycan, it won't be hard. I can hold it down with Tyler."

"No," Rourke said, shaking his head. "There's barely any room for us to maneuver around with that thing in this hallway. Your job will be getting us into the rooms."

Ray went shoulder to shoulder with Rourke. "This thing is going to be like a bucking bronco," he commented. "Sounds like my idea of good time." He grinned and rubbed his hands together, his irises jumping to silver.

Tyler stood right behind them. "On three," Rourke said, turning to Lili. "You get its attention, toss the vial and the shirt, and then we'll spring."

Lili took a step forward, her voice low and soothing. "Here we go, boy," she coaxed. It snarled and shook its heads. "You love this stuff." She shook the vial in front of it. "Remember? The last time you woke up you didn't remember a thing and the sleep is so very peaceful."

Last time?

The orthrus paced to the side like a crab as Lili took a step closer. One of its heads extended and right as it snapped its jaws, the demoness tossed the vial.

There was a crunch, and she took several paces forward and threw Rourke's T-shirt at its two heads.

It grabbed the shirt and shook it like a puppy with a rag toy. Worst plan ever.

"Crap!" I yelled.

"Doesn't matter," Ray shouted. "We're going in."

All three sprang at the same time.

Ray landed right in front of it, grabbing a snout under each arm. Rourke dove for the tail as I held my breath. Tyler took the flank, shoving the beast up against the wall with his shoulder right as it started to bellow.

Rourke was fierce, his back bending, muscles flexing as he took the tail right below its head with both fists. It lashed out at him, but he held on, turning his back into the flank to help Tyler. Sweat glistened along his chest, which was easy to see without his shirt on.

That man was pure heaven even in the midst of Hell.

"You're not... going to win," Ray ground out. "I can hold my own against you." As the beast bucked its long necks, it repeatedly tossed Ray into the wall. "I'm not letting go, you dickweed, no matter how many times you bang me... up... against... *ow*."

Once the beast was significantly pinned and had started to slow its efforts, Tyler yelled, "Go! Get into the rooms. We'll follow you as soon as we can."

Lili leaped forward, slipping by the howling beast at an angle. I followed, grabbing Selene by the arm and tugging her along with me. "Where's the entrance?" I yelled.

"It's camouflaged in the rock," Lili answered. "My magic should still be able to break the code, but if not... you will have to do it."

"Of course I will," I grumbled. "You keep making this stuff sound easy, except it's not. What's going to be waiting for us inside, a griffin?"

"There will be nothing inside, except for relief," she said. "Nothing is allowed to enter these rooms without permission, something the Prince does not give to anyone."

Lili ran her hands over the rock ten feet from where the boys were still struggling with the orthrus.

"How long is the spell going to take to activate?" I asked, glancing back with trepidation. The snake tail was still giving my mate a run for his money, and if he was bitten, I was going to lose it all over this hallway. We'd already encountered venom from the Underworld in the form of rabid bats. This would likely be much worse, judging by the size of the beast. I had no idea if I could cure Rourke if I needed to.

"It should be weakening soon," Lili said, irritation in her voice. After a few more failed attempts to find the door, she dropped her hands. "The passageway is not here."

"What do you mean, *not here*?" I moved up beside her and ran my hands along the wall, searching for anything I could find. "A doorway doesn't move." Well, it usually didn't.

"The Prince has guarded against my attempts more than he ever has before. Even after all our many spats, this entry was still accessible to me through magic. I don't understand it." She appeared genuinely confused as she shook her head. "It should be here, and I should be able to sense it."

I edged her out of the way and took over. "The relationship between you two is clearly over. He's giving you no more chances. That's why he has a huge, scary beast blocking your path." A beast who was still struggling. "Lili?" I asked. "If the Prince thought you might come back here, and he bothered to mask the door, don't you think he'd make damn sure the orthrus wouldn't fall to your magic too?"

"It's not possible for him to do so," she answered, her face appearing struck at the notion. "I am the strongest spell caster in Hell. No one here can best my magic."

"That may have been the case before, but something has obviously changed." I shouted over my shoulder to the boys, "I don't think Lili's magic is going to work on that beast! We're going to have to come up with a plan B if I can't find this opening quickly."

Rourke gritted his teeth as the snake rattled in his grasp. "We'll have to take it down. There's no other way."

Tyler's face was red with effort. "This thing is not even close to slowing down; if anything it's gaining its second wind." The thing bucked and raged.

Instead of trying to find the door, I rushed toward the head of the beast, where Ray struggled with both heads locked under each of his arms. He was holding on, but it wouldn't be long until the beast finally bashed him off.

I grabbed the neck of one of the heads and the thing immediately tossed me off, slamming me into the wall. I recovered my footing and launched myself at it again. Its hair was coarse and warm under my grasp and its neck was about the size of a watermelon. I had to sling my elbow around it to hold on. Tyler was right, the beast was not even close to waning.

I glared at Lili as I yelled to the guys, "I'm going to throw some magic into it and see if I can do something." *We need to find a way to take it down. What do you see?* I asked my wolf as my magic filtered in. This thing was all blackness. It was a true beast of the Underworld. I used my demon magic to prod it, and it pushed me back. But it wasn't stronger than I was. *We have to find something to hurt it or disable it.* This thing had to have a heart somewhere. If I concentrated a blast of my magic there, it might work.

"Go for the stomach," Lili called. "It will trigger a mass effect."

"The stomach?" I questioned. "Why wouldn't I try to stop its heart?" The thing roared in my ear, as if it knew my intent.

"Hannon," Ray said through a clenched jaw, "can you hurry it up? I can't hold this thing still much longer." I noticed for the first time that Ray had pivoted himself up against the wall and had braced his legs across the cave so I could hold on to the neck without getting thrown again.

"I'm working on it, Ray," I muttered. "I'm looking for something to hurt inside this thing, but I'm coming up short. It's all darkness inside. Like a void."

"The orthrus doesn't have a working heart," Lili explained. "It has no veins. Go for the stomach. It does eat. If it explodes, it should shut down the rest of it."

"Where is the stomach located?" Rourke shouted as he turned, keeping a firm knee pressed into the beast's flank. Tyler had spread his entire body up against its side, grunting with effort as he struggled to keep it pinned.

"I don't know why it has not gone to sleep," Lili cried. "I find it unbelievable. The stomach is on the bottom of the beast—"

Rourke rammed the snake's head against the wall hard enough to shake it silly for a few precious seconds while he drove his other hand into the beast's underbelly with so much force the hallway shook.

The thing shrieked like a pterodactyl.

One more concentrated punch to the belly and the beast opened up.

The orthrus stumbled, losing its footing as black sludge poured out of the wound. Without hesitation, Rourke stuck his hand farther into the mess.

"*Be careful!*" I covered my mouth and nose. The smell was ridiculous. "I hope the blood isn't poisonous."

"I found it." Rourke's jaw was clenched and fierce concentration lined his face. "Just…one second…more." With a final yank, the beast's insides flooded onto the ground in a huge splash.

The beast crumpled to the ground as its legs gave away. The boys and I jumped back as it fell. I glanced over at my mate, who was covered with the equivalent of black tar all the way up his arm and down the front of his chest.

He smiled grimly at me. "Sometimes all you need is strength concentrated in the right place."

Tyler panted, leaning against the far wall away from the beast. "That was badass," he said to Rourke. "I'm just glad it was you and not me who had to go there."

Rourke grunted, sluicing the sludge off his arm with his other hand and flinging it to the ground. "You wouldn't have been strong enough, wolf." He grinned. "It took all my strength to get through that thing."

Tyler stood straight up, ready to refute my mate until he saw the twinkle in Rourke's eye. "Well," Tyler said good-naturedly, "I concede it might've taken me a few more hits than it took you, but I would've gotten through. No doubt about it."

"By that time, we all would've been dead," Ray guffawed. "It's nice and handy to have an ancient cat around when you need him."

It was also nice to see my mate smile. It was a rare event. But it was time to get back to business. I turned to Lili. "You have one more chance to get this right. How do we get in?" I jabbed my thumb at the rock wall behind me.

"I don't know," she said, panic in her voice. She knew this was it. "If the door is here, it's cloaked from me. I've sent my power out all over this wall to no avail. This is all very distressing."

I walked over to where we'd stood before and placed my hands on the wall. "How do these walls seal themselves up like this?" There were no cracks in the stone. "It looks like nothing was ever here."

"The walls are alive, much like the ones you saw with veins earlier. With a proper spell they will grow together in a matter of hours. It doesn't take much coaxing," she replied.

"Well, I guess we'll just have to coax it back open again." I scoured the wall. *Wait, did you sense that?* My wolf had concentrated our power and tossed it outward. It had finally struck something. That something had a taste. And the taste was familiar. *Good gods, how can this be?*

I dropped my hands and turned around.

Selene was positioned farther down the hallway, leaning with her back against the tunnel, her head down. Rourke picked up on my unease.

"What is it?" he asked. "What'd you find?"

"Something has indeed spelled the wall, but unfortunately the signature is all too familiar." I glanced down the hallway again. I cleared my voice. "Selene, have you been here recently? Did the Prince bring you here?"

Selene's head came up. "What?"

"I asked you if you'd been in this hallway recently. Did the Prince task you to spell this wall?" I rapped it with my knuckle. It made sense the Prince would've used the only thing that might trump Lili's magic or at least give it a run for its money.

Selene glanced around her like she'd just discovered she was down here. She shrugged. "How should I know? These tunnels all look the same to me. It's like one big caveman subway system around here. I've been through plenty of them during my stay in the land of awful."

"Selene, I'm asking you because I detect your spell signature in this wall. But it's a little...off." I had no other way to explain it.

"What do you mean, *off*? What's wrong with it?" Ray asked, moving forward and placing his hand on the wall.

"I'm not sure, but it feels like an echo of some kind," I said.

Selene came forward. She placed her palms on the hard surface and gasped. "That's not *my* magic."

"Are you sure?" I asked. No two magics were ever the same. "Selene, this feels too close to yours to be someone else's. I've felt your magic firsthand." I probed along the wall again to make sure. "The spell is red, just like your signature. Everything about it is yours. It's just not as...precise." Maybe the Prince had tapped her to do it after he'd had most of her magic drained?

She dropped her hand. "It's not mine." Her voice held a dull ring.

I turned to Lili, who had her brows drawn. "What gives?" I asked.

A dark look came over Lili's face. "He must have made a clone."

18

"Please run that by me again," I demanded. "A clone of Selene? How is that possible?"

"The results are...unpredictable at best, but we do have the technology and magic to make a demon clone," Lili answered as she turned toward an emotionally deadened Selene, who had taken a few steps back. "It makes more sense to me now why you are like you are." She ran her eyes over Selene's body. "Clones are made directly from your power and magic—like sucking the life out and leaving a shell—but when the demons finished making your clone, I'm certain you were supposed to die, but somehow you prevailed. I had not thought it possible to survive a cloning, so I never even suspected it."

Ray whistled. "That's a pretty shitty way to go, but it explains why she's still here." By the inflection in his voice, I could tell I wasn't the only one who felt a little sorry for the villain in our midst. That made me feel better. Selene had basically caused Ray's brutal death by convincing Eamon she loved him, so if he could find a way to forgive her—any of us could. It made me immensely proud of him.

If Ray managed to hold on to his humanness, as I did, I believed he would fare much better in the long run.

"If the Prince had Selene's doppelganger spell the entrance, then there's a good chance the clone is awaiting us in his chambers," Lili intoned. "We must tread with caution."

"Sounds like there's a new mistress in town," Tyler muttered. "And if she's exactly like Selene"—he eyed the former goddess—"except more powerful, we're going to have another epic battle on our hands."

"I can break the spell in the wall. It's enough like Selene's," I said, "and I'm familiar with her signature. But once it's broken, is there a way we can quietly sneak up on this clone if she's in there?" She had to be in there. The Prince of Hell needed a new resident spell caster to protect what was his.

Selene finally seemed to understand what we were saying and elbowed me out of the way. "If anyone is going to break this spell and kill this imposter, it'll be me. I deserve retribution more than any of you, and think I know the best way to defeat myself." She smacked her palms against the wall and closed her eyes.

Selene had little more than an echo of magic inside her, but as I watched, it seemed to be enough. The wall began to vibrate.

"How are you doing that?" I whispered, my head next to hers. "You shouldn't be strong enough."

"I created these spells. They were mine even if I didn't wield them. This is one of my less extraordinary ones. It's meant to mask something's true nature. The door is here, it only seems as if it's not."

I stepped back and gave her room, turning to the group. "We've been lucky so far, no demons have found us. The Princess must still have them on lockdown, but I'm sure that will be over soon.

When we get in, we deal with imposter Selene and figure out how to help the Princess defeat the Prince."

That sounded easy, right?

Rourke gestured at Lili. "And once we get in there, I want to know exactly what's in the new Scriptures you found, demoness." He narrowed his eyes. "No evading our questions. We need to know what we're dealing with and why the demons will go to war with each other—especially why the Princess of Hell is willing to help us escape. If you leave anything out, you will feel my wrath."

Lili appeared uncomfortable. She wasn't going to share the information willingly. I put a hand over my nose to block the increasing stink of the dead orthrus as I added, "Lili, there's no way to get away from this. We need to know everything."

She shifted on her feet. "What is written in the Scriptures is for demons only. We are not allowed to...share with others. It is forbidden."

Rourke took a step forward, still bare-chested, his forearm tattoos jumping as he fisted his hands. "I don't give a rat's ass about your demon rules or laws. My mate's name is written in your history books and I want to know what we're dealing with, do you understand? I didn't arrive in Hell to free her, only to find myself here"—he motioned around the tunnel—"for nothing. The only reason we haven't escaped and gone back to our plane is because Jessica wants to be done with this ordeal. I agree, but only up to a point. Now it's going to be your job to tell us what we need to know." He bared his teeth.

She shrank back from his anger, but before she could answer, the wall wavered and the spell melted away to reveal a door.

"See." Selene had a grim smile on her face. "I told you I could break it."

Ray came up from behind and guided Selene by the waist,

maneuvering her out of the way, and remarkably, she let him. "Great," he said. "We'll take it from here."

Once she was relocated, she placed her hands on her hips. "You don't need to treat me like a child. I'm strong enough to take my alter ego down on my own."

"We'll see about that," Ray said, his face set. "We go in first, and if we need your assistance, we'll let you know. If that lady in there is anything like you, it's going to be one pissed-off clone."

I glanced at the door warily. He was right. I'd already defeated Selene once and I had no desire to do it twice. "Is this the front door?" I asked Lili.

"No," Lili answered. "We are entering from the back. If this other . . . woman . . . is indeed his new mistress, she will be keeping his house in the main rooms. If we go quietly we might gain a small advantage. Certainly she will sense us at some point—if she is *indeed* that powerful."

Spoken like a true woman scorned.

Ray stood in front of the door. I glanced behind me. My brother and Rourke appeared ready to do some damage. "Okay, let's go," I said. "The smell out here is killing me."

My brother waved his hand in front of his face and then leaned over to sniff Rourke. "Jesus, dude, you need a shower."

"Working on it," Rourke growled. "There's not exactly a public restroom nearby."

"The Prince's rooms are palatial," Lili replied. "You will be able to clean up once we are inside."

Ray edged his shoulder up against the door and grunted as he pushed. It gave, but only about an inch.

"What's wrong? Is it too heavy?" I asked.

"No." He pulled back. "There's something blocking it from the inside."

"If you can, try to pry it open it a little more so I can see what it is," I told him, craning my neck around, trying to get a good angle.

Tyler nudged by me. "Let me see," he said. "You go stand next to stinky."

I chuckled, letting him do it, moving back by Rourke. I didn't care how bad he smelled. I leaned my back against his chest and sighed. "Nothing can cover your natural scent for me." I inhaled and grinned like a teenager. "Molasses and cloves. Just the way I like it."

His body rumbled with pleasure as his arms enfolded me. He leaned down to my ear. "You're a handful, you know that?" His fingertips electrified me, sending currents of energy racing through my body.

"*Mm*, I know," I replied, laying my head against his shoulder, gazing up at him. "But that's the way you prefer it. If this were easy, you'd be bored. I know you adventurous types like life filled with action and I'm happy to oblige."

He chuckled. "I could take nice and boring with you right now." He growled low and ran his lips across my neck. "Long, boring... and slow."

Chills raced up my spine and my heart skipped a beat, right as Ray shouldered the door again. He pushed his weight against it and there was a snapping sound as the door finally moved in a few inches.

"What was that?" I asked, moving reluctantly out of my mate's grasp to investigate.

He growled his displeasure but let me go.

"I don't know," Tyler said. "It sounded like broken bones to me. I can't really get a good look."

Ray changed positions with Tyler and glanced into the opening. "I have no idea what the hell that is, but we need to start referring to this entire place as the Mad Fucking House of

Horrors, because there are no explanations for what goes on here."
Ray grumbled, peering into the doorway again. "I think that's...
a remnant of a human being of some kind, but I can't tell either."

Ray stepped back and I moved in. It actually resembled a
mummy, of all things. "What"—I paused as Ray pushed the door
open a little more, ignoring the crunching sounds, to expose what
appeared to be a withered-looking human—"is that thing?"

Lili cleared her throat from behind us. "That is a golem. A
human golem."

We all stared at her.

"It's like every time you speak, it's in tongues," Ray said. "What
exactly is a *human golem*?"

"The Prince has taken a liking over the last century to necromancers. He's lured quite a few to the Underworld with promises
of riches and as many dead souls as they'd like. But he ensnares
them and makes them do things...such as this." She gestured at
the mummified broken thing behind the door.

"You've got to be kidding me," I muttered. "That dead human
was resurrected as some kind of guard? Looks like it did a bang-up
job. It broke into pieces at the first attempt to get through the door."

Rourke shook his head and moved into the doorway, examining the golem. "No, it didn't break because of that. It broke
because it was linked to the door spell. It was a two-for-one
combo." He glanced at Selene. "Did you know you were disarm-
ing this thing when you broke the passageway spell?"

"I didn't know what it was specifically," she countered with
some hostility. "I felt something back there, so I did what any
witch would do—I sent a spell backward to fry whatever it was."
She raised her eyebrows. "It didn't really have any brains to fry,
but it worked anyway." She looked smug.

"It sure did," I commented. "But that thing doesn't look like it
would've put up much of a fight anyway."

"It's only the watchdog," Lili said. "It was supposed to alert its master if someone broke through the spell."

"Well, Selene seems to have circumvented the alarm," Ray snorted, "so what are we waiting for? Let's go."

Rourke led the way through the narrow chambers. Tyler stayed behind and made sure the passageway door was firmly shut. We traveled through several short tunnels before we ended up in a small atrium. It held a huge bed in the center, draped in ornate cloth. The color scheme in here was decidedly feminine: the room was decorated in rich gold and yellow hues. The walls were covered with tapestries that appeared to be from our plane, and likely priceless at that.

I raised an eyebrow at Lili. "Is this space yours?" The bed was made. It appeared not to have been touched in a while, so that was a relief.

"Yes," Lili said. "It was...ours."

Doing the nasty with the Prince of Hell sounded like the most detestable thing I could possibly think of. But I reminded myself I wasn't a demon. Or even a half demon. I needed to get some perspective or I might start gagging. "How do we get to the Prince's rooms?" I asked.

"These rooms are mine," Lili answered. "We have to travel a bit farther to get to his quarters. Down the next hallway we're going to come up on a big door made of iron."

Rourke moved through the room, pacing around the huge bed, motioning for us to follow. We passed through another beautiful space decorated in plush scarlet couches, and chandeliers that hung from smooth stone ceilings.

I noticed something peculiar about this space that made it different from the others I'd seen in the Underworld. "The interior here looks like it was made from human textiles and furniture, not like the other smooth, glossy stuff I've seen," I said. "Whatever is manufactured in Hell is all weird and shiny."

"Our raw materials are much different from those found on your plane." Lili nodded. "We use pure minerals only found here. Everything that grows in Hell is alive, even the metals, and it makes them smooth and somewhat moist." She glanced around her old rooms wistfully as we passed through. "I much prefer human decorations, so the Prince spared no expense. They were last updated a century ago, but I will miss them."

"How far underground are we, by the way?" Ray asked as we entered another hallway, this one with walls resembling polished granite. "These walls are solid rock."

I hadn't thought about that much. The buildings I'd first seen were obviously on the top, but my suspicion was we were deep underground.

"Demons have always lived below the surface," Lili answered. "We are cave dwellers by nature. The sun above burns our skin, so it is out of necessity as well. We are about six levels under right now. This level is called the *Hodoseod Dyjyd* and is reserved for Demon Lords and their accommodations only. That's why you don't see any low-level demons milling around. Only their servants are allowed to come here."

Rourke finally stopped in front of an imposing door.

"Sweet, another door for us to bust through," Tyler quipped, coming up behind us. "That one looks easy enough."

"Once we open this, it will alert...whoever resides in there," the demoness said quietly. "The doors and walls are very thick, so they likely can't hear us, but once we break the seal they will be able to both hear and scent us."

"Unless the Prince has spelled the area," I countered. "Or has it booby-trapped."

Selene interrupted, surprising me by shaking her head and saying, "There are no spells here."

"How can you be so sure?" I asked. I didn't want any golems to jump out at us.

Selene looked at me like I was a moron. "I may be dead, but I know how to detect a spell, especially if it was one of mine. I sense nothing in the air or on the door."

"She's right," Lili said, appraising Selene. "I detect nothing as well."

Rourke placed his hands gently on the door, testing. Nothing zapped him, so that was a good sign. "This door is thick," he said. "But to bust it open will make a lot of noise." Instead he grasped one of the two big handles and depressed it.

It didn't move.

I asked Lili, "How did you two lovebirds go back and forth? You didn't have to come through this locked door every time, did you? Shouldn't there be a key in some secret cubbyhole or something?"

"There is no key." Lili sighed. "I used magic, of course. He has found a way to block me already, but I will try."

She moved in front of Rourke and placed her palms on the door, caressing it as she pressed one cheek to it, listening for something.

Then she sprang back. "There's something on the other—"

Before she could finish, the door burst open in front of us.

"Looking for me?" a very bored and familiar voice intoned.

19

The fake Selene stood sentry, dressed in her predecessor's former glory. She wore a black leather corset with metal studs and a pair of the tightest leather pants I'd ever seen. Her hair was long, gorgeous, and bright red, and there wasn't a mar on her perfect porcelain skin. She had the balls to cross her arms and lean up against the door frame like it was no big deal that three shifters, one former goddess, and one witch-demon were standing there waiting to take her out. "We knew you'd try to come here, Lili. You are so very predictable." She shook her head with a pitying expression.

Lili's power jumped and cold fury whipped off her. "Of course I came back." Lili calmly placed her hands on her hips, belying the inner turmoil I knew raged inside her. This had to burn. "I left some of my most cherished treasures here and I can't leave this plane until I retrieve them." Then, without so much as flinching or signaling her intent, Lili sprang, grabbing the doppelganger by the throat with one hand and by the hair with the other.

Hair that came out in Lili's fist as they went down.

They were on the floor before anyone could blink. The clone struggled, but Lili was too quick. We all watched, our mouths slightly agape as they rolled twice more, and then, with one swipe, Lili tore out the doppelganger's jugular and plunged her fist down her throat.

There was an awful sucking noise, followed by gushing and gurgling.

None of us had moved from the doorway.

"Well." Ray chuckled. "I didn't see that one coming." He angled his head to the side. "That demoness has good form. Selene Two never had a chance."

"Lili has good form because she's a cold-blooded killer," I commented. "This is another reminder that she's dangerous."

"You got that right," Ray said.

After a few more seconds the clone went totally still and Lili rose, clutching something slimy in her hand. Before she could explain how she'd gotten the jump on the clone so quickly, the real Selene grabbed her own throat and stumbled forward, gasping for air.

Tyler stood the closest and managed to catch her in his arms as she collapsed, dragging her into the room and laying her out on the stone floor.

I knelt by her side. "What's happening to her?" I asked Lili as Rourke and Ray came up beside me.

Lili went to a side table, plucked an ornate bowl from its resting place, and dropped something into it that landed with a squish. She bent over it for a moment, like she needed to examine it, and after finding it adequate she turned back to me, wiping blood off her hands and onto her jumpsuit. "I'm not sure. They must've been linked together somehow. The cloning has obviously gone awry." She walked over, holding the bowl. "Maybe that's why she couldn't die in the first place? The two bodies are connected."

I stood slowly, blinking. For a single second I felt like I was watching this entire scene from outside myself. I glanced into the bowl Lili held. "Is that her heart? You ripped it out through her *neck*?" I grimaced. It was smaller than a human heart. "That can't be Selene's heart. It's too small."

"It's a demon heart, and it's located higher on the chest than a human's, which is why I opened her throat." Lili said it like it was commonplace to rip someone's heart out. "That clone was ninety-five percent Selene, five percent demon. Take out the five percent and it cannot function in the Underworld. The stronger the demon heart, the more powerful the clone. This was a fairly powerful heart, from one of our highborn demons, but not enough to deter me." She shook the bowl and the mass slipped around. "The Prince underestimated me if he thought I could not disarm this clone in less than three minutes."

I shook my head. "You know, you could've told us you had this handled. Or at the very least we could've held her down or something." I peered at Lili out of the corner of my eye. "Constantly keeping us in the dark is not helping you."

Lili shrugged. "If the clone had been smart, she would've used a spell. But the five percent demon gave her a big disadvantage. I had to act quickly to make it clean. Some demons can sense intent before it happens and I didn't know which demon heart they'd used, so I cloaked my feelings."

The real Selene continued to roll on the ground, her hands still tearing at her neck, her eyes wide. I knelt down next to her again as she rocked, her face turning a very dark shade of scarlet. I had no idea what to do.

"What's happening to her?" Ray asked, kneeling next to me, his face a mask of confusion. "Can't we stop this somehow?"

"I honestly don't know." I glanced over my shoulder at the list-less, very dead clone lying a few feet away. "Ray, I think the bodies are connected somehow—possibly with one soul. It's the only thing you detected keeping the real Selene alive, but wouldn't the demons need her soul for the clone? I mean, that's what demons always want—your soul. Taking it must be what allows the power shift to happen." It was remarkable, really. Transferring a supernatural's raw magic and power was unheard of in my world. If the sorcerers had truly teamed up with the demons and gained this knowledge, it would be a supernatural game changer.

Ray immediately raised his head in the air and his eyes shone silver.

I knew the moment he figured it out. His gaze snapped to mine. "The soul is split. You were right." He shook his head, his forehead crinkling in concentration. "This is very wrong. My body is telling me it's not supposed to be like this." He rubbed the back of his neck. "It's highly unusual, and the universe doesn't like when things like this happen. Very bad chi."

"But that explains it, right?" I said. "Neither Selene can survive with half a soul. When the demons make a clone, I bet they take the whole soul. But Selene's immortality must have torn it in two somehow." Her godhood had tried to save her. My bet was that Selene had been the first goddess to ever make a deal with Hell, and that the demons had had no idea a goddess couldn't die.

Now they did.

Ray angled his nose in the air again, sensing something else. His head turned back and forth like a bloodhound on the scent. He leaped up and rushed over to the clone and lowered his mouth over hers and inhaled.

I rose and took a step back.

Tyler and Rourke gathered behind me and Lili stood off to the side, all of us waiting to see what would happen next.

After a moment Ray lifted his head up, his eyes cascading to full black as his incisors snapped down. His vampire and reaper sides together as one. It was a bit chilling to see. He was a formidable supernatural who was currently on a mission. And his mission was to save Selene. It was the unlikeliest scenario I would've ever guessed would happen during my trip to the Underworld.

My wolf howled in my mind, urging us to stop him. *I'm not getting involved*, I told her. *It's not up to us any longer. If her immortality tried to save her soul, there has to be a damn good reason behind it. We're going to have to wait this out. If she lives and comes back from this at full strength, out for revenge, we'll deal with it then.* My wolf clacked her jaws at my foolishness. *I know you disagree, but eradicating a proposed threat is not the answer. Clearly something else is going on here.*

Ray staggered over to the real Selene, who had stopped struggling and appeared to be unconscious. Ray placed his lips over hers and blew.

Her chest heaved once, twice, and by the third time she coughed and sputtered, bringing her arms over her head. She blinked her eyes open as she gasped, recoiling away from Ray. "What are you doing? Get away from me!" She shoved him back hard enough for him to lose his balance.

He thumped onto his backside and took in a few breaths of his own, resting his elbows on his knees, clearly worn out from his efforts. "Lady, I just saved your life," he panted. "Don't ask me how it happened, because by all rights that piece of your soul shouldn't have lingered so long. But it did. And I wasn't sure your body would take it back"—he paused—"but it did. I don't know what the hell's going on, but you have a powerful force working for you. And honestly, for the life of me, I have no idea why, because you're a royal pain in the ass most of the time." He rose, shaking his arms out. "And next time, a simple thank-you would suffice."

Selene sat up, clearly bewildered.

I half expected her to start healing from all the previous demon torture immediately. But we all waited and nothing happened. Her hands flew to her head and her face. She leaped up and ran to a huge mirror mounted on a nearby wall. "It's not working," she wailed. "I feel more like myself, but my magic is not returning."

I pushed my senses out to check for myself, but she was right, her signature hadn't changed at all. I sighed. "Why don't you give it more than seven seconds? You just got your soul back together and it may need some time to mend before anything starts regenerating." I cleared my throat to put emphasis on the next part. "But I'm warning you, Selene, if your magic does come back, and you decide to pick up where you left off back at the arena, I will not hesitate to have Ray suck your soul right back out, like that." I snapped my fingers. "And once he does, it's all over for good."

She glared at me in the mirror but kept her mouth shut. I took that as her accepting my mandate. At least for a few minutes.

I turned and addressed Lili, saying, "How long before you can get word to the Princess?" I was bone-tired, but there was no time to rest. "We need to let her know what's going on. We will aid her, and once we do that, we leave this world behind for good."

"The Prince will likely be by the Princess's side for the rest of the day, as our rules dictate. Once she dismisses him, he will call a meeting with the Council of High Demon Lords to figure out what is to be done about you. He will not come back to his quarters until daybreak. Demons need very little sleep, so we do not use our homes like you do." Her voice held a wistful note. "But I have the Princess's private number and will try it now."

Rourke stood next to me. "Where does the Prince keep his important information, demoness?" We were all standing in a foyer of sorts. It had tall, vaulted ceilings and was very clean. There were very few personal items scattered about, save some knickknacks on various tables. Some of the items looked as though they'd been collected from different planes, set around to remind the Prince of his travels.

My eyes narrowed for a moment as I spotted something perched on the table under the mirror where Selene had just stood. "Is that a shrunken head?" I pointed to what looked like a withered pygmy head. "From our plane?"

"Yes," Lili replied, not even bothering to glance where I gestured. "Before he was the Prince of Hell, and was only a high-ranking demon, he was summoned to your plane often, by many. He brought back...a souvenir each time."

"That head doesn't look like it was given freely."

She shook her head. "No, unfortunately for some summoners, most of his trinkets were not. The Prince has always been a very fierce, very proud demon. He was meant to rule, not to be called upon like a slave." She turned abruptly and started walking through an entryway. "His personal rooms are this way."

We all followed, including a pensive Selene, who kept running her hands over her face, hoping for a miracle. *Keep an eye on her*, I told my wolf. *I want to know if she suddenly generates a lot of power.* My wolf gave me a "no shit" look and shook her head. *Well, lately we've been on opposite sides of the argument. I'm just trying to keep it real.* She huffed at me and turned her back. My wolf was such a good sport.

We strode through a huge living area decorated in straight lines and smooth textures. There were several long black couches made out of some kind of demon material. It was all very orderly. I didn't see a kitchen or any place to prepare food. "Where does the Prince eat?" I asked, thinking about the horrid gazebos. I knew for a fact that the Prince of Hell did not eat with the common demons.

Lili stopped. "In the main *kefefr laat*, of course. That's where all the Demon Lords and demonesses eat."

"What's a kay-fay-frea lay-at?" Ray asked.

"It's the main dining room. We have four meals a day there. Each feast is a very elaborate event."

"Is your food always...alive?" I asked, wondering if I really wanted to know. "From what I've seen, demons prefer to have their meals wiggle and fight."

"Yes," she said. "We prefer our food breathing, but we do... mix it up on occasion. Freezing the main course and letting it thaw just before we partake of it is a recent favorite."

I shivered. That was just plain gross.

"That's fairly disgusting," Tyler commented, not having to read my mind on that one. "Even in my wolf form, I make a clean kill before I eat."

"We are...not like you, if you haven't noticed," she said. "It took me time to adjust to it too, but my demon side takes great joy in food that...puts up a struggle." Her pupils elongated, radiating her pleasure. "It's an acquired taste."

"Well, it's one that none of us will be acquiring any time soon," I finished.

We continued down a long hallway with a beautiful bowed white ceiling, and at the end was another elaborate door.

Lili pushed it open without incident. "This is where the Prince conducts his business while he is home. Do not touch any of the buttons on the desk if you do not wish for company." She went across to the far wall and pressed a lever, and a sheet of material cascaded down one wall. She turned back to us. "There you go. No prying eyes. Once this is down there can be no surveillance."

Rourke strode immediately to the Prince's desk, fingering all the notes and books piled there. "I know the Prince will have specific demon law books as well as High Law books that cover the rights of all supernaturals. If the Prince of Hell is also the judge and jury of the Underworld then he must have access to all information and I want to see it."

Lili walked behind the desk and opened a large cutout in the wall to expose row after row of orderly books. "You are welcome to look here, but all these demon books are written in Demonish. I doubt you know the language well enough to read it."

Rourke grunted his response.

All the books were adorned with strange characters on the spines, like hieroglyphics.

"If he has High Law books," Tyler stated from the doorway, "they will be footnoted in English as well as all the popular European languages."

Tyler and I only spoke English, since we'd been raised in America and we were very young on the supernatural age scale. I had no idea how many languages Rourke spoke, but my guess was many.

"I know some Demonish phrases," Rourke said. "But of course the written language will be a challenge. But the demons have close ties with the Shamans of the East, correct? They worship the Underworld and speak many European languages. I know a lot of those."

Lili appraised my mate with a calculated gaze. "Yes, the Shamans do have a strong connection to the Underworld. Unfortunately, they are not involved in any of our laws. We use them for...ceremonies."

I followed Lili and Rourke behind the desk and sat down in the chair. It was ridged and cool. "There has to be something here we can work with, Lili. We need information, specifically about the Scriptures."

Lili strode back to the entryway where Tyler stood. Ray and Selene had stayed outside the office. I could hear them bickering about something in the hallway. "I will check the other rooms and see what I can find."

I nodded toward Tyler. "Go with her and see if you can come up with anything." *Watch her like a hawk*, I said. *Something's up.*

I'm on it. He turned and followed her out, closing the office door behind him.

I swiveled in the chair and met Rourke's heated gaze. It was the first time we'd been alone since he'd arrived. Shivers raced up my spine and a calm heat spread over my entire body.

Instead of speaking, he simply extended his hand.

I took it and energy immediately zinged up my arm in a delicious current. He tugged me out of the chair with a gentle pull and led me back around the desk toward a door I hadn't noticed before. It wasn't one of those concealed cutout doors but looked like a regular working door.

"Before we continue our investigation, I need you to help me clean this crap off," he said, grinning. He had a point, as he was still covered in dried blood from the orthrus.

We reached the door and he turned the knob. It gave easily. He swung it wide.

To reveal the biggest bathroom I'd ever seen.

20

"How'd you know there was a bathroom here, you tricky beast?"
I laughed.

"I didn't." He chuckled. "I was actually hoping it was a
bedroom."

Before I could respond he had me pressed up against the
doorjamb, mouth slanted over mine. It was a needy kiss and I
responded in kind, my tongue delving deeply into his mouth,
matching him stroke for stroke.

His hands slid down my body, electrifying everything along
the way. He broke the kiss with a growl and ran his delicious
blond stubble along my jaw and down my neck. "My beast went
crazy without you," he whispered. "I couldn't think. I couldn't
function. I craved your smell. I needed to have it back inside me.
You make me totally irrational"—his voice was low—"and I *like*
it that way. You're not allowed to take off without me again. Do
you hear me?"

I shivered. "I—" His tongue found its way to the hollow of my neck and as it licked, a small sound erupted from the back of my throat. "—I . . . promise."

He shook his head as he gazed up at me, his eyes slightly unfocused. "I realized something huge when you left." His irises radiated their emotion like tiny prisms of the most beautiful emerald. "I can't take a backseat where you're involved. We're either in this together—as a team—or it doesn't happen. My beast can't stand it and neither can I." He ran his tongue up my jaw, stopping a hairbreadth from my lips. "Deal?" he purred.

With his passion and love pressed against me, my wolf howling in pleasure, there was no way I could say no. He was right. This was where we needed to be. We were a team, bonded together in the most primal way possible. I gazed up at him, knowing my eyes were full of the same emotions, a kaleidoscope of violet. "Deal," I whispered.

His lips took mine again as he slid his hands down my back until they were firmly planted around my backside. In one motion he picked me up, and I obliged by wrapping my legs around his waist. He walked us into the large room covered in an intricate mosaic of black and white tile, kicking the door shut behind us.

I broke the kiss as I glanced upward. Everywhere I could see were row after row of what looked to be sprinkler heads. I gazed back down at my mate with one eyebrow arched. He flashed me a devious smile and reached a hand over and flipped a large switch on the wall.

Demon water cascaded down around us in heavy currents, coating us completely in seconds.

It was thick and warm, instantly eating off all the nasty grime as it went. Rourke leaned into me, his cinnamon-laced breath on mine. "No one will begrudge us a quick shower break." His eyes twinkled. "I smelled like old roadkill. A demon would scent me a mile away, making our getaway much too risky."

"I hadn't noticed any nefarious smells," I replied coyly. "You always smell like heaven to me." I cupped a hand around his jaw as I moved forward and took his mouth slowly, enjoying the feeling of the wetness coupled with his heat.

Once our kiss deepened, he walked me over to a ledge that ran around the large showering area. My backside fit perfectly onto the shelf and he pressed his way between my thighs, flattening himself against me.

Gods, he felt so good.

My hands splayed along his now-clean torso and I leaned over and bit his bottom lip. No other man in the history of the universe was as hot as he was. I would dare anyone to say otherwise. My wolf barked her agreement.

The shower continued to rain down as I covered his mouth with mine, my tongue plunging deeply. He returned my kiss with a sigh, tilting our heads together, melding them perfectly. His full warm lips felt ridiculously good against mine. He took his sweet time exploring my mouth, making my toes curl in pleasure. I ran my hands up his neck and into his hair, grabbing fistfuls and forcing us together even closer. I had missed him an insane amount.

I broke the kiss reluctantly, pressing my forehead against his, sliding my hands down his neck, my nails raking his bare shoulders as I murmured into his lips, "We only have about three minutes left to spare in here, you know. We are in the bowels of Hell and it's imperative we stay focused. People are waiting for us. As much as I regret it, this is not the time for loving."

"I *am* laser-focused," he answered in a serious tone, his voice raw. "This is the most important mission I've had in days."

I laughed into his lips. It felt so good to relax for a few precious moments. "It would be *highly* inappropriate for us to lose ourselves right now. I know how we operate, and if we give in, we will be lost for hours."

He gave me a throaty growl. "I'm up for making this quick if you can manage it." Water rushed down his face and throat and it was hard for me not to lick it off him. The demon water had no taste, and other than being thicker, it was a lot like our regular water. "After all, you're the one with the problem. Always wanting more. It's all I can do to keep you satiated."

"Quiet!" I squealed, smacking his chest right as the water magically shut off. It must've been on a timer, but that was fine because we were squeaky clean. "That's so unfair. You're the one who never seems to be finished. Don't you ever get tired?"

"Not when I'm around you." He nuzzled my throat. "I'm sure that's a *huge* hardship for you."

I laughed as his hands wandered their way up my chest. "It totally is. I'm drained most of the time."

"I want to be drained," he growled as he thumbed my sensitive peaks through the jumpsuit.

"*Ahh*," I moaned as my head angled back against the wall. "Rourke, honestly, you have to stop. There will be time for this when we get home. If the Prince comes back here before—"

There was a polite knock on the door and I straightened up.

Tyler cleared his voice politely. "Um, I think we found something that may help us. Lili said it's important. Also, is that the bathroom? I could use a rinse-off."

"Yep, it's the bathroom," I called. "We'll be right"—Rourke tweaked me deliciously hard—"*out!*"

"Gotcha," Tyler said, amusement in his voice.

"You win this time," Rourke whispered in my ear as he tugged me off the ledge, "but all bets are off the next opportunity we get to ourselves. Being connected to you is the most important thing and I don't give a shit about anything else." He held me tightly against his length. "I'm taking you." He leaned over. "Make no mistake about it."

I slid my hand all the way down and cupped him, giving him a gentle squeeze. A low growl issued out of the back of his throat ending on a moan.

"I'm all in." I rose up on tiptoe to his ear. "But only if the timing's right. I want to *enjoy* you."

"Oh, there will be much enjoyment to be had." He grabbed my hand and led me to what had to be a wall of dryers, even though they looked more like trumpets erupting from the wall. "Now we dry off. After all, we can't go save the world sopping wet." He grinned as he punched another button on the wall and the dryers sprang to life. "And I just may have to take that jumpsuit off you to make sure there's not a drop of water left clinging to it."

I laughed as he slid me backward, pressing me firmly up against the tile.

A girl had to get dry somehow.

"What's in your hand?" I asked my brother as I walked up behind him. The dryers had been ridiculously effective and we'd been dry within a minute, much to Rourke's chagrin. I'd had to drag him from the bathroom, promising to do delicious, naughty things to him later.

"It's an official written warrant for your arrest in the Underworld," Tyler answered, waving the parchment in the air.

I snatched it from him and scanned it quickly. "It says I've committed 'small, answerable crimes' to be judged if 'the defendant arrived to the Underworld of her own volition.'" I walked around and sat on one of the black couches, which didn't give an inch. Ignoring the rigidity, I asked, "Who issued this? I doubt it was the Prince of Hell."

"No," Lili answered. "The Prince did not have a hand in that.

That was issued by the magistrate, but in order for you to be charged with a crime here someone had to file the appropriate paperwork citing your crimes in detail. No demon here would know about the two imps on your plane or the *Camazotz* you killed, because to us they simply disappeared. If any demon was upset by the loss, one could rationalize that the Lunar Goddess had purchased them, so therefore they were her responsibility. But in reality, no one would've gone looking for them."

"So what does that mean?" I asked. "The Prince filed a complaint with the magistrate because he had his own agenda?" That wasn't exactly surprising. "According to this, he went against his own law to lure me here."

"Not exactly," Lili replied. "Demons are wordsmiths of the highest degree. That piece of paper does indeed accuse you of crimes. It makes me wonder, however, why he would go to such great lengths to get you to come here. But either way, the Prince has fulfilled the prophecy by luring you here. If you had not arrived, there would be no uprising."

"That's what I've tried to tell the Prince all along, but he's too pigheaded to understand. If he would've left me alone, none of this would've happened. Now I want to know what the new Scriptures say," I said pointedly, arching an eye at Lili. "That's information we desperately need."

"I told you already," she answered, appearing uncomfortable once again. "I cannot tell you the exact wording, it is forbidden."

"Forbidden why? And what do you care?" I said. "You're only half demon and you want to leave this plane behind and never look back. Why would you worry about protocol now?"

"It's not protocol, it's superstition," she replied. "Demons are highly superstitious about only a few things, and repeating the Scriptures to a non-demon is one of them. If I tell you, I potentially place a hex on the Underworld. I won't do it, so don't ask me."

I begrudgingly understood superstition. Wolves are highly superstitious about many things, including myths and legends, which had made my life much harder than it needed to be for a very, very long time.

"Fine," I said, crossing my arms. "Don't tell us in exact words, just give us an idea. Paint a picture."

Her face was grim. "Fine." She strode over to a far wall in the room and turned. "It says that your being here will ignite a civil war, and once that war is over, there will be a new rule and that's it in a nutshell."

"You've already said as much," I retorted, unimpressed. "And the Prince happened to find out about these new Scriptures *after* you showed them to the Princess? Not before? Correct?"

"That's correct," Lili said. "I didn't tell him. He was not supposed to have this knowledge, but it was somehow leaked. The other demons who discovered this secret were very nervous and afraid of his wrath."

"But if my presence here was supposed to ignite a war, why would the Prince think parading me around in front of the court was a good idea? Why not keep me locked up where no demon could see me? Keep it all under wraps and keep an eye on me?"

"He is prideful." She shrugged. "And I may have told him... a few lies once he had me arrested." She smirked. "He could not find the new Scriptures, because I had hidden them well, so he interrogated me as to what was in them—and I told him... some truths and some falsehoods."

"So you basically made up enough stuff to make sure a war would indeed start," I said. "And you took me through the Sholls, and everything else, to make sure we ended up where we needed to be? That seems risky on your part."

"I took you through the Sholls because your only objective was to get to your brother. There was no other way. And if you remember, we did find him. I didn't have an ultimate plan at the time, but I knew if we didn't leave this plane immediately you would be apprehended sooner." She shrugged again. "It didn't really matter to me, because I believe wholeheartedly in the Scriptures. Whatever is meant to happen, will. It's that simple."

"Simple, my ass." I stood. "You could've told me what was at stake from the very beginning, especially if you wanted to earn my trust. You did no such thing."

"I earned your trust by repeatedly putting myself at risk," she argued. "How else would I go about it? Everything I've done thus far has been for your betterment." Her eyes pulsed in her anger.

"You stuck your neck out for your own cause, and nothing more," I answered. "Don't fool yourself." I waved my hand in the air, dismissing the conversation. "We're not getting anywhere with this and we need to move forward. I ignited a war, the damage is done, and now I want to prove that I don't want anything more to do with Hell by helping the Princess ascend to the throne, and then I want to go home. In that order."

"The only way to do that will be to convince the demon population that you seek no rule while the Princess announces the new Scriptures into law," she said firmly.

Before I could question how we were supposed to do that, Ray's voice floated into the room. Then he shouted. "What do you mean, leaving? Where in the hell are you going to go?"

21

"Anywhere but here," Selene replied in a haughty tone. "I have my soul back but not my magic. I'm going to force them to give it back to me."

I walked into the foyer, followed by Rourke and Tyler. Ray and Selene stood glaring at each other. "Selene," I said patiently, interrupting them. "That's not how things are going to work." I gestured to the still-very-dead doppelganger lying on the floor. "She had your power and magic. I felt it. If it didn't revert back to you, there's a reason."

When the Alpha or leader of a Sect dies, oftentimes their accumulated power seeks out the next in line, making the new Alpha or master the strongest of their kind. I had no idea what happened with true immortals—gods and goddesses were the very strongest of our kind, and if Selene's power did not willingly go back to her there was likely no way she could reclaim it.

"As a goddess, it should've gone back to you," Rourke said,

mirroring my thoughts. "There's nowhere else for it to go. So, like Jessica said, there must be a damn good reason why."

"But it's not fair. I need to heal and they need to pay for this," she snipped.

"Marching back into the belly of the beast is not the way you want to handle this," I told her. "You're still their property, lest you forget. They will toss you into a cell and keep trying to kill you. Or make a new clone. Or something equally hideous." I couldn't believe I was arguing with Selene about keeping her safe. It was like my worlds had collided. My wolf growled.

Selene threw up her arms. "I don't believe this. I can't be an immortal with no power; such a thing doesn't exist. I'd rather die than be left as an undying human until the end of time."

"Well," Ray snorted. "We could've easily arranged that about fifteen minutes ago."

"Selene," I said in the most patient tone I could possibly muster. "If you were back to full power and magic we'd be forced to act—and do something drastic, like throw you into the Sholls or have Ray suck your soul out. Be thankful for once in your sorry life that you are no threat to us, especially after everything you've done."

I watched as emotion fluttered across her features, and just as quickly it was gone. "I did what I had to do," she accused. "You all had it coming."

"You don't really believe that." I squinted at her, assessing. "I think you might actually be gaining some empathy from this ordeal. I just saw a flicker of it now. Are you starting to care, Selene? I know it's hard for you to *feel* anything, but I promise you it will be a welcome addition to your former power-hungry vanity-filled world."

"I have empathy! Just not for fools who don't deserve it."

I strode up to her quickly, backing her into the wall. It was immensely satisfying to see her shrink before me. "This is how this is going to work," I said through a clenched jaw. "Listen carefully, because I'm only going to explain it once. You will help us escape with every fiber of your being, and if you cooperate, we will take you with us. When we get home you will be put under arrest and kept by the witches. You will answer for every single crime you've committed against us, and you will do your time. And there won't be a single dissent on your part. If at any moment you retaliate, from here on out, we either leave you behind or have Ray kill you. Do you understand me, Selene?" She opened her mouth and started to speak, but I shut her down. "Before you even think about answering, I'd suggest you mull it over. We're giving you something you would never allow us in return." I leaned forward until there was no more personal space left. "We are giving you a *chance*. And for that, I want you grateful. If you so much as snicker at me, I will toss your ass out the front door before you're finished speaking. The demons can tear at your flesh for an eternity, because this is it for me." I bared my teeth just to be sure she got the message. My wolf was close to the surface, snarling her warning in tandem.

Selene opened her mouth and snapped it shut it.

I stepped back and she swallowed once before answering, "Fine. I'll do what you say, but only because I want to get out of this hellhole for good and nothing more."

I narrowed my eyes and she dropped her gaze. I knew it. Something was shifting inside that broken mind of hers. I deliberately turned my back on her and walked away. "Ray," I called over my shoulder. "You're in charge of her. Make sure she doesn't do anything stupid. And if she does, throw her out the door and leave her to rot."

"Got it," he replied. He addressed Selene as I left the room. "Listen, lady, if you so much as blink at me wrong I'll feed you to the dead orthrus, so get your goddamn act together and start behaving like an adult."

"As if you could," she muttered.

I walked back into the main room. "Lili, did you get ahold of the Princess?" Lili had been on her own with Tyler the entire time we'd been in the showers.

"No," she answered. "She was not in her rooms and I could not risk trying to track her down. That would have given our location away."

I glanced over at Tyler and he nodded. "I've been thinking," I said. "You mentioned earlier that when the Prince left the Princess he'd call a meeting with his Council of High Demon Lords, right? What would be better than confronting the Prince's rule in front of an audience? If the Princess can insist on gathering a demon assembly for a public announcement, in the guise of calming the masses down, we could hijack the proceedings and announce I have no intention of ruling, and support her ascension to the crown according to the Scriptures. I think doing this publicly might be the only chance we have to end this entire ordeal."

The demoness's eyes went wide. "That would be an elaborate hoax, something I'm not sure we could pull off on such short notice. But, yes," she said hesitantly. "That may work."

"I agree," Rourke said. "If we do this publicly, in front of everyone, once and for all, that gives us the best chance." He turned to address Lili. "But we have to do it tonight. We need to meet with the Princess as soon as she can get away, but we can't meet her here."

"That's correct," Lili said. "She cannot come here."

"Maybe it's best we head back to the auditorium and camp out there. That way, when she decides to call in the demons to make her announcement, we're already located in a strategic place. I've mastered being in the right place at the right time over the last few hundred years." He glanced at me and winked.

Rourke had done that exact thing the first time we'd met, effectively throwing us all off his trail. He'd gone to the bar ahead of us and slept on the roof, sneaking down without being seen or scented.

"Is there an adequate place to take cover in the arena?" Tyler asked. "It was a fairly open space. I don't like the sound of this."

"There is one place," Lili said, drumming a fingertip against her lip. She seemed to be deep in thought. "The judges' benches are hollow below." Then she smiled like a shrew. "The space is small, but you can hide in there, and once you're in place, I will slip out and contact the Princess. I'm sure she will be eager for our plan and come at her first opportunity."

A little worry crept into the back of my mind, but I had to shake it off. We didn't have a lot of options. If we couldn't convince the Princess to call in the demons to prove to them I was no threat, there was no way we could solve this on a big scale. And we needed a big scale. "If we're going to hide essentially under everyone's nose," I said, "they're bound to scent us or feel our power the moment they arrive."

"That's not a problem. I can spell the area," Lili said. "A masking spell will make you all smell like demons."

"You can't possibly cover up all our power signatures," Tyler said. "I think being that close to the action is too risky."

"Not if the Demon Lords and the Prince come in last," Rourke said, turning to Lili. "If the Princess is on board, she can convince them to enter last. By that time the audience will already be there and it will be too late."

Lili nodded. "The Prince always makes his entrance last anyway, and I'm sure the Princess will agree. You are helping her bid for the throne sooner than expected, and I'm certain once she meets with you she will have some good ideas of her own. Confronting the Prince, and doing so in front of the demon population, I believe is the right decision. Without doing so, you will certainly be in Hell for a lot longer. If the demons stand convinced, he will have a hard time justifying his case against you, and will have no choice but to let you go."

I didn't believe it would be that easy, but it was a step in the right direction. "Okay," I said. "That's the best plan we've got. The quicker we can get settled in the auditorium, the better."

The walk to the auditorium was uneventful. We encountered no clones and no orthruses. It was almost too quiet.

"Where is everyone?" I asked as we came to a stop outside the door Lili had told us was the entrance to the bottom part of the arena. "This feels wrong. There should be some activity. The Princess couldn't have kept all the demons occupied this long."

Rourke growled. "I agree. I don't like it."

Lili's face showed her irritation. "Throw your power out. Do you sense anything? There's no one here. The Princess has kept the Prince well occupied, and you should be grateful." I sent my power out, and she was right. I didn't feel anything strange at all. "This was your plan, remember?" She stopped short of rolling her eyes. "I led you here per your request. If this doesn't work, we will have to come up with something else, but for right now this is it. I'll get you inside and go find the Princess." Lili placed her hand on the door and pushed it open.

The auditorium was quiet. My wolf growled, throwing our power out to make sure. Rourke went first, scouting. "It looks okay," he said. "How do we get under the benches?"

Lili led us in. The arena was bigger than I remembered from just a short time ago, stretching far up into the back rows. It was hard to believe it had been full of demons a few hours ago and would be again if we were lucky. "You can enter through there," Lili gestured, ushering us to an opening at one end of the benches. "This is a small space, but you should all fit."

Rourke went first, unlatching the wooden door. He stuck his head in and turned to Lili. "Once we're inside, spell the area. Selene will know if it takes."

Lili nodded. "I know exactly what I have to do. I'll take care of everything."

Selene grumbled as she made her way in after Rourke. "This is the dumbest thing I've ever done. This is worse than a Trojan horse. It's more like a rat stuck in a cupboard."

"Quit your grumbling," Ray said, following her in. "Under the radar is where we need to be. We have to get out of here in one piece, so for now we play along. If it doesn't work, we fight."

I went next; Tyler brought up the rear. He paused at the doorway. *Jess, I don't like this. It feels wrong.*

I had to admit I was getting the same vibe. My wolf had started pacing in earnest. *Like Lili said,* I told my brother, *this was our plan. Not hers. Being here feels both right and wrong at the same time. I can't explain it. It's like I'm getting a mixed message. But as far as I can see, we have no other choice but to play this out.*

I don't want to wait around and see what happens, he said. *I think we should hightail it back to our plane right now while all the demons are still occupied, and if the Prince of Hell comes looking for you, we tackle the problem then.*

Tyler, I'm exhausted and I don't want the demons on my list anymore, not while I have a chance to make an alliance with the new ruler. If we help the Princess ascend to the throne, we have a chance to leave here without looking over our shoulders. She will owe us.

He gave me a long look. *Okay. But I promise you, we're going to be fighting our way out of whatever comes next. Even if the Princess takes the throne, there's very little chance we're walking out of this without using our fists.*

That may be true, but we're in too deep to go back now. Our decision has been made, for better or worse.

He nodded once and ducked in after me. The space was no bigger than a human bathroom. I edged my way over to my mate and leaned my back against his chest. He placed his hands on my shoulders.

Lili stuck her head in the door. "I'll be back as soon as I can with the Princess. This will work out for the best, don't worry." She shut and latched it behind her, speaking a few words in Demonish.

Energy immediately bounded around in the air. For a moment I couldn't breathe.

Then I doubled over, coughing. "What was that?" I sputtered. Everyone was having the same reaction. I shook my head, trying to clear it, but it felt like I was waking up from a bad dream.

Selene was the first to speak, her voice stunned. "That was us waking up from an enchantment spell. That's not a good sign."

"What do you mean?" I asked. "What *enchantment*?"

"It means Lili had already spelled us, and now she's decided to wake us up," Selene stated grimly.

"How can you be sure?" Tyler coughed, hitting his chest with his fist.

Selene arched her eye at my brother. "She probably did it while I was out, likely right after she killed the clone, with blood on her hands. For demons, fresh blood is a potent amplifier to their power. It must have been her lucky day when I collapsed, because I'm the only one who would've noticed. The situation presented her with an opportunity, and she took it. It's very hard to detect a spell when a very powerful witch hits you with one. You can only sense it at the very beginning. There's a slight tingle and nothing more."

"No. Please tell me you're wrong," I breathed. "We can't have been spelled that entire time." My mind raced back to when Lili was holding the demon heart she'd torn out of the clone. She'd done something over that bowl, and then I'd felt a little off. *Dammit, we were so stupid! How could we not have noticed?* My wolf howled in anger, but I knew she'd been fooled too or she would have warned me.

Tyler rubbed his neck. "Man, Jess, this is bad. Much worse than I thought."

Rourke snarled, stalking to the doorway. "Only a few supernaturals in the world could pull such a trick on me. This means Lili has been lying and seeking an opportunity to change the game for a long time." His voice was low and furious. He took the door handle and depressed it.

It was locked tight.

Then I heard it. Thousands and thousands of voices. I met Ray's eyes and they echoed the same thing.

The auditorium was already full of demons.

We were indeed rats trapped in the cupboard.

22

"This is my fault," I said, joining my furious mate at the doorway. When we agreed to allow her to lead us away from the arena, even after we knew who she really was, we'd made a huge mistake, and now we were paying the price. "My wolf has been at me to tear Lili's throat out since we first met, and I've ignored her, repeatedly." My wolf huffed at me, spinning in a circle. *I know, I know. But you wanted me to tear out Selene's throat too.*

"No, this is not all on you." Rourke's voice was like steel. "I've been alive for centuries. I am one of the strongest supes on the planet. If anyone should've felt an enchantment spell, it was me. Lili duped us all. And the reason she was so successful was because we *wanted* to believe her. We needed an ally here and we chose not to scrutinize the only help we had too closely." He rattled the door and pushed into it with his shoulder. Nothing. It didn't even crack. "We have to assume all of our interactions with Lili starting from the Prince's quarters were false. One of the reasons we might not have detected the spell is it may be a very subtle one. She may have guided us in small ways only."

I ran a hand through my hair and cursed. "Selene," I asked, turning, "what does an enchantment spell do, specifically?"

"The demoness has essentially created an alternate reality and made us all believe it. We have seen only what she wanted us to see and nothing more."

"That means she probably never called the Princess, and the piece of paper that was key to making our decision was likely a blank sheet of paper."

Selene nodded. "Yes, and I agree with"—she nodded at Rourke—"him. It was a powerful spell, but a small one. Only our direct interactions with her were affected."

The voice decibel level had increased outside.

Tyler rammed his weight against one wall, and Ray took the other. It had no effect. We were sealed in. "Thinking back to everything that's happened," I said, "Lili has been guiding us on a very well-orchestrated wild-goose chase. But what's her angle?" I was so angry at myself for putting what little trust I had in Lili. She was the daughter of Lilith, for chrissake! I pressed my fingertips to my temples. "She obviously wanted the civil war to happen, so she must have something to gain. When we suggested we come back here, she'd been almost giddy. She must have needed us here, or someplace very public. Dammit! I can't believe I've been so stupid."

Rourke leaned against the door and crossed his arms, fury etched across his features. "This isn't over. Whatever her end game is, she won't win. We all lowered our guard and now we're paying the price. But she's not smarter than we are."

"Selene," I said, turning to the goddess. "Can we create a witch circle here?"

She shook her head. "Impossible. We would need all the right ingredients and the circle has to be dug into raw earth."

I glanced beneath us. The ground was covered in huge stones. It would take longer than we had to get to any soil—if there was even any under there.

The crowd outside started to chant.

"I think we're in the middle of some kind of ceremony," Tyler said, his hands running along the walls, searching for a way out. "This doesn't sound like another trial, Jess. The demons out there are calling for something specific. Maybe they're going to try and steal your power or magic?"

The door burst open behind Rourke with no warning.

Before he could react, five demon guards, these in full battle regalia, with breastplates covering their silver jumpsuits, blasted him with huge ugly-looking guns. He flew forward in a shower of sparks and crashed into the wall, falling to the ground out cold.

I knew he was alive, and that was all that mattered, but my rage was now full-blown.

Demons swarmed the doorway, forcing us all to take a step backward in the cramped space. I morphed into my Lycan form, a red film of fury cascading over my eyes. *We take them all down*, I told my wolf. She growled her agreement, snapping her jaws furiously.

Tyler and Ray sprang first, Tyler's fist meeting the side of a demon guard's face. The demon crumpled instantly. I lowered myself into a fighting stance just as I caught sight of Lili.

I rose back up to a standing position slowly.

"That's right, take it in." She laughed as her hair flowed out behind her. The guards in front of us parted so she could come forward. She was dressed in an incredibly detailed gold gown, decorated in demon glyphs that glittered as she moved. On top of her head sat a pure gold crown covered in gilded serpents. "You were so easy to manipulate." She clapped her hands in glee. "But I already knew you'd be, based on your prior actions with the Prince, and your desperate need to save your dear brother. A soft-hearted female Lycan. What an embarrassment to your forebears. The last female Lycan was tough as nails. In fact, if you must know, she was the one who sent me here." She spread her arms wide. "But enough chatter. Now it's time for me to mete out my ultimate revenge, and by doing so I finally gain the power owed to me for these many years. It's going to be a very good day."

I made a move to spring as she lifted up her palm. Her hand radiated so much power, it looked like she was holding a pure ball of energy. Then she aimed it at Tyler's heart.

"One wrong move and I will kill your entire family," she said. "Which I can do, because I'm powerful and dangerous. Just like I told you all along. If you cooperate, I might decide to let them live once I'm finished, but I haven't made up my mind yet."

"Finished with what?" I asked, my vocal cords straining, my Lycan form making it tough to be clear. "Taking my blood? Killing me? Making me your slave?"

She smiled like a shrew. "Oh, by all means I'm going to kill you. That's what the ceremony calls for. It demands piles and piles of your blood. See, I'm going to make a *clone*. Something only *I* can do. I neglected to mention that the first time, didn't I? And once I reanimate your clone, all your delicious power and magic will be mine to control. Then I will be crowned the new Queen of Hell. A title I've waited much too long for."

"Everything the Prince did to get me here and everything that has happened since my arrival was a ruse to make you *Queen*?" I asked.

"Oh, no," she answered dismissively. "The Prince acted of his own accord, but he was doing so to follow the altered Scriptures." She leaned in like we were coconspirators and whispered, "I actually uncovered the *real* Scriptures a long time ago, but I changed them to my liking, and then pretended the ones I altered were the newly uncovered ones. The Prince has believed *you* to be the real threat, not me. The true Scriptures state that if the female wolf arrives in Hell a new reign shall begin. They think you are that reign, but of course, that's not true—*I* am the new reign. You are here to ensure that I ascend to the throne, and of course, to give me your magic. It has all been fairly easy to orchestrate, but it's taken much too long. I've been waiting for this day for hundreds of years, but now it's finally here."

It was hard to battle someone who'd had plans for your demise in place for hundreds of years. Lili had been scheming for a long time to get me here. And if she'd really encountered another female wolf, like she'd told us, Lili was older than any other supernatural I'd ever known.

And I had played right into her hands.

She was a skilled actress, I'd give her that. "So to get the Prince to play along, the Scriptures you altered must state that if I come to Hell the Prince will keep his rule—or some such thing."

"It's much more delicious than that," Lili answered with obvious glee, moving methodically toward me. "They actually state that if the Prince *himself* leads you here, he will be the supreme ruler of Hell for all *eternity*. But, in order for this to work, you had to be a full Lycan. No swiping the *Daughter of Cain* before she shifted for the first time." Her mouth spread into a grin. "And believe me, I celebrated your birth like that of none other before you."

Breath left my body.

Lili had been behind the Cain Myth. She had wanted everyone

to fear me, including the Prince of Hell, and it had worked incredibly well. She'd left me vulnerable within my Pack with very little backup.

Anger filled me. She thought I was weak.

My wolf urged us to attack, her eyes as feral as I'd ever seen them. But I had to negotiate for my family first. I didn't believe for a second Lili would keep them alive once I was dead. I glanced over at Selene and met her dead stare. Her face was devoid of any emotion. This news was bigger than any war between Selene and me. If we didn't work together, we all lost. I turned back to Lili. "Spare my family and I will come willingly," I grated. "But do not, and I will fight."

"I don't care if you fight," she scoffed. "Remember, demons love to play with their food. I prefer you kicking and screaming."

"I want in," Selene interrupted as she took a step forward, "to whatever you're going to do to her. In fact, I want be part of it. This mongrel has ruined my life, robbed me of my future, and sent me to this godforsaken plane." She smirked at me. "I will take great pleasure in seeing her *suffer*."

Lili appraised Selene with a cool glance. "I don't trust you. You have too much at stake to betray her now."

Selene took another bold step forward. "I have *nothing* at stake. There is no life for me anywhere. I have no magic. I have no status. I am nothing but a shell of my former glory. The only joy left for me in this lifetime is to see her die"—she pointed a finger at me—"in the most cruel and unusual way you can dream up." She was gleeful. "Inflicting pain is what I have always loved the most. Have you not heard anything about me in all these years? All my cooperation up until now has just been a show, much like yours, and because of that I can appreciate your deception like no other. Death and destruction are what I truly crave. I always have. So where do I sign up to see the female wolf fry?"

Ray spat in disgust. "I knew there weren't any redeeming qualities left in you. You're nothing but a useless coward! A shrew, a waste, and a burden. I hope you rot in the Hell forever."

"I never claimed there was anything redeeming about me," Selene replied, unfazed. "Now"—she nodded to Lili—"how do you want me to show you I want nothing more than to see her suffer?" Selene waltzed up to me, my wolf snarling fiercely.

Well, I guess it appears you were right about Selene too. From now on, I will not second-guess you. My wolf clacked her jaws.

"How about this?" Selene reached up, cool as could be, and tried to rake her fingernails down my face.

I batted her hand away so hard she spun, smashing face-first into the wall behind me, collapsing to the ground. It was lucky my mate was still down or he would've torn her head off for the second time. "Selene," I growled. "Do not test me—"

"Fine," Lili chirped, my head snapping back to hers. "Selene, you can attend the ceremony, but one wrong twitch of your fingers and I'll *fry* you in your seat. You may not die from my assault, but I'll just kill you again. Your knowledge of witchcraft, once I become Queen of the Underworld, will be beneficial. If you aid me without error, you may find a welcome home in the Underworld after all."

Selene picked herself up off the floor and made a show of dusting herself off. "I've spent my entire life crafting unique torture spells. They are a particular favorite of mine. They are ... absolute perfection. I would gladly share them in return for a safe haven in this wretched place. There is nothing for me on the human plane."

"I'll find a place for you among my staff," Lili replied. "And with good behavior, who knows, maybe I'd let you up to the surface for a little fun and chaos once in a while." Selene's face broke into a wide grin. She hadn't looked that happy in a long time. She edged by Lili in the doorway, smiling a particularly evil smile back at me.

A perfect match made in Hell.

I placed an arm out toward my brother, halting his forward motion. *Don't attack Lili*, I told him. *Let me go, and once I'm gone, formulate the best plan you can. When Rourke wakes up he's going to be in a rage, but don't let him come after me until you make sure you have something solid that might actually free us from here.*

We can take them, Jess, Tyler insisted. *The demons aren't good fighters.*

No, if you haven't noticed, Lili has been cloaking her power the entire time. I knew she was strong, but now I sense something else. Plus, by my best guess, there are several thousand demons already out there in the audience, and the guards she has now are skilled. I nodded once to Tyler so he knew I was serious and took a step forward. "What can I do to ensure the safety of my family?" I asked Lili. "I will do anything."

"Nothing," the demoness replied in a flat tone. "Seize them all and bring them forward," she barked at her guards as she met my gaze. "If anyone resists you shall see why they call me *the Unforgiving* here in Hell."

Demons streamed in around us in the cramped space. I nodded at Ray to comply. We were going to fight, there was no question, but we would fight to our advantage.

Two demons took me by the arms, jostling me forward. "Lili, you certainly went to great lengths to make me believe that the only thing you wanted was a ticket back to my plane," I said wryly. "I think you might deserve an Oscar for that performance."

"Oh, I am going back to your plane," she gloated. "Once I am the most powerful supernatural the world has ever seen, I will have the freedom to punish those who have wronged me. I have waited for this for almost a thousand years. It will be the sweetest revenge. But I've never lied. I told you I could go back to your plane on my own, and once I'm the Queen of the Underworld, and ruler of *all* supernaturals, it will be my right to go as I choose."

We filed out of the small space into the back of the arena. I couldn't see the crowd yet because the benches were in the way.

As we rounded the corner, I pulled up short, causing the demon guards to stumble beside me.

The coliseum was packed.

Three times as many demons were in attendance as last time and this time they varied in size and shape as well. Lili had called the entire Underworld in to see her spectacular rise to unmatched supernatural power. The unglamoured ones stuck out the most, appearing decidedly reptilian, with luminous skin, scaly but smooth, and beady eyes.

The crowd quieted as it took me in for the first time.

The demon guards firmly escorted me to the front, where I'd stood before during my short trial. The demonesses' chairs had been cleared away and there was a lone chalk circle etched into the stone floor. To the right of the circle sat a table covered with paraphernalia—lots and lots of sharp-looking blades and some crude buckets, likely to gather my blood. "You've been a busy girl, Lili," I said as the demons shoved me over the chalk line and centered me inside the circle.

"I've had a millennium to plan this. When you've had that long, there's really nothing left to orchestrate. Tie her up," she commanded with a swish of her hand as she turned to address the large audience. "Behold! I have captured the female wolf! Justice will reign and a new demon order will begin!"

The crowd went wild. Cheers, growls, snarls, cackles, and thundering applause came from every inch of the coliseum.

"So where's the Prince of Hell?" I asked over the din, knowing Lili could hear me, no problem. "Surely you want your former lover to witness your crowning moment." For the first time in my entire life I hoped the Prince of Hell would make an appearance and try to stop all this. But I knew she'd taken care of him. He hadn't been busy with his Princess at all, like Lili had told us. He'd probably been captured and restrained.

Rourke? Nothing. *Tyler, can you hear me?*

Yes, Tyler replied. *The demons are taking us back to some kind of holding cell. Your mate is coming around and he's about to go apeshit crazy. And I, for one, can't wait.*

Change of plans. You have to find the Prince of Hell and get him here.

What?

The Prince of Hell is the only one who can stop this, and I know Lili's stashed him someplace. You need to find him. I can't believe I'm saying this, but we need him.

Got it. We'll get free, but I'm not sure how long it will take.

Lili turned to me as the audience excitement died down, her face flashing some emotion I couldn't name. Exhilaration? Regret? "The Prince of Hell will not be the ruler of Hell for much longer," she hissed low under her breath. "He will bow to me when this is over. Or he will die."

She stalked to the table that held all the pointy implements, while the demon guards wrestled to chain me. I put up a struggle to give everyone a good show. That's what Lili demanded, and if I was going to gain the upper hand, I needed to act like I was playing along with the program. The demon guards finally clasped me in chains, and once they were secure, a loud rumbling erupted under my feet.

The guards leaped out of the circle as it began to lower into the ground, separating cleanly from the rest of the floor. After a few feet it came to a grinding halt.

Lili paced to the lip and grinned down at me, then turned dramatically, her hands flying up in the air as she addressed her minions once again. "I give you the female Lycan! The vessel of my power! You will all stand witness to the undoing of Hell, and when I'm finished, a new reign shall begin. We will call it the Era of Splendor, a time when every demon will be free!" There was massive cheering. "No more glamour! No more separation! We will unite as the One True Underworld and all other worlds will cower under our will!"

The applause was so loud, I almost missed the sound of my mate waking.

Almost.

23

Jessica, where are you? Rourke roared in my mind. I could hear scuffling and knew he was already locked in a fight with his captors. *I'm coming for you.*

Rourke! Wait a second. There's a new plan. You have to find the Prince of Hell before you come here. Lili has him stowed somewhere and I think he may be the only one who can stop this. More grunting and scuffling. *There's no way the Prince would willingly give up his crown, and if nothing else, it will buy us some needed time.*

Got it. More fighting. *I'll be there as soon as I can.*

The applause quieted and the demoness sauntered back and forth across the floor, parading herself in front of the demons, clearly enjoying her time at center stage. She spoke in Demonish first, and then English. "The Underworld will never know such power! When I am ruler, we will control all supernatural races, and humans will cower before us!"

The crowd went wild again, and the six other demonesses, including the Princess, strolled into the arena, streaming in to stand next to Lili as one united front. They all wore the same high-collared identical black dresses as before.

This was turning into a true feminist movement. Too bad Lili's rise to power was supposed to cost me my life or I might've enjoyed it. From what I'd witnessed, Hell could use a vast improvement in leadership.

Rourke's voice shot into my consciousness again. *We'll find the Prince, but it's going to take me...a minute*, he panted. *These demons are trying to use those fucking guns on us again. They are spelled... but now*—I could hear a crunching sound—*they're all gone.*

Lili turned to face me. Her expression was cruel, with an added measure of joy. This was her crowning moment. Literally. I couldn't imagine waiting for anything for a whole year, much less a thousand of them. "Now the Lycan will suffer!" she crooned. "But rest assured, her agony will not be without purpose." She leaned in like a conspirator. "You will be doing what you were born to do," Lili announced, half to me, half to the crowd, as she paced down a few stone steps that led into the circle I was in. They must use it for their ceremonies.

There was a pungent scent of leftover blood all over.

My wolf paced in my mind, wanting to strike the moment she reached us. Power zipped along my spine. I had morphed back into my human form, but my wolf sat at the very edge, waiting not so patiently. *We don't attack until we have an opportunity to win this or she forces us to act.* The chains were spelled, but it was nothing we couldn't break. Lili either underestimated me or she was hoping for a show. *I'm sure she's guessing we'll try to escape*, I told my wolf. *She would love an opportunity to show all the demons in attendance that she is fit for the job as their new leader by striking us down. So instead of fighting back, we're going to bide our time and try to make this game turn in our favor sooner than later.*

As Lili edged closer, I responded, projecting loudly enough for the first few rows to hear, "I'm not planning on suffering for your cause, Lili, but I'm sure your faithful demons here would love to start off the ceremony by having you read the real Scriptures aloud." Then I made my voice carry dramatically. "I mean, what better way to kick off a new reign than by reading the *real* words to your adoring fans?" I nodded up to the crowd. All eyes were riveted on me and the murmurs had quieted to whispers. "Am I right? Who wants to hear the real demon prophecy? I know I do!" There was tentative clapping. "Come on, you can do better than that. Let's give it up for hearing the Scriptures!" The clapping turned into a wild round of applause.

Lili looked murderous.

Before she turned back to the crowd, she steeled herself, plastering a smile on her face. She whipped around in glorious motion, her golden dress whirling as her arms lifted once again. "I will do better than that! You have all been fooled by the Prince for far too long, and after this ceremony is complete, I will personally post the *true* Scriptures, the ones I uncovered, in our Great Square, encased in glass for all to see."

The crowd cheered and hooted at the news, satisfied for now.

She paced back up the steps, out of the circle, and reached her hand out, gesturing to one of the demonesses, who immediately moved forward and handed her an ancient-looking scroll. To my surprise, it was the Princess, and as she turned she was careful not to make eye contact with me. It made me wonder what stake she had in all of this. She couldn't be happy that Lili, her husband's lover, was nabbing her rightful spot as ruler. But what did I know? Lili's signature was stronger, so maybe the Princess had to acquiesce or die? But, honestly, losing her husband and the crown to his mistress had to suck no matter what.

The room hushed as Lili unrolled the parchment, which was covered in Demonish markings. She walked toward a stand someone had set up and hooked the roll to the top, unwinding it slowly. "For now, here they are in all their glory! The original Scriptures passed down from our forefathers for eons," she announced to massive applause. "These are yours! For every demon to read. No more hiding, no more secrets, no more inequality! The new reign starts today and begins with the truth!"

She spun around, meeting my eyes, pure satisfaction racing through them. But before she could mask it, I glimpsed a small, fleeting measure of uncertainty.

It flickered for only the briefest of seconds, but I saw it.

I grinned, my smile wide. Lili wasn't sure if she could pull this off. That was the reason for all this pomp. She needed support from every demon in this room to ascend to the throne. I quickly scanned the rows again. There were so many demons. It would be impossible to know how many were on board with her new leadership plan and how many were not. And since every single audience member was male, it was doubtful she had full support. She was counting on their superstitions and their unflinching belief in the Scriptures to make this happen.

About ten rows up I noticed a group of demons all wearing what looked to be metallic robes. They were unglamoured and their skin was iridescent, their features sharp and hawkish. *I bet those are the spell casters*, I told my wolf. *And they aren't clapping.* It was too early to know, but seeing Lili's uncertainty had bolstered me immensely.

Jessica, Rourke called in my mind. *Things out here are chaotic. It looks like Lili didn't have a plan in place for everything. Demons are running all over and all the Demon Lords are missing. We took a few of the demon janitors prisoner, but we're having a tough time convincing them to help us. They keep saying their Prince will smite them or some such crap. I have the Prince's recent scent and we're going to start searching now, but I want to know you're okay first.*

I can't stand the thought of leaving you in the middle of all this. It's going against my instincts not to come and break you out.

I'm fine at the moment. Lili's putting on quite a show, but I just discovered she has no real idea if this is going to work. But, that said, I suggest you hurry. My guess is she's going to be picking up some sharp implements next.

He growled fiercely in my mind. *Can you break out on your own if you have to?*

Yes, but I'm going to be patient as long as I can. The bottom line is, I'm not sure we can win without the Prince's help. And once we start fighting, we don't stop until we're all free. I paused for a minute. *Rourke, I'm not sure any of us is strong enough to kill Lili. I don't think she was lying when she said she couldn't die. We can try to stop her, and maybe bring her down temporarily, but I don't think we can kill her outright. She was cloaking herself before. Her signature is off the charts. I'm hoping if we act with the Prince, something can be done.*

Before my wolf could correct me and tell me how wrong I was, and that we could indeed kill her, Lili plucked several tools from the table and waved them in the air, declaring to the crowd, "It's now time to prepare for the cloning. Once I take the female wolf's power, I shall control both the Heavens and Hells!"

At once, several demons dressed in white jumpsuits wheeled out a strange-looking gurney. It appeared to be like the ones we use on our plane, except this was ornate, made of some kind of gilded material. It was empty and they parked it right in front of the cheering crowd.

To my utter astonishment the Princess walked over and gracefully lay down, clasping her hands across her abdomen and closed her eyes.

The crowd went berserk.

But on top of the excitement, I sensed some hesitation. Fear began to permeate the room. Demon fear smells like rancid eggs, on top of already rancid eggs. It was enough to make me gag. It appeared that some of the demons were clearly worried about their beloved Princess.

Lili also interpreted the change in the crowd, because immediately, in both Demonish and English, she announced, "Have no fear, my fellow demons! This is what the Scriptures intend. The new reign shall begin. With the wolf's power and magic, coupled with the Princess's heart, we will become the most powerful force in the entire universe!"

There was a smattering of applause and some cheering.

Lili nodded her head at the demons manning the gurney and they skillfully lifted the contraption, along with the unmoving Princess, to the edge of the circle and walked it down the steps. They rolled her next to me, and Lili followed, easing down the steps, starting some kind of chant.

I gazed over at the Princess, but her eyes were firmly closed. Because she was clearly cooperating, the crowd calmed down and its fear eased. Everyone was waiting to see what came next, including me.

Curious about the Princess, I pushed my power out toward her, testing. She wasn't as strong as Lili, but there was something else. Something unique that I couldn't place.

I had no idea how cloning worked. It was obviously a transfer of power, but other than that it was baffling.

My wolf snarled. *Don't worry, I'm not planning on finding out, but aren't you the least bit curious?* She flashed a picture of us tearing Lili's head completely from her body. *I guess not as much as I am, but you have to admit none of it makes sense. Maybe we were spelled and only thought the clone looked like Selene?* Before my wolf could become even more irritated with me, another gurney was wheeled out. This one had a body on it.

As it was wheeled closer, I gasped.

There was no sheet covering the unmoving form. It was lying on its back with its eyes closed.

It looked exactly like me.

"What's going on?" I asked, alarmed. "How did you get that?"

Lili laughed at my discomfort. "You gave your DNA so nicely when I asked. Your handprint was so generous, as it gave us so much good data. We just needed time to grow the shell, but we had that in spades as I ran you through the Sholls, and even better when you spent all that time in jail worrying about the fate of your brother."

Ohmygods, I said to my wolf. *All those times she asked me to help her she was collecting DNA samples.* I was nauseous. *That can't really be me.* My wolf's ears were pinned back, canines exposed, nose scenting. My lifeless clone had no smell. *That's a good sign, right?*

"The best part was that your signature was already mixed with demon essence—due to your own stupidity, which made the growth extremely easy. Usually it takes much longer to copy a non-demon, but this was a piece of cake." She clapped her hands together as the crowd cheered at her brilliance. "Now we just have to transfer your life-force into the clone, along with the Princess's heart, and I become the most powerful supernatural the world has ever seen."

Rourke, I said urgently. *We have a definite problem here. Where are you?*

Just… breaking down… a few doors. It seems the Prince is being held in… some place they keep their animals.

Lili made a clone of me.

What? I sensed his body still.

I don't quite understand. I swallowed. *But you need to get up here. Now.*

I'm on my way. I'll leave Tyler and Ray here to get the Prince. I felt him running. *Hold tight, Jessica. She's not going to get away with anything.*

We can't leave my clone alive, I whispered. My attention was riveted back to Lili as she waltzed over to me. "This will only hurt for about fifteen minutes." She smirked. "But it will hurt like the fires of Hell are raging through your body, tearing you apart and sizzling you from the inside out."

My wolf had already wrapped us in ribbons of magic, forcing it outward to create a barrier against her. I began to push the demon essence that we'd separated out past the shell, coating it all around us to make an oily bubble, which I hoped would be a direct repellent against Lili's demon magic.

I gritted my teeth as I spat, "Go ahead, Lili. I'd love to see how this is all going to turn out."

She smiled as she lifted her hands, her magic shooting forward. Only to be rebuffed.

The reverberation of the backlash forced her to take an inadvertent step backward, which caused instant chatter to erupt in the audience, especially among those closest to us, who had seen what had actually happened.

She recovered quickly, her eyes narrowing.

But instead of trying it again, she spun with a flourish. "I just tested my magic on the female wolf, and she is primed and ready. But first, we must take the heart from your beloved Princess and place it in the host body." She nodded toward two demons and they proceeded to maneuver my cloned body into the circle, so it was situated right next to the Princess, the two gurneys side-by-side. New fear emanated from the demons in the audience, and Lili responded with "Have no fear! Your Princess will rise again in this new form, as all clones do. Her heart will feed the body. She will not be lost!"

After selecting a knife from the table, Lili sauntered back into the circle and over to the Princess, who I witnessed from my proximity stiffen ever so slightly. The Princess was nervous. Something was up. *This is not going to end well*, I told my wolf as Lili positioned herself over the demoness, the wicked-looking blade clutched tightly in her hands. It was long and sharp—the kind you use to skin a hide.

Lili flourished the knife over the Princess's heart and brought it down, and as the tip of the knife entered her chest, the Princess's glamour began to drop with a loud rushing noise. She had remained perfectly still as Lili struck her with the knife, but now her body undulated beneath the blade.

Lili had no choice but to bring the blade up to give her room.

The crowd took in a collective breath. I took one in along with them. *Holy crap!* I was too stunned to move.

The Princess's hair flowed outward, longer and thicker. Her lips thinned as her skin took on a different sheen, almost opalescent. It was beautiful. She continued to undulate on the table as a demon yelled from the crowd, "The true Princess! *Swy sliy hlefpyzz!* She should be Queen!"

Lili's face turned dark, but she hid it quickly. "Yes, our beloved Princess. She is so important in our world. But there can only be one true Queen of the Underworld." Lili turned her head toward the crowd, raising the knife above the Princess, ready to pierce her once more. "Have no fear, my fellow demons, the new reign will choose the demon who is most worthy. This has always been our way. Make no mistake!"

The Princess's body was shifting in earnest now.

I tried not to gape. *What's going on?* My wolf had no answers for me. *Demons aren't shifters. Has she been glamouring her size all this time?*

There was a collective *ooooh* from the crowd as her chest definitively rose on the gurney. *Good grief! Are those wings?* The

Princess's skin turned luminescent, like beautiful see-through scales, as soft, black, feathery wings erupted out of her back, spreading over the sides of the gurney.

Wings were something Lili was sorely missing.

"The true Queen!" a demon yelled from the crowd.

"Raise her up!"

"She shall rule us all!"

Some of the comments were shouted in both Demonish and English and there were many more, one on top of the other as fast as the demons could spout them off.

"Silence!" Lili cried, turning to the unruly crowd, spreading her arms wide, blood the color of motor oil dripping off the knife blade. "Your Princess and I will rule Hell together, with both strength and power!" There was an instant hush and Lili smiled, before continuing, "She will not die as long as her heart is preserved. Only the Princess is strong enough to give this powerful clone life. It is written that a female shall rule, and with her heart and the Lycan's power, we shall together be undefeated! The supernatural world will bow to us!"

The crowd cheered their agreement, even though Lili was selling the same thing in different words.

There was no chance Lili would step down, and any demon who believed that was a fool. She would kill my doppelganger, power and all, with the Princess's heart inside, before she'd let that happen. But the crowd had bought it.

It was time to throw a wrench in Lili's plans. "Prove it!" I yelled, my voice clear and strong. "Prove to your demon constituents that the Princess will live on!"

"There is no way she can prove it," an icy voice bellowed from the top of the stairs, the anger carried across the entire arena, silencing all in attendance. "Because she has always been full of lies!"

24

The Prince strode down the long stairway, his fury palpable. It pressed down on everyone. His magic whipped forward, swift and menacing. Lili stiffened, her hand still gripping the wicked-looking knife, which now hung by her side.

I guess you found the Prince, I said wryly to Rourke when I spotted him at the back of the auditorium looking grim.

The boys broke him out of this frozen mold right after I left, and then I got lost in this fucking place. He was angry. *Your scent is everywhere and it's like a sick maze of tunnels. When I circled around for the second time, I met up with them. We couldn't get the Prince to agree to anything, but he owes us for freeing him. He wanted to run the show once we got here, so we had no real choice but to let him. When this place erupts into madness, which it will, we'll come to you on the floor.* His voice was firm and commanding.

Got it. I'm working on these spelled chains. I'm almost free.

"Step away from my bride, you piece of filth," the Prince snarled as he descended. "You will never rule Hell. You are not

241

even a full demon! The power of Hell will never choose you. You are the spawn of evil, and have been wiggling under our skin for far too long. You thought you were clever, but you were wrong."

"If you come any closer, I will kill her," Lili said in a cold tone, raising the knife above her head once again, its jagged end only a foot above the Princess's heart. Lili had only pierced the Princess's skin before, and the Princess hadn't moved or reacted since her glamour dropped, though I knew she was alive because her chest lifted with each breath she took.

Why isn't the Princess moving to defend herself? I asked my wolf. *She needs to start fighting back. Get off that gurney and slap Lili silly or do something. Why is she letting this happen?*

There was something bigger happening here that I didn't understand.

"You cannot kill the Princess of Hell," the Prince scoffed. "She is a true demon and can regenerate from any injuries you inflict."

"Possibly." Lili shrugged. "If she hadn't sworn me a promise. Spelled in blood. The very same promise that is attached to this *nfeby*." She shook the knife. "Once I pierce her heart she will be gone forever. She will not regenerate. So if you want your bride to remain alive, I suggest you stop moving."

"You speak lies!" the Prince roared as he shot his magic outward. It flowed ahead of him like a gust of hot wind, causing waves to ripple in the air. All the demons in the audience visibly cringed, and some of them ducked. "You are not stronger than I!"

Lili raised her hand in answer, and redirected his flux of power with only a few words. The energy arced around her and raced to the side, smashing into the nearest column, exploding it and sending pieces flying everywhere.

With that, the crowd jumped out of its seats, alarmed and bewildered by the sudden change in direction. Seeing their current leader opposed to Lili, even though she had told them what the Scriptures said, and their beloved Princess at risk of death, rocked the arena and sent it into chaos just as Rourke had predicted. This time the audience wasn't filled with minions who blindly followed the rules of She'ol, it was full of *all* demons, from everywhere in the Underworld. Now every demon in this room knew something had gone wrong.

Terribly wrong.

Rourke eyed the Prince, who was almost down to the floor. Tyler and Ray stood behind him. They would all follow soon.

Lili lifted her knife higher when the Prince did not slow his pace. "Say goodbye to your beloved." Lili lowered the knife, and right before she plunged it into her chest, the Princess's arm snapped out, her hand stilling Lili's wrist.

That was enough of a cue for me to intervene, and I was closer to her than the Prince.

My wolf snapped the spell on our chains and I leaped forward to aid the Princess. Lili was muttering under her breath, but just before I could reach them, she plunged the knife deeply into the Princess's heart.

I watched in horror as the demoness's body arched and she uttered one long, hollow scream. She thrashed for a moment, then went totally still.

The Prince landed at the bottom at the same time I swung my leg around, connecting with Lili's back with enough force to send her hurtling over the gurneys. She crashed onto the floor of the circle.

Pandemonium in the arena continued. Demons raced everywhere, shouting about their Princess while they tried to escape. The Prince rushed to his bride's side, picking her up and cradling her in his arms as I squared off against Lili. Demons swarmed the aisles all around us as my angry mate barreled down the stairs trying to reach me.

Lili hissed at me as we rounded on each other. "I will use your heart to revive her and I will be hailed a savior!" she declared. "Nothing is going to stop me. I will be Queen one way or another."

"Wrong," I retorted, crouching low, my claws at the ready. "I think your new plan may need a few more thousand years to marinate, because no one is going to herald you as anything other than a cheat and a liar after what they just witnessed. You just ruined every chance you may have had in Hell by killing their beloved Princess, and you've sealed your fate as a traitor. They might have bought the whole 'the Princess lives on in my clone' idea for a while if your plan had worked, but never now."

She maneuvered around me, edging around the outside of the circle, her back to the fleeing audience. The demons were making a rapid exit away from us, no one wanting to come in contact with their furious Prince. From the little I'd seen, he ruled his realm with little warmth and lots of pain. None of these demons wanted to see the inside of a mending room.

I spied something out of the corner of my eye, and then, almost like they had mystically appeared, a ring of spell caster demons dressed in shimmering robes was standing behind Lili.

"Meet my family." She grinned as she spread her arms. "Lilith was my mother, the most powerful witch on every plane, but my father was a spell caster demon. She chose very wisely. I'm ten times more powerful than even she was—or any Princess or Prince of Hell for that matter—and I was born to rule, not only the Underworld, but all supernaturals. The new reign was meant for *me*."

The spell caster demons closed their eyes, and before I could do anything a thick wave of blackness engulfed me. I dropped to my knees, my eyes sliding shut. *What's going on?* I asked my wolf. She was howling, but I couldn't see her. Whatever the spell caster demons had thrown at me was different from any other demon magic I'd taken in before. A blankness invaded every part of me, wiping out everything in its path. The spell had evaded my protective magic shield and my demon essence like they hadn't even been there.

Lili laughed as I fell. "You cannot best our power, especially since it has been tailor-made for you—"

"Sorry to interrupt the party, but you know, I do love my galas," Selene snickered, and a moment later I heard Lili gasp. As the two of them struggled, the blackness inside my head hung like a drape in front of my eyes. "And you were doing so well up until the end, Lili. I was rooting for you, I really was." Whatever Selene was doing, she must be winning, because the darkness eased slightly.

There was a loud gurgle and my eyes suddenly cleared to see Selene holding Lili by the throat on the ground.

Selene leaned in close, her eyes sparking with violence. "I don't care how strong you think you are," she snarled. "You pale in comparison to my former glory. You should've practiced your spells like a good little witch rather than depended on your false glory. I had both glory *and* power before it was stripped from me—by you!" Lili's eyes rolled back in her head. Selene had managed to spell her with the little magic she had left. "You are no goddess, so you don't get to act like one."

With Lili down, the demon spell casters seemed to snap out of their trance, but before they could transfer their attack from me to Selene, Rourke barreled into them from behind, sending most of them flying. A second later Ray landed in front of them, his fists swinging.

These demons may have been able to cast spells, but they were no fighters.

Once the spell caster demons had been all taken care of, the remnants of the spell inside me snapped completely. I was relieved to see my magic intact. It seemed the spell had been able to cloak my own magic from me. *Lili said the spell had been made especially for me. I'm fairly certain it had our signature attached*, I told my wolf. *I think it fooled our body into thinking we didn't want to access our magic.* She snarled. She'd been unable to react or grab our magic either.

I rose and took in what was happening around me. Tyler had come up from behind Rourke and was helping to eradicate the last few stray demons, making sure none came too close. There weren't too many demons left in the entire arena. The demonesses had also left. I would've thought they'd stick around, but seeing their Princess die must've been too much.

Rourke and Ray were busy tossing the out-cold spell casters behind the benches. I turned to Selene, who still had a firm hold on Lili, who was curled in a fetal position on the ground.

"How are you keeping her down?" I asked, amazed. "You have very little magic left." I strode toward them. "She should be stronger than you are, so I don't get it. Not that I'm arguing, mind you, but it doesn't make sense."

"It's true," Selene replied. "She has more strength and power than me, and I have very little magic left, but psyche spells have always been my greatest masterpiece. And they happen to take very little concentrated magic. My spell has infiltrated her mind and she believes she is dying a very horrid death. But she will eventually break—" Lili's fist shot out and connected with Selene's jaw, efficiently breaking the spell.

Selene staggered backward, her arms cartwheeling, before collapsing against the edge of the circle.

"You interfering bitch," Lili raged as she stood, her eyes wild. "You think you're very clever, don't you?" She addressed Selene. "But you're nothing! I stripped you of your power in under one day and gave it to your clone, whom I then sacrificed with pleasure. You want to know where your power and magic went? It went into me." She grinned, pointing to herself. "That's right, when I killed your clone all the residual magic gathered in the clone's heart, as it's supposed to, which I consumed as I spelled you all. After that, you only saw what I projected. You will never regain what you've lost, and it only proves you were never strong enough to keep it." Lili lifted her palm and her magic shot Selene squarely in the chest. Selene flew backward out of the circle like a sack of flour, but her progress was halted before she hit the ground by a very familiar, very welcome face.

I almost cheered out loud.

Danny held Selene in his arms like she weighed nothing. He gaped down at her, and when he tilted his head back up, surprise laced his features. "So what has happened here, then? Shall I toss her away like trash or set her down gently?" His eyebrows shot up as he glanced around the group. "Since we've just now arrived, I'm not gathering a clear understanding of what's gone on, but it looks a bit...complicated."

One pissed-off Vampire Queen stood right behind him, her arms crossed, pale hair perfectly coiffed and a perplexed expression on her delicate features.

"Complicated is a good way to describe it," I answered. "Just set her down behind you. She's not going to die." I had no idea how Tally had gotten them here, but I was ecstatic. The timing couldn't have been better.

"It figures we would appear right in the middle of complete and utter madness," Eudoxia complained. "Which I have no doubt was brought on by you." Her eyes were accusing. The Vamp Queen had never shied away from telling me she didn't like the way I did things, and she wasn't going to begin now.

I didn't have time to respond, because Lili was on me before I could turn my head.

We rolled on the ground a second before her hand dug sharply into my chest, her nails like daggers. "*Ow!* You don't get...to have my heart," I sputtered as she started to chant a spell. The pain was intense. I turned my head to shout, "She's going to—"

Rourke's fist connected with her face. It effectively cut off her words, but she hadn't loosened her grip on me. Instead, she regenerated—as fast as I've ever seen a supe heal—and we continued to roll, amid shouting.

"You're not going to win this," I raged, knocking her against the edge of the stone circle, banging her head hard. "Your interpretation of the new reign . . . was the wrong one."

Her eyes were crazed as she plunged her hand farther into my abdomen, radiating her power outward. My wolf howled and I gasped. The pain was searing—like nothing I'd ever experienced before. But no sooner had she'd done it, than her hand faltered, and she withdrew it.

My body convulsed in pain as I healed the wound as quickly as I could.

I glanced up to see a seething Vampire Queen, her own hand deep in Lili's body from behind. "Lili, it's so nice to see you again." Eudoxia's lips curled into a tight smile, pursed in concentration. "It appears I landed on this cursed plane just in the nick of time. I heard someone say something about a heart? I think yours will do nicely."

Lili squirmed, screaming, "Get off me, this is not your battle, vampire!" Lili's grip on my shoulder loosened as one of the Queen's fae spells shot forward. It traveled through Lili, and into me, tasting like crab apple.

But Lili repelled it quickly with a burst of her own concentrated power, and Eudoxia was knocked backward.

My wound had already healed, but I knew Lili would be back at it for another try. She wanted my heart and she wasn't going to stop until she got it. My jumpsuit was in tatters and I was covered in blood, but I managed to wrap one leg around Lili's torso. With my strength back, and in my full Lycan form, I whipped her over, effectively pinning her to the ground.

Rourke, Tyler, Ray, and Danny all hovered around us in a circle, waiting for a chance to take her out. But it wasn't going to be that easy. Lili was strong and determined. I slid my hand up around her neck and gritted my teeth as I gave it a tight squeeze. "I will find a way to get rid of you, Lili. Just give me a few minutes to figure out your weaknesses."

Lili began to laugh. A high-pitched chortle. Not the response I'd been hoping for. "I have no weakness! I've told you that all along. I take what I want, and I get it. This is far from over, wolf." Her hand shot to my side as she uttered a spell, and as she said the words they echoed behind her.

The spell caster demons had recovered. My mind shot to darkness in the next instant, but this time my head felt like it was going to explode. It wasn't the same spell, but it had also been keyed to my signature. There was no way to fight against it. I heard the guys shouting and running as my wolf did her best to fight against the void, but our magic wouldn't respond. My hold on Lili dropped, and she rolled me over, settling herself over me triumphantly.

There were crashing sounds all around as Lili's victorious laugh rang out into the air. "It's too late, you can't save her."

Her voice cut off abruptly as she was tossed off me. Rourke took me in his arms, his voice reedy. "Jessica, I need you to wake up. Right now." His hands fell against my hair, his lips next to my ear. "Come on. You can do this. We took those assholes down again and this time we made sure they won't wake up."

I heard him, but I couldn't respond out loud. *Rourke*, I managed internally. *I need more . . . magic. These guys have my signature . . . the spell is coded to me.*

I can barely hear you, he replied frantically. *Jessica, what's going* on? *We took them down again. Why aren't you waking up?* He leaned over me, his anxiety coursing through my veins. *What do I have to do to wake you up?*

What I needed was more raw magic, something to change my signature. *Need . . . magic.*

Power rushed in from Rourke, but power wasn't the problem when I couldn't access my own magic. *I'm giving you power!* Rourke's voice was on edge. *Why isn't it helping?*

Need . . . new magic, I told him.

What I needed was the Prince of Hell.

There were muffled shouts in the background. I grabbed Rourke's shirt, and with everything I had, I whispered, "Get the Prince of Hell."

Rourke moved with me in his arms. "He's busy trying to revive his bride. There's no way he's going to help us. We have to think of something else."

"Tell him I have a plan"—I gasped—"to save his bride."

"He heard you," Rourke growled. "But he's choosing not to respond."

Eudoxia's voice was close. "Lili, you fight the same as you always have. Nothing has changed." She was the one keeping Lili away from me.

"And you're just as weak as ever, Vampire Queen," Lili retorted. "You have chosen the wrong side yet again, which isn't really a surprise."

"No, it has always been you who has chosen unwisely," Eudoxia answered. "If one never learns from one's mistakes, one can never grow stronger. If it's not a proverb, it should be. It's been four hundred years since our paths last crossed, and it seems you are no smarter for it after all this time."

Eudoxia had likely come to the Underworld kicking and screaming, but now that she was here, I knew she would do her best to earn her blood reward. She needed my blood to ascend to godhood, something she desperately wanted. And I'd made a deal to give it to her if she helped us.

I started to convulse, my body betraying me. I couldn't see my wolf. All my magic was masked. I had nothing to fight this spell with. Rourke roared, "Get over here, demon king!"

I felt, as well as heard, the Prince's anger at his summons. "I will not kneel before the female wolf," the Prince barked. "She is no concern of mine any longer. I hope she dies, and once you're gone I will deal with Lili myself."

"Stop your damn posturing," Ray's voice shot out. "Didn't you hear her the first time? If you want your bride to rise again, I suggest you listen to her. If Jessica has a plan, it will work. And maybe if you help, and stop being a stone-cold asshole, you might be able to get the Underworld back under some semblance of control." I could almost picture Ray's face as he finished with "This place is a fucking madhouse. Too many clowns showed up to this rodeo, and if you don't act soon, it's going to all be over, and then you'll be left with absolutely nothing."

The Vampire Queen struck Lili. I knew because the darkness wavered for a moment and I snapped my eyes open. It hadn't been the spell caster demons spelling me this time, it had been Lili. She'd hit me with a spell while we'd been struggling.

My eyes landed on the face of a very angry Prince of Hell, who was hovering over me. My mate tightened his hold around my waist as the Prince accused, "This is all because of you. The Scriptures were right. It doesn't matter which ones were correct. Your birth has caused a ripple in my world—one that cannot be undone! You should die in agony for this."

I blinked a few times, forcing myself to answer. "None of this was mandated by me. Your precious Lili deceived us all. The power in the Underworld is shifting…whether you like it or not,"

I gasped. "I can feel it and I know you can too. So the question is, will the power of the Underworld go to her?" I nodded toward Lili, who was struggling with the Eudoxia. "Or your Princess?"

The Vampire Queen had almost lost her power to Valdov when she died for that brief moment—the power of the Sect chooses the most fit to rule—and right now the power of the Underworld was shifting, sensing a change, searching for the most powerful. If Lili succeeded in becoming the strongest supernatural on earth, the power would shift to her, but if I could change it and give that power to the Princess, there might be a way to stop it.

The Prince appeared taken aback and finally responded through a grim look, "I will not relinquish my crown to *anyone*, so you are wrong on both counts." Even through all of this insanity, I noticed that not one hair on the Prince's head was out of place. His glamour was impeccable.

"It's funny you still think this is your…choice," I managed as the spell pushed at me once again. Lili was occupied, but she wasn't down. I still couldn't access my magic, but at least I could see. "It's already begun and I know you can feel it. You've probably felt it all along. That's why you've been running scared—searching me out, wrongly accusing me, breaking the rules, and going against your own code. You *knew* this was coming. The power of the Underworld is leaving you. Your Scriptures were right about that. So, again, I ask you, will it go to your wife or your mistress?"

Lili snickered, and then chanted something in Demonish. My eyes slid closed again. "Those are big words coming from a defeated pawn. You're not even strong enough to break my spell—the spell I created from the very fiber of your being, strands from your very DNA. The power of the Underworld will choose me. The Princess is dead. There is no other."

Rourke snarled as the Prince of Hell roared and lunged at his former mistress. Power accumulated quickly in the room. He grabbed her by the throat and my eyes snapped opened. They began to battle, and Eudoxia was by my side in the next instant.

"If we want to get out of this alive, I need your blood," the Vamp Queen insisted, leaning over me in hushed tones. "Lili is the most powerful being on this plane right now, and she's right. The power will choose her. To defeat her, it will take all of our magic combined." Her face was as intense as I'd ever seen it.

"How do you know that?" I asked.

As the Prince battled Lili, the spell lifted a little more, but I knew it wouldn't completely disappear unless I forced it out with magic or Lili died. Magic I couldn't access.

"Because I know all about Ardat Lili. I'd hoped she was dead, because no one had heard from her for hundreds of years, but I can see we were not that lucky." She narrowed her eyes on the fighting duo.

"How do you know her?" I shook my head. "I don't understand."

Rourke still had me in his arms. "Vampire Queen, explain yourself."

"Lili is one of the *Five*." Eudoxia's words were harsh in my ears and not above a whisper. "She can only be defeated by one of the other four. But I think I may have a way around it. As a fae child I learned that there are ways to defeat the Five, but to do it you must have powers numbering five and the ability to control magic." She cocked her head at me. "And you happen to be able to do such a thing. And there just so happens to be five different supernaturals in this room. A coincidence? I think not. I have learned there are no coincidences when it comes to you." She shook her head like I tried her patience as her fangs snapped down. "If I had not been forced against my will to follow you to this wretched plane, all would've been lost. You would've surely died, and now, because

I am here, saving your sorry life, you will owe me more than just blood for this."

I tried to put the pieces of what she was saying together in my mind. "Are you telling me that Lili is part of the *Coalition*? Is that what the Five is?" If it was, that news was nothing less than completely staggering. I'd had no idea the Coalition was made up of only five supernaturals.

"Yes," the Vampire Queen hissed impatiently. "Can't you keep up? She is one of the Five, and has been for centuries. But she did something very bad to someone—quite possibly your predecessor—and was cast here as punishment. Lili has managed to escape over the years, but can only stay on our plane for a very short time before she is automatically pulled back. That is where I encountered her. As I said, I think we can defeat her here and now and finally be rid of her forever, but we must hurry."

"How?" I asked.

"Why did Fate have to play such a cruel joke on the rest of us by having you be the one we must depend upon?" she scoffed, clearly irritated I wasn't following along quickly enough.

Instead of answering, Rourke's voice sounded low in my ear. "She means by giving you magic from the five most powerful supernaturals at the same time. The strongest Sects are: shifter, vampire, demon, witch..." He glanced up at the Vamp Queen.

Her eyes shot to silver. "And fae."

25

I couldn't fight it any longer. Lili had broken free of the Prince, and her prime motive was to keep me down. The spell dragged me under once again and I couldn't respond to my mate. Rourke's and Eudoxia's hands landed on my body, both of them transferring power to help me best the spell, but it wasn't enough.

Now I knew why.

Lili was a member of the Coalition.

One of the five most powerful supernaturals in the world. She was more powerful than I was. There was no contest. I knew I wasn't alone in my confusion as I tried to process all the information. Most supes had no idea who sat on the Coalition, not to mention how many. It was clear Eudoxia had knowledge not every supernatural had. My guess was the Vamp Queen had made it her life's goal to gather as much information as she could on everything, and her cunning had paid off. The members of the Coalition were cloaked in secrecy for a reason.

My wolf snarled, but I couldn't see her. She managed to flash me a fuzzy picture of us glowing with power, eradicating the spell. *It won't be enough. This spell is attached to our DNA, just like she said. Our body thinks we don't want to access our magic.* My wolf snapped her jaws together. *There's a power order in place for a reason and the top is the Coalition. Lili is stronger. Eudoxia is right. It's going to take all of us to defeat her. I just hope there's enough time—*

"Jessica!" Rourke called, his voice frantic. "Answer me."

I couldn't respond. I hadn't even heard his question.

My wolf howled, but she was fading from me quickly. Through my haze, I heard Eudoxia bark some orders. Then her fangs entered my wrist. There was nothing I could do to stop her—and even if I'd wanted to, Fate was in control now. I said a silent prayer that the direction we were heading in would save me. I wasn't ready to die yet.

There were depressions on my chest, hands all around me.

Lili's manic laughter echoed in my ears. "Try all you want, but you won't succeed. Once she dies, I will have her power. It is written. She was the last obstacle in my path to greatness. Once she is gone I will be the One. There will be no more Five. All will answer to *me.*"

My chest arched up, my backbone close to breaking as a huge blast of magic entered me, strong and fierce. It came at me from all points of my body, and strangely, each piece had a different signature, texture, and scent.

"No, you must do it like I'm telling you," Eudoxia barked. "It has to be together, as one. And with your magic, send your power to aid her."

Once again, there was a huge pulse of magic, along with enough power to generate it all. It entered my psyche like a starburst, lighting up my mind, making my head spin like I'd just inflated a balloon the size of a Mack truck in one breath. Dizziness consumed me as the magic streamed into my body unchecked. It was enough to push the spell back a bit. I could see my wolf. My signature was changing as I absorbed more magic, and my wolf and I took it in greedily, my wolf working furiously to combine it with our own to create something brand-new and parcel it away as fast as she could. The time in our cell had paid off. I joined her and we worked in tandem.

One more blast of energy and I coughed.

The onslaught of magic was changing me. Lili's spell was no longer tailored to me, as my new magic signature was nothing like my old one. But I could still see her spell lingering and I heard chanting now in earnest. *We need to eradicate the spell completely*, I told my wolf. *We take the combined magic and launch it at the spell.* She barked her agreement. I took a breath before focusing all the magic inward in one concentrated shot.

My body jumped like it had been detonated from the inside as raw magic from five different supernaturals raced through my system at once. It destroyed the spell, smashing it to pieces.

I blinked my eyes open to see five faces peering down on me. Eudoxia, Rourke, Ray, Selene, and a very disgruntled Prince of Hell.

"Is that what you wanted, Queen of Vampires?" the Prince spat through his razor-sharp teeth. His glamour flickered for the first time, his reptilian side clamoring to be seen. "Now make good on your promise to me. Immediately!" He rose and stalked off.

I gazed up at the Vamp Queen. Her eyes were matte black and red tears had formed at the corners. She was in some kind of transition. "You made a promise to the Prince of Hell?" I croaked, trying to shake off the headiness of the combined magic buzzing through my body.

Eudoxia's eyes were on me, but they were hollow and vacant. "I did what I had to." Her voice sounded strange, both far away and close at the same time.

Rourke hauled me up. I wobbled a little but managed to keep my balance. "Are you okay?" he asked. "That wasn't a normal reaction to any spell I've ever seen."

I gripped his forearms. "The spell was made for me, out of my own signature. Without what you all just did, I think it would've choked the life out of me. Lili wasn't lying when she said she was an expert spell crafter." I glanced around the room, willing my body to cooperate.

Everyone had fanned out beside me, and we all faced Lili, who stood in the middle of the circle by herself.

Her face was inscrutable. "I don't care if you've momentarily shaken off my spell. I am confident you still cannot defeat me." Lili's voice commanded the room. She turned to address the Vamp Queen. "Eudoxia, I had not expected you to show up in the bowels of Hell, but that does not change anything. My place on the Coalition is sound, and as the last surviving daughter of Lilith, I carry her magic inside me. As I said before, I will be the *One*. Nothing can change that."

"That will only happen if you can defeat the female wolf, as you well know," the Vamp Queen stated in a bored tone beside me. "And as you can see, we have healed her completely."

Lili waved her hand in the air dismissively. "Then I will simply put her down again until it's done. There is no time frame here. This is not a battle—it's a sacrifice to ensure power. One that can continue for as long as it takes."

As they spoke, new magic zapped along my nerve endings. My wolf was working overtime to harness it—but it kept spiraling together, separating again, and then colliding. If Rourke hadn't had a sure grip on me, I wasn't sure I would still be upright. As my wolf stored the magic, she raced back and forth howling with delight, rejoicing in the strength it had given us. It seemed she'd been waiting for this and was treating it like a homecoming of sorts.

I, on the other hand, was grappling with the meaning of it all.

The Vampire Queen laughed cruelly, bringing me back to the conversation. "Dear Lili, it doesn't seem you are comprehending what I'm patiently trying to explain to you. It's not that she *is* healed, but *how* we've healed her. Or shall I say *given* freely to her, so she could heal herself. Do you grasp my meaning yet, or do I need to spell it out even further for your small mind to grasp?"

Lili's face clouded. "It doesn't matter how she is healed. She's not strong enough to defeat me." Her hands drummed her hips, her blonde hair flowing out around her.

The Vampire Queen took a bold step forward. "It seems the brilliant Ardat Lili, the Seductress of Hell, last surviving daughter of Lilith, may have some things to learn about the world even after all these years." Eudoxia clasped her petite hands, her dark-purple gown shimmering almost like it had been demon-made. "For your information, we have just given the female wolf the *power of five*. Together, as one, of our own free will. We have chosen to give this"—she cleared her throat—"*wolf* supreme power, but it wasn't really for us to decide, because it was her birthright after all, as you well know." Eudoxia glanced at me with a knowing look—except I had no idea what she was talking about, as usual. "Regardless of whether any of us like it, the female wolf is now the most powerful being in the room, not you. Do you grasp what I'm saying to you *now*?"

"That is impossible," Lili said, storming forward, her hands fisted. "You cannot just make a supernatural the *most powerful*. They are born that way, as I was!"

"Wrong," Eudoxia retorted, cackling with glee. "I only know legends of Jessica's predecessor, but I know you knew her intimately." The Vamp Queen narrowed her eyes. "The female Lycan was part of the Coalition in her time and was given a special ability, making her unique for a reason. Do you remember why that was, Lili? Or have you blocked it from your mind on purpose?"

"This one doesn't have that kind of ability or power," Lili sputtered, thrusting her head at me. "She is weak," she spit. "Her signature barely triggers notice in comparison to mine."

"No, she is young," the Vamp Queen said with a sigh, "but she has never been weak—untrained and so very, very ignorant, it's true, but it can't be helped. I have finally come to accept what Fate has set in front of us, and it's time you did too. This female wolf possesses the same abilities as her predecessor. She has not utilized them properly... up until now." The Vamp Queen held one hand up, dismissing Lili's rebuttal before she could begin, the Queen's pale skin glowing with a new power, one my blood had given her. "This wolf now has the power of five inside her, and it has made her... unparalleled." She cleared her throat again, because admitting I was powerful was still a hard pill for her to swallow. "And if you don't believe me, send your power out to her now. Her signature has changed. The female Lycan has the ability to mold magics, and she will stand as the new justifier, just as her predecessor did. It is her role to enforce the High Law and her rebirth has triggered all that has come in its wake." She opened her arms wide to indicate the predicament we were all in now. "I have tried my best to deny it, it's true, but it has done me no good, as you can plainly see. I find myself standing here next to her, enduring her foolishness, but the truth cannot be avoided any longer. The female wolf has just become more powerful than you and is now ready to take her rightful place on the Coalition."

I was so flabbergasted by the news, I turned to openly stare at the Vampire Queen with my mouth wide open. I made a small noise in the back of my throat as Rourke tightened his grip on my waist. None of us had ever guessed such a thing. The Coalition? It was shocking.

The fae must be record keepers of some kind, or if Eudoxia's aunt Alana was any indication, they must have their fair share of oracles. The wolves had no idea a female Lycan had existed before, much less sat on the Coalition. My father was only five hundred years old, and when our records were entrusted to him they'd been damaged. Now I knew why. Keeping this information from the wolves had allowed Lili to keep the upper hand. She had perpetuated the Cain Myth and had destroyed our history.

But that all stopped today.

Anger jumped out ahead of Lili and my head snapped back to her. "She will not sit on the *Coalition*. Even with the power of five she does not have the power to stay my hand. And even if she did, this is not what Fate intended for me—I am sure of it." Lili had taken the Vamp Queen's advice and her power assaulted me now, testing my signature. I rebuffed her easily, a gridlock of new magic fortifying me. "I've studied the Scriptures and it says a powerful new reign shall begin once the female Lycan arrives in the Underworld. And I've waited for centuries to take my rightful place as the *One*. I am that new reign, there is no one else."

I took a step forward and Rourke let me go reluctantly. "I have to correct you there, Lili. I don't fully understand everything yet, and I don't have any insightful knowledge about the past, but I am putting the pieces together and I do know that Fate would never allow just *One* to rule. The Coalition has been the same for thousands of years—for a reason. In order for it to work, it has to have one representative from each of the most powerful supernatural Sects. But I'm thinking you know that already, don't you?" I glanced at Eudoxia to my left and Rourke to my right. Everyone else stood behind us. Lili had been sentenced to life in Hell, and if my predecessor had put her here, there had to have been a grave reason why. I narrowed my gaze at her. "This is exactly why you were sent to the Underworld in the first place, right? You fought to become the One before...and lost, and your punishment was exile."

One look at Lili's face, and I knew I'd put the pieces together correctly. Out of the corner of my eye I spied the Prince of Hell. He stood near his bride with both his hands fisted. It was strange to know he couldn't defeat Lili, even if he wanted to. I glanced between him and his bride and something incredibly important struck me.

Lili still couldn't take control of Hell without my magic, combined with the Princess's powerful heart. Without them, the power of the Underworld would not choose her and she knew it. But, with them, there was indeed a possibility that she could become the One and wreak havoc on us all.

I couldn't let that happen. And to stop it, the first thing I needed to do was save the Princess—and I'd already figured out a way to do it when Lili had spelled me the first time. I hadn't lied to the Prince when I'd said I had a plan. Lili had told the demon audience that the Princess wouldn't die if her heart lived on in the clone's body. But the Princess didn't need her heart to bring her back—she just needed *a* heart. I sprang forward, shouting, "Ray, make sure the Princess's soul is still in her body! If it's not, find it!"

"I'm on it," Ray answered without pause.

I moved so fast I was a blur. All the magic inside me coalesced as I raced forward, tightening and strengthening, making me faster than I'd ever been. Eudoxia had been right. I had craved this, but I'd had no idea I needed it or where to get it. As I moved toward my prey, I finally felt like the supernatural I'd been born to be. My wolf howled in agreement.

As I reached Lili, the magic snapped inside me, blooming into one multicolored sheet in my mind. I pushed it outward to protect me without thought, my wolf urging me on. I took hold of

Lili by the throat, bringing her down to the ground swiftly, not even pausing to hear her words. My wolf slid into control and we both knew what had to be done.

In order for the new reign in the Underworld to begin, it had to start with Lili's death. I was a hundred percent certain. With the new magic churning inside me, I was aware like never before and I wasn't here to usher her into a new reign, I was here to make sure she died. Something my predecessor hadn't been able to do for whatever reason. The Prince of Hell hadn't sat on the Coalition for a reason, and I'd realized why as I'd watched him stare down at his bride. It wasn't because the Prince wasn't strong enough to have his own place as the demon representative.

It was because the Coalition was made up entirely of females.

Demonesses were rare and powerful for a reason. The Princess's power had been eclipsed by Lili's for the last thousand years in the Underworld, but only because Lili had been sent here by my predecessor. It was time to fix it and I was the only one who could do it. If this demon princess, the rightful heir to the throne, died, I knew everything that was supposed to happen would be lost.

In order for the Princess to become the new ruler of Hell, and take her rightful place on the Coalition, she had to gain Lili's power—not the other way around—and once she did, a new reign would truly begin, just as the demon Scriptures predicted.

This was the reason I was here. I knew it with every part of my being. My new magic pulsed with certainty.

"Sorry to put a crimp in your plans, Lili," I snarled down at her. "But your interpretation of the Scriptures was wrong. The new reign in the Underworld will happen, but only because we are all gathered here at the *same* time, and you made that happen. Your death will give the rightful heir of Hell power to rule." My fist plunged into her chest and grabbed ahold of what it needed quickly. I was careful not to let my claws shred it. Lili began muttering a spell, struggling beneath me, but my new magic kept her out like armor.

She gritted her teeth as she fought against me. "This...is not going to work," she panted. "I *will* come back. I can't die."

"I don't think so," I countered. "It's taken me entirely too long to grasp what's been going on here—what's been right in front of my face the entire time. But gaining the power of five has given me the insight already. Something like this must only happen once a millennium. A female shifter is born, a demoness rules the Underworld, the fae rise—and now it will begin again, thanks to you. The Coalition is in rebirth, isn't it?"

"You know nothing!" Lili shouted, trying to push me away, her fingernails swiping at my face. "I outlasted them all for a reason. It is I—the last one to sit on the Coalition—who will rule. It is *my* birthright, not yours!"

"Wrong." I shook my head. "You're the last, but I believe you were left here for one single reason"—my voice caught as images began to assault me out of nowhere—"you are the catalyst for the next cycle of power, and after I take your heart and give it to the Princess, it will begin—" The pictures flickered through my mind almost too fast to track.

I couldn't focus on anything but the images. I gaped as I saw Ardat Lili locked in battle with my predecessor, who had been glorious. My breath hitched as I witnessed her strength. She had efficiently cut off Lili's rise to power with cunning and skill. I had been right. Her hair had been dark like mine, her features softer, her expression harder. She'd lived in a far crueler world than I. Lili was true evil, and she had never been meant to sit on the Coalition. Pictures of Lili killing her sisters one by one flashed through my mind. Their grisly bodies were mutilated and left to rot. Another image made its way to the forefront. Lili locked in an epic battle with her mother. The images continued and I moaned, unable to hold them back.

Lilith knew she would lose the fight against her daughter. In the end, she willingly gave Lili her power, handed it over with glee, because she *knew* the Coalition would have to accept her daughter once she was gone. They had no choice; there was no witch more powerful.

But this was not what Fate had intended.

Instead Fate had been forced to shift and adapt. The road had curved once Lilith made her decision, and in order to balance the scales, and avert complete disaster, the female Lycan had been granted new skills. She had become *adaptable*. She took on the role of the Coalition's Enforcer, and when the time came, and Lili challenged them all, the female Lycan sent her to Hell.

Lili's long life in the Underworld had culminated in this very point in time.

There was no doubt about it now. The horror of what I'd just witnessed assaulted me on every level. Lili was cruel with the blackest of hearts, and I couldn't take any more. But just as I'd made my decision to end it all and rip her life-force from her body, something tried to push back, staying my hand, urging me to wait.

I fought against it, resisting.

There was no way Lili could remain alive after what I'd seen. She was too dangerous. She would bring evil to my world if she was allowed to live.

Then one final image burned itself into my brain, releasing with a snap of power.

I opened my eyes and gasped. I hadn't realized they'd been shut. I was panting and everyone was yelling. I glanced down. Lili was gone. Totally gone.

The only thing left of her was cradled in my open palm.

The last image had seared itself into my soul forever. I blinked, trying to understand what had happened. I glanced down at the pulsing mass in my hand.

That's when I realized I'd made a terrible mistake.

26

I stood, staggering to regain my balance, clutching Lili's heart carefully so I didn't harm it. I shook my head and the world slowly came back into focus, my senses opening up once again. It was clear to me now that I'd been in some kind of trance-like state, but I hadn't realized I'd been under.

Rourke and Tyler stood beside me, each of them holding an arm to steady me. I made my way to the Princess, who lay unmoving on the gurney.

Ray stood sentinel by her head, his face as serious as I'd ever seen it. "It's there," he said. "Her soul is there and it hasn't tried to leave."

"I'm not surprised," I responded as I met his questioning stare. "You're going to have to assist me with this. As of right now, I believe this is the sole reason you were created. If this doesn't work, I don't want to know what will happen."

His eyebrows rose, but he nodded gravely, taking his cue from my tone. Everyone in this place had just realized something incredible had happened. And none of us knew its true meaning.

I picked up the knife Lili had used to stab the Princess. There was no spell on it any longer, but I could feel the residue. She had indeed spelled it to kill the Princess. I stood over her listless body, and lifted it high so I could plunge it into her chest when a firm hand stayed my wrist.

"Let me do it for you," Rourke said, emotion in his voice. I knew he understood the magnitude of what had just occurred, and without hesitation he took the knife from me and drove it into the Princess's chest, drawing a clean, straight line down from her breastbone to her abdomen.

Had the Princess been awake for this, I might've passed out. But she hadn't moved and I was thankful.

The Prince of Hell stood behind my right shoulder, his mouth pursed in a straight line, hands clasped in front of him. He had to realize what was at stake, and knew his bride would surpass him in power, yet didn't try to stay my hand. He had likely come to the same conclusion I had—this was out of our hands. The power of the Underworld had to go somewhere, and if it didn't choose his bride, or she couldn't be revived, it would probably choose me.

With the power of five supernaturals inside me, I had surpassed him in power.

His Princess was the lesser of two evils.

Suddenly Tyler was next to me. He reached over and parted the demoness's chest so I could place the heart inside. My love for both my mate and my brother almost took me to my knees. I swayed but stood my ground, knowing I had to complete this task.

I brought my empty hand down and reached into the opening in her chest and clasped it around her deadened heart. "Ray, as I take this out," I ordered, "make sure her soul stays rooted. It's the only way I believe she will heal once we're done."

"Got it," he said, placing his hands alongside her temples gently. "The quicker this is over, the quicker we can get the fuck out of here. I've had enough of this place to last an entire lifetime."

"I hear you," I replied. "I want out of here just as bad." I tugged at her damaged heart, trying not to tear the tissue around it too much. It wasn't the same shape as Lili's. It was smaller and I could only feel three ventricles.

One more tug and it came out. I tossed it to the end of the gurney.

The Princess's blood was like the Prince's, thick and amber, not like Lili's, which was red. With my other hand, I slowly guided Lili's heart into the Princess's chest cavity, positioning it as best I could. When I felt like it was in the right place I glanced up and met Ray's gaze. "This is going to be the hard part. I have no idea what I'm doing, but I'm going to try to spread the magic I just received around her heart. You do whatever you have to do to get her soul to accept it, including any sweet talk you may have stored away in there."

"I don't think that will be a problem," he grunted. "This soul seems to be waiting for something."

I gathered the new magic in my mind. It was a mass of lightness mixed with dark, all the different signatures creating a kaleidoscope of energy twirling around inside me. It made me feel strange, not quite myself. My wolf yipped. *I hope that means this will get easier to handle later. My brain feels scrambled right now.* I concentrated on pulling what I thought I needed, amassing it and sending it out into the Princess's body, down through my arm.

Her body accepted it immediately, almost greedily, and as my magic spread into her chest cavity, the new heart gave a tentative beat, and then another. Once I felt her body start to heal itself, I withdrew my hand. I hoped it would be enough.

"If she does not come back, as promised to me by the Queen of Vampires," the Prince of Hell said quietly behind me, "your kin will feel my wrath. They are not stronger than I." His voice was hard, but I heard his feeling behind it. He wanted her to survive. I did too.

I glanced over my shoulder. "Not only is she coming back, but when she does, she will surpass you in strength." I stated the obvious so he couldn't manipulate the situation. "And when I'm done healing your bride, we will all leave this plane unharmed and you will publicly declare your fight with me finished. You and your Princess owe me a life debt, if not more. I will consider it paid if you agree everything between us is completely resolved. As you can see, I never wanted to rule this plane and if this doesn't prove it, nothing will."

The image Fate had burned into my mind flashed again, making me shudder.

The Prince's pupils elongated and anger radiated outward. "I owe you no such promise—"

"You shall leave this place unharmed," an unfamiliar female voice interjected. "With my blessing and thanks."

I glanced down, startled. I hadn't expected her to heal that fast.

The Princess's voice had been surprisingly refined. She had a regal stature about her even while lying flat on her back. Her long jet-black hair flowed carelessly over the gurney, her features precise, much like the Prince's, but her skin was pearlescent—not quite scaly, but not regular skin either. Depending on the angle, it shimmered, like everything else around here. She couldn't have been holding her glamour in death, so it surprised me that her real appearance seemed almost human—if you discounted the wings. I knew the Prince of Hell would look much less human if he dropped his own glamour. "You look more human than I'd thought you would without your glamour," I commented a little stupidly as she continued to stare up at me.

Power radiated out of her as she finished regenerating from her wounds. I stepped back and watched as her chest wound healed. Once it was done she reached up and pulled her dress together as neatly as she could, and sat, her wings retracting into her back seamlessly. Her pupils were definitely reptilian, however, and they expanded and contracted as she continued to adjust herself.

"Yes," she said, her English laced with a thick Demonish accent. "The Prince has mandated that everyone in the Underworld conform to the likenesses of humans, but the demonesses don't have to glamour themselves as much." She said it with some disdain, which led me to believe her new rule would likely mandate some immediate changes in the glamour department. "Female demons are born to supernaturals, bred by Demon Lords, so their gene pools are stronger by nature than those of their male demon counterparts, which are hatched from what are called 'birther demons,' whose sole job it is to populate our species. My mother was a nymph, so my appearance favors her." She swung her legs over and motioned to the Prince to come to her side. She turned and addressed him. "You have been very patient, my love," she cooed in a surprisingly nurturing tone. "This has been a long road, but you must understand my deception was necessary. Without it, Lili would have ruled in my stead. And because you stood by me, instead of siding with"—she purposefully omitted Lili's name—"the other, you will be rewarded. I could not share what Fate had intended once the new Scriptures were unveiled, or the Underworld would have been tossed into chaos, as you well know. My only concern was with our race and keeping them all safe."

The Prince's face was stony, his eyes fully reptilian. He nodded once, accepting her words, but it was going to take more than that to get him to come around. I wondered if they had Underworld therapists.

I cleared my throat and glanced at the Princess, meeting her gaze. Her irises were a beautiful mossy green. "So you knew what Lili was up to the entire time and you went along with it, having no reservations?" I asked.

"Of course," she replied, shrugging. "Ardat Lili has been conniving, but fooling no one but herself for centuries. I am Princess of this realm for a reason." Her irises lit with a snippet of light green, which must be from her nymph side. Demons didn't seem to have the same internal spark as other supernaturals. "When Lili brought me the Scriptures she had uncovered, along with a plan to overthrow the Underworld in her favor, I saw the words as they were intended—for me, not her." The Princess's power radiated outward. Surprisingly, I found it almost as heady as mine. "I spent that time planning my own ascension to the throne, undermining Lili at every turn, but making sure she believed I pandered to her. She never doubted my intent for a moment, but it was easy to fool her, as she'd always been consumed by her own ego and strength. She held more power than I did, so she never considered me a threat."

"Still, you willingly let her kill you," I pointed out. "That was incredibly risky. What if I hadn't figured out how to revive you?" It hadn't exactly been an easy conclusion for me to reach.

She shrugged as she slipped off the gurney. She stood a head shorter than I was, but she held herself with quiet determination. "I had no doubts. If my interpretation of the Scriptures had been incorrect, then death was what Fate had intended for me all along—something I could not argue against. I made my peace with it long ago."

Eudoxia strode forward and I glanced between the two women, a shared power now swirling between us. I had given the Vampire Queen my blood, and in turn she had given me her fae magic, and I had revived the Princess with it. I nodded toward Eudoxia. "Did you have any idea what was going to happen here?" I asked the Vamp Queen. "That we would end up sharing power like this?"

"No," Eudoxia admitted, her voice ringing with its regular petulance. Her skin softened as I watched, taking on a peach tone. It had lost most of its bone whiteness. She appeared... almost human. "I'd only had a chance encounter with Ardat Lili many, many years ago. In the short time we were together she hinted about her place on the Coalition, as well as the female Lycan who had sent her to Hell, and of one who would be born again. She sought information from me, and gave me just enough to make me eager to learn the truth. But I had to dig for that truth for centuries. I hired an army of spies, and even with all my resources, I never gained a clear picture." Her voice became irritated. "Not much is known about the Coalition for a reason. Its inner workings are well kept by the Guardians of our Lore, as supernaturals would clamor to get near them. As I was forced to accompany you here"—she nodded toward me—"against my will, none of this was in the forefront of my mind. How could I have known Lili was still alive? Or predicted such a thing? But once I saw her, and realized what she'd been up to, the pieces came together easily. The new regime of our time has begun, triggered by the events that have happened here today. Now we have no choice but to wait and see what comes next."

"There's something else," I said quietly. I wasn't exactly ready to divulge what I'd seen, but I had to. What I'd done now affected us all. "I was shown some images when I held Lili's heart. You're right, a new regime has begun, but it wasn't supposed to happen now"—I drew in a deep breath—"it was supposed to happen a hundred years from now." There were several utterances of surprise. Rourke growled low and Ray whistled, all of us knowing the impact of my words. I glanced at the Princess, who did not look the least bit surprised. "Did your demon Scriptures tell you something would go wrong if Lili died right now, instead of later?" I asked. "Please tell me there is a stipulation in the Scriptures for changing Fate's plan by one hundred years."

The image replayed in slow motion in my mind and I cringed.

Rourke sensed my distress and reached out to me. I slid into him for comfort, his chest bracing me and calming me instantly.

The Princess glanced at the floor. "I could not stop her. Lili had been on a tangent for years. Once you made your first shift into a wolf, and the supernatural world found out, she was adamant about luring you here. She had a special influence over… the Prince." She would not meet his eyes. "It was out of my control. I let Fate move us forward as it saw fit. If Fate hadn't willed this, then I was content to believe we would not end up here. It was as simple as that."

"I don't think that's exactly how Fate works," I said, shaking my head. "Eudoxia's aunt, who is an oracle, told me once that we had choices, and you can choose wrong. To keep things on track you have to listen to your heart. And right before I took Lili's life, a moment of doubt stayed my hand, but I deliberately chose not to listen. I actually don't think I was coherent enough—I was too upset by the images of Lili killing everyone she'd ever met—but in the end that's no excuse." I dropped my gaze to the ground. "I think…I made the wrong choice. I believe that's why Lili disappeared completely. Fate has erased her from existence. All of this was supposed to happen, but not right now, and I think it's because none of us are ready for this. I set something into motion that we may not fully recover from."

"I don't believe that," Eudoxia stated, crossing her arms. "I am ready. I have been ready for eons."

"It doesn't matter if you're personally ready," I said. "I'm talking about all supernaturals not being ready for such a huge change in leadership." I turned to meet the Vamp Queen's silver-edged stare. "The turmoil I just unleashed will be felt in every Sect. I saw it. Lili was supposed to have completed something before she died. Something major. And when I killed her, Fate was forced to shift again." I glanced around the room and met each pair of eyes. "I know you all felt it."

"I felt it," Danny admitted. "It was as if someone punched me in the stomach and took all my breath away for a solid minute."

"What was it?" the Princess asked. "What was Lili supposed to do?"

"She was supposed to birth a child." I closed my eyes for a brief moment.

"I don't understand." Rourke said. "What was so special about the child?"

I turned to my mate, my emotions rising to the forefront. "When Lilith willingly gave her power to Lili, Fate tried to intervene. I saw it happen. It was awful, and one of the vital peacekeepers of Fate was killed in the process. Lilith and her daughter were too strong. And the only way Fate could right this wrong was to set something else in motion. A soul for a soul. A child would have to be reborn to Lili, an egg implanted for the one who was lost."

"Who was this child to become?" Eudoxia demanded. "What kind of power are we talking about?"

"One of the Three Hags," I answered in a hushed tone. "To be born into the world again. The one who was killed trying to stop Lilith in order to keep Fate on the right path for all of us."

There was a collective breath taken in around the room.

Danny spoke as he started to pace. "Naomi told us that story about meeting one of the Hags in the flesh. That Hag spared her life and told her she would meet you one day. They are very powerful deities. The keepers of our knowledge, as far as I know. This is incredible news."

I shuddered, and the vision I couldn't erase clouded my eyes once more. "Yes, apparently the Hags are the gatekeepers of Fate, but they only interfere when they are forced to, according to the brief glimpses I was given. But they've been separated for too long and they are very angry with me. I felt their wrath." I flinched, thinking about the ripple effect this was going to have. "They're going to seek retribution, and when they do, we're all going to feel it."

"How can we change this?" the Princess asked, moving forward. "There must be a way to fix it."

I shook my head. "I have no idea. I only saw what they chose to show me, and the last vision I had before I took Lili's heart was carnage. Everywhere. The supernatural world had been turned upside down."

"If the three of us are part of the next Coalition," the Vamp Queen interjected, "then we should become powerful enough to change this in time. Or at least guide the path of Fate to a more desirable outcome."

I bit my lip. "I think we are part of the next Coalition, but as I said, it's not supposed to begin for another hundred years. I don't think we're strong enough yet to rule and we have no idea who the other two are who make up the Five. By killing Lili before she birthed her child, we've interfered in a way I'm not sure we can right. From what I gathered, from the brief snippets I was given, and from what little I understand, Fate has one true path.

But that path holds many intersections and side roads. You can veer from the path, as you make wrong choices, but you're not supposed to be able to alter the true path. I have no idea if I've detoured us or tampered with something critical—something that was not meant to change."

"How do you think Fate might seek its retribution?" the Princess asked.

"I have no idea," I said. "I just saw a flash of carnage. Blood, killing, death, and destruction. And anger. I felt the Hags' anger." I shook my head, glancing around the group. "I should've listened to my heart, but my mind was determined to mete out justice for all the wrongdoings Lili had perpetrated."

"Well," Ray snorted. "Death and carnage don't paint a very pretty picture—and I'm not one to know anything about Fate—but I do know I'm bonded to Jessica for a reason. It's not just you three who have to fight this, it's all of us." He motioned around him. "We're all in this together. If I'd been given the same choice as you, I would've sucked Lili's soul out in a red-hot minute, no regrets. That woman was pure evil down to her toes. But we can't look backward; the only thing to do that makes any sense is move forward."

I nodded at Ray, acknowledging him. Then I glanced around the huge arena. All the demons were long gone. Selene sat quietly on the edge of the circle, her face showing no emotion. The Prince of Hell stood stoic, arms crossed. Rourke's face was impassive, but I knew what was going on behind those beautiful green eyes. He was just as worried about this as I was. Raw emotion ran through my veins and I felt his connection, and surprisingly I felt something from the Vampire Queen.

She had taken my blood, and now it seemed we'd forged some kind of a connection between us.

But it wasn't like the others.

Instead of emotions, I felt a stark line of power running between us. I glanced at the Princess. Her body was still regenerating, but her strength had grown tenfold. My connection to her wasn't as strong as the one to Eudoxia, because we hadn't exchanged blood, but something definitely tethered the three of us together. Once we found the other two supernaturals who would join us on the Coalition, I knew we would all share power once again.

And this time it would be The Power of Five.

Finding out I was going to serve on the Coalition was both terrifying and exhilarating. I could see now that it was the role I was destined for—the very reason I'd been born. There was no use arguing against it, because I had no choice in the matter.

I was the Enforcer.

27

"What do you mean it's dead?" I asked. We had all gathered around the circle Rourke and Ray had landed in. The other witch circle, the one Eudoxia and Danny had arrived in, was also dead. "How can all the circles be inactive?"

"It means no one is manning these circles on your plane," the Princess answered patiently, an array of demon guards surrounding her.

After our discussion in the coliseum, the Prince of Hell had promptly left and had not returned—but not without threatening to end my life if he ever laid eyes on me again.

The feeling was mutual.

The Princess had left for a while but had returned with her faithful guards to escort us out of the Underworld. Rourke had insisted on taking care of my clone himself. I knew my doppelganger was only a shell with no working parts, but it was awful to think about. The Princess had assured us that in order for the clone to have been successfully reanimated with my magic and power, it first would have needed her heart, along with my blood, and a powerful spell that had died with Lili. It was a relief to know that no more clones could be made in the Underworld with Lili gone, but we still had to get rid of mine.

In the end, Tyler had insisted on accompanying Rourke, and the Princess had taken them somewhere. When they'd all returned they seemed satisfied. I didn't ask. I didn't want to know how they'd disposed of me, and I trusted them completely, so the details weren't necessary.

Now it was time for us to exit the Underworld.

None of us knew how to deal with the Hags, or the fallout, so all we could do now was head home and wait for their move. It wasn't ideal, but we weren't going to wait around in Hell any longer to figure it out.

"How can no one be manning the circle on our plane?" Danny complained. "The witches literally just sent us down here."

"Time works much differently here," the Princess responded, her voice sounding harsh as her Demonish accent mixed with the English words, making them sound clipped at the ends. "While you are here, time on your plane goes both forward and backward with no regularity. It has to do with our plane being in constant motion. But time is not the issue here. The witches are not sending power down to fuel the circle, so we must find you another way back."

We had voted to bring Selene back by a four-to-two margin. She was going to have to serve jail time for her misdeeds, which she had neither agreed to nor protested. Ray hovered near her, accepting his role as her guard without dissent. I addressed Selene directly, as she'd been a witch. "What does this mean?" I asked her. "Why aren't they manning the circle?"

"I'd assume it means something catastrophic has happened." Her voice was callous. "If what you said is true, they should be on a twenty-four-hour watch. They would be powering it at all times. So"—she smiled slyly, enjoying this—"it means they're gone. And if they can't keep the circle manned, it likely means trouble."

"Or perhaps they are temporarily without a leader and have completely fallen apart," the Vampire Queen interjected. "When Ardat Lili died we all felt something. Lili was the witch portion of the Five, and a very powerful one at that. She will have to be replaced by the next most powerful witch in line. Is there any witch in the world more powerful than Tallulah Talbot?"

"I don't know," I confessed. "If Tally is the most powerful, that means she's the next female witch in line for the Coalition. Possibly the shift in Fate triggered something and Tally had to leave quickly—or was forced to leave." I didn't know of another witch as powerful as Tally, but that didn't mean there wasn't one.

The world was a big place.

"It doesn't really matter," Eudoxia said flatly. "The witches are otherwise occupied, so it looks as though there is no one to get us off this godforsaken plane."

"There is another way. I can escort you to a portal," the Princess said. "But the location on your plane will vary each time one of you goes through. You will not be gathered in the same place upon your return, and you will likely be far from home."

"How many can travel together at one time through a portal?" Rourke asked. I knew there was no way he would go without me. His grip on my hand tightened as he awaited her response.

"Technically there is only supposed to be one traveler at a time, but we have learned that if two seem as one it will work," the Princess replied.

"What does that mean?" Ray asked. "Two seem as one?"

"It means you must be thoroughly connected while traveling," she answered.

"Connected how?" Danny interrupted. "And please don't tell me that means what I think it means."

"Your brain is dangerous territory, Danny." I chuckled. "I'm sure it's not what you're thinking, and it means something like we have to be tied together in some way."

"Yes, you must be bound together." The Princess nodded. "We have something called *torep lahy*, which means 'spelled rope,' and it's used for just this purpose. Only imps can use the portals. A full demon will be ripped apart upon entry. But with this rope the imps can go by twos."

"That doesn't exactly seem safe," Tyler said. "Being ripped apart doesn't sound appealing. How do you know we can go through without danger?"

She smiled. "These few portals were created by witches on your plane long ago. They made them for themselves with the intent to travel here. They were meant for your species, not ours. It has taken us many centuries to figure out ways for the imps to travel through them, but they are still unpredictable and dangerous for demons, and therefore banned in She'ol. Many from this era do not even know of their locations."

"Okay," I said, making the necessary decision. "Heading to a portal sounds like the only viable plan we have. If they were made by witches, they have to be okay for us. We'll pair up. Ray and Selene, Tyler and Danny, Rourke and me…" I paused when my gaze landed on the Vamp Queen.

"If you think I'm going anywhere tethered to one of you, you're sadly mistaken," Eudoxia said with a fair amount of malice. "I will go on my own." Since the intake of my blood, her ears had become a bit pointed, forcing her to change her hairstyle to cover them. It was strange to see her pale locks hanging down around her shoulders.

"Fine," I said. "You can go alone, but once we all make it back, we meet up and strategize."

"That's not happening," she retorted. "I agree we will come together...eventually, as the necessity of our position dictates, but I have pertinent business of my own to attend to once I get home. I am Queen of a Sect, in case you've forgotten."

"The witches will be our first order of business," I said pointedly, my head arched at her. "We have to figure out what happened to Tally. They did us a favor by sending us here and we owe them our help."

"I owe no one. Tallulah Talbot was simply doing her job. The witches are not my first order of *anything*," the Vamp Queen challenged me, her arms crossing. "My flock has been without my guidance for far too long. I will go to them first and oversee building a new rule. Then, when that is finished...I will have other business to attend to. There is no way you can mandate my participation in your games. If the Hags descend, you have my permission to call upon me, but otherwise I will be dealing with things in my own world and will not be forced to deal in yours."

Arguing at this point would be fruitless. The Queen's stubborn mind was made up. "I shouldn't have to remind you that our new job descriptions require us to keep peace in the supernatural world. If something major has happened to the witches, that means we must step in."

"You are ahead of yourself as usual, little wolf girl," Eudoxia snipped, leaning forward, her eyes flickering silver. "You are not the master of the supernatural universe and it's best you remember that. We have not been anointed into the Coalition yet. These things take time. There must be a ceremony, oaths given, promises made—but until then we are on our own, to do what we please. And as you've pointed out already, this was not supposed to happen for a *century*." The rest was left unsaid, because I was the one who had screwed it up and I would be the one to try to pick up the pieces. And it seemed I would be doing so without the Vampire Queen's support.

I shook my head as the vision of chaos shown to me by the Hags surfaced once again. Rourke's hand tightened possessively around me, tugging me closer as he sensed my distress.

"Eudoxia," he said. "It's no surprise to me that you would choose to let us fight this battle ourselves. We will be in touch when necessary, and we will expect you to reply in good time to a summons, if one is needed."

"Correct me if I'm wrong, but it's your job to do the fighting. You are the most feral—the animals of the supernatural world." Her eyes were as fierce as I'd ever seen them. "And it's my job to be the most cunning. And that's precisely what I will continue to do. When the time arises for the new Coalition to be called upon, I will be ready. And when I arrive, I will bring the best arsenal of information I can arm myself with. Until then, my life is my own."

"Those are lofty words, Eudoxia. My life hasn't been my own since the night I first shifted," I said. I'd been pulled in every direction imaginable since that fateful day. But if Tally needed my help, I would help her, just as she had done for me. There was no question. "We'll have to agree to disagree. For now. If there's an uprising we will see each other shortly; if not, we won't."

I was done arguing and anxious to get home. I hoped not too much time had passed in our absence. I turned my attention to the Princess, who had been standing by, waiting for us to finish this. "We're ready to go."

"I have sent a runner for the *torep lahy*," the Princess said. "When he returns we will go. The nearest portal is a long walk, so prepare yourselves."

"*That's* the bloody portal?" Danny sputtered once we'd finally arrived at our destination, which had indeed been a long hike. "It looks like a broken advertisement board." He bent over to investigate an old, weathered piece of what looked to be a billboard—from when billboards were actually made of wood and hand-painted. "Is that a clown's face?"

"It is an old billboard," I said. I could make out a clown, as well as a faint outline of a circus ringmaster and some yellow stars on another end of the panel. The boards were chunked together at a haphazard angle to the ground. This was obviously an abandoned place outside of She'ol. There was nothing but a wasteland for miles around. Once we had gotten through the creepy yellow worm-grass, we carefully made our way along a demon-made path through another enormous field, this one with brown, wilted grass, that seemed to go on forever, then there'd been nothing but rocks and dust for the rest of the journey.

Kind of like how I pictured Mars.

The Princess had doubled her guards for the journey, each of them carrying the bizarre-looking weapons that resembled bazookas. It was night, but the winged devils, and anything else that went bump in the night, stayed well away from us. I was certain the demon bazookas could vaporize anything that dared to bother us, or the demons wouldn't have ventured here with us.

"I have not heard the word 'billboard' before, but yes, I've been told this was used as an advertisement in your world," the Princess said. "It was the first portal ever into our world, and it was created from the town you refer to as New York City. The witches spelled this"—she gestured to the broken pile of wood barely resembling a billboard—"for some reason. Half of it lies here and half remains on your plane. But as I stated before, the exit location constantly changes. The portal is spelled to go where there will be no witnesses, never in the same place twice. I've been told these kinds of boards are common in your world and will not be considered suspicious. Is that correct?"

I glanced at the sign. "Technically it's correct. This is an old billboard, likely made circa the eighteen hundreds. If it pops up in rural America, it may be overlooked, but if it lands in the Arctic Circle it may drum up some questions. But the witches chose well. If it did happen to show up in an odd place, people would be curious, but it wouldn't cause alarm." Witches were crafty, and my mind raced to Tally and I hoped she was all right. I knew whatever had happened to her was tied to what I had done here, and it was hard not to feel responsible.

"So, um, exactly how does this portal thingy work?" Ray couldn't help grumbling. "We jump through a busted-up billboard and end up somewhere nobody inhabits on our plane? What if it dumps us in the middle of the ocean?"

The Princess shrugged. "I do not know. I have never used it."

"Don't worry, Ray," I said. "You can fly, remember. However, if we end up in the ocean"—I gestured between Rourke and myself—"it'll be one hell of a swim. So on that note, who wants to go first?"

"We will," Tyler volunteered. "I want to go in ahead of you. We don't know what the time frame will look like once we arrive or what may have happened while we've been gone. If I can get back home and secure the area by the time you arrive, that would be ideal."

I nodded once. "That sounds good. You and Danny go first. We'll plan to meet up at home." I turned to address the Princess. "Are you positive there's no definitive way to calculate the time change?"

She shook her head. "The time is ever-changing. It is because our planes do not relate in time, only in space."

The Princess had given me her summoning name before we'd begun our walk here, which meant I could summon her instantly to my plane if there was a dire emergency. I had sworn only to use it if absolutely necessary.

Two demon guards stepped forward. Tyler and Danny turned so they stood back to back. The demons went to work binding them with the spelled rope. The Princess uttered something harsh in Demonish, then said in English, "Make sure it is secure."

These demons appeared comfortable around her. She had chosen only those who had been loyal to her in the past. The Underworld was going to be in upheaval while the reign changed from Prince to Princess. We'd discovered that the demons who had fled the arena had ended up gathering in the square, and the Prince had gone to address them and likely calm them down. The Princess would have a battle on her hands if the Prince tried to fight her to keep his throne. But she hadn't asked for our help.

"So now what?" Danny asked. "Once we're tied up you're just going to toss us through the advertisement and it's done?"

"Nobody is going to toss us anywhere," Tyler griped, irritated by his circumstances. He was trying not to move too much while they tied him up, but it was hard for him. "We can get close enough and jump through on our own."

"I'm not sure jumping will be in the cards once they secure your ankles. We may have to push you through." I chuckled. "But I promise to do it gently."

"One more question," Danny asked. "How do we get out of this magic rope once we hit our side of things?"

"Our magic will fade quickly on your plane," the Princess replied. "It may take a moment or two, so be patient. Make sure you are clear of the portal or the magic may linger for longer. Once it fades the ropes will disintegrate."

"That sounds easy enough," Tyler grumbled. "Just so long as we don't get dumped into a volcano."

"No matter where you end up, I'm positive you'll find your way home. You have innate wolf senses," I reminded him. "Plus, the witches had to have put in some precautions. They wouldn't risk hot lava either. The main objective will be for all of us to make it back to the Safe House. I'll call there as soon as I can find a phone; you do the same. Make sure Nick or Marcy monitor the office phones at Hannon & Michaels if you make it back before us."

"Will do," Danny said, trying to give me a small salute but only managing a flick of his wrist since he was firmly tied up. "Just do us a favor and keep yourselves safe. I don't like that the witches are unresponsive. That spells nasty trouble." Danny was the head of security in the city. Trouble for the witches meant trouble for the city. "We won't know what we're getting ourselves into until we reach home, but that also means we could be plowing headlong into danger."

"Jess, Danny's right. Stay vigilant," Tyler said. "And I never had a chance to ask you what happened right after I was taken. Did Dad go after the fracture pack? The Made wolves have to be stopped or it could turn into the worst supernatural breach the world has ever seen. From what I saw they had no control, no leadership, and there is no way they can be corralled for long without it being catastrophic."

I shook my head. "No, as far as I know Dad hasn't gone after them," I answered. "But, like you, I have no idea how long we've been gone or what's happened in our absence. My trip here ended up being...a little unexpected, and I didn't have the opportunity to check in with Dad before I left." Rourke grunted at my understatement. "He was sending wolves down to do recon, I do know that." I actually hadn't let myself think about the Made wolves, because that situation was another huge complication I didn't have any no control over while I was here. "But you're right, whatever is going on with that will have to be our first priority." Pack came first. Always.

Tyler nodded. "Making contact with Dad will be the first order of business. I know the Hags will be an issue at some point, but before we help the witches we deal with the wolves."

"Agreed," I said. The sorcerers were going to be another obstacle. They weren't going to stop their pursuit. I needed them off my back. I turned to the Princess. "Do you know anything about the deal the demons struck with the sorcerers about finding me?" I asked.

"Yes and no," she answered. "I was aware of what was happening, and a deal was being brokered, but I was not consulted on the details."

"Is there any way you can offer them another deal or make them back off permanently? Or threaten them in some way? They're trying to steal my power, just like Lili was, and I need something that will scare them off the chase." The sorcerers were desperate for a way to increase their magic, and they weren't going to back off without a substantial threat.

"I owe you a life debt and I will work to see it done," she agreed. "I gave you my summoning name, but I also want to give you this. It's called a *zplexy zsafy*, which translates to 'scribe stone.'" She reached into a pocket of her long dress and drew out a perfectly round, flat stone with a metallic sheen, and placed it in the palm of my upturned hand. "If you rub this with salt while saying only my first name, it will connect us. There are several ways to use the stone, but the easiest way is to place it against what I've been told is called a telephone."

I couldn't help but throw my head back and chortle. "Are you really telling me"—I flipped the stone into the air and caught it—"I can make a phone call to Hell with this? That's the craziest thing I've ever heard. How can that possibly be true?"

She smiled. Her teeth were not human, and it reminded me she was a demon, even though she was cooperating with us. "It works as a transmitter across planes. You can put it up to anything that transmits a sound wave. It took us a very long time to perfect the technology. In the past imps used them with radios until the invention of the telephone. There are spelled metal particles inside that *zplexy zsafy* that transmit sound waves to our plane. It is not always foolproof, but it will serve in the meantime."

"Got it," I said. The demons were proving to be very technologically savvy. "I'll use it in case of an emergency."

"For the journey to your plane you must place it under your tongue or it will be lost. The stone is made up of organic demon minerals, but it needs to be inside your body."

"Um, hello, my arms are falling asleep over here," Danny interjected. "This rope seems a little on the tight side." He flexed his arms and the bindings didn't give at all. "I think it's time to get a move on."

"I'm sure the demons tied it tight so you wouldn't be lost in the vortex forever, Daniel Walker," I replied. "And I'm thinking that's a good thing."

"That may be so." He chuckled. "But if all my limbs fall off between now and then it's going to cause some egregious problems." He and Tyler were as close as they could be to the portal.

"I hear you," I said as I walked up to them. "Safe travels, boys." I kissed both of them on the cheek, Danny preening a little more than necessary. "Stay safe and we'll see you when we get home."

"Did you see that, cat?" Danny said, peering around me and waggling his eyebrows. "She gave me a kiss. It was a wet one too."

"If you weren't like a brother to her, I'd kill you right now just for enjoying it," Rourke rumbled. "But as it stands, I see that as a pity kiss. I feel sorry for you two. A couple of guinea pigs in wolf clothing. If we see flames erupt out of the portal, we know to go home a different way. And, Danny, I want to personally thank you for trying it out for us like a champ. That takes guts."

"There aren't going to be any bloody flames!" Danny retorted, turning to crane his neck back at the Princess. "Right? This is a safe way to travel. You said so yourself!"

Before she could respond, Rourke chimed in, "She also said that if you weren't the right species, you'd be ripped apart." He was clearly enjoying himself. "So I hope for the love of everything holy, you are."

"What do you mean by 'the right species'? Shifters have human DNA, just as witches do. It should be safe enough, right?"

The Princess was clearly bewildered by the banter. From what I'd seen, demons didn't have much of a sense of humor. "Just ignore them," I urged her, waving my hand. "So, I just shove them forward? No need to say anything special?"

"They just need to go in," she said.

"Okay, boys, this is it," I said as I shoved. "See you on the other side."

As they fell forward Danny screamed, "Please be kind to me, portal gods! I love each and every one of my parts!"

28

Eudoxia went next. She flung herself through without looking back. It was agreed that Rourke and I would go next, followed by Ray and Selene. The demons were in the process of tying us all up at the same time. Rourke and I faced each other, Ray and Selene were back to back.

Rourke's hands slid tightly around my lower back, edging me closer. "Make sure you tie it extremely tight," he growled to the demons. "I want every body part firmly connected." His eyes shone as he gazed down on me. "There's no room for error."

I could sense his unease. It fluttered through me like butterfly wings stuck in my veins. My hands tightened around his broad neck, my fingertips pressing against his skin. "Don't worry, we're going to be fine. I just really hope we don't end up out to sea. That would really suck."

"This portal doesn't look like it's been used in a hundred years or more," he murmured quietly. "We're taking a big chance doing this and I don't like taking unknown risks."

"If I thought the Princess was leading us astray, I'd agree with you. But like it or not this is all we've got. No witches on our plane means no circles. It's either this or stay, and I'm not a fan of sticking around in hopes the witches come back. The tides could turn easily if we stayed."

"I'd like to think there'd be a few more options if we searched harder, but I agree, we don't have time to figure them out." His voice held frustration. My man was not used to being at anyone's beck and call. Being with me was a decidedly different life for him, and in the scope of things, he was continuing to handle it like a champ. "I just want us back on our plane, our feet firmly planted on the soil. This is the first and last trip we're ever making to the Underworld."

"I agree with you a thousand percent," I said. "Hell is not becoming our next vacation spot."

"Are you both ready?" the Princess gently interrupted. "We can move you through now."

"Yes," I said, craning my neck to the side. "Ray, make sure you touch base with me as soon as you can. If Selene gives you any trouble, feel free to rip whatever soul she has left from her body. She's going to atone for her misdeeds once we get home."

"I'm not an idiot," Selene countered. This was the first time she'd spoken since the long walk here. "I have nothing left, so why bother fighting the inevitable? The witches can roast me at the stake, and I hope they try. If I die, it will be far better than whatever life I'm going back to without my magic."

"Selene," I said. "You should be thankful you're even coming back. Fate is involved and you should count your blessings. If you hadn't lost everything, we would've left you here to rot. You might want to try and act a little grateful." Naomi was going to have something to say about my allowing her archnemesis to come home. I had a lot of explaining to do.

To make the news easier to swallow, I planned to put Naomi in charge of Selene's punishment, at the very least.

" 'Grateful' is not a word I have in my vocabulary," Selene snipped. "Everything I've gotten in life I've fought tooth and nail for. I've *earned* it. There were no handouts, nothing to be grateful for."

"Maybe that's where you got it wrong," Ray interrupted. "You should've been less of an asshole and more of a nurturer. Maybe then you'd have some people who actually cared if you lived or died—people who'd fight for you, people you could depend on."

"*Nurturer?*" Her voice was nothing short of aghast, and I bit my tongue trying not to laugh. "I've never needed anyone to fight for me. I can do that myself. I will make it my life's goal to regain my former status—or I will die trying."

"You're already dead, lady," Ray snorted. "Remember? And if that doesn't make you change your tune, nothing will. Your stubborn soul is hanging on by a single thread. The demons couldn't kill you because they couldn't take your soul, but I can. It may do you well to remember that."

Selene's mouth snapped shut.

Having a vampire reaper as her guard was the best stroke of luck ever. Well, it was either luck or Fate, and at this point I was betting on Fate. It was hard to know how each and every piece of the crazy puzzle fit together. But I knew that bringing Selene back was the right choice. For now. And having Ray here had been no coincidence.

"Okay," the Princess chimed in, this time with exhaustion in her voice. We were all tired. "We are ready. You must go now. It's been many minutes since your brother left."

I inclined my head at her. "One last thing." I held the summoning stone out to her, my hand stuck between the ropes. The Princess picked it up and placed it under my tongue, nodding her head at me, her pupils expanding.

"I owe you much," she said, acknowledging everything that had gone on between us. "Have a safe journey. I will do my best here with the sorcerers and launch my imp spies. I will be in contact."

"Thank you. If I need you, I know where to find you," I replied. "We'll be ready to go on three."

Rourke counted down as two demons placed their hands on our shoulders, glancing at their Princess for her okay. "One, two...three!" he yelled as they pushed us with enough force to send us flying into the billboard.

Once we were through, the free fall was immediate.

It was much colder than the witch's circle and we began to twist and spin quickly. "Hold on!" Rourke yelled.

Doing my best, I said internally, keeping my mouth closed tightly, which wasn't a problem since the force made it difficult to do much else.

As we twirled through the vortex it began to get hotter and hotter.

"*Jesus!*" Rourke roared, his voice echoing in space.

We were spinning so fast I couldn't get my bearings. The air around us started to shift and move, hurricane-like winds tore at our bodies and clothes. The ropes held, but just barely. I couldn't see or hear anything except my howling wolf.

After a few more minutes, just when I thought I couldn't take it anymore, we slammed into the ground with surprising force, hitting so hard we broke apart, each of us tumbling in different directions.

Once I stopped I couldn't move for a full minute.

"Holy *shit*." I coughed. I moved my body and cried out. The pain was intense. "I have so many bones broken," I moaned. "This is going to take a while." I gritted my teeth as my body began to mend itself. As the bones popped and knitted back together, I forced my mind to think about something nice, like getting my hands on my man again.

"Christ," Rourke muttered from a few feet away. "That was the worst way to travel ever."

Once the pain had ebbed somewhat, after what felt like an hour but was likely only about three minutes, I finally raised my head up.

I was totally naked.

The portal had literally stripped us of everything, including our clothing. My scalp tingled as new hair began to grow back. I hadn't lost it all, but there were definite patches missing. I reached an arm up to feel my head, assessing the damage. Sand trickled down on my face. "Hey," I said, spitting the tiny grains out of my mouth as I realized where we'd landed. "I think we're on a beach, which isn't the worst place we could've been sent."

"I don't care if we landed in the middle of a five-star resort. We're never doing that again." Rourke eased his massive frame up. I knew he hurt as much as I did, but he hadn't complained once. He was behind a screen of scrubby brush and I couldn't get a good look at him. He was healing faster than me because he was older, but I wasn't too far behind. "Are you okay?" he asked as he stood. "All your pieces back together?"

"Working on it," I said, trying not to groan as I leaned my head back and closed my eyes. Another cascade of pain rippled through me as more bones set and the gashes healed. Hard shells and rocks poked me from underneath and the ocean roared not too far away. "I think we're behind a dune or something," I mumbled. "I don't scent any humans."

He rose and walked out from behind the brush—I opened my eyes and he took my breath away, effectively making me forget any pain I was in. He was so perfectly made, with his incredibly defined abs, broad shoulders, those muscles that made a delicious vee toward his very ample...parts. His body glowed with energy. The heat from the portal, coupled with the quick healing, had covered him in a sheen of sweat. It didn't even matter that half his body was covered in sand.

The man was magnificent.

"We are indeed at the beach." He grinned down on me. "It's almost dusk and the ocean is right over that hill." His head inclined to the right. "I don't hear or scent anyone either, but you're proving to be quite a distraction right here. I don't think I need to investigate anything else." His eyes flashed with intensity as he knelt down beside me. "Are you still in pain?" His hand lightly caressed my forearm. "Your body looks well on its way to being healed."

I angled an arm up to caress his chest. "I'm not in pain any longer," I replied. "Everything is finally right with the world."

He growled as he scooped me up.

His lips met mine, our tongues intertwined instantly, and our kiss deepened as he lifted me like I weighed nothing. I moaned in pleasure. Without stopping, or looking back, Rourke walked us over the dune and straight into the ocean.

My hands tugged at his hair as the cool water lapped deliciously around our naked bodies, rinsing us clean in a single instant. There were no big waves, only beautifully calm turquoise waters. "You know," I teased, breaking our kiss, "we could've landed in the middle of the desert. Possibly during a migration of wildebeests. Or maybe in a den of hungry hyenas. But instead we landed on a deserted island. This was a very lucky break." I didn't bother to dwell on the fact that nothing in my life thus far had been lucky.

Except for meeting Rourke.

Fate had played its part in us coming together, but I also knew how very lucky I'd been that it'd happened when it did. Or at all. Our paths could've been separated for much longer, but now, looking at him and feeling his closeness, I couldn't imagine finding my way through this life alone.

"Luck may have had something to do with it." He grinned. "Or Fate has finally decided to give us a five-minute break. But I plan on showing you exactly how *lucky* we are right this minute." He readjusted me in his arms. I gripped his shoulders as he slid me down his chest. I wrapped my legs tightly around his waist as his hands kneaded my backside.

My mouth connected with his, my tongue seeking his as he positioned me over his hardness. He wasted no time, both of us already frenzied, as he guided himself into me in one motion. I was more than ready, my head falling backward as he filled me, a cry of pleasure on my lips.

We both needed this so badly.

As my body arched in ecstasy, his mouth latched on to me, sucking hard. I could feel his need, which matched my own. We'd been apart too long. I rocked forward and backward, building a rhythm, the cool water lapping against us, earning a moan from him. "Jessica," he whispered, his hands running up to my shoulders and back down. "I can't be apart from you this long again."

"I know," I replied. His hands found their way to my hips and he gripped me firmly, rocking us together hard. "But if you keep that up, it's going to end quicker than I'd like." I wrapped my hands around his neck and smiled into his lips, resting my forehead against his as my eyes slid shut. "You feel so good."

"There's a lot more where this came from." He slowed to a more languorous rate, which made my toes curl. "You realize we can't think about getting off this island until morning. Once it's full dark, it will be impossible." He growled into my lips, his possession making me shudder with pleasure. "So I'm going to make this night as enjoyable as I can." He punctuated that statement with a firm thrust.

I answered by covering his mouth with mine and taking him deep, my body responding in kind. I rocked against him, my abs flexing against his with each thrust. I moaned.

"Let go, Jessica," Rourke whispered, his hands gripping me tightly, increasing the rhythm, pounding against me, each thrust more delicious than the last.

I threw my head back as I did exactly that, ceasing to care about anything in the entire universe.

Except for him.

I squinted into the morning sunlight. We were curled up under a palm tree, one of my arms casually draped over Rourke's torso. I yawned, turning to nuzzle my face into his neck.

"Um, excuse me, ma'am." A polite voice interrupted the silence. "I'm sorry to bother you, but we're about to set this beach up for a wedding. You may want to head back to the main island before more...people arrive. There should be a ferryboat coming in about fifteen minutes. There's a nude beach on the main island, on the north side."

"*I'm sorry, what?*" I shot straight up, shielding my delicate parts with my arms as best I could. I was so surprised by the sudden appearance of what looked to be a very nice waiter, the question had come out much louder and harsher than I'd intended.

The poor worker, who could not have been more than twenty-one, took a surprised step backward at the alarm in my voice. He was dressed all in white, his uniform crisp and formal. "Um...I was telling you about...the ferry..."

Good grief, we *had* landed in a five-star resort.

Rourke opened a lazy eye next to me, a full grin playing on his lips. He had known this guy was coming up on us and I socked him in the arm for not warning me sooner. He chuckled as he rose to a sitting position. I leaned behind him to further conceal my nudity as he addressed our poor shaken waiter. "Glad you found us. We got a little tipsy last night…after the last ferry ride… and seem to have gotten lost. We decided it was safer to stay here instead of trying to find our way back."

"It's no problem at all, sir," the waiter answered gravely. "I have some linen on my cart and you can use it…to cover up." He gulped as Rourke flexed his arms to brush the sand off. "I think the tablecloths will be big enough to conceal most of you. But you both should head out before the others start coming. I…" he stammered, "I…don't want you to be…"

I nodded, trying to swallow and not choke on my tongue from laughter. "It's no problem, really," I managed. "We'd be grateful for the linens, and then we'll be on our way lickety-split. If you could be so kind as to direct us back to the docks, since we got turned around last night, that would help immensely."

As he scurried away, Rourke let out a bellow of laughter in a delicious deep bass and I slapped him on the shoulder, giggling myself. "That wasn't funny! I think we scarred that poor boy for life."

"I'm sure he's seen worse, especially if there's a nude beach on the main island." He chuckled. "I heard the boats this morning, so I knew we weren't alone. It was only a matter of time."

"Good grief," I muttered. "Why didn't you wake me up?" I scooted back to the base of the palm tree, pulling my knees up tight and wrapping my arms around my legs, making sure everything was covered. At the last minute, I piled some sand around my bottom.

"Because you hadn't slept in days," he replied, arching an eye over his shoulder at me. "The only time your body can truly shut down is when you're with me. Your wolf knows I will protect you.

And don't sit there and tell me you didn't need it, because that's bullshit. You slept like the dead, snoring with your mouth open, and I enjoyed every minute of it."

I couldn't argue. Just that little bit of sleep had invigorated me. Not to mention all the other relaxing releases I'd had during the night. I actually felt great. "Grab the summoning stone. It's by your foot. And I don't snore." After we'd finished in the ocean, I'd realized the stone had popped out of my mouth upon impact. We'd found it a few yards from where we'd landed. It gave off a wave of otherworldliness, so it hadn't been hard to find.

Rourke palmed the rock right as a throat was politely cleared beside us. "Um," the waiter said, approaching slowly. "Here you go." He held out two nicely folded tablecloths. "If you exit the beach by my cart, just over the rise you'll hit a path to the ferry dock. It's about two hundred yards through the vegetation on the other side. The ferry should be there once you arrive."

I took one of the proffered linens from his outstretched hands and Rourke took the other. "Thank you so much," I replied. "We'll head out right away. And we're so sorry to have bothered you."

"Really," the waiter said, "it's not a problem. You aren't... even the first I've seen here. Overnights... do happen."

Rourke shot me a pointed look as he stood, wrapping the cloth around his waist and tying the ends.

I shook the cloth out before I stood, rising behind it. Then I fashioned it into a toga, looping the ends in a bulky mess over my shoulder. Thank goodness it was thin enough to tie. Once I was done, I shook out my hair and readjusted myself, smoothing the front, trying to find some grace in this awkward situation. "Again," I said as I stepped forward. "We truly appreciate the help... and the linen."

I glanced up to find the waiter's eyes fastened on me, his mouth slightly ajar.

Rourke scowled, coming up behind me, wrapping one arm around my waist as he nudged me forward. "We've got it from here. Thanks."

Almost like a spell had been broken, the boy shook his head. "Um, yeah, no problem."

As we started to walk away, Rourke whispered in my ear, "One more look at you like that and he was going to find himself taking an impromptu swim in the ocean. Facedown."

"Don't forget, you let that very same boy see me with all my bits and pieces hanging out, so you can't possibly be angry with him now." We found the small path by the cart and followed it.

"The kid wasn't looking at any of your parts, he was looking into your eyes." There was more possessiveness in his voice than I'd expected, especially over a human waiter. "I watched him fall in love with you in that very instant."

"Shut up." I laughed. "You can't fall in love in one glance."

"Wanna bet?"

29

The ferry was nothing more than a very expensive speedboat meant for shuttling guests to and from the main island, which was located less than three miles away. The captain had merely raised an eyebrow as we'd boarded and said nothing.

Explaining to the front desk that we had somehow misplaced our room key and "couldn't remember" our villa number took more energy than I had once we arrived. I left it to Rourke and went to find a courtesy phone.

Ignoring the passing looks from the other hotel guests, I folded myself into one of the nearby couches in the lobby, pressing the phone against my ear as I dialed. "Marcy?" I asked as soon as the collect call was accepted. "Is that you?" I was so relieved to hear her voice I almost wept.

"Who else would it be?" She had answered with her usual sarcasm, and I wanted to kiss her on the lips.

"I guess I didn't expect you to be at work," I replied lamely.

"Why wouldn't I be at work?" she said. "It's nine o'clock on a Wednesday morning, of course I'm here." Because Marcy was in such a good mood, and she was acting like it was just another normal day, she clearly had no idea what was going on with the witches. Before I could answer, she added, "Are you calling me direct from the Underworld? Or is this caller ID correct and you're actually calling from a place called Rum Cay?"

We were in fact on the tiny Bahamian island of Rum Cay. The island name had been scrawled on the outside of the resort, which had been helpful. I'd been relieved we weren't farther out of the United States. "We are in the Bahamas, but how we got here is a long story and there are far more pressing things we need to discuss at the moment."

"Like the fact you're alive," she snarked. "When you went through that circle unexpectedly, that man of yours nearly decapitated us all with one swipe of his meaty paw. It was touch and go there for three solid minutes. I hope he found you, or there's one pissed-off cat roaming around in Hell right now killing things."

"He's with me." I glanced over to see both receptionists batting their eyelashes at him. It was hard to look away from his bare chest, so I could hardly blame them, and because only I knew what lay underneath the tablecloth, I let it go. I planted my eyes firmly on the table beside me. Whatever yarn he'd spun, we'd be lucky if they bought it. There was no need for jealousy, even though my wolf was emitting a low, continuous growl. "Marcy, I'm going to need you to wire money to this resort pronto. You're also going to have to call the front desk back on behalf of your 'clients' and bitch and moan about the service, and blame their lack of check-in records on some kind of computer glitch."

"Got it," she answered. I heard her scratching notes on paper. "How are you getting off said island with no passports or ID? Need me to book you a private plane?"

"Can you do that?" I'd never needed a private anything before.

"Of course. If you throw enough money at anything no one asks any questions. But the funds will have to come out of Pack moneys, since you are currently stone-cold broke."

"Fine," I grumbled. "Get in touch with Nick, then. He has access to the Safe House and he'll give you the bank numbers you need."

"Um." She hesitated. "I can't really do that right now."

I sat up straighter, detecting the cadence in her voice shift. "Why not?"

"He's sort of gone…along with the rest of your Pack."

"Marcy," I said, wrapping my fingers around the edge of the table, trying not to break anything. "Gone where? What's going on?"

"You've been gone kind of a long time," she said. "Things have been…happening."

"How long?"

"Ninety-six days."

Ninety-six days. Shit. "Where are they?"

"The last I heard from James, a day ago, they were circling a nonexistent town not found on any map, deep in the Everglades. It seems the horrible man-eating wolf predators were hurting humans or something. They're trying to contain the damage before everyone is found out. All hands on deck."

"Why are you still at home?" I couldn't believe she'd willingly leave her new man's side. A mated pair didn't go very far without each other, especially when danger was involved, and now I knew firsthand why.

"He made me swear an oath, that big, fat hunk of a potbellied weasel." Then she swore, which was highly unusual for Marcy. "And I promised I'd stay home—that is—until you got home. And you can bet I'm counting Rum Cay as home. So now I'm free to find him and you better believe I'm going to."

"Erm, there's something else you need to know before you go," I said quietly, cupping my hand over the receiver as a couple walked by, the woman eying my getup with interest. "Have you been in contact with Tally since I left?"

I heard her slump back in her chair. "No, those witch asshats threw me out of the Coven after you left. They said they needed more time to decide whether or not I was 'qualified' to join them, even after I'd done everything they'd asked—and I'd done it perfectly, I might add. So I stomped out and haven't been back since. I'm still pissed. Why?"

"Something's going on. I think Tally may have . . . disappeared."

"What do you mean, disappeared?" I heard her sit up, her stack of pencils clattering. "I would know if my old battle-ax of an aunt had left the country. She would've found a way to tell me, even though I wouldn't have taken her calls. She could've sent an owl. Or a honey badger with a note attached to his collar. That would be more her style."

"When we tried to come back from the Underworld the circle was dead. We were forced to take a portal back, which is why I'm sitting here wrapped in a tablecloth on a small Bahamian island. Tyler and Danny came through before us, but I haven't tried the Safe House phone yet. They may have gotten stuck in a worse locale than we did—"

There was a jumble of muffled noises as Marcy covered the phone with her hand and spoke with someone else.

"Who are you talking to?" I asked. "Is that Naomi?"

More rustling, and then Marcy came back on the line. "Yes, that vamp has turned out to be one very talented investigator. Someone had to do your job while you were on vacation, so I added her to the payroll. I just sent her to the Coven to check it out. There's been no gossip about the witches deserting at all. *Damn.* If they're gone, the entire supernatural community should know about it. If you're right, and they've split, quiet spells huge trouble."

"Let's not get too worried yet. Jumping to conclusions won't help us." Marcy had no idea what had gone on in the Underworld and I didn't have the time or desire to worry her about the Coalition, Hags, or anything else right now. "It might be nothing at all."

"Nothing, my cherry-red lipstick," she quipped. "If that circle was dead it means she's gone. Or something dreadful has happened. Leave it to those wenches to not contact me. I'm her only living, breathing relative—and, oh my goodness, Maggie! Listen, Jess, I'll take care of things on your end; expect a plane out in less than twelve hours from whatever landing strip is closest to you. And I'll call the front desk as soon as I hang up, but I need to get on this. I'll contact you as soon as I can."

"Sounds good," I said. "And, Marcy?"

"Yeah?"

"It's great to hear your voice."

"Of course it is, because it's getting your rump out of Rum Cay."

Dad, can you hear me?

Nothing.

Tyler, are you back yet?

Nothing.

I slammed my fist into the pillow in frustration. It broke on impact and feathers burst into the air like I'd blown the top off a dandelion. "Dammit." I tossed it on the floor.

"I take it no luck again?" Rourke asked as he tied the complimentary bathrobe around his waist. It barely closed, but it was a big step up from a tablecloth.

We were in the fanciest villa they had, but it had taken Marcy an hour to convince them they'd somehow lost our reservation. I had no idea if she'd used magic, but I didn't care.

"No, no luck. I wish they'd answer."

"We need to be patient," he said. "Tyler is probably back, but too far away for your communication to work. Your dad may be fighting, and we know that takes up brainpower. Not to mention your habit of blocking him."

"I just hate not knowing." Marcy hadn't called us back since we'd arrived in the room, and it'd been four restless hours. We'd known when the money transfer had gone through, however, because once it showed up, the staff had bent over backward for us. They'd even brought an assortment of clothes to our room from the resort boutique when we'd loosely explained that our luggage had been somehow stolen.

Rourke had looked delicious in the white linen pants, but he refused to wear them, preferring the robe. I had on new capris and a navy blue T-shirt. It was the best combat outfit they had, seeing as I couldn't fight in a sundress.

Rourke strode over and opened the double doors to our massive balcony, which jutted right over clear sapphire water. "I want you to try to enjoy the last few hours left of any real downtime we've ever had. If I had my way, you'd be sleeping right now. Well"— he paused to glance back at me with a grin—"after some nice, relaxing one-on-one time." His voice had turned throaty and it sent chills racing up my spine. "And a long soak in that double Jacuzzi."

I rubbed my arms. "That does sound like heaven. I guess there's no harm in considering this a honeymoon of sorts—"

There was a whooshing noise and half a beat later Naomi landed cleanly on the balcony in front of the open door, her familiar voice chiming in, "*Ma Reine*, I am glad to see you. I hope I am not interrupting anything." She stood with her hands crossed demurely in front of her, like she hadn't just flown over the ocean to find me.

"Naomi!" I cried as I jumped out of bed and ran to hug her. Rourke scowled as I raced by, but I knew he was as relieved as I was to see her. "Of course you're not interrupting anything. It's good to see you again." I pulled her into my arms.

She hugged me back tentatively, clearly not used to physical affection. "Marcy sent me here as soon as I returned from the Coven," she said. "I've brought you your things." She slipped off a small backpack and handed it to me. "Along with some other incidentals Marcy thought you might need. There is no airstrip here, so you are booked out on the five a.m. ferry. It will take you to a bigger island, where a plane will be waiting."

I set the backpack on the ground and unzipped it, my eyebrow rising as I immediately spotted a scrap of material no bigger than a hanky sitting on top. I drew it out on my index finger to reveal a pink, lacy thong. Naomi blushed. "She felt...you might need, and these are her words, 'to put some sexy back in your life after being forced to wear those awful fatigues.'" A pink thong was indeed better than witch fatigues, and most definitely better than a demon jumpsuit.

"That sounds like Marcy," I said, tossing it back in. The bag also contained all our identification, which Marcy would've taken from the Coven when she left. A new outfit for me—my usual spandex—and a set of new toothbrushes. I zipped it back up and led Naomi by the hand to a cute table and chairs with an umbrella on the balcony. "Is the sun hurting you?" I asked.

"*Non*," she said. "In fact, it feels wonderful." Her skin was a nice rosy pink and didn't seem to be blistering too much.

"Okay," I said, once we were situated at the table. "Fill me in. Let's start with the Coven. What did you find out?"

"The manor was empty when I arrived," she said. "I could not get very close, as the exterior was still spelled and warded, but I detected no sound or movement inside for the time I was there."

"Damn," I said, rubbing the back of my neck absentmindedly. "What did Marcy say when you returned to the office?"

"She was on the phone most of the time trying to track down her aunt and small cousin. Once she was finished, she had me gather some supplies and sent me here."

"What about my father and my Pack?" I asked. "When did they leave for Florida?"

"They left a little less than three weeks ago. I was not included in any of the planning or events, so I have very few details to share. Marcy has been in touch with her mate throughout, but I do not know their exact location." She leaned in. "I do not think Marcy knows either. He has kept it secret for fear she would break her promise and follow him there."

I nodded. James would've had to be crafty, knowing full well Marcy would follow if she could find a way to shimmy out of her end of the deal. James knew the Made wolves would kill her instantly if given a chance, and he wouldn't take that lightly. "Is the plane she booked ready to take us anywhere we wish?"

"I believe so, though Marcy said they would have to log a flight plan ahead of time, so she said, 'Tell her to keep her pink undies on while they figure it out.'" I nodded. Marcy knew we'd plan to follow my father, and she'd likely told the pilot we would be going somewhere in south Florida when she booked him.

"I'm going to need you to do some more investigating for me, Naomi. Marcy said you had a knack for it, and I believe it. It's actually the perfect job for you." She smiled and that made me happy. "The Made wolves and the fracture pack are someplace in the Everglades. It's a huge area to cover, but I want you to try and find them. Start with the smallest city and go from there.

The towns you're going to be looking for won't be on any regular maps, they'll be more like homesteads. Search for lights and stay well out of the way, and don't touch ground if you don't have to. If you don't have any luck, go to the nearest populace and try to inquire about any rumored voodoo in the area. There is an abundant amount of Haitian voodoo in Florida. The locals will know what you're talking about, and if they give you blank stares, move to the next town. Once you have any information, or detect any supernatural activity, I want you to turn around and come back. Don't go in alone. Meet us at the plane tomorrow regardless of what you find and we'll go the rest of the way together."

Her eyes sparked with adventure. "I will see it done. I hadn't thought I would enjoy what humans call private investigating, but I am finding it quite adequate. Since I am a tracker by nature, this is, how do you say, right up my alley?"

I tossed my head back and laughed. "I'd say you're finding it more than adequate, and I'm happy Marcy was smart enough to give you the job."

Naomi stood. "I will leave now. The ferry ride tomorrow should take you approximately forty-five minutes. Once you are on the larger island, there will be a taxi waiting to take you to the landing strip. I will see you there, *Ma Reine*. Stay safe."

I stood and grabbed her wrist before she could take off. "Wait, there's one more thing I need to share with you before you go."

"What is it?" she asked.

"I had to make a very tough decision while I was in the Underworld. You need to know Selene is alive and she and Ray are on her way back to this plane together."

Naomi let out a small gasp. "I don't understand. Why would you allow her to come back into our world?"

"There are so many things I have to share with you." I gripped both her wrists. "And I understand you've put trust in me time and time again, and I'm asking you to do it again now. If I thought Selene could harm us, I would not have brought her back. I swear that to you. She's lost all her magic and is essentially dead. The demons stole almost everything from her. Except for one piece. For some unknown reason her soul won't leave her body. She's a walking shell of what she used to be, and because of that she needed to return with us."

Naomi's face was inscrutable. We hadn't known each other for that long and it was hard to know what she was thinking.

She remained quiet as Rourke moved forward and added, "Listen, I know how you feel. Hearing that has to be a blow. I wanted her dead just like you. No more chances. I actually voted not to bring her back here, but Jessica is right, the demons tried and they couldn't kill her. Something else is going on here and we're going to have to wait and see how it all plays out whether we like it or not."

"Naomi," I said. "I'm putting you in charge of her incarceration. It will be up to you how long she needs to serve her time and what her punishment will be. We can talk about it later, but just because she's coming back to this plane doesn't mean she's absolved of her crimes. She will pay for them, however, and for however long you deem fit."

"I understand what you're both saying," Naomi finally answered, her voice quiet. "I appreciate it, but it will take some time for me to adjust to this news. I'm certain I will come to see your viewpoints, but I'm finding it hard for my mind to grasp giving her a chance"—she shuddered—"for she has made my life so miserable for so many centuries."

I reached out and embraced Naomi again, and she let me. "I know," I whispered. "And I'm so sorry. The only answer I have is that I felt compelled to bring her back with us. She has a role to play yet. This road we're on is going to be full of twists and turns, and some of them are going to be extremely hard—but I promise you, if she misbehaves, she will die. You have my oath." I held Naomi at arm's length and looked in her eyes. "Ray is likely the only supernatural in the universe who can truly end her life, which I find ironic since his life could've ended in her cave. And if it hadn't been for you, we wouldn't be here right now, because Ray would've died. There is something bigger than us at work here, and I believe bringing her back to this plane is the right choice for now. We will have to do our best and be patient as we see how this unfolds."

As we separated, Naomi nodded. "Okay, I understand," she said. "I can handle this. Thank you for preparing me. I will see you tomorrow morning and I will hopefully have news to share."

"Travel safe," I said. "And remember, I don't want you to take any unnecessary risks."

"I won't. I will see you soon, *Ma Reine*." She paced to the edge of the balcony and shot up into the sky. She went so fast, there was no worry that a human would see. If anything, they'd think it was a passing bird. And once they did a double take, she would be long gone.

Rourke came over and slid his arm around my waist. I leaned my head against his shoulder. "Do you think she's going to be okay with all this?" I asked him.

"Jess, she's a supernatural," he said, kissing the top of my head. "She's not a human. The things she's seen in her lifetime would shatter most. She's a fighter and that's one of the main reasons why I like her."

"I'm glad you like her, because I do too," I replied. "She has the ability to turn on the badass when she needs it. And I actually can't wait to see how Selene deals with that. Naomi will have her justice yet, and my guess is she just might enjoy it."

30

Jess! Are you on this plane yet?

I shot straight up in bed, panting. *Tyler? Is that you?* I brought both my hands to my head and pressed, glancing at the clock next to my bedside. It was 3:47 a.m.

Yes, it's me, he said impatiently. *Where are you?*

In the Bahamas, if you can believe it.

The Bahamas? We just landed about five minutes ago. How can you already be settled?

Rourke had risen beside me immediately. "Who is it? Is it your dad?" he asked.

I shook my head. "No, my brother. Apparently they just landed."

I addressed Tyler. *I have no idea why we arrived before you. The Underworld is freaky like that. Do you have your location yet?*

Danny thinks we're somewhere on Shenandoah Mountain. But he only thinks that because one time he met a Virginia girl and she had the same flower smell in her hair. But we're definitely in a forest

314

of some kind. Very remote. We're going to shift and run. I don't smell people yet, but as soon as we do, we will figure it out.

If Tyler couldn't scent any people they were very remote. *Just keep running and head south. We're on our way to the Everglades in the morning. You were right. Things have blown up with the Made wolves in our absence. The entire Pack is circling the Everglades trying to take them down. I haven't been able to get ahold of Dad, but that's not unusual for me. Have you tried?*

No, I dialed you up first. Once I'm in my wolf form I should be able to contact him.

Sounds good, I said. *Keep me informed.*

Will do. Any word about the Hags or the witches?

"Where are they?" Rourke asked as he slid from the bed.

"Possibly in Virginia. I told them to meet us in Florida." I slipped out of bed and donned a robe. *No,* I answered Tyler. *The witches are indeed gone, but we don't know where to yet. The entire Coven is empty. But Marcy—*

The phone rang by my bedside, jarring me out of my conversation.

What is it? Tyler asked, sensing the shift in my thoughts. *Is something wrong?*

It's just the phone, but I have to go. I'll let you know where the plane lands tomorrow and we'll rendezvous before we head in. I want us to have strength in numbers.

I'll be in touch. He clicked off.

The phone rang twice more and I eased away from it. Something strange was coming off it.

"I'm not sure you should answer that," Rourke said, meeting my gaze from across the room.

"I'm not planning on it," I responded.

It stopped ringing.

I walked around the bed and by the time I rounded the end it rang again.

We both turned to stare at it. "That phone is giving off a serious magic signature," Rourke said as he approached it slowly, moving me out of the way. "It doesn't feel like anything I've ever encountered before, and I've come in contact with almost every species of supernatural on the planet." The moment he got close enough to answer the phone, it abruptly shut off. He glanced up at me, his eyes alight. "We are leaving here *now*."

I wasn't going to argue.

Scrambling to the other end of the room, I snatched up the backpack Naomi had brought and raced toward the bathroom. I yanked on the outfit Marcy had packed, sans the underwear in favor of the cotton pair I'd just bought. Rourke was on the phone with the front desk in the other room.

"I don't care how much it's going to cost me," he yelled. "Yes, a fishing boat is just fine. We want to leave immediately. Yes, we'll be there in four minutes." He hung up right as I exited the bathroom. I finished tying my hair up in a ponytail and stood facing him. Thankfully I'd had a chance to shower and shave.

"They're going to charter us a fishing boat," he said. "The marina is on the other side of the island a little farther than the ferry dock."

"I'm all set," I said.

He made a frustrated noise as he slid into the white linen pants and the button-up shirt. "These clothes are a joke. I won't be able to move in them."

I walked up to him and adjusted his collar. "I think you look hot. You can pull off white linen extremely well. It makes you look island sexy." I bit my lip, trying not to smile. The man looked unbelievable, but he had a point. The idea of trying to fight rabid wolves in white linen was enough to make me crack up. "Don't worry." I patted his chest. "Once we're on the mainland, we'll find you some appropriate fighting gear."

Before I could move away he pulled me close, his delicious stubble rubbing the side of my cheek as he murmured, "This was the best mini-vacation I've ever had in my entire life. I hope this can last us until the next time we get another moment to breathe."

"I hope so too," I said, threading my arms around his neck. "Sleep...and fulfilling recreation has made me feel like a brand-new woman."

"Jessica," he said, meeting my gaze. "We haven't really had a chance to talk about anything that happened in the Underworld, but before we race out of here I need to know you're really okay. You seem the same, except you have a hell of a lot more magic. I saw the transfer happen with my own eyes, and I can feel it inside you now, but I keep thinking your signature is going to change, or morph, or ignite. Instead you've essentially stayed the same. I'm not going to pretend to understand it, and I'm fine with it as long as you're okay."

The power of five had settled in and become a part of me with little fuss, like the demon essence before it. It was dormant at the moment, but I knew I could call on it when I needed it. Either all at once, or independently. But I had no real explanation of what was going on inside me, or why my body worked the way it did. "Honestly, I think my special gift just happens to be adapting magic. It's as simple and as complicated as that. Tyler can run faster than any other supe, James can heal faster, Nick can use persuasion, and my body just happens to take in the magic of other supernaturals."

"Seeing you work the new magic on Lili was an amazing thing to witness," he said, leaning down to kiss me lightly on the lips, and then he deepened the connection, his lips firm and full against mine. I opened up to him as naturally as taking a breath.

The phone rang, shrill in our quiet room, and we sprang apart. Rourke met my eyes as he gently tugged me out of the room.

We arrived at the big island an hour earlier than scheduled. The fishing boat had delivered us in less than forty-five minutes, and it was still only 5:04 a.m. There had been no taxi waiting, but the nice fisherman had driven us to the airstrip, where we now stood talking to our sleepy pilot. "The closest available place to land on the west coast of Florida is in the town of Everglades," he said. "It's all national park down there. Lots of swampland and little else."

"That's fine," I told him. "We don't have a better location at the moment. We're waiting for a friend to show up. Chart a course for Everglades and we'll go from there."

He left. The pilot had asked us zero questions and didn't seem upset we had woken him early. Marcy had been right: if you had enough money no one questioned you. I didn't want to know what this was costing the Pack, but from now on I would get used to spending Pack money. That's what it was there for. And I was Pack.

"Do you see her anywhere?" I asked Rourke for the second time that morning, craning my neck up to the sky as we walked toward the parking lot to wait.

"No," he replied. "And I don't have to remind you we'd only see her if she wanted us to see her. But we're early, so don't start worrying just yet."

"Worry is my middle name. And before you start complaining, I like my humanness. It keeps me grounded in this crazy super-natural world. Worrying feels normal and useful. I care about Naomi and if something happened to her it would be my fault. Thus I worry." My wolf yipped. *I know you don't agree, but I'm not asking you.*

Rourke stopped abruptly and turned me toward him. "Jessica, I love your humanness." He pulled me in and I rested my forehead against his clean white shirt. He placed a hand on my shoulders and his warmth felt good.

"I'm glad you do," I mumbled. "It would be hard if you hated it."

"Before I met you any scrap of humanness I'd ever possessed was almost gone." His chest rumbled as he spoke. "You brought it back, and because of it, it's made me start rethinking things."

"Maybe that's why Fate bound us together?" I lifted my head and glanced up at him. "You're clearly the best supernatural on the planet to teach me how to become an Enforcer, and I'm the best supernatural to keep you human."

He stepped back slightly, his hands sliding down to my waist. "I swear to you that I'll make you into the greatest supernatural fighter the world has ever seen."

"I'm so lucky—"

There was a noise in the trees to our right. I broke away from Rourke immediately, expecting Naomi. But knew I was wrong the moment his scent hit me. "Ray?" I called, moving forward. He stepped out of the trees looking clean, showered, and ready to go. "What are you doing here?" I couldn't mask the confusion in my voice.

"Um, I guess you could say I'm reporting for duty?" he answered musingly. "Why the hell else would I be here?"

I glanced around him into the woods. "Where's Selene?"

"We landed right in our own backyard about six hours ago, in the middle of a fucking lake," Ray groused. "We were about a mile from the Safe House. I took Selene there first. She was beat up from the trip and wasn't healing. No one was there. So I took her to your office. Marcy was just leaving, and let me tell you, that secretary of yours is a spark plug"—tell me something

I didn't know—"and she had a solution in about seven seconds. We took Selene to the local shaman house and they agreed to heal her for a fee, and then deliver her to the nymphs for safe-keeping. I guess nymphs are only second in heavy artillery to the witches or some such thing? Anyway, Marcy had a contact there and made all the arrangements. We'll pick Selene up once we get back." I started to interject and Ray held up his hand. "Just a minute. Before the interrogation starts, I have one more thing to tell you." He strode toward us right as a horn tooted in the distance, from what sounded suspiciously like a golf cart. "In order for her to help us, Marcy made me promise—"

"To bring her with you," I finished. "I know, I figured that out the moment you mentioned you saw her." I turned as a little white golf cart darted into view, containing a spunky and slightly disheveled redhead.

She flung out of the cart before it came to a full stop. "You didn't honestly think I'd miss this party for anything in the whole wide world, did you?" She smiled like a shrew as she made her way toward us. "But I can promise you, my hand to the goddesses above"—she struck her chest with her right hand—"I'm never flying Vamp Airline again. That was the most hideous experience I've had in a long time. I'm still picking the bugs out of my teeth." She mocked spitting on the ground.

I laughed as I walked to meet her halfway. "Well, once Naomi arrives," I said, "the gang is mostly all here. It only makes sense you'd tag along. The boys are heading down from Virginia last I heard." I embraced her. "The plan is to meet up in Florida. Any word on your aunt?" I asked as I stepped back.

She shook her head. "I haven't been able to find out much, which is irritating my nails to the quick. I called all the European Covens. It took a long time to find someone who would actually talk to me. Some chick in Romania told me there's some sort of magic disruption in Italy and there's been a convergence of supernatural activity there in the last week, and everyone seems worried."

"Italy?" I commented. "That's where the Mediterranean Pack is headquartered." Julian de Rossi was the Pack Alpha of the biggest European Pack, located in Florence, and was my father's ally.

Marcy shrugged. "That's all I have. But as much as I love my aunt and my little cousin-niece, I'm going to make sure my mate is alive and well first. Once that is done, we can figure out the next Big Bad. My aunt is powerful and fights dirty. She'll be okay until we can get to her."

"Agreed." I nodded. "Pack comes first, everything else is second."

I'd fill her in on what had happened in the Underworld during the flight. I also needed to pick her brain for everything she knew about the Coalition. The witches kept better records than we did—in fact, it seemed everyone kept better records than the wolves did, but that was about to change if I had anything to do with it.

The pilot exited a small building next to the runway and walked toward the plane. I turned to Rourke. "Do you want to let him know we've added a few flyers to the list?"

"Sure," he said. "I'll be right back."

"No need," Marcy chirped before he turned. "They already know five of us will be on the flight. There was no way you were leaving here without me. And if Vamp Airline had failed, your little plane there would've been delayed by an hour or two until I could've made it conventionally, as I have the final payment right here." She reached into the pocket of her cherry-red jeans and said, "*Voilà*" as she brandished a card in the air. It was black.

"Is that the Pack credit card?" I asked.

"Yep." She smirked. "My man is crafty. I got in touch with him after we talked and he told me where his was. He also told me where they were in Florida."

"That makes things easier," I said.

"But we can't get to their exact location by plane."

"Okay, how do we get there?"

"We need to fly into Florida City, and then we have to rent one of those swampy hovercraft boat things. The boys are somewhere smack in the middle of the godforsaken Everglades."

"What she says is correct," Naomi called as she walked out of the trees. None of us had heard her land, but that was likely because she had landed farther away and walked in. Humans were now showing up for work, pulling into the parking lot in front of us. "It took much searching, but I have located them. You were right, *Ma Reine*, the fracture wolves are not in a town but are in the middle of the swamp. Your Pack lies just outside their boundaries, but they have been forced to wait before they can strike."

"Why do they have to wait?" I asked.

She shook her head. "I'm not entirely certain, but I did over-hear some of the wolves talking when I hovered over for a brief moment. The news did not seem especially good."

"What did you hear?" Rourke's voice held a command.

"It seems the Voodoo Priestess has taken some of your Pack as prisoners." She cleared her voice with a small cough before she continued. "And your father was discussing giving himself over in exchange for their release."

Of course he would. He was their Alpha. He was much more powerful than any of his wolves and had less chance of dying. The situation must be dire if he felt he needed to make an exchange.

"That's not the news I wanted to hear," I said. "Let's hope we can get to him before he decides to go through with it. It's time to move out. I need to contact my brother and hopefully he can make a connection with our father to let him know we're on the way."

The plane's engines started and we headed toward it. The stairs were down. I turned toward Marcy. "We told the pilot Everglades, but you said Florida City."

"It's all taken care of." She waved her hand. "The moment Ray and I landed here I called them and they changed it." She patted her back pocket and I saw her cell phone sticking out.

We boarded the plane.

It was small but nicely appointed. All the seats were leather and I could smell the coffee brewing. I took a recliner next to Rourke, facing Ray and Marcy. Naomi scooted in behind us. I could've sent her and Ray to the Pack ahead of time, but the flight was only going to be an hour or two at the most and we needed the time to come up with our next plan. Plus, the wolves were not familiar with the vamps, so it was better to wait.

Tyler, I called in my mind. *Can you hear me?*

Yes, he answered. He was running and I could sense his short breaths through our connection. He had to be tired. It was going to be a long run.

Were you able to get in contact with Dad?

Not really, he answered. *I've been trying for the last hour, but the connection is too fuzzy. I think it's because you and I swapped blood. I think whatever causes you to block him is starting to affect me. Maybe it's a built-in protection thing?*

I don't know why it happens—

Marcy's cell phone rang, interrupting our conversation.

She'd set it on the small tray table between us, along with the black credit card and some other things she'd brought.

Marcy's eyes shot to mine, mild panic filling them. "That phone is not ringing for me."

"Do you know who it is?" I asked, effectively cutting off communication with my brother. I knew without a doubt that whoever was calling Marcy's phone was the same caller who had tried our hotel room.

"Well," she answered, "I know whoever is calling is not human, that's for sure. The magic coming off that phone"—she pointed to it with a shaky index finger—"is off-the-charts crazy."

It kept ringing and we all stared at it, none of us daring to reach for it.

It stopped suddenly and I commented, "I don't know who would be trying—"

A message began to flash across the screen.

Rourke leaned over.

"What the hell does it say?" Ray asked.

When Rourke frowned, Marcy plucked it up using only her fingernails. She turned it toward herself first and her eyebrows shot to her forehead as she read the message. Then she slowly turned the phone around so I could see it.

The screen was flashing the words *PICK THIS UP, CHICA! PICK THIS UP, CHICA! PICK THIS UP, CHICA!*

The message scrolled across the screen like ticker tape.

There was only one person in the entire universe who called me Chica.

I snatched the phone out of Marcy's grasp, punching it on, and put it to my ear. "Juanita?"

"Oh, Chica, I'm so glad you finally picked up! I was getting worried you would keep ignoring me." Her voice sounded exactly the same as it always had, even though I knew now there was no way Juanita could possibly be human. The magic signature coming through the phone, now that we'd made a connection, was crazy intense. It was so powerful it prickled at my face as I held the phone to my ear. "You are in a dire emergency. I had no other choice but to contact you. I am breaking all the rules, but I will gladly pay the price to help you."

"The price for what, Juanita?" I asked, trying to keep the worry out of my voice. "I don't understand. What's going on?"

"Your life es in danger, Chica. That's what's goin' on."

Acknowledgments

I want to thank, as always, all my readers and fans. You inspire me every single day. To my awesome husband, Bill, you light up my life and everything in it. To Paige, Nat, and Jane, you continue to grow into amazing human beings. I am so proud. To my parents, Daryl and Koppy, your support is unparalleled and I appreciate it more than you will ever know. To all my writerchicks. You know who you are and I love you all.

extras

orbit

meet the author

Paige Carlson

A Minnesota girl born and bred, Amanda began writing in earnest after her second child was born. She's addicted to playing Scrabble, tropical beaches, and IKEA. She lives in Minneapolis with her husband and three kids.

Find out more about Amanda
at www.amandacarlson.com
or on Twitter at @AmandaCCarlson.

introducing

If you enjoyed
RED BLOODED
look out for

THE HOUSE OF THE RISING SUN

Crescent City: Book 1

by Kristen Painter

Augustine lives the perfect life in the Haven city of New Orleans. He rarely works a real job, spends most of his nights with different human women, and resides in a spectacular Garden District mansion paid for by retired movie star Olivia Goodwin, who has come to think of him as an adopted son, providing him room and board and whatever else he needs.

But when Augustine returns home to find Olivia's been attacked by vampires, he knows his idyllic life has come to an end. It's time for revenge—and to take up the mantle of the city's Guardian.

Prologue

New Orleans, Louisiana, 2040

Why can't we take the streetcar?" Walking home from church at night was always a little scary for Augustine, especially when they had to go past the cemetery.

"You know why," Mama answered. "Because we don't have money for things like that. Not that your shiftless father would help out. Why I expect anything from that lying, manipulative piece of…" She grunted softly and shook her head.

Augustine had never met his father, but from what Mama had told him, which wasn't much, his father didn't seem like a very nice man. Just once, though, Augustine would like to meet him to see what he looked like. Augustine figured he must look like his father, because he sure didn't look like Mama. Maybe if they met, he'd also ask his father why he never came around. Why he didn't want to be part of their family. Why Mama cried so much.

With a soft sigh, he held Mama's hand a little tighter, moving closer to her side. Unlike him, Mama only had five fingers on each hand, not six. She didn't have gray skin or horns like him, either. She didn't like his horns much. She kept them filed down so his hair hid the stumps. He jammed his free hand into his jacket pocket, the move jogging him to the side a little.

"Be careful, Augustine. You're going to make me trip."

"Sorry, Mama." The sidewalks were all torn up from the tree roots poking through them. The moon shone through those big trees with their twisty branches and clumps of moss, and cast shadows that looked like creatures reaching toward them. He shivered, almost tripping over one of the roots.

She jerked his arm. "Pay attention."

"Yes, Mama." But paying attention was what had scared him in the first place. He tried shutting his eyes, picking his feet up higher to avoid the roots.

Next thing he knew, his foot caught one of those roots and he was on his hands and knees, the skin on his palms burning from where he'd scraped them raw on the rough sidewalk. His knee throbbed with the same pain, but he wouldn't cry, because he was almost nine and he was a big boy. Old enough to know that he must also control the powers inside him that wanted to come out whenever he felt angry or hurt or excited.

"Oh, Augustine! You ripped your good pants." Mama grabbed his hand and tugged him to his feet.

"I'm sorry about my pants." He stood very still, trying not to cause any more trouble. Mama got so angry, so fast. "My knee hurts."

With a sigh, Mama crouched down, pulled a tissue from her purse, spit on it, and began to dab at the blood. "It will be okay. It's just a little scrape. And you heal . . . quickly."

The dabbing hurt worse, but he kept quiet, biting at his cheek. He looked at his hands, opening his twelve fingers wide. Already the scrapes there were fading. It was because of his fae blood, which he wasn't supposed to talk about. He dropped his hands and stared at the tall cemetery wall next to them. On the other side of that wall were a lot of dead people. In New Orleans, no one could be buried underground because of the water table. He'd learned that in school.

The wind shook the tree above their heads, making the shadows crawl toward them. He inched closer to her and pointed at the cemetery. "Do you think there's ghosts in there, Mama?"

She stood, ignoring his pointing to brush dirt off his jacket. "Don't be silly. You know ghosts aren't real."

extras

The cemetery gates creaked. She turned, then suddenly put him behind her. Around the side of her dress, Augustine could see a big shape almost on them, smell something sour and sweaty, and hear heavy breathing. Mama reached for Augustine, jerking them both back as the man grabbed for her.

The man missed, but Mama's heart was going *thump, thump, thump.* That was another fae thing Augustine wasn't supposed to talk about, being able to hear extra-quiet sounds like people's hearts beating.

"C'mere, now," the man growled. Even in the darkness, Augustine's sharp fae eyes could see the man's teeth were icky.

Mama swung her purse at him. "Leave us alone!"

"Us?" The man grunted, his gaze dropping to Augustine. Eyes widening for a second, he snorted. "Your runt's not going to ruin my fun."

"I'm not a runt," Augustine said. Fear made his voice wobble, but he darted out from behind his mother anyway, planting himself in front of her.

The man swatted Augustine away with a meaty hand.

Augustine hit the cemetery wall, cracking his head hard enough to see stars. But with the new pain came anger. And heat. The two mixed together like a storm in his belly, making him want to do...something. He tried to control it, but the man went after Mama next, grabbing her and pushing her to the ground. Then the man climbed on top of her.

She cried out and the swirling inside Augustine became a hurricane dragging him along in its winds. Without really knowing what he was doing, he leaped onto the man's back. The hard muscle and bone he expected seemed soft and squishy. He grabbed fistfuls of the man's jacket—but his hands met roots and dirt and shards of concrete instead.

336

Mama's eyes blinked up at him, wide and fearful. She seemed a little blurry. Was he crying? And how was he seeing her when he was on the man's back? And why had everything gone so quiet? Except for a real loud *tha-thump*, *tha-thump*, *tha-thump*, everything else sounded real far away. He pushed to his knees, expecting them to sting from his fall, but he felt nothing. And the man attacking his mother was somehow...gone.

"Don't, Augustine." She shook her head as she scrabbled backward. "Don't do this."

"Don't do what, Mama?" He reached for her but the hand that appeared before him was too big. And only had five fingers. He stuck his other hand out and saw the same thing. "What's happening to me, Mama?"

"Get out of him, Augustine." She got to her feet, one trembling hand clutching the crucifix on her necklace. "Let the man go."

He stood and suddenly he was looking down at his mother. Down. How was he doing that? He glanced at his body. But it wasn't his body, it was the man's.

"I don't understand." But he had an idea. Was this one of the powers he had? One of the things he was supposed to control? He didn't know how to get out. Was he trapped? He only wanted to protect his mother, he didn't want to be this man!

The storm inside him welled up in waves. The heat in his belly was too much. He didn't understand this new power. He wanted to be himself. He wanted to be out. Panic made bigger waves, hot swells that clogged his throat so he couldn't take deep breaths. The thumping noise got louder.

The man's hands reached up to claw at Augustine, at his own skin.

Mama backed away, her fingers in the sign of the cross. He cried out to her for help. He was too hot, too angry, too scared—

337

A loud, wet pop filled his ears and he fell to his hands and knees again, this time covered in sticky red ooze and smoking hunks of flesh. The thumping noise was gone. Around him was more sticky red, lumps of flesh and pieces of white bone. All he could think about was the time he and Nevil Tremain had stuffed a watermelon full of firecrackers. Except this was way worse. And blowing up the watermelon hadn't made him feel like throwing up. Or smelled like burnt metal. He sat back, wiped at his face and eyes, and tried to find his mother. She was a few feet away, but coming closer.

"You killed that man." She stood over him looking more angry than afraid now. "You possessed that man like a demon." She pointed at him. "You're just like your father, just like that dirty fae-blooded liar."

Augustine shook his head. "That man was hurting you—"

"Yes, you saved me, but you took his *life*, Augustine." She looked around, eyes darting in all directions. "*Sturka*," she muttered, a fae curse word Augustine had once gotten slapped for saying.

"I didn't mean to, I was trying to help—"

"And who's next? Are you going to help me that way too someday?"

He was crying now, unable to help himself. "No, Mama, no. I would never hurt you."

She grabbed him by his shirt and yanked him to his feet. "Act human, not like a freak, do you understand? If people could see what you really looked like..." Fear clouded her eyes.

He nodded, sniffling, hating the smell of the blood he was covered in. He didn't want to be a freak. He really didn't. "I can act human. I promise."

She let go of his shirt, her lip slightly curled as she looked him over. "This was your father's blood that caused this. Not mine."

extras

"Not yours," Augustine repeated. Mama looked human but was part smokesinger, something he knew only because he'd overheard an argument she'd had with his father on the phone once. He'd learned other things that way, too. Like that his father was something called shadeux fae. But not just part. All of him. And he'd lied to Mama about that. Used magic to make Mama think he was human. To seduce her.

"I never want to hear or see anything fae ever again or I will put you out of my house. I live as human and while you're under my roof, so will you. Am I clear?"

The thought of being without her made his chest ache. She was all he had. His world. "Yes, Mama."

But keeping his fae side hidden was impossible, and five years later, put him out is exactly what she did.

1

Procrastination assassinates opportunity.
—Elektos Codex, 4.1.1

New Orleans, 2068

Augustine trailed his fingers over the silky shoulder of one of his mocha-skinned bedmates. He dare not wake her, or her sister sleeping on the other side of him, or he feared he'd never get home in time for lunch with his dear Olivia. He felt a twinge of guilt that he'd spent his first night back in New Orleans in the

339

company of "strange" women, as Olivia would call them, but only a twinge. A man had needs, after all.

The woman sighed contentedly at his touch, causing him to do the same. Last night had been just the right amount of fun to welcome him home. He eased onto his back and folded his arms behind his head, a satisfied smile firmly in place. The Santiago sisters from Mobile, Alabama, had earned their sleep.

Outside the Hotel Monteleone, the city was just waking up. Delivery trucks rumbled through the Quarter's narrow streets, shopkeepers washed their sidewalks clean of last night's revelries, and the bitter scent of chicory coffee filled the air with a seductive, smoky darkness. Day or night, there was no mistaking the magic of New Orleans. And damn, he'd missed it.

His smile widened. He wasn't much for traveling and that's all he'd done these past few months. Things had gotten hot after he'd given his estranged brother's *human* friend entrance to the fae plane. Ditching town was the only way to keep the Elektos off his back. The damn fae high council had never liked him much. Violating such a sacred rule as allowing a mortal access to the fae plane had shot him to the top of their blacklist.

Smile fading, he sighed. If two and a half months away wasn't enough, then he'd have to figure something else out. He didn't like being away from Livie for so long. He could imagine the size of her smile when he strolled in this afternoon. She'd been more of a mother to him than his own had, not a feat that required much effort, but Olivia had saved him from the streets. From himself.

There wasn't much he wouldn't do for her.

With that thought, he extricated himself from the bedcovers and his sleeping partners and began the hunt for his clothing. When he'd dressed, he stood before the vanity mirror and finger-combed his hair around his recently grown-out horns. They followed the curve of his skull, starting near his forehead, then arching around to end with sharp points near his cheek-bones. He preferred them ground down, but growing them out had helped him blend with the rest of the fae population. Most fae also added ornate silver bands and capped the tips in fili-gree, but he wasn't into that.

His jeans, black T-shirt, and motorcycle boots weren't much to look at, but the horns were all it took for most mortal women to go positively weak. Standard fae-wear typically included a lot of magically enhanced leather, which was perfect for a city like NOLA, where being a little theatrical was almost expected, but you had to have plastic for spendy gear like that.

Satisfied, he walked back to the women who'd been his unsuspecting welcome-home party and stood quietly at the side of the bed.

Pressing his fingertips together, he worked the magic that ran in his veins, power born of the melding of his smokesinger and shadeux fae bloodlines, power that had blossomed when he'd finally opened himself up to it. Power he'd learned to use through trial and error and the help of a good friend.

He smiled. It would be great to see Dulcinea again, too.

Slowly, he drew his fingers apart and threads of smoke spun out between them. The strands twisted and curled between his fingers until the nebulous creation took the shape of a rose.

Gentle heat built in the bones of his hands and arms, a plea-surable sensation that gave him great satisfaction.

The form solidified further, then Augustine flicked one wrist to break the connection. With that free hand, he grasped the stem. The moment he touched it, the stem went green and royal purple filled the flower's petals. He lifted it to his nose, inhaling its heady perfume. Fae magic never ceased to amaze him. He tucked the flower behind his ear and quickly spun another, then laid the blooms on the sisters' pillows.

Pleased with his work, he picked up his bag, pulled a black compact from the pocket of his jeans, and flipped it open to reveal a mirror. The mirror was nothing special, just a piece of silver-backed glass, but that was all any fae needed to travel from one place to another.

"Thanks for a wonderful evening, ladies," he whispered. Focusing on his reflection, he imagined himself back at Livie's. The familiar swirl of vertigo tugged at him as the magic drew him through.

A second later, when he glanced away from his reflection, he was home.

Harlow Goodwin held paper documents so rarely that if the stark white, unrecycled stock in her hands were anything else than the death knell to her freedom, she'd be caressing it with her bare fingers, willing to risk any residual emotions left from the person who'd last touched it—it wasn't like she could read objects the way she could people or computers, but every once in a while, if the thing had been touched by someone else recently, something leaked through. In this case, she kept her gloves on. This wasn't any old paper, this was the judgment that was about to bring an abrupt and miserable end to life as she knew it.

They couldn't even have the decency to wait to deliver it until after she'd had her morning coffee. For once, she wished it had been another of her mother's missives pleading with her to come for a visit.

She read the sum again. Eight hundred fifty thousand dollars. Eight five zero zero zero zero. She'd heard it in court when the judge had pronounced her sentence, but seeing it in black-and-white, in letters that couldn't be backspaced over and deleted, made the hollowness inside her gape that much wider.

How in the hell was she going to pay off eight hundred and fifty freaking thousand dollars? Might as well have been a million. Or a hundred million. She couldn't pay it, even if she wanted to. That queasy feeling came over her again, like she might hurl the ramen noodles she'd choked down for dinner. Moments like this, not having a father cut through her more sharply than ever. She knew that if her mother had allowed him into her life, he'd be here, taking care of her. He'd know what to do, how to handle it. That's what fathers did, wasn't it?

At least that's what Harlow's father did in her fantasies. And fantasies were all she had, because Olivia Goodwin hadn't only kept that secret from the paparazzi; she'd also kept it from her daughter.

Oh, Harlow had tried to find him. She'd searched every possibility she could think of, traced her mother's path during the month of her conception, but her mother had been on tour for a movie premiere. Thirty-eight cities in twelve different countries. The number of men she could have come in contact with was staggering.

Harlow's father, whoever he was, remained a mystery.

Heart aching with the kind of loss she'd come to think of as normal, she tossed the papers onto her desk, collapsed onto her unmade bed, and dropped her head into her hands. The five-monitor computer station on her desk hummed softly, a sound she generally considered soothing, but today it only served to remind her of how royally she'd been duped. Damn it.

The client who'd hired her to test his new security system and retrieve a set of files had actually given her false information. She'd ended up hacking into what she'd belatedly guessed was his rival's company and accessing their top-secret formula for a new drug protocol. Shady SOB.

She shuddered, thinking what her punishment might have been if she'd actually delivered that drug formula into her client's hands, but a sixth sense had told her to get out right after she'd accessed the file. Something in her head had tripped her internal alarms, something she'd be forever grateful for if only it had gone off sooner. She'd ditched the info and hurriedly erased her presence. Almost. Obviously not enough to prevent herself from being caught.

Times like this she cursed the "gift" she'd been born with. Well, the first one, the ability to feel people's emotions through touch, that one she always cursed. And really it was more than emotion. She saw images, heard sounds, even picked up scents from people. Which all added up to an intense overload— sometimes pleasurable but too often painful—that she preferred not to deal with. The second gift was the way she seemed to be able to read computers. She didn't know how else to describe it, but they responded to her like she could speak binary code without even trying. Finding her way into a motherboard took no more effort than opening a door. That gift had given her a career. A slightly questionable one at times. But a job was a job. Except when it brought her clients like this last one.

A client who was now in the wind, the twenty large she'd charged him not even a down payment on her fine. She should have known something was up when he'd paid in cash, his courier a shifty-eyed sort who was probably as much fae as he was something else. She shuddered. That cash, tucked away in a backpack under the bed, was the only thing the court hadn't been able to seize. Everything else was frozen solid until she paid the fine or did her time.

She flopped back on the bed and folded her arms over her eyes. She was about as screwed as a person could get.

Her eyes closed but it didn't stop her brain from filling her head with the one name she was doing her best not to think about.

The one person capable of helping her. The one person who'd been the greatest source of conflict in her life.

Olivia Goodwin.

Her mother.

Harlow hadn't *really* spoken to her mother in years. Not since their last big fight and Olivia's umpteenth refusal to share any information about her biological father. For Harlow, it was difficult to say what hurt worse—not knowing who her father was, or her mother not understanding the gaping hole inside Harlow where her father was missing and yet her mother somehow thinking she could still make things okay between them.

The cycle usually started with Olivia barraging Harlow with pleas to move to New Orleans. Harlow ignored them until she finally believed things might be different this time and countered with a request of her own. Her father's name. Because that's all she needed. A name. With her computer skills, there was no question she'd be able to find him after that. But without a name...every clue she'd followed had led to a dead end. But that small request was all it took to shut Olivia down and destroy Harlow's hope. The next few months would pass without them talking at all.

extras

Then Olivia would contact her again.

Harlow *had* made one attempt at reconciliation, but that had dissolved just like the rest of them. After that, their communication became very one-sided. E-mails and calls and letters from her mother went unanswered except for an occasional response to let Olivia know she was still alive and still *not* interested in living in New Orleans.

She loved her mother. But the hurt Olivia had caused her was deep.

If her mother was going to help now, the money would come with strings attached. Namely Harlow agreeing to drop the topic of her father.

The thought widened the hole in her heart a little more. If she agreed to never ask about him again, she'd have to live with the same unbearable sense of not knowing she'd carried all her life. And if she didn't agree, her mother probably wouldn't give her the money, which meant Harlow was going to jail. A life lesson, her mother would call it.

A deep sigh fluttered the hair trapped between her cheeks and her forearms. Was she really going to do this? The drive from Boston to New Orleans would take a minimum of twenty-four hours, but flying meant being trapped in a closed space with strangers. It also meant putting herself on the CCU's radar, and until her fine was paid, she wasn't supposed to leave the state. At least she had a car. Her little hybrid might be a beater, but it would get her to Louisiana and there'd be no one in the car but her.

Another sigh and she pulled her arms away from her face to stare at the ceiling. If her mother refused her the money, which was a very real possibility, Harlow would be in jail in a month's time. Her security gone, her freedom gone, forced to live in a cell with another person.

346

She sat up abruptly. Would they let her keep her gloves in prison? What if her cell mate…touched her? That kind of looming threat made her want to do something rebellious. The kind of thing she'd only done once before at a Comic-Con where her costume had given her a sense of anonymity and some protection from skin-to-skin contact.

She wanted one night of basic, bone-deep pleasure of her choosing. One night of the kind of fun that didn't include sitting in front of her monitors, leveling up one of her Realm of Zauron characters to major proportions. Not that that kind of fun wasn't epic. It was basically her life. But she needed something more, the kind of memory that would carry her through her incarceration.

One night of *careful* physical contact with another living, breathing *male* being.

The thought alone was enough to raise goose bumps on her skin. She'd do it the same way she had at Comic-Con. A couple of good, stiff drinks and the alcohol would dull her senses and make being around so many people bearable. With a good buzz, she could stand being touched. Maybe even find it enjoyable, if things went well. Which was the point.

She was going to New Orleans. The city was practically built on senseless fun and cheap booze, right? If there was ever a place to have one last night of debauchery before heading to the big house, New Orleans seemed custom made for it.

On her Life Management Device, the one she could no longer afford and that would soon be turned off, she checked the weather. Unseasonably warm in New Orleans. Leaving behind the snowpocalypse of Boston wouldn't be such a hardship, but she wasn't about to ditch her long sleeves just for a little sunshine. On the rare occasions she had to leave her apartment, she liked as much skin covered as possible.

She jumped off the bed, grabbed her rolling bag, and packed. Just the necessities—travel laptop with holoscreen and gaming headset, some clothes, toiletries, and the cash. Not like she'd be gone long. She changed into her favorite Star Alliance T-shirt, set her security cameras, locked down her main computer and servers, and grabbed her purse. She took a deep breath and one last look at her apartment. It was only for a few days. She could do this.

A few minutes later she was in the car, a jumbo energy drink in the cup holder and the nav on her LMD directing her toward Louisiana.

introducing

If you enjoyed
RED BLOODED
look out for

THE SHAMBLING GUIDE TO NEW YORK CITY

The Shambling Guides: Book 1

by Mur Lafferty

A travel writer takes a job with a shady publishing company in New York, only to find that she must write a guide to the city—for the undead!

Because of the disaster that was her last job, Zoë is searching for a fresh start as a travel book editor in tourist-centric New York City. After stumbling across a seemingly perfect position, though, Zoe is blocked at every turn because of the one thing she can't take off her résumé—she's human.

Not to be put off by anything—especially not her blood-drinking boss or death goddess coworker—Zoë delves deep

*into the monster world. But her job turns deadly
when the careful balance between humans and monsters
starts to crumble—with Zoë right in the middle.*

1

The bookstore was sandwiched between a dry cleaner's and a shifty-looking accounting office. Mannegishi's Tricks wasn't in the guidebook, but Zoë Norris knew enough about guidebooks to know they often missed the best places.

This clearly was not one of those places.

The store was, to put it bluntly, filthy. It reminded Zoë of an abandoned mechanic's garage, with grime and grease coating the walls and bookshelves. She pulled her arms in to avoid brushing against anything. Long strips of paint dotted with mold peeled away from the walls as if they could no longer stand to adhere to such filth. Zoë couldn't blame them. She felt a bizarre desire to wave to them as they bobbed lazily to herald her passing. Her shoes stuck slightly to the floor, making her trek through the store louder than she would have liked.

She always enjoyed looking at cities—even her hometown—through the eyes of a tourist. She owned guidebooks of every city she had visited and used them extensively. It made her usual urban exploration feel more thorough.

It also allowed her to look at the competition, or it had when she'd worked in travel book publishing.

The store didn't win her over with its stock, either. She'd never heard of most of the books; they had titles like *How to*

extras

Make Love, Marry, Devour, and Inherit in Eight Weeks in the Romance section and *When Your Hound from Hell Outgrows His House—and Yours* in the Pets section.

She picked the one about hounds and opened it to Chapter Four: "The Augean Stables: How to Pooper-Scoop Dung That Could Drown a Terrier." She frowned. *So, they're* really *assuming your dog gets bigger than a house? It's not tongue-in-cheek? If this is humor, it's failing.* Despite the humorous title, the front cover had a frightening drawing of a hulking white beast with red eyes. The cover was growing uncomfortably warm, and the leather had a sticky, alien feeling, not like cow or even snake leather. She switched the book to her left hand and wiped her right on her beige sweater. She immediately regretted it.

"One sweater ruined," she muttered, looking at the grainy black smear. "What *is* this stuff?"

The cashier's desk faced the door from the back of the store, and was staffed by an unsmiling teen girl in a dirty gray sundress. She had olive skin and big round eyes, and her head had the fuzz of the somewhat-recently shaved. Piercings dotted her face at her nose, eyebrow, lip, and cheek, and all the way up her ears. Despite her slouchy body language, she watched Zoë with a bright, sharp gaze that looked almost hungry.

Beside the desk was a bulletin board, blocked by a pudgy man hanging a flyer. He wore a T-shirt and jeans and looked to be in his mid-thirties. He looked completely out of place in this store; that is, he was clean.

"Can I help you?" the girl asked as Zoë approached the counter.

"Uh, you have a very interesting shop here," Zoë said, smiling. She put the hound book on the counter and tried not to grimace as it stuck to her hand briefly. "How much is this one?"

The clerk didn't return her smile. "We cater to a specific clientele."

"OK...but how much is the book?" Zoë asked again.

"It's not for sale. It's a collectible."

Zoë became aware of the man at the bulletin board turning and watching her. She began to sweat a little bit.

Jesus, calm down. Not everyone is out to get you.

"So it's not for sale, or it's a collectible. Which one?"

The girl reached over and took the book. "It's not for sale to you, only to collectors."

"How do you know I don't collect dog books?" Zoë asked, bristling. "And what does it matter? All I wanted to know was how much it costs. Do you care where it goes as long as it's paid for?"

"Are you a collector of rare books catering to the owners of...exotic pets?" the man interrupted, smiling. His voice was pleasant and mild, and she relaxed a little, despite his patronizing words. "Excuse me for butting in, but I know the owner of this shop and she considers these books her treasure. She is very particular about where they go when they leave her care."

"Why should she..." Zoë trailed off when she got a closer look at the bulletin board to the man's left. Several flyers stood out, many with phone numbers ripped from the bottom. One, advertising an exorcism service specializing in elemental demons, looked burned in a couple of places. The flyer that had caught her eye was pink, and the one the man had just secured with a thumbtack.

Underground Publishing
LOOKING FOR WRITERS

Underground Publishing is a new company writing travel guides for people like you. Since we're writing for people like you, we need people like you to write for us. Pluses: Experience in writing, publishing, or editing (in this life or any other), and knowledge of New York City.

Minuses: A life span shorter than an editorial cycle (in this case, nine months).

Call 212.555.1666 for more information or e-mail rand@undergroundpub.com for more information.

"Oh, hell yes," said Zoë, and with the weird, dirty hound book forgotten, she pulled a battered notebook from her satchel. She needed a job. She was refusing to adhere to the stereotype of running home to New York, admitting failure at her attempts to leave her hometown. Her goal was a simple office job. She wasn't waiting for her big break on Broadway and looking to wait tables or take on a leaflet-passing, taco-suit-wearing street-nuisance job in the meantime.

Office job. Simple. Uncomplicated.

As she scribbled down the information, the man looked her up and down and said, "Ah, I'm not sure if that's a good idea for you to pursue."

Zoë looked up sharply. "What are you talking about? First I can't buy the book, now I can't apply for a job? I know you guys have some sort of weird vibe going on, 'We're so goth and special, let's freak out the normals.' But for a business that caters to, you know, *customers*, you're certainly not welcoming."

"I just think that particular business may be looking for someone with experience you may not have," he said, his voice level and diplomatic. He held his hands out, placating her.

"But you don't even know me. You don't know my qualifications. I just left Misconceptions Publishing in Raleigh. You heard of them?" She hated name-dropping her old employer—she would have preferred to forget it entirely—but the second-biggest travel book publisher in the USA was her strongest credential in the job hunt.

The man shifted his weight and touched his chin. "Really. What did you do for them?"

Zoë stood a little taller. "Head researcher and writer. I wrote most of *Raleigh Misconceptions*, and was picked to head the project *Tallahassee Misconceptions*."

He smiled a bit. "Impressive. But you do know Tallahassee is south of North Carolina, right? You went in the wrong direction entirely."

Zoë clenched her jaw. "I was laid off. It wasn't due to job performance. I took my severance and came back home to the city."

The man rubbed his smooth, pudgy cheek. "What happened to cause the layoff? I thought Misconceptions was doing well."

Zoë felt her cheeks get hot. Her boss, Godfrey, had happened. Then Godfrey's wife—whom he had failed to mention until Zoë was well and truly in "other woman" territory—had happened. She swallowed. "Economy. You know how it goes."

He stepped back and leaned against the wall, clearly not minding the cracked and peeling paint that broke off and stuck to his shirt. "Those are good credentials. However, you're still probably not what they're looking for."

Zoë looked at her notebook and continued writing. "Luckily it's not your decision, is it?"

"Actually, it is."

She groaned and looked back up at him. "All right. Who are you?"

He extended his hand. "Phillip Rand. Owner, president, and CEO of Underground Publishing."

She looked at his hand for a moment and shook it, her small fingers briefly engulfed in his grip. It was a cool handshake, but strong.

"Zoë Norris. And why, Mr. Phillip Rand, will you not let me even apply?"

"Well, Miss Zoë Norris, I don't think you'd fit in with the staff. And fitting in with the staff is key to this company's success."

A vision of future months dressed as a dancing cell phone on the wintry streets pummeled Zoë's psyche. She leaned forward in desperation. She was short, and used to looking up at people, but he was over six feet, and she was forced to crane her neck to look up at him. "Mr. Rand. How many other people experienced in researching and writing travel guides do you have with you?"

He considered for a moment. "With that specific qualification? I actually have none."

"So if you have a full staff of people who fit into some kind of mystery mold, but don't actually have experience writing travel books, how good do you think your books are going to be? You sound like you're a kid trying to fill a club, not a working publishing company. You need a managing editor with experience to supervise your writers and researchers. I'm smart, hardworking, creative, and a hell of a lot of fun in the times I'm not blatantly begging for a job—obviously you'll have to just take my word on that. I haven't found a work environment I don't fit in with. I don't care if Underground Publishing is catering to eastern Europeans, or transsexuals, or Eskimos, or even

Republicans. Just because I don't fit in doesn't mean I can't be accepting as long as they accept me. Just give me a chance."

Phillip Rand was unmoved. "Trust me. You would not fit in. You're not our type."

She finally deflated and sighed. "Isn't this illegal?"

He actually had the audacity to laugh at that. "I'm not discriminating based on your gender or race or religion."

"Then what are you basing it on?"

He licked his lips and looked at her again, studying her. "Call it a gut reaction."

She deflated. "Oh well. It was worth a try. Have a good day."

On her way out, she ran through her options: there were the few publishing companies she hadn't yet applied to, the jobs that she had recently thought beneath her that she'd gladly take at this point. She paused a moment in the Self-Help section to see if anything there could help her better herself. She glanced at the covers for *Reborn and Loving It, Second Life: Not Just on the Internet*, and *Get the Salary You Deserve! Negotiating Hell Notes in a Time of Economic Downturn*. Nothing she could relate to, so she trudged out the door, contemplating a long bath when she got back to her apartment. Better than unpacking more boxes.

After the grimy door shut behind her, Zoë decided she had earned a tall caloric caffeine bomb to soothe her ego. She wasn't sure what she'd done to deserve this, but it didn't take much to make her leap for the comfort treats these days—which reminded her: she needed to recycle some wine bottles.

The Shambling Guide to New York City

THEATER DISTRICT:
Shops

Mannegishi's Tricks is the oldest bookstore in the Theater District. Established 1834 by Akilina, nicknamed "The Drakon Lady," after she emigrated from Russia, the store has a stock that is lovingly picked from collections all over the world. Currently managed by Akilina's great-granddaughter, Anastasiya, the store continues to offer some of the best finds for any book collector. Anastasiya upholds the old dragon lady's practice of knowing just which book should go to which customer, and refuses to sell a book to the "wrong" person. Don't try to argue with her; the drakon's teeth remain sharp.

Mannegishi's Tricks is one of the few shops that deliberately maintains a squalid appearance—dingy, smelly, with a strong "leave now" aura—in order to repel unwanted customers. In nearly 180 years, Akilina and her descendants have sold only three books to humans. She refuses to say to whom.